DARKTOWN

ALSO BY THOMAS MULLEN

The Last Town on Earth

The Many Deaths of the Firefly Brothers

The Revisionists

DARKTOWN

A NOVEL

THOMAS MULLEN

37INK

ATRIA

NEW YORK LONDON TORONTO SYDNEY NEW DELHI

ATRIA BOOKS   37INK
An Imprint of Simon & Schuster, Inc.
1230 Avenue of the Americas
New York, NY 10020

First 37 Ink/Atria Books hardcover edition September 2016

37INK / ATRIA BOOKS and colophons are trademarks of Simon & Schuster, Inc.

For information about special discounts for bulk purchases, please contact Simon & Schuster Special Sales at 1-866-506-1949 or business@simonandschuster.com.

The Simon & Schuster Speakers Bureau can bring authors to your live event. For more information or to book an event, contact the Simon & Schuster Speakers Bureau at 1-866-248-3049 or visit our website at www.simonspeakers.com.

Interior design by Kyoko Watanabe

Manufactured in the United States of America

10 9 8 7 6 5 4 3 2 1

Library of Congress Cataloging-in-Publication Data

Names: Mullen, Thomas.
Title: Darktown : a novel / Thomas Mullen.
Description: New York : 37 Ink/Atria , 2016.
Identifiers: LCCN 2015041687 (print) | LCCN 2015044852 (ebook)
Subjects: | BISAC: FICTION / Mystery & Detective / Police Procedural. |
   FICTION / African American / Mystery & Detective.
Classification: LCC PS3613.U447 D37 2016 (print) | LCC PS3613.U447
(ebook) |
   DDC 813/.6—dc23
LC record available at http://lccn.loc.gov/2015041687

ISBN 978-1-5011-3386-2
ISBN 978-1-5011-3388-6 (ebook)

For Jenny

"I must tell you, it was not easy for me to raise my right hand and say, 'I, Willard Strickland, a Negro, do solemnly swear to perform the duties of a Negro policeman.'"

 —*Officer Willard Strickland, Atlanta Police Department,*
  Retired, in a 1977 speech recalling his 1948 induction
  as one of the city's first eight African American officers

IT WAS NEARING midnight when one of the new lampposts on Auburn Avenue achieved the unfortunate fate of being the first to be hit by a car. Shards of a white Buick's headlight fell scattered across the sidewalk below the now-leaning pole.

Locusts continued their thrum in the thick July air. Windows were open throughout town, the impact no doubt waking many. The lone pedestrian on that block, an old man on his way home from sweeping floors at a sugar factory, was no more than ten yards away. He had stepped back when the car jumped the curb but now he stopped and watched for a moment, in case the pole should come crashing the rest of the way down. It didn't. At least not yet.

The Buick reversed, slowly, the front wheel easing off the curb. The movement caused the pole to lean the other way, too far, and then back again, a giant metronome.

The pedestrian could hear a woman's voice, shouting. Something about what on earth do you think you're doing, just take me home, that sort of thing. The pedestrian shook his head and shambled off before something worse might happen.

Whether or not the lampposts were *new*, exactly, was a matter of perspective. It had been a few months now, but considering how many years it had taken the leaders of Atlanta's colored community to convince the mayor to install them, and considering the many, many years in which Negroes had walked down even their busiest and most monied street in darkness, the celestial presence of those lampposts still *felt* new.

None of which was known to the Buick's driver.

He had been attempting to turn around in the middle of the otherwise empty street but had misjudged his turning radius, or the width of the road, or general physics. He also perhaps hadn't noticed that two blocks away were two Atlanta police officers.

Five minutes earlier, Officer Lucius Boggs finally confronted his partner, Tommy Smith, about his limp.

"You did not hurt yourself playing baseball. Own up."

"It was a hard slide," Smith said.

"But you told McInnis you were rounding third."

At roll call, Smith had assured their sergeant, McInnis, that his knee was fine, just a tweak he'd felt in a game he'd played with some buddies. *You know how those sand lots are, sir, no traction.* McInnis had listened to this stone-faced, as if experienced enough at hearing colored flimflam but deciding the truth of this matter was not worth prodding into.

"I fell out a window," Smith now admitted to Boggs. They were standing on Hilliard Street, three blocks from the Negro YMCA whose basement served as their makeshift precinct. At that hour the sun was long gone but it had left more than enough heat to last until it felt like showing up again. Both officers had sweated through their undershirts, and even their uniforms were damp.

"Yours?"

"What do you think?"

Boggs folded his arms and couldn't help smiling. "And who was the lady you were impressing with your acrobatics?"

"I was *in the middle of entertaining her* with my acrobatics, matter of fact. When her man busted into the apartment."

"Are you crazy?"

"She'd told me he'd left her, pulled up stakes for Detroit. She talked about needing some lawyer to do her divorce papers or something."

Atlanta police officers were ordered to abide by a strict moral code—no drinking, even at home, and no womanizing—but that had not entirely sunk in with Tommy Smith. The Negro officers dutifully avoided alcohol, as they knew all too well that a witness could report them and get them suspended, but for Smith the idea of suddenly becoming a chaste man was altogether too much.

"You're going to get yourself killed."

"I do *not* go after the married ones."

"Except for her, and the girl who did that thing with the candied pecans, and—"

"That's different, she and I went way back."

They started walking again.

"So then what happened?"

"What do you think? Pulled on my britches and jumped out the window."

"What floor did she live on?"

"Third."

"No!"

"One of them places with no fire escape. I'd say I'm walking remarkably well, considering."

"What happened with the husband?"

"I did not linger around to eavesdrop."

"Aren't you at least worried?"

"She struck me as the kind of gal knew how to handle herself and think on her feet."

Boggs was the son of a minister, and though he had chosen not to follow in his father's footsteps, the idea of tomcatting across town the way his partner did was utterly foreign to him. His own experience with women had been limited to innocent dates with well-mannered, well-raised young ladies of the Negro intelligentsia, and he was coming off a recent broken engagement to a girl who'd finally told him that the stress of knowing her fiancé might be shot or beaten on any given night was too much for her constitution to handle.

A squad car approached, the headlights strangely off. Hilliard had neither lampposts nor sidewalks. They stopped talking and stood there, each wondering if they should back up a few steps, or would that look weak.

Then the car accelerated, and each of them did indeed take a step back onto the small plot of grass and weeds that served as someone's front yard. The squad car feinted toward them, swerving a bit, then screeched to a stop.

They caught glimpses of two white officers whose faces they didn't recognize—cops from other beats who just happened to be driving through, apparently.

The white cops yelled, *"Oooh-oooh-oooh!"*

"Aaah-aaah-aaah!"

Monkey sounds and orangutan sounds and maybe some gorilla thrown in.

"Woo-woo-woo-boogga-boogga!"

"Watch your asses, niggers!"

Then the squad car sped off, the white cops laughing hysterically.

You couldn't show fear. They acted like it was all a harmless prank, even when they gunned their engines at you when you were crossing the street, even when they nearly grazed against you. More than once Boggs had stood in the road to flag down a squad car, needing assistance for an arrest, when the car had accelerated toward him until he'd had to leap out of the way. Laughter in its wake. Surely, if the day came when they actually *did* run over one of the colored officers, they would insist it was an accident.

Neither Boggs nor Smith felt like telling stories anymore as they reached the corner of Auburn, the night silent but for the almost mechanical churn of locusts and the call-and-response of crickets. The marquee over Bailey's Royal Theater was off, as were the lights of the jeweler and tailoring shops; someone had left on a third-floor office lamp at Atlanta Life Insurance Company, but other than that and the streetlights, all was dark. Then they heard the crash.

They turned, each half-hoping to see that the squad car had hit a fire hydrant or perhaps a brick wall. Instead they saw a white Buick two blocks away, on the curb, and the light pole dancing almost, or at least swaying drunkenly. They watched as the light flickered once, then again, just as each of their homes' electricity did during thunderstorms.

The Buick backed up. They couldn't read the tags from so far away. Then it started driving toward them.

They had been police officers for just under three months now, walking the beats around Auburn Avenue (the neighborhood where both had lived all their lives save the war years) and the West Side, on the other side of downtown. Although Atlanta's eight Negro officers had not yet been entrusted with squad cars, they did have uniforms:

black caps with the gold city crest, dark blue shirts on which their shiny badges were pinned, black slacks, and black ties (Smith being one of two cops on the team who went with the bow-tie option, which he found rather dapper). Their thick belts were weighed down by a heavy arsenal of weapons and gear, including firearms, which terrified a number of white people in Atlanta and beyond.

Boggs stepped into the road and held out a palm. The white cops may have enjoyed trying to run over their colored colleagues, but civilians were another matter. Or so he hoped. The Buick was driving slower than was normal, as if ashamed. Its headlights glinted off his badge.

The Buick stopped.

"He's not turning his engine off," Smith said after a few seconds.

Boggs walked over to the driver's door, Smith mirroring him along the sidewalk and stopping at the passenger door. The soles of Smith's shoes hardly made a sound because the cement had been meticulously swept by someone that very morning, not a twig or cigarette butt in sight.

The glare from the streetlights had prevented the officers from getting a good look in the car until now. All they had been able to discern were silhouettes of a driver with a hat and a passenger without.

Boggs opened his mouth and was about to ask for the driver's license and registration when he saw that the driver was white.

That he hadn't expected. What he *had* suspected, that the driver was drunk, was correct. Boggs was bathed in alcohol fumes as the portly white man gazed at him with something between annoyance and contempt.

"May I have your license and registration, please, sir?"

White people were not often found in Sweet Auburn, the wealthiest Negro neighborhood in Atlanta—possibly in the world, boosters liked to say. Adventurous whites looking for gambling or whores in the darker parts of town would normally troll along Decatur Street, by the railroad tracks, a half mile to the south. Or they'd find one of the other, more nefarious areas that the colored officers patrolled. This fellow was either lost or so drunk and stupid that he figured any colored part of town offered the vices he craved, when in fact this neighborhood mostly held churches, real estate firms, banks, insurance companies, funeral parlors, barbershops, and the sorts of restaurants long closed at this hour. A couple of nightclubs did grace the streets, yes, but they were respectable places where respectable Negroes gathered, and they only opened their doors to whites on Saturdays, when Negroes weren't allowed in.

The driver's gray homburg was tipped high, as if he'd been rubbing sweat from his forehead. Which he needed to be doing more of, because his skin was still shiny. Hair light gray, blue tie loosened, linen jacket wrinkled. He seemed sweatier than a man driving a car should be, Boggs thought. Like he'd just been doing something strenuous.

On the other side of the car, Smith visually frisked the man's passenger. She wore the kind of yellow sundress that always made him so thrilled when spring came along, and even here in the depths of summer he was not a man to complain about the kind of heat that allowed the women of Atlanta to walk around half naked. She was short enough to cross her legs in the front seat, the hem above her knee. Light glinted off a small locket that looked stuck to the dampness at the small of her throat.

She made eye contact with Smith for only the briefest of seconds, just enough for him to gather a few facts. She was light-skinned and young, early twenties at most. The right side of her lip looked a shade of red that didn't match her lipstick. Red and slightly puffy.

Although Smith could not yet see the driver, he divined the man's race based on the subtle change in Boggs's voice when asking for the license. Not exactly deferential, but more polite than was otherwise warranted.

The driver answered, "No, you may not."

Boggs was cognizant of the fact that the man's right hand was at his side, on the seat, and therefore out of view. Boggs decided he need not comment on this yet. Hopefully Smith could see it. The man's left hand casually rested on the steering wheel, the engine still running.

"You hit a light pole, sir."

"I mighta glanced against it." Not even looking at Boggs.

"It's leaning over and will need to be fixed, and—"

"You're wasting my time, boy."

Nothing but a crescendo of katydids for a moment, and only then did the white man deign to look at Boggs. Just to check out how that had registered on this uppity Negro's face.

Boggs tried not to let it register at all. His face, he knew, was very good at being blank. This had been commented upon by parents, schoolteachers, girlfriends. *What are you thinking right now? Where are you? Penny for your thoughts?* He'd always hated those questions. *I'm right here. I'm thinking thoughts, any thoughts, who knows. And no, you can't buy them.*

Normally you weren't supposed to look white folks in the eye. But Boggs was the police. This was only the third time he and Smith had dealt with a white perpetrator. Colored officers only patrolled the colored parts of town, where whites were infrequent visitors.

"I need to see your license and registration, sir."

"You don't need to see anything, boy."

Boggs felt his heart rate spike and he told himself to stay calm. "Please turn your car off, sir," he said, realizing he should have started with that.

"You don't have the power to arrest me and you know it."

On the other side, Smith took this as the proper time to beam the backseat. He didn't see anything there, other than a road atlas on the floorboards. The car was prewar but in good condition, the vinyl shining. Smith aimed his light at the front seat, where the woman had been staring ahead, her hair blocking his view. He had hoped the light would startle her into looking at him, so he could better study her injury and look for others, but she turned farther away.

Smith, unlike Boggs, had a good view of the space between driver and passenger. He saw that the man's right hand was resting protectively atop a large brown envelope.

"I do have the authority to issue you a traffic citation, sir, and I intend to do that," Boggs said. "I also have the ability to call white officers here, should your arrest be required. I wouldn't have thought that necessary for something as minor as a traffic violation, but if you want to push things up the ladder with your tone, then I can oblige you."

The white man smiled, entertained.

"Oh. Oh, damn. You're one of the smart ones, huh?" He nodded, looking Boggs up and down as though finally laying eyes on a new kind of jungle cat the zoo had imported. "I'm very impressed. Y'all certainly have come a long way."

"Sir, this is the last time that I'll be the one asking you for your license and registration."

Still smiling at Boggs, still not moving.

On the other side of the car, Smith asked, "What's your name, miss?"

"*Don't* you talk to her," the white man snapped, turning to the side. All he could have seen from his vantage was Smith's midsection, his badge *(yes, we really are cops, sorry for the inconvenience),* and perhaps the handle of Smith's holstered gun *(yes, it's real).*

"Are you all right, miss?" Smith asked the woman. *Let's see how the white man likes being ignored.* Her face he still couldn't see, though her breaths occasionally made her hair move just enough for him to see the right, bruised side of her lips. Yet she refused to turn.

Smith glanced up at his partner over the car roof. Both of them would have loved to see this blowhard arrested, but they weren't sure if Dispatch would bother sending a white squad car for an auto accident whose only victim was an inanimate object. And Atlanta's eight colored officers hated calling in the white cops for any reason whatsoever. They did not appreciate the reminder that they had only so much power.

Smith leaned back down and said, "Your friend isn't very friendly, miss."

The white man said, "I *told* you not to talk to her, boy."

"*Sir,*" Boggs said to the back of the man's hat, trying to regain control (had he ever had it?), and annoyed at his partner for escalating the situation, "if you do not show me your license and registration, then I will call in—"

He didn't get to finish his pathetic threat, the threat he was ashamed to need and far more ashamed to use, because in the middle of his sentence the white man turned back to face the road and shifted into gear, the Buick lurching forward.

Both cops stepped back so their feet wouldn't be run over.

The Buick drove off, but it didn't even have the decency to speed. The white man wasn't fleeing, he simply had tired of pretending that their existence mattered.

" 'Stop or I'll call the real cops'?" Smith shook his head. "Funny how that don't work."

Atlanta, Georgia. Two parts Confederate racist to two parts Negro to one part something-that-doesn't-quite-have-a-name-for-it-yet. Neither city nor country but some odd combination, a once sleepy railroad crossing that had exploded due to the wartime need for matériel and the necessities of shipping it. Even after the war, all those factories and textile mills and rail yards were still churning, because normalcy had returned and Americans were desperate for new clothes and washing machines and automobiles, and the South was very good at providing cheap, nonunionized labor. So Atlanta continued to grow, the trains continued to disgorge new residents and the tenements grew more crowded and the moonshine continued to be driven down from the mountains and the streets spilled over with even yet more passion and schemes and brawls, because there on the Georgia piedmont something had been set loose that might never again be contained.

Twenty blocks away from Boggs and Smith, Officer Denny Rakestraw was dividing himself in two again.

Standing in an alley off Decatur Street, a colored section of town, though he and his partner were white. Staring up at the sliver of moon above him, perfectly framed between the tops of the two brick buildings. Listening to the sound of an approaching westbound freight train slowly, slowly trudge its way from the downtown yards. Then looking at his shiny cop shoes. Then turning to look behind him at the squad car they had left on the side of the road, lights not blinking because his partner, Lionel Dunlow, said he didn't want the attention.

Dunlow hit the Negro again. "I said, did you hear what I said, nigger?"

The Negro was trying to say something, Rakestraw could tell, but Dunlow was holding him too tightly around the throat.

Then the sound of soles scuffing, and Rakestraw's attention was drawn to the mouth of the alley again. Two silhouettes were watching them.

"Dammit, clear that out," Dunlow instructed his young partner.

Rakestraw took a step toward the two silhouettes. They were either young men or teenagers, tall but slight, hardly a threat. Drawn here by the sound of the beating, not any desire to intervene.

"Beat it!" Rakestraw yelled in his lowest register, bass notes practically shaking dust from the mortar in the brick walls. The shadows beat it.

Then another swing from Dunlow and the Negro was on the ground.

"Thought we didn't want attention," Rakestraw said.

This constituted a significant workout for Officer Dunlow. Sweat ran down his cheeks, and his cap was askew. His belt was strained by his forty-some-odd-year-old belly, and he was panting even though he'd thrown only five or six punches. Failed physicals were in his immediate future.

Rakestraw hadn't thrown a punch himself, had in fact barely moved, yet beneath his uniform his skin, too, was slick. Not from exertion but the opposite, the stress of holding himself back, the anxiety of watching this again.

"You're right," Dunlow said, catching his breath. He stepped closer to the loudly breathing mound that, minutes ago, had been a Negro walking alone, a man Dunlow suspected of bootlegging moonshine. Dunlow looked down at the mound. "We come to an understanding, boy?"

This was a phrase Rakestraw had heard his partner use so often now that it echoed in his sleep. Dunlow and perpetrators *came to an understanding,* Dunlow and witnesses *came to an understanding,* even Dunlow and the judges before whom he testified *came to an understanding.* The man seemed confident that he possessed a vast reservoir of knowledge, which he in his goodwill shared with those around him.

"Yeah, yeah. I unnerstand." It sounded funny because some teeth were missing.

Rakestraw saw that flicker in his partner's eyes, something he'd seen a few times now. It foretold very bad things indeed. So Rakestraw stepped forward and put a hand on his partner's shoulder. Dunlow was taller by two inches; that and the age difference made this feel uncomfortably like a son trying to coax his drunk daddy back from the brink of slapping Ma around some.

"Dunlow," Rake said.

Dunlow looked back at Rake like he barely recognized him for a second, like maybe he'd actually expected to see a son and not his partner.

Dunlow did have sons, two of them, in their teens and by all accounts hell-raisers who lacked rap sheets only because of their father's occupation. The veteran cop's eyes were fiery and he appeared on the verge of taking a swing at this junior interloper, the way he probably had numerous times to his sons. Then he recognized Rake and returned to where he was.

Rake said, "Made yourself clear, I think."

"Yeah."

But not before a final kick in the gut for emphasis, and the lump on the ground hissed a long inhalation, then silence, like he was afraid to let it out. By the time he exhaled, the two cops were gone from the alley.

Rake chose to believe that his partner's extreme response to the bootlegger was due to a passionate desire to enforce the city's alcohol ordinances. He chose to believe a lot of things about Dunlow. Such believing took work, not unlike religious faith, the devout belief in things that could not be proven. Because in the case of the not-terribly-godlike Dunlow, there often was strong evidence to the contrary. In the weeks since Rake had taken his oath, he had seen Dunlow beat at least a dozen men (usually Negroes) rather than arresting them, had seen him instruct a few men on what to say if and when they needed to stand witness at a trial, and had seen him take a handful of bribes from bootleggers and numbers runners and madams.

There was a lot that Rake was learning about his new occupation. He had survived against steep odds for years in Europe as an advance scout, had been alone for long stretches and had wisely figured the difference between threats and opportunities, collaborators and spies. Back home in Atlanta, however, he was finding the moral territory more difficult to chart than he'd expected.

Rake wondered if there was a particular reason Dunlow had beaten this Negro, a particular message he'd been sending, and, if so, was it any more nuanced than the message Rake's own dog sent whenever he lifted his leg on the neighborhood walk. In such cases, Rake rationalized that his job was just to hold on to the leash, hold on to the leash.

So Rake stood there and tried to divide himself in half. One half of him would hold tight to his moral compass, that small wobbly thing that prevented him from beating a stranger without cause. The other half of him would learn everything he could from Dunlow and his fellow officers, the surprising and often counterintuitive pieces of advice on how to survive in Darktown.

"I'll drive," Rake said, opening the driver's door before his elder could object.

Dunlow sat in shotgun and peeled off his gloves, sucking in his breath.

"Y'all right?" Rake asked.

"Bastard had a hard head."

"Sounded like it."

"You know the average nigger skull is nearly two inches thicker'n ours?"

Rake wasn't the type to indulge such comments. But he didn't feel he had much choice around Dunlow, so he went for the neutral, "I did not know that."

"Read it in a journal. Phrenologists."

"I've been reading the wrong journals, I guess."

"I ain't surprised, college boy." Dunlow called him that even though Rake hadn't graduated, doing only two years before the war changed everything. Fluent in German thanks to an immigrant mother and two years of courses at UGA, his skill had been prized indeed. "Anyway, explains a lot, don't it? Not just the lack of room for a fully evolved brain, but, you know, your basic hard-headedness and all."

"His skull looked plenty malleable to me."

Dunlow made a fist, then extended his fingers. He had double-jointed thumbs. He could extend them all the way back to his wrists, a gruesome circus trick—he liked to surprise newcomers by doing that after opening a bottle of Co-Cola, crying in pain for a moment, receiving a horrified reaction from the witness, and then he'd bust a gut laughing. He bragged that he'd been the greatest thumb wrestler in his elementary school, which was exactly the sort of bizarre accomplishment only he would boast about.

It also meant that, when wrapping his hands around someone's throat, he had an extra couple of inches of grip, an advantage which he'd just employed.

Dunlow made a fist again. Rake heard a tendon pop.

"Ah, shit. That's better."

Then Dispatch came over the radio, mentioning how Negro Officer Boggs was reporting a traffic violation, and did any real cops feel the need to assist? Dunlow picked up the mike and said he'd love to.

After the white man had driven away, Boggs and Smith had walked to the nearest call box, requesting a squad car to make an arrest. Dispatch had mercifully refrained from commentary as he relayed the information over the wires, and a white squad car, D-152, had immediately called in to say it was coming. Smith and Boggs were surprised—usually the white cops took their sweet time responding to anything the colored officers requested. D-152 must have been mighty bored that night.

Five minutes later, they were walking a few blocks south of Auburn, approaching the National Pencil Factory and its ever-present smell of wood shavings, when they saw the Buick again. It was actually stopped at the end of the next block, obeying a stop sign. It lingered there.

"What's he doing?" Boggs asked. "Circling around for something?"

Boggs imagined himself shooting the Buick's tires. Which of course would get him fired, or worse. No colored officer had yet discharged a firearm in the line of duty.

"Maybe he's given up?" Smith asked. He hurried toward it, not quite running but moving fast enough that his injured knee was very displeased.

He and Boggs were only ten feet away when they saw the white man hit the girl. Even through the back windshield it was unmistakable, the white man's gray sleeve lashing out, the passenger's long hair flailing to the right. The whole car seemed to jump.

Then the Buick drove on again.

"Let's keep after it," Boggs said.

The Buick was moving south, and in two blocks they would be near another call box. They could at least update Dispatch as to the car's location, in case D-152 really was on its way.

They ran. The Buick still wasn't going a normal speed, as if it was on the prowl for something. Clearly the driver didn't see the two cops giving chase.

Smith's knee was giving him a rather clear and unadulterated warning that this whole running business had best stop soon. After another block they reached the intersection with Decatur Street, just north of the train tracks. Again the Buick obeyed a stop sign.

Then its passenger door opened. The woman darted out, her yellow sundress a tiny flame in the dark night until she vanished into an alley.

The Buick stayed where it was, the door hanging open like an unanswered question. Then the white man leaned over, his pale hand appearing outside the car and grasping drunkenly for the handle. He closed the door and drove on.

"Chase him or follow her?" Boggs wondered aloud as he and Smith stopped.

They could have split up. Smith could have pursued the woman and Boggs could have continued his chase of the Buick. But Sergeant McInnis had warned them many times against separating themselves from each other. Apparently, the Department felt that a lone Negro officer was not terribly trustworthy, and that a second Negro officer somehow had a restraining influence on the first. Or something. It was difficult to discern white people's reasoning.

"I want to see the son of a bitch written up," Smith said. "Or arrested."

"Me, too."

So although only one of them had seen her face, and that just for a second, they let her disappear into the night, which would never release her.

Boggs sprinted east on Decatur. A half mile ahead of him, the downtown towers were dark. Nearby he could hear freight cars being hitched and unhitched, other behemoths wearily making their way through the night. Smith kept after the Buick, which was headed south now, driving into the short tunnel that cut beneath the tracks. He was losing it. Rats darted in either direction as the Buick splashed a stagnant puddle from that afternoon's twenty-minute storm. Smith was just about to give up when he heard the familiar horn of a squad car.

He ran through the tunnel and into a scene strobed by blue lights: the tracks curving away to his left, garbage loose on the street and sidewalk, and a squad car pulled sideways to block the path of the Buick, which had finally pulled over.

The white cop who'd been driving jumped out of the car, left hand held high, right hand lingering on the butt of his holstered pistol.

"It's Dunlow," Smith said when Boggs made it beside him.

Dunlow ranked high on Boggs and Smith's list of most hated white officers. Not that there was an actual list. And not that there were many white cops who did *not* rank high. Maybe it wasn't so much that Dunlow was worse than the others; the trouble was that he was an ever-present problem. The colored officers were only allowed to work the 6–2 shift, and there were only eight of them, so white officers still had occasion to visit what was now the colored officers' turf. No white cops had ever had Auburn Avenue as a beat before, they'd simply dropped by the neighborhood when they needed a Negro to pin a crime on, or when they felt like taking out their aggressions on colored victims. Otherwise, white cops had avoided the colored neighborhoods. Dunlow, however, seemed to feel rather at home here, though the residents did not feel nearly so warmly toward him.

"Let me handle him," Boggs said. He was the more diplomatic of the two, a notion Smith did not like to acknowledge. Even if he knew it to be true.

They adjusted their caps and ties, made sure their shirttails hadn't come out, and straightened their postures as they slowly walked up to the white Buick.

Dunlow arrived at the driver's door, trailed by his young partner, Rakestraw. Dunlow seemed to look at the driver longer than necessary before speaking. Perhaps he thought this was intimidating. The days when his bulk had been mostly muscle were gone, but he was still a man accustomed to cutting quite a wake.

"License and registration, please."

Boggs had spent his entire life giving such white men as wide a berth as possible. Now he had to work with them.

So Boggs concentrated on Dunlow's partner. He walked up beside Rakestraw and leaned into his ear. If Rakestraw was offended at the prox-imity, he did not show it. They didn't have much opinion on Rakestraw, who tended to hide in his partner's long shadow. He likely would prove to be as much of a bastard as Dunlow once they got to know him.

"He had an adult Negro female in the car with him. She fled on foot, at the corner of Hilliard and Pittman. He'd hit her in the head a block earlier."

"You saw it?"

"They'd been circling around. It just happened a minute ago."

Rakestraw offered a neutral expression and the slightest of nods, which could have meant *Interesting* and could have meant *Who cares?* and could have meant that he would recommend to the colored officers' white sergeant that Boggs and Smith be reprimanded for not pursuing the woman.

The driver handed Dunlow his papers and joked, "They got you babysitting the Africans?"

"Understand you fled the scene of an accident," Dunlow replied.

"Wasn't no accident. You hear any other car complaining 'bout an accident?"

"It was a lamppost on Auburn Ave," Boggs said.

Dunlow glared at Boggs. He did not seem to appreciate the colored officer's contribution to the conversation. He extended the paperwork to Rakestraw, who walked back to their car to call in the information. Then Dunlow said to the colored officers, "That'll be all, boys."

Boggs glanced at his partner. Smith was dying to say something, Boggs could tell, but was holding himself back. They hadn't yet told Dunlow about the assault they'd witnessed. The victim was gone, sure, but a crime is a crime.

Boggs opened his mouth. He tried to choose his words carefully. But before he could do so, the driver chimed in again, in a drunken singsong, "Back to the jungle, monkeys!"

Dunlow cracked a smile.

That approval was all the driver needed: he launched into a rousing chorus of "Yes! We Have No Bananas!"

Dunlow was grinning broadly at the performance as Boggs met his eyes. Boggs held the look for a moment, hoping that he was passing on silent messages but knowing, despite all his effort and anger, that those messages would not be received.

The song was getting louder. Boggs couldn't even look at his own partner, as he would see the rage there, would see the reflection of himself, and he could not abide that.

Boggs and Smith walked away. The flashing blues painted the top of an eastbound freight train on the crossing.

"Son of a bitch," Smith cursed.

Boggs spat on the ground. A cockroach half as long as his shoe scuttled across the sidewalk.

"Two bucks says they don't even ticket him," Smith said.

Boggs would not take that bet.

A six-year-old boy named Horace was three blocks from his house when he saw the lady in the yellow dress running. She was pretty, he thought, even though he couldn't much see her face. Then why did he think she was pretty? He would wonder that, later, when thinking back to this moment.

He was walking alone late at night because his mother had woken him up and commanded him to. She was very sick and needed the doctor. She'd given Horace careful directions. He had to hurry, for her sake and because if he took too long, he might forget the directions.

The lady was banging on someone's front door.

Horace watched her as he passed, and she must have heard him because she turned and looked at him. Looking at him and then not looking, the way adults do when they realize you're just a kid and they can forget about you now.

He walked on. She stopped knocking.

At the next corner, he looked both ways to cross the street. Then he decided to turn around and see what that lady was up to. He saw her step off the front porch and walk around to the backyard, at which point he couldn't see her anymore.

He looked both ways to cross again. This time a car was coming, so he waited.

The car pulled up to the curb, right where Horace was standing. The door opened on the opposite side, the engine still on, the headlights still too bright in Horace's face.

A thin white man walked up to him, a white man in a light gray suit.

"Hello there, son. What are you doing out at this hour?"

It was the kind of voice that adults who aren't used to talking to kids use.

Horace mumbled something about his mother.

The man squatted down so his eyes were almost at Horace's level. His eyes were very blue. His hat matched his suit.

"Slow down, son, and enunciate those words."

Horace had felt mostly confused when the man had stepped out of the car. Now he felt mostly scared. Something about those eyes, and the man's waxy white face, and the way he looked at Horace. Like he was very *interested* in Horace.

"Mama's sick. I'm fetching the doctor."

A loud banging sound, like a garbage can falling over a block away, and then the laughter of coyotes.

"I'm sorry to hear that. Now, I have another question for you, son. Have you seen a colored lady out here tonight, with long hair? In a yellow dress?"

Horace nodded. The man smiled. His teeth were like the drawing in a magazine.

"She went into that building over there, didn't she?"

"She knocked but couldn't get in, sir." He remembered to say "sir." He had forgotten earlier. "She went 'round back instead."

Rakestraw sat in his squad car, calling in the license and registration and watching as his partner chatted with the driver. What were they talking about? It seemed more conversation than would normally be taking place right now.

The driver's name was Brian Underhill and he was forty-three years old. The license listed a Mechanicsville address a short drive away.

Dispatch radioed back that Mr. Underhill did not have any record, warrant, or probationary status. Rakestraw was about to jot out the ticket when he stopped himself. He wasn't clear on how his partner wanted to proceed. So he stepped out of the squad car and walked toward the Buick.

Dunlow had been saying something, but he stopped as Rake handed over the papers.

"Thank you," Dunlow said. "I was just telling Mr. Underhill here to be more careful about his driving."

"Yes, sir, Officer." The driver seemed slightly amused by something. So did Dunlow.

"All right," Dunlow said. "You have a good night."

Underhill turned his Buick back on. After it was a block away, Rake asked, "No ticket?"

"Me and him came to an understanding."

"That understanding involved us not ticketing him for being drunk and knocking down a city light pole?"

"What light pole? You see any light pole?"

"Boggs and Smith say they saw it."

"Don't recall the darkies saying they actually witnessed it. Though they may have. Even so, it's one less light in Darktown. Practically a civic service the man performed for us."

Dunlow walked back to the car, taking the driver's side this time.

"Wonder who the girl was," Rakestraw said as he got in, trying not to sound too accusatory.

"Again, I myself do not recall seeing any girl. Darkies say they did, I'm sure they're sniffing around the bushes for her right now."

Dunlow probably believed that the colored cops did indeed possess such heightened powers of smell. Among other powers.

"And when Boggs and Smith file a report about it?" he asked.

"They're dumb, but not that dumb. Niggers know if they step on my toes, I kick hard." He turned on the car. "Let's patrol a more respectable area of our fair city."

The white man in the light gray suit had been smiling at Horace for longer than felt normal.

"You're a good little boy, aren't you?"

"Yes, sir." Horace's mother had warned him about white people, that he should never speak to them unless they spoke first, and that if he did, he needed to say "sir" and "ma'am" and not be rude but to get away as quickly as he could before they did something terrible.

She had refused to say what it was people like this did that was so awful. Horace figured they ate colored people, or at least colored children.

What else had his mother said? That's right, not to look into their eyes.

Yet Horace had looked into the man's eyes the moment the man had crouched down, and he could not look away. They were so blue and empty he felt himself being pulled in more deeply to fill that void. Horace shifted on his bare feet.

The man reached out and patted Horace's head. Once, two times. The second time, the hand lingered there. Then it moved, slowly, to the base of Horace's neck.

Horace flinched.

The man's hand slipped behind Horace's right ear, then reappeared again. Between the man's forefinger and thumb was a shiny dime.

"You can pay the colored doctor with that."

Horace realized he should be reaching out with his hand, so he did, and the man placed the coin in his palm. Then the man stood, and without that eye contact it was like he vanished.

Horace hurriedly crossed the road.

He was still clutching the coin and had walked another block when he realized that he had indeed forgotten his mother's directions to the doctor's, and he was lost now, and so very tired.

2

THE NEXT MORNING, Rake and Dunlow were on the prowl for an escaped convict.

They were pulling an earlier watch than usual, having clocked in at ten a.m., due to some strange personnel shift that no one really understood. Overtired and overcoffeed, they were in search of one James James Jameson—his real name—who had escaped state prison in Reidsville the previous day. APD had just been notified. Triple James, as he was known on the force, had been sent away for attempted murder two years ago, back when Rake was a disgruntled civilian adjusting to postwar life at a textile mill and doing a poor job of it. The trial had attracted much local coverage and even some national attention, as there were many in northern areas who felt the Negro had been unjustly persecuted, in that way of far-off people disapproving of how you deal with your own.

"Boy's been bad news since before he was born," Dunlow said as they sped down side streets.

"How'd Reidsville say he got out?"

"Official story is prison break. Shots fired from a tower, speedy nigger escaping nonetheless, you know the story. But it so happens a buddy a mine retired out there, and story he heard is that Triple James and two other niggers were on highway cleanup, with just two guards. And one of them guards takes a walk or something, and the other guard, who's now the only guard, decides this is a good time to take a leak off to the side of the road. Only he has one of them infections makes pissing take forever. And hurt like blazes. So I'm told. Anyway, Triple James had apparently freed himself from his foot links, Lord only knows how, and as the guard was huffing and puffing with his little man in his hands, poof, off runs Triple James into the piney woods."

"You have got to be joking."

"Son, don't ever overestimate the intelligence of our partners in law enforcement."

"With you around, I never will."

Officers had been assigned different locations to check first. Ex-girlfriends' apartments, last known associates, poor old parents, and aunts and uncles and sundry relations. Apparently Dunlow knew that Triple James's sister had moved recently, and he'd kept this information to himself during the briefing, not sharing it with Rake until they were in their car. The sister lived in a crowded Negro neighborhood a few blocks south of Auburn Avenue.

This was one advantage to Dunlow's propensity to wander into the colored neighborhoods: he knew the streets, the characters, the histories, and could predict the future with surprising accuracy.

Atlanta was a strange city, and Rake was realizing that he'd not fully appreciated that strangeness before the war, as this was all he'd known. Yet he'd known only parts of it. Downtown had the towers, the wide avenues crowded with streetcars and trolleys and cabs, small triangular parks at confusing intersections, and unexpected one-ways that baffled the newcomers. Grand hotels and office buildings and fine theaters and, in the dark interstices between, narrow alleys that could turn dangerous after dark. During his time in Europe he'd seen London and Paris, where he realized just how small Atlanta was, but his city didn't like admitting that, and indeed every year a new ten- or fifteen-story building seemed to add itself to the skyline. Go too far in any direction and the tall buildings were replaced by either mills or factories or rail yards, most of them surrounded by cheap worker housing, and beyond those borderline shanties the neighborhoods were buffeted by shotgun shacks or bungalows or Queen Anne's or Tudors, depending on how poor or well off the area. Outside the city center, the trees were omnipresent, a canopy of oaks blocking out the sun most of the time, and thank God for it in the summer. Go farther beyond those neighborhoods, though, and you were in the country, farmland and the occasional small-town Main Street, mule-drawn plows and cotton and vistas unchanged over decades. Even within the city limits Rake had found himself in scenes so rural he was amazed they were still within a few miles of the capitol, with crumbling old farm buildings and outhouses and livestock giving funny looks to his passing squad car.

It was the areas east and west of downtown that Rake had known especially little about. To the east was the Auburn Avenue corridor, and immediately west of downtown was the West Side, both of them Negro neighborhoods.

The street Dunlow now drove them to was only a few blocks south of Auburn and was flanked by rows of narrow, two-story clapboard houses. Crape myrtle branches sagged in the heat, their lavender blooms hanging like ripe fruit. The cloudy sky was darkening at midmorning, rain on the way.

"His sister lives here with her husband, second floor," Dunlow said.

"Let me guess, her name's Jamie Jamie Jameson?"

"Belle. Just moved here a couple of weeks ago. Husband's more or less clean as far as having a record, but with a gal like that . . ."

"What's her record?"

"Ain't got none, but you know how blood is. I'll knock kindly on the front door, and you can sneak in back."

Great, the back door. Though going in the back may seem to benefit from the element of surprise, and therefore be an advantage, Rake had learned it was usually the opposite. Back doors opened into kitchens. Kitchens had knives. Two months ago, on a similar surprise backdoor entrance, Rake had been sliced in the arm by a drunk man who outweighed him by fifty pounds, and who had needed three blows from Rake's club to finally fall down.

No one was on the sidewalk as Rake walked through the narrow side yard, creeping beneath clotheslines. No dogs barking, yet. In back, an old wooden fence enclosed their yard, and it wasn't in any condition to support the weight of a full-grown man. In the neighbor's fenceless backyard sat an assortment of boxes and crates, so Rake dragged a wooden crate that reeked of rotten peaches to the fence. He stood upon it and, in the second before the wet wood crumpled beneath him, hoisted himself over the fence. Nearly castrating or at least causing himself severe damage, but managing to avoid it. He did not avoid landing on his backside, however. Fortunately he did not have an audience.

This was the part of police work that remained unknown to those who would glorify it. As far as Rake could tell, the job consisted of about nine parts of this to one part of the other stuff.

He was about to step in the other stuff.

He crept up the back stairs as silently as he could, which wasn't very silently, as the creaky planks did not enjoy being stepped upon. It had taken him so long to get up here that he figured Dunlow was already inside, beating up Triple James's brother-in-law without probable cause.

A thin curtain at the back door's window prevented Rake from getting much more than a gauzy view of a dark-skinned person in the kitchen.

Rake knocked on the door, hard enough to make things in the kitchen shake. The figure turned.

At the front, Dunlow hit the door like it owed him money.

"Police, open up!"

The door did not obey. He pounded it again and could see the gaps around the door widen with each blow. Niggers couldn't afford decent doors. Even the ones who moved to the better neighborhoods, he'd noticed, had weak doors. The ones who wanted to act white and let you think they were above the fray. Just pound on the door and the truth revealed itself right quick.

"I'm coming, I'm coming!" a man said from within. Freddie, Dunlow recalled. He'd spoken to him once or twice, never anything important, just enough to remember the name. A nigger who marries a gal who happens to be sister to a murderer is someone to keep your eye on.

The door finally opened, and it was free of any annoying door chains. Dunlow entered like the conqueror he was.

Freddie was slender and short. Dunlow figured a harsh word would knock him over. How the little ones like this managed to reproduce and send on their genes was a mystery, as was so much about these people.

"Freddie, right? Freddie the man who has Triple James's sister's heart."

Freddie looked down. "What can I do for you, Officer?"

Because the little man barely deserved his attention, Dunlow scanned the room. Perfectly tidy. Suspiciously tidy. The walls were bare but for two photographs, one of a happy Negro bride and groom and lots of their well-dressed relations. It looked new. The other picture of Freddie in army khakis. Christ, Dunlow hated seeing them in uniform. Maybe he'd find a reason to knock the picture down before he left.

A plant by the window leaned toward what little sunlight squeezed between the tightly packed buildings. No toys or crying babies, so they had yet to get around to that. Glasses of what looked like Coca-Cola were sweating on a salvaged coffee table in a small room. An electric fan sat there, aimed at no one.

"You can tell me where he is."

"Who's that, Officer?"

Dunlow inhaled slowly, which, he'd learned, made him appear that much larger, especially around smaller men. And most men *were* smaller.

"You know who I'm looking for."

Freddie's eyes were darting around the room, but whenever they returned to Dunlow they stayed no higher than his chest. Sometimes they appeared to fix on the gun in Dunlow's holster. Perhaps Freddie had never seen one so close. Dunlow doubted that.

"I'm sorry, Officer. I'm a little confused."

Dunlow placed his large left hand on the Negro's right shoulder. He could feel Freddie's trapezius muscle twitch.

"Don't make his problems your problems, boy."

Freddie didn't answer.

"What were you doing before I got here, huh? Ain't got no job to be at?"

"I, uh, I had to take today off. Haven't been feeling that well."

"Really now? That's a shame. Don't you breathe no nigger germs on me." Dunlow smiled, but Freddie didn't seem to see the humor in it.

Rake should be kicking in the back door right about now, Dunlow was thinking. He heard something coming from the kitchen, a tapping.

"Who's that?"

"My wife, Belle. She's fixing my lunch, sir."

"She's home sick, too, huh?" Dunlow's hand was still on Freddie's shoulder.

"Taking care of me, yes, sir."

"You don't seem that sick to me."

A pause. Freddie was wearing only slacks and a sleeveless under-shirt, and Dunlow was in full uniform, yet it was the Negro who was sweating.

"Well, I did nap most of the morning, sir."

There was a narrow hall behind Freddie, and past that a door leading to the bedroom, and past that the kitchen, just out of view.

Dunlow raised his voice. "Why don't you stop that chopping in there, Belle, and walk out here nice and slow so we can all talk together."

The tapping stopped. Freddie looked nervous. Dunlow, in truth, had thought there was only a tiny chance Triple James had come this way, but those odds seemed to be increasing by the second.

"Y'all been home all day, that right?"

"Yes, sir."

Finally Dunlow heard Rake pounding on the back door.

"Just you two newlyweds, taking the morning off?"

"Yes, sir."

"Then tell me why you got three glasses set out?"

The closet door beside him swung open, hitting his elbow. A whirl-wind of panicked Negro sprang out of the closet and Dunlow barely had a chance to see Triple James's face before the convict planted a prison-tested fist square on Dunlow's nose.

Dunlow stumbled back. He reached for his gun with his right hand, thumbing back the hammer, but something clamped on his forearm and prevented him from drawing the pistol. A spell of numbness was working its way from his neck into his hands from that blow—Christ, the nigger could hit—and then Triple James popped him a second time.

Dunlow couldn't reach up with his right to deflect the blow, or he'd relinquish his gun to Freddie, who was clawing at it. He stepped back again and may well have fallen down if not for the fact that he came against the wall then, which was a godsend, and he swung wildly with his left hand, not hitting anything but at least inspiring Triple James to move.

That bought him a second, so he leaned with his right shoulder and drove forward, knocking little Freddie out of the way. Dunlow and Triple James squared off then, the convict with both fists up like a goddamn boxer. Only Freddie wasn't as out of the way as Dunlow had thought—the black twerp had been knocked down, but not completely flat. Freddie reached up, seeking Dunlow's holstered firearm, and somehow managed to pull its trigger.

Rake had been waiting for the figure to open the door when he heard the shot.

Jesus Christ. In his months on the force, he had not yet drawn his weapon in the line of duty. For target practice at the firing range, sure. And he had many years of awful experience firing weapons of various sizes in Europe. But this was the first time he had to reach into the holster and draw, to say nothing of doing so while also taking a step back, then putting all his weight into a lunging kick at the door just beside its knob.

The door-kicking part he excelled at: it was busted clean from its hinges. The drawing part, though, he hesitated at. Because as he entered the small kitchen he saw the figure, now an actual person, a thin, tall Negress with her hair pulled in a bun. Her eyes were large, the kind of large that weren't usually that large but were now because a man had just charged into her house and someone else had fired a gun. There was, of course, a sharp knife in her hand. She was standing at a chopping block, diced tomatoes glistening in their juices.

His fingers were touching the handle of his revolver. But he hadn't drawn it yet, despite the gunshot. Signals were competing in his brain, and the thought of drawing on a cook seemed wrong. He would regret this decision.

"Put your hands up!" he yelled.

She dropped the knife—didn't put it on the counter but actually clean dropped it to the floor—and grabbed from the counter what appeared to be a revolver.

He hadn't seen it. Now it was aimed at his heart. His fingers closed around the handle of his own gun and he began to slowly pull it out, even as he felt something cold place fingers around his heart.

"I need you to put that down," he managed to say.

She managed to shake her head.

"Let go of that!" she said, glancing at his gun, still mostly holstered.

Many a weapon had been trained on him in Europe but never from this close, and never with eye contact. They stared at each other and breathed.

It was actually a good thing this was happening so quickly. He would be much more nervous later. Now, though, he said with a miraculously unshaking voice, "Belle, you need to put that down."

She shook her head. Sweet Jesus she looked scared.

"Don't make me!" she yelled.

He slowly lifted his hands, palms out, *just keep very calm, girl.* He didn't raise them very high, though, his elbows bent. Putting his life at even greater risk, mainly because he still didn't quite believe this was happening. And because he knew he wouldn't have been able to draw fast enough anyway, with her already aimed at him. It was a small room, potential shooter and potential victim maybe seven feet from each other. Seven feet was awfully close to miss completely.

"You haven't been in any trouble, and you don't want to be now." His throat had become parched in an instant. "This is about your brother, not you."

A pot was on the stove. He smelled garlic. He could hear the water in the pot hissing from the pressure.

"Leave us alone." Gritted teeth. She had backed up a step, but now she was against the wall with nowhere else to go.

The lid of the pot started doing that jitterbug thing.

Rake could hear sounds of a scuffle from the other room. Whoever might have been shot was still putting up a fight. But if Dunlow had pulled the trigger, there wouldn't be any scuffling.

"Don't come no closer! You aren't going to do me like you done James!"

"Please put it down and let's talk."

Another shot from the other room. It made Rake jump, not sky-high but a quick twitch like an infielder as the pitcher releases.

It also made Belle's finger twitch.

The gun in her hand fired.

He heard it twice, or maybe she fired twice, he wasn't sure. All he knew was that it was very, very loud in here and that he didn't seem to have been hit by anything.

She'd not expected the kickback, and her arms jolted at the elbows, the pistol no longer aimed at him but at the ceiling.

He grabbed the pot handle and threw.

The pot hit her and she screamed, or the boiling water hit her and she screamed, or both. Her hands were raised to her face and she was bent half over now and she'd dropped the gun. The wall behind her was a different color than before, dripping with something, and she kept screaming, the worst screams Rake had heard in a long while.

He unholstered his gun and scrambled forward for hers. It was coated in hot, gummy grits and he had to shake the damn stuff off.

Footsteps, rushing. He looked up just as a small Negro was darting into the room, eyes wide with horror. The girl's husband, no doubt. Unarmed. Rake sprang up and aimed his revolver at him.

"Don't move! On the ground, now!"

The Negro's eyes were wide, and he obeyed only Rake's first command. They were no more than a foot apart.

"Belle! What did you do to her?!"

Rake could have shot him, or if he'd had a hand free, he could have pushed the man down to the ground, then spun him to cuff him, but he had two guns in his hands. So he swung with the grits-gun and hit the husband crosswise with its butt and down he went.

Rake kneeled on the man and cuffed his hands behind his back. Then he stuffed Belle's gun into his pocket.

Belle was absolutely wailing, half lying on the floor and leaning against the grits-covered wall, her legs kicking out in agony. She was clawing at her face, pulling the stuff off. He couldn't tell if she was pulling out her own skin, too, and had to look away.

More gunshots, four of them, not as loud as before. From the front entrance, maybe?

"Dunlow!?"

"I'm all right!" Dunlow shouted. Sounding not exactly all right, but not dead either. "He ran out the front!"

She was still screaming, yelling about her face and the heat and sweet Jesus. The smells of cooking had been replaced by something far worse.

Rake ran into the hallway.

After Freddie had coaxed Dunlow's gun into going off in its damned holster, things got sort of hard for Dunlow to follow.

He hopped into the air, both in shock and from fear that he'd maybe blown off his foot. He hadn't, luckily, and the shock of the gunshot had finally been enough to persuade Freddie to let go. Dunlow landed with one of his feet on Freddie, or maybe that came later, but anyway at some point Dunlow stomped the little bastard while attempting to box one-handed with Triple James.

He took more punches than he could remember ever having taken in one day, indeed more than in most years, but he was so much taller than the punchy little convict that he'd managed to lean on Triple James, then wrap his left arm around the nigger's neck, trying to choke the fight out of him. He swung Triple James into the wall and probably would have knocked him out if Freddie's apartment had stronger walls. Instead the convict made a person-sized hole in some cheap wallpapered plywood.

With his free hand, Dunlow reached for his holster. He was still holding Triple James in a headlock and wondering if he should shoot him point blank or just pistol-whip him when Freddie, whose hands seemed goddamn magnetized to Dunlow's pistol barrel, knocked the gun from Dunlow's hand. It hit the floor, firing once more.

Even in the headlock, Triple James kept swinging at Dunlow, landing a few. But those fists had a lot less juice to them now, so Dunlow released him, pushing out with his knee to knock the convict onto the floor. Dunlow turned to Freddie, hitting him with a roundhouse that literally spun the little man in a circle. Freddie was almost exactly in the same spot when the spin ended as he'd been before, and then he collapsed.

A crashing sound got Dunlow's attention. Dunlow turned, looking for Triple James. The apartment door was open. Dunlow's gun was still on the floor.

Outside, Triple James was scrambling out of the large azalea bush he'd landed in from his second-floor leap. Dunlow ran back for his gun, returned to the doorway, and saw the convict darting across the street. He pulled the trigger as many times as the gun would fire. Some asphalt kicked up and the back windshield of an old Ford exploded, but the only effect the shots had on Triple James was to make him run even faster, until he was out of sight around the corner.

Dunlow was about to give chase when the world spun on him a bit and he leaned against the doorjamb. The adrenaline was kicking in and his heart was doing things it had never done before and perhaps shouldn't when he finally felt the delayed force of every punch he'd taken.

He slid to the floor, a woman's awful screams the only thing that cut through the fog in his mind.

An hour later, Rake was sitting on the sidewalk in front of the building when Dunlow planted himself there, too.

Four squad cars blocked off the road in either direction, lights flashing. Neighbors had gathered, been shooed away, and now peered through their windows.

The ambulance had come and gone by then, though it hadn't taken Belle with it. She was being arrested, along with her husband, so treatment for her burns would have to wait. Rake still had the acrid singed scent of her in his nostrils.

"That's police work for you," Dunlow said. "All the work and none of the glory."

The sun was hot on their backs, unveiled by the black clouds that must have deposited their wrath nearby but had left this neighborhood unscathed.

"Who was it?"

"Timpson. Got him with a single shot. Set up with a Winchester."

"Heard he was a sniper in France."

"I'd say he just proved it."

Rake had run to their squad car to call in a report. He'd wanted to pursue Triple James himself, but Dispatch had told him there were other cars in the area, and he had to stay in the apartment to watch over Freddie and Belle. And Dunlow, who had been on the verge of consciousness. The big fellow had revived somewhat by the time the other cops showed up, and he'd refused medical attention despite the fact that with every passing minute his face looked more and more like some awful melon gone bad.

Dunlow asked, "You all right?"

"Fine." In truth, Rake's hand hurt like hell. The pot handle had been hot, apparently, and he'd scorched his palm. Hadn't even noticed until ten, twenty minutes later.

They sat there for a moment. The rush had long faded and they were mentally exhausted from explaining the series of events to their superiors. The sun, seeming to sear their flesh like a pan, pressed into their necks.

"I cannot believe I let a woman get the drop on me."

"Happens. The grits, though, will be harder to explain."

"Story must be halfway across the Department by now."

"Don't sweat it. Hell, we're the ones found him. Somebody else got to open the jar, but we pried it loose for 'em."

Some reporters lingered by the squad cars but they were being kept at bay.

"You could have lied," Dunlow said.

"Couldn't think of one fast enough."

Dunlow laughed. "Need to work on that. It's an important skill in this line of work."

Rake realized his hands were shaking. He hugged them to his chest, not realizing that made him look even more unwound.

"*Fuck,*" he breathed, amazed at what was happening to his own body.

"Just wait on it to pass," Dunlow said quietly.

Rake had never been much of a drinker but Lord Jesus he could have used one then. He felt a shiver in his body, but the opposite of the way they usually work, this one starting from his hands and working its effect up until it reached his neck. He swiveled his head a few times as if trying to unscrew it from his neck. His teeth were chattering.

"Been doing this a long while," Dunlow said after a minute, "and I've only stared down the barrel one time. Long while ago. And he sure as hell never pulled the trigger like she just did."

How had she missed? Lord, the luck.

As amazing as her missed shot, Rake realized, was the fact that, of all the cops in Atlanta, it was Dunlow who'd correctly deduced where the convict would be. Every other officer had been chasing down dead leads and outdated information, but Dunlow knew better. Why hadn't

Rake walked in with his gun drawn? Why hadn't he shot her? Because
he didn't think Dunlow could possibly have been right about this apartment harboring Triple James. He had believed to his bones that Dunlow
simply wanted to bully some poor Negroes, far from the real action.
Rake had refused to play along by walking in with his weapon drawn.
He did not want to be party to terrorizing innocent people. As a reward
for that attitude, he'd wound up grievously injuring a woman instead.

Dunlow clapped him on the shoulder. Almost hugging him. That
bit of human contact, not at all what Rake would have expected from
his partner, proved to be exactly what his own body needed. His nerves
seemed to stop firing. He took a breath and his rib cage relaxed.

"You did good," Dunlow said.

Later there would be ample time to deconstruct the myriad ways in
which they had each fucked up. But for now they sat there, while other
cops cleaned up the mess and joked about Triple James's agility and
cleaned grits from the kitchen wall and floor.

"She's burned to all hell." Rake's jaw started to behave itself again.

"That she is," Dunlow said. "Like burnt bacon."

"If I'd walked in with my gun in my hand, she never would have
picked hers up."

"Or she would have tried it and she'd be dead now and you'd be sitting here feeling guilty for killing a nigger girl instead of just maiming
her."

The phrase *maiming her,* the finality of it, was not what Rake wanted
to hear. He sat there and tried not to fixate on the images of her head,
the smell of skin burned liquid.

Dunlow hit Rake in the muscle of the shoulder. Hard enough to
snap someone out of a coma. "Hey. Don't you feel guilty for a thing. You
might be dead if you'd done different, or she might be, or both. This
ain't on you. This is on Triple James and them that harbored him. You
hear me?"

Rake nodded.

"Say it."

"It's on them."

Dunlow's eyes had been focused and intense, probably the same
way they were whenever he told his linebacker sons during halftime to

hit harder goddammit. Then they softened, and he gave Rake another shoulder clap.

"You did good, kid. You lived to tell about it, and every bad joke another cop tells about you maiming her is one more bad joke you wouldn't have gotten to hear if you were dead."

Rake tried to untangle that sentence while he looked at the palm of his right hand, the blister already forming, a bunched whiteness emerging from all that red.

3

SUMMER WEATHER IN Atlanta came in one size: big. There were big storms and big winds when those storms came and sometimes a big tornado afterward, then big floods. Or it was big heat, as though the sun had veered out of orbit and was pressing closer and closer, determined to exert itself on the personal space of everyone in the city, get right up next to you, breathe in your face, and laugh at your inability to do anything about it. The one fortunate thing about being on the night shift, Boggs figured, was that it was *slightly* less grueling to be walking around the city in the dark.

He and Smith were walking the beat on a quiet Tuesday night. Lightning occasionally streaked the sky like a distant, silent warning.

Then another flash, closer still, and the sound was not thunder.

"Gunshot." Smith said what Boggs was thinking. Then a second shot, and glass breaking, and a woman's scream.

They stood at the intersection of Edgewood and Howell, and the sounds were coming from the south. They unholstered their pistols and raced down the street, where in the distance they could see a figure escaping into the night. They heard shouting closer by, and as they ran they saw two people standing on the front porch of a two-story brick apartment building. A man leaned on the porch railing, a woman holding something to his forehead.

"Were you shot?" Smith called out at them, stopping.

"Mind your own business," the woman hollered back, not even looking at them.

"Police!" Smith tried again. "Have you been shot?"

She looked up now, surprised. "No. We fine."

"Stay there," Boggs instructed them, then he and his partner continued to run down Howell, but that brief pause was enough: whoever they were chasing was gone.

Five minutes later they returned to the couple on the porch. They said their names were Wilma and Raymond Moore, they appeared to be in their late thirties, and they seemed more annoyed than alarmed at whatever had just occurred. She wore a loose gray dress and her hair was pulled back in a bun with a red kerchief that matched the one she was pressing into his forehead. He wore a janitor's blue uniform shirt and tan pants, and his forehead was giving out more blood than his wife could clean right then. They claimed someone had been trying to climb into their first-floor bedroom, where she had been sleeping, when Raymond, who was returning from work, happened upon the would-be burglar. He'd wrestled the man from behind, taken an elbow to the forehead, and at some point the assailant had fired the errant shots and escaped. This scant information came from them grudgingly, and the officers could sense there was more they weren't being told. Plus, Wilma appeared to have some makeup on—she did not look like a woman who had been asleep a moment ago—and Raymond had liquor on his breath.

"Did you see his face?" Smith asked.

"Look, we're fine now," Raymond said. "We're okay."

"Why you even bothering about any of this?" she asked.

"Because we're police officers," Smith replied. "It's what we do."

"We didn't call you here," Raymond said.

"We heard the gunshots."

"Whyn't you mind your business?" she asked.

"This *is* our business," Smith said. "Enforcing the law is our business."

"Law?" Raymond laughed. "Law ain't never concerned itself with us before, less'n they want to jail one of us for something somebody else done."

"Well," Boggs explained, "it's different now."

"I ain't remember saying I wanted it any different. I want you off my porch."

"We have a right to be on this porch because we heard gunshots and I'm looking at a man with a busted forehead," Boggs said. "That's called probable cause."

"Look, folks," Smith said, speaking slowly, "I know everyone's all revved up right now so let's just calm down a spell. We're here to help you. Because we're two crazy men who actually like to help people for a living. It's like being preachers except we get to carry these," and he lightly tapped the handle of the sidearm in his holster.

"You don't need to be dealing with people who cause you trouble on your own porch and try to break in and shoot you, all right?" Boggs said. "You don't need that. You can tell us who it was, and we'll take care of it. We can help you."

"I don't need your help. I see that sumbitch again, *I'll* take care of him."

"*No,*" Smith said. "That's what *we* do."

"You beat folks up?"

"No, but we arrest people who've broken the law and we put them in jail."

"I ain't want him in jail, I want to beat his ass, and that's exactly what I'll do next time I see him."

"A second beat-up person is not what we want," Boggs said. "We want you to stop beating on each other every time you disagree about something."

"Don't you talk to me like I'm some child."

"Sir, I'm trying to help you and—"

"I told you I don't need your help! I ain't some child, I'm a man. I know how to uphold my honor when some fool like that try and mess with me. He think he got away with it but he don't. Next time I see that Emmett Jones, I'm gonna—"

"His name is Emmett Jones, good," Boggs said. "Where does Mr. Jones live?"

"You stop playing those police tricks on him!" the man's wife interjected. She removed the kerchief from her husband's forehead. "See how he done that trick on you?"

"It's not a trick, ma'am," Smith said. "If you say this Emmett Jones assaulted you and shot at you, we can have him in jail tonight. He'll be tried, and if he's convicted he'll—"

"Dammit, I said I didn't want him arrested, I want his ass beat." He took the kerchief from his wife and again tried to stanch the bleeding.

"I don't need some pretty-talking boy in a nice uniform to be doing no convicting for me. You saying I ain't my own man? I know how to defend myself. Last winter when Moody Hills come by and stole all my firewood, what you think I did to him? I tracked him down and clocked him with a piece of that same firewood and that took care of that."

"*You're* the one who assaulted Moody Hills?" Smith asked. "He was unconscious three days." They'd never made any progress on that one; they'd simply come upon a man lying outside his home beside a pile of logs, back during their first week on the force.

"I didn't say that! I didn't say that!"

"You see!" his wife hit him in the chest. "He playing those police tricks on you again! You gots to stop talking!"

"That was a different time Moody got sent to the hospital anyway!" Raymond shouted at the officers. "Time I hit him was different from that time!"

Boggs folded his arms and began rapidly losing the desire to talk to this couple. Yet talk he did, for a few more minutes, and if this had been the debate club at Morehouse College, then surely the judge would have awarded Boggs all the points. But here on this dilapidated and unlit porch in the darkness of night, the verbal sparring won him nothing. Trying to introduce the concept of law and order to a people who had never been given reason to trust it, and who therefore found justice in blood feuds—they were so much more honorable, and interesting, and, well, bloody—was a terribly long and frustrating process.

Boggs jotted down snippets in his small notebook. More questions, fewer answers. The couple adamantly refused the need for medical care, and they didn't want to file a report, thank you, but the gunshots alone dictated the following of certain procedures. Boggs walked down the street to call in the gunshots from the nearest call box, and Smith began knocking on the other doors of the apartment building, hoping for witnesses and already knowing the kinds of half-asleep nonanswers he would receive.

※

Two hours later they were walking again when the skies opened and they took shelter beneath the awning of a hardware store. The monsoon was intense and the wind soaked their pant legs as they stood there otherwise protected, the tang of wet asphalt thick in the air already.

Power flicked off, power flicked back on. Thunder rattled old windows.

Of the eight, seven had served in the war. Two had medals to show for it, including Smith, awarded a Silver Star for carrying two badly burned fellow soldiers out of a demolished tank and through hostile fire. Six had attended college and four, including Boggs, had diplomas (a graduation rate exponentially higher than the white cops'). All were Atlanta natives. Before swearing their oaths, one had been a typesetter at the Negro *Daily Times,* one had been a butcher, two had sold insurance, one had been a handyman, one had taught, and two had been janitors. Xavier Little played a mean fiddle and was ruthless at chess. Wade Johnson was a skilled artist and had once hoped to be an architect before seeing that particular door closed due to his color. Champ Jennings was six three, had once been an amateur boxer, and carried, instead of a billy club, the sawed-off handle of an ax. All were Christian, six of them attending services regularly. Three were fathers. Their ages ranged from twenty-one to thirty-two. Each of them wondered how many of the others were seriously considering quitting.

One of them was currently on suspension: Sherman Bayle, the ex-butcher. A kindhearted fellow, whom each of the others feared might be a bit too soft for this line of work. At twenty-nine, he was the second oldest, with three kids. Two weeks ago he was brought before Sergeant McInnis; someone had lodged a complaint that Bayle had been seen drinking in public. Bayle told McInnis it wasn't so, he hadn't even been at the nightclub in question. Yet a white officer, off duty, had driven past the club and he swore he'd seen Bayle leave the premises stumbling drunk. It was a white cop's word against a colored cop's.

An investigation was ongoing. Bayle was suspended without pay. Most of his fellow colored officers had dropped by his house to offer their support, though there wasn't anything that could be done.

All of the other seven believed Bayle was innocent, but that hardly mattered.

They were not detectives, only beat cops. They had no squad cars and were forbidden from entering the white headquarters. Their job was to enforce peace and arrest those observed to have broken the law, but they could not conduct investigations. One day, they each hoped, there would be promotions, but not now. Probably not for a very long while.

Although Sweet Auburn boasted far more wealth than most white folks realized, and, on the other side of town, the West Side offered renowned Negro universities that many white folks didn't even know existed, most of Atlanta's colored neighborhoods were in dire condition. Few lampposts, sporadic-to-no garbage collection, several unpaved roads, no enforcement of housing codes. And, until months ago, no cops. The end of the war had brought a population boom to the city, with so many farmers fleeing sharecropping to find something only slightly less horrible. Families lived packed into one-room apartments, multiple families sharing a bathroom in some buildings, others in ramshackle dwellings tucked into the alleys lining the more decrepit blocks. Some of the neighborhoods still lacked plumbing, and more than once Boggs and Smith had the unfortunate experience of pursuing a suspect who wound up trying to hide in an outhouse. These neighborhoods were minutes on foot from the street where Boggs had lived all his life, but his family had assiduously avoided them. It was like entering another world.

The area was in desperate need of policing. Since the white cops ventured over only when they needed a Negro to conveniently arrest for some crime, the residents had no protection from pickpockets and thieves and burglars, scofflaws and roughnecks, moonshiners and drunks and rapists. Even the fine homes on Auburn Avenue were not immune from break-ins and the occasional sighting of a prostitute strolling past. And the sheer amount of alcohol in this until-recently officially dry city was enough to keep the rest of the South at least half drunk at all times.

So they had started by going after the booze. They busted pool halls that kept moonshine. They busted stills, literally tore them apart with crowbars and set fire to the piles. They shut down barbershops that sold illegal booze, pharmacies that sold illegal booze, even an old lady who ran a small nursery school but sold booze on the side. The closest thing to an actual investigation they'd pulled off had been a prolonged surveillance of several low-level bootleggers to get a better sense of the underground market's supply chain. That had led to a handful of arrests; one of the bootleggers' trial was just days away. Otherwise, their work involved being put in the middle of awful family situations: this son stabbed his father, that husband put his wife in the hospital, this wife is selling herself at night and now the husband found out and is chasing the pimp down the block with a cleaver in his hand.

His second day on the job, Boggs had been trying to help a woman whose wayward sons' friends had broken into her place and robbed it. He'd asked, *"Ma'am, can you tell me what time it was when you were out?"* and *"What other things were taken, ma'am?"* when her face turned into a scowl and she'd demanded, *"Why you keep calling me 'ma'am'?"* He'd been thrown at first, no idea what she meant. The second time she'd said it, he replied, *"Well, I can't very well call you 'sir.'"* Which had not been what she wanted to hear; she launched into a tirade, accusing him of playing some trick on her. It took him a moment to realize that no one had ever called her "ma'am" before. Boggs had heard his own mother so addressed countless times, as she was a regal Auburn Avenue matriarch, wife to a preacher. But to this poor woman, it was a word for someone else. *"You blind, son? You see a 'ma'am' here? I look like a white lady to you?"* It had broken his heart.

A few months later, it had happened so many times he'd grown used to it.

Hours later, another storm had come and mostly gone, fading to a drizzle. Boggs and Smith walked in their ponchos, gutters playing their percussion all around them. Vast puddles sometimes forced them to walk in the middle of the road, and the city was glistening and new and everyone but them was asleep.

They walked down Krog Street, passing bungalows painted red and yellow and blue. Another block north and they'd reach a small textile mill across the street from an empty, overgrown plot where a few weeks ago they'd helped two lunatic white men from the country retrieve a couple of stallions that had fled the men's trailer after the men had pulled over in front of a nightclub for a few drinks.

Their shift had more than an hour to go and Boggs was yearning for sleep when Smith stopped.

"Oh, Lord." He was sniffing, so Boggs did, too. Even in the damp air it was unmistakable.

They walked in little circles, seeking its source.

Smith knew the smell far more intimately than Boggs, whose war experience had not involved combat, much to his chagrin. But Boggs had come to learn that scent on two occasions these past few months, once when they'd helped a landlord kick down the door to an apartment whose tenant had not been heard from in days and once when they'd come upon a local drunk who'd had his final, lethal jolt of bad moonshine in an alley.

Smith walked through the high grass of the abandoned lot, risking snakebites and red bugs and God knew what, using his long flashlight to see where he was going and to push back the overgrowth.

As they neared the brick wall of a two-story building, their feet started crunching upon wrappers. They beamed the ground and saw that this was an unofficial trash dump; garbage spanned the length of the building, several feet high in places. The overall stench was even worse, and more varied now, but still that tang of death clung around them.

Amid the weeds was some bamboo, and Boggs snapped off two shoots. He handed one to Smith and they used them to sift through the trash. Their beams illuminated paper bags and bottles and decaying food and worse things, all of their smells loud and radiant, made all the worse by the fact that the lot had been baked by the sun and soaked by rains and reheated and resoaked over and over again.

Boggs's bamboo hit against something solid. He pushed at the trash and moved it off whatever it was. Then he saw her. He didn't recognize the skin as skin at first, because it was so discolored. But he recognized her canary-yellow dress.

While Smith hurried to the nearest call box, Boggs said a prayer for her. He asked that the Lord keep her spirit, whoever she was. He asked that she find peace. And he prayed for the Lord's forgiveness, because he had seen her in that car with the white man who hit her, and he hadn't done anything to help her.

4

SERGEANT MCINNIS WAS the first to join them at the site. Two of the other colored officers, Wade Johnson and big Champ Jennings, made it minutes later.

"You're sure she's the same girl?" McInnis asked.

"Pretty sure," Smith replied.

"Thought you said you couldn't see her face that night."

"Can't really see her face anymore either, Sergeant. But she has the same dress and locket and hair."

McInnis crouched beside the corpse while Boggs shined a light. The body was bloated and purpled and not recognizably human. Pieces of it were missing, sometimes in chunks and sometimes little pecks, in accordance with the size of the scavengers that had feasted on it.

"Damn. Couple days, I'd say." McInnis stood back up. "Garbage collection is supposed to be once a week in this neighborhood, ain't it?"

"That might be official policy," Smith said. "But I live a few blocks away, and it ain't the case."

"Well, I want you to call in to Sanitation and find out the most recent time they've been by."

"Yes, sir."

After three months of working under McInnis, none of them knew quite what to make of him. He had the exasperated air of a man who was perpetually one card shy of a royal flush, his patience thinned by that one maddening, missing card. He had a wife and, they'd heard somewhere, kids, yet he never spoke about them. His short dark hair had never noticeably grown or been cut, which meant either he trimmed it incessantly or it just somehow didn't grow. The hair was free of gray, though he had wrinkles around his eyes, the weathered look of a fellow who'd been scowling for years until it became permanent. He was thin and—the few times any of them had occasion to see him pursue a subject on foot—startlingly fast. He was their boss. He called all of them by their last names and never asked about their home lives. None of them had ever heard him say "nigger" or "coon" or "monkey" or "ape," yet they all felt certain those words were familiar to his tongue. He didn't smile much. He ate meticulously constructed sandwiches that his wife (they assumed) wrapped in waxed paper for him, never going out for a meal, which (they assumed) was because he did not want to patronize the local colored establishments. He was in all likelihood the only sergeant in Atlanta who had eight rookies to deal with, regardless of race. They each sensed that he hated his job, at least since they'd been hired.

"You'll have to take the body out," he said. "And then you'll have to go through this whole mess for the murder weapon or anything else."

"Should we wait for Homicide, sir?" Jennings asked. "We don't want them criticizing us for disturbing a crime scene."

"They'll criticize you regardless of what you do. And this crime scene appears pretty well disturbed already. Besides, if we wait on them, we could wait so long the sanitation trucks beat them to her."

They didn't need him to translate: white detectives couldn't care less about a dead colored girl, especially one found in a dump.

"Someone should question the fellow she was with that night," Johnson chimed in.

"Brian Underhill," Boggs said.

"He was in your report?" McInnis seemed interested in that name.

"Yes, sir. Dunlow and Rakestraw took over once he was pulled over the second time."

"I'll look into it." McInnis considered something, eyes down. "C'mon, take her out."

Boggs and Smith exchanged a quick glance, then got on with the unfortunate business. The body was rock hard, and they heard ugly snapping sounds, what might have been bone or tendons, and the gross expulsions of gas as they wrestled her out. They carried her past the dump and the jungle of weeds, lowering her to the alley floor as gently as they could manage. Boggs trying very, very hard not to think about what they were doing, not to fully grasp it.

The body was filthy, covered in everything from coffee grounds to wet newspaper to what appeared to be maggots. Jennings backed up a step, hand raised to his mouth.

McInnis, handkerchief covering his nose and mouth, knelt down beside her. He tried to move her head, couldn't, and settled for rearranging the hair that had been covering her face. It was foul and nightmarish and despite all the missing flesh there didn't seem to be anything shaped like a bullet hole.

He moved to her chest now, and there it was, a bullet hole leading to her heart. Not difficult to find at all, since the top of her dress was soaked black. There only appeared to be one, and the sight of it seemed enough for McInnis, who apparently figured the coroner could look for any others.

McInnis used his flashlight to beam the ground, looking for a blood trail, evidence she'd been dragged, anything. But the area was so unkempt that the search was useless. If she'd been dragged and bled somewhere, the blood was long since washed away.

Clock-out time was supposed to be two, but it was nearing seven and Boggs and Smith were still filling out paperwork on their Negro Jane Doe in the basement of the Butler Street YMCA.

The Y was a six-story brick structure that, in addition to serving as a gymnasium, rooming house, neighborhood meeting place, and political headquarters for the colored community, had for the past three months also become the de facto precinct for Atlanta's eight Negro police officers. The same city fathers who had finally extended the badge to Negroes still could not imagine a world in which colored cops *sat beside* white cops, or ate with them, or showered and dressed in the same locker rooms, or defecated in the same toilets. Surely a riot would ensue.

The fact that the Y was their HQ had spawned a range of slang terms among the officers. Walking a beat was "running laps." Being chewed out by McInnis was "getting benched." Doing paperwork was "lifting weights."

The Y was managed by Herm Eakins, an older man who'd come down from New York ten years earlier. He told people he wasn't a political sort, but he'd been spurred into action by the white cops, who frequently busted his door down and demanded that he admit them into the rooms of his various boarders, whom they suspected of having committed some crime or another. The cops never had a warrant and seldom even had a name, and Eakins seldom seemed to have any rights. He had reinstalled his door *twelve times* after cops had kicked it down, the story goes, one for each tribe of Israel. After the *twelfth time* he'd had to replace it—had to painstakingly rebuild the entryway and put in new screws and chisel the side of the wall and install new anchors—that twelfth time was the last. He reached out to Reverend King, Reverend Holmes Borders, and Reverend Boggs, informing them that whatever they needed from him to help get some Negro cops in this neighborhood, he was their man.

That's when Lucius first met him, more than a year ago, at one of the Citizenship School sessions Reverend Boggs helped organize. The white primary had just been abolished by the Supreme Court, which meant white people could no longer bar Negroes from voting in the Democratic primary, the only election that mattered. At least, *in theory* white people couldn't bar them (the ruling didn't stop Governor Talmadge from proclaiming that the best way to keep Negroes from voting was "with pistols"). Mayor Hartsfield, a moderate on the race issue, had promised the colored community leaders that he would hire colored cops only if they registered enough voters to make an impact in the municipal elections.

Lucius had been back from the war for a year and a half by then, working at the same black-owned insurance company as his brother Reginald and still seeking his purpose. At the Citizenship School, he had stood in front of nearly a hundred people of varying ages and explained to them how voting worked, where they needed to go to register, what they had to bring. Which nasty questions to anticipate and how to deflect them. How to dress and conduct themselves, what not to say.

Twenty thousand registered Negro voters later (countless pamphlets and endless meetings and long speeches and miles of shoe leather worn down all across the colored neighborhoods of Atlanta) the community had their officers. And because those officers needed a place to change into their uniforms and file their reports, Eakins offered them the Y's basement.

White officers had proven quite uninterested in knocking down—or even knocking *on*—the Y's door ever since. They grumbled that the Y's boarding rooms were no doubt a hive of illicit activity with nothing but *Negro-quote-cops-unquote* to stop them, but Eakins didn't mind the chatter. At least he didn't have to hang another gotdang door.

The ramshackle precinct consisted solely of this subterranean space, badly heated in the winter (so they had been warned) and so humid in the summer that the concrete walls actually sweat. Eight desks were crammed in the room like some rural Negro elementary school. The concrete floor was cracked in places, dirt from below seeping upward, so much so that no matter how well Boggs shined his shoes, they looked dusty when he hit the streets. In the back some Sheetrock and a thin door had been installed to create an office for McInnis, who had asked his own superiors repeatedly if this cup could pass from his lips, but no, someone had to be the martyr and oversee the Negro cops, and it was him.

The showers were three floors up, the toilet was one flight up, and there was often a line for both. Lack of paper and paper clips was a problem. Rats were a larger problem.

On one wall, thumbtacks denoting crimes and suspects' addresses adorned a map of their district. Even at this early hour, Boggs could hear a basketball bouncing on the first-floor courts.

That there were eight Negro officers did not alter the way the Atlanta police department went about identifying Negro Jane Does. The first step was shipping the body to the morgue, in the basement of the white headquarters, far removed from the colored officers. The second step was waiting for someone to show up asking where his girl was. If that didn't happen, the third was throwing away the body when space was needed for another dead Negro. The coroner had finally shown up in his wagon to take the body, but, as McInnis had predicted, Homicide never showed.

Most of the bodies Boggs had dealt with were found at crime scenes where the perpetrator was still present, or where the victim lived, or at a venue with several witnesses. This was the first time any uncertainty had been involved. There was no missing persons report matching her description. The yellow dress she'd been wearing and the simple necklace—steel cord and a silverlike heart-shaped locket, empty—were the only things on her person that might prove identifying, other than a birthmark on her right shoulder.

"You done with that report yet, Boggs?" McInnis asked. He was not a fan of Boggs's report-writing. During their first week, he had read one of Boggs's reports to the others during roll call. "The subject *vehemently* defended himself," he read, with sarcastic emphasis, and "the witness's *aquamarine* blouse had become *translucent* from spilled moonshine," and "the hilt of the blade *protruded* at a ninety-degree angle." Then the sergeant had tossed the report in the trash, saying, "You're not impressing anyone with the ten-dollar words, Boggs. Fewer adjectives, please. No one's giving you a PhD for this." Since then, Boggs strained to be as succinct as possible so as not to offend his GED-holding boss.

As he typed, he thought of the facts he wished he knew, information a white cop easily could acquire by going to the Records department. If the Negro officers needed to access files that were stored at headquarters, they needed to place a call asking for the file, since they weren't allowed on the premises. The file would then be added to a stack that was picked up daily by McInnis, who frequently complained to his officers about that chore. *I am not your errand boy.* Which made them that much more reluctant to make such requests.

Boggs didn't even know what charges Dunlow and Rakestraw had cited Underhill with the evening they'd pulled him over. But he had a feeling McInnis didn't want him to bother with finding out, as it would have only made the paperwork take longer.

Boggs was nearly finished when McInnis excused himself to use the john, which was one flight up. (The Y had been paid by the police department to turn an existing closet into a small, whites-only restroom for McInnis's sake.) Boggs picked up the phone. He identified himself to the police switchboard operator and asked for Records. Muffling the receiver, he turned to his partner and asked, "Cover for me, Tommy."

Smith shook his head, but he walked over to the stairs, in better position for a warning whistle if McInnis approached.

The voice of a middle-aged woman came over the line: "Records."

"Yes, I need the arrest record for Brian Underhill on July ninth."

"Who's speaking?"

He gave her his name and badge number, which included the suffix identifying him as a Negro officer. He was put on hold for a while. At least she hadn't hung up on him. *McInnis better have slow bowels,* he thought. Finally, she was back on the line. She told him there was nothing to be found.

"Not even a traffic citation?"

"Nothing. No record of anything involving that name."

"I'm sure that's a mistake. Could you check the logs for Officers Dunlow and Rakestraw? They would have made the arrest."

She sighed loudly into the phone and put him on hold again. Minutes passed. McInnis was still in the john, poor bastard (or maybe he'd fallen asleep on it?), when her voice finally came back on.

"Nothing in the recent logs for those officers about any Underhill."

So not only had Dunlow and Rakestraw not cited him for striking the lamppost, they hadn't even made note of the fact that they'd pulled him over.

"While I have you," Boggs said as politely as he could before she hung up on him, "I was hoping you could pull Underhill's records. Does he have any priors?"

"I've done enough for you, boy. There was no arrest, there's nothing for you to worry about, so go patrol your nigger neighborhood." She hung up.

Boggs held on to the receiver for an extra moment, his cheeks burning.

A minute later, McInnis returned, and Boggs handed over his report. McInnis skimmed it, his eyes red above the gray bags in his skin.

"I'll take it over in the morning. Next shift, I mean." He yawned. "Lord, it's late. Go home, everyone." He left without a thank-you.

Boggs and Smith each showered upstairs for a good fifteen minutes. They saw garbage whenever they closed their eyes. Garbage and a body. They put on their civvies and stuffed their rancid blues into trash bags. They had only one spare each, so they'd need to get these washed immediately. Boggs had his mother—financial good sense and practicality meant that he still lived with his parents—while Smith paid a woman on his block to do his.

Boggs was on his way out, nodding a good morning to Eakins at the front desk, when he heard the basement phone ringing. He stopped, considered for a moment, then jogged down and unlocked the precinct door. The phone was on its sixth ring by the time he lifted the receiver.

"Officer Boggs."

"This is Records." It was a woman's voice, so hushed he could hardly hear her. "Did you call about Underhill?"

"Yes. Yes, that was me."

"Well, we never had this conversation, but what do you need to know?"

It had been hard to tell because of her whisper, but now he was sure of it: this wasn't the same lady who'd told him off earlier.

"I had thought he was cited for a traffic violation the night of the ninth, but she told me there wasn't anything—"

"I know, I heard that part. But what else? You'd best hurry, she'll be back soon."

"His arrest record. Any priors. And his address, occupation. Anything."

"He's ex-APD."

Boggs sat down. "When was he on the force?"

"Until '44 or '45. Toward the end of the war, I remember."

The facts and ramifications were coming too fast for Boggs to assemble at once. If Underhill was ex-APD, then Dunlow must have known him. Which at least partially accounted for the easy rapport between the two of them that night, the way Underhill's singing taunt had won a familiar smile from Dunlow.

But also: *McInnis* likely knew Underhill. Which would explain the look on the sergeant's face when Boggs had said the name a few hours ago.

"He looked a little young for retirement," Boggs said.

"He didn't retire. He was forced out."

"Why?"

"Shoot, I gotta go. I'll try and get you something."

"What's your name, ma'am?"

But she'd already hung up.

5

THE NEXT NIGHT, Rake was filing a report at headquarters when he heard someone say *"Dead girl."*

"What dead girl?"

Girl used to make him think *woman* but now that he had a daughter the word had forever changed. He heard *"dead girl"* and thought of a toddler in a pink dress. A car accident, a stray bullet, a drowning. One little life ended and so many others permanently scarred.

The other cop clarified: "girl" as in nigger adult female.

Rake read the report. In a trash heap. Yellow dress, locket. One bullet wound in the chest. No name or ID, nothing physically distinguishing save for a birthmark on her right shoulder. Filed by Negro officers Boggs and Smith.

"Anybody been to the brothels?" Rake asked out loud, to no one in particular.

"Not tonight, but maybe later," someone joked. Laughter from the others.

"I mean, is she a whore or just somebody who got shot?"

Another beat cop sighed as he walked past and said, "She came in all covered in garbage. I don't imagine any detectives will be lining up to take that one, but I'm sure you're welcome to sniff around."

"We are born naked and covered in shit, and so shall we exit," someone else mused.

"She wasn't naked, according to this," Rake said.

"Well, she's naked now."

Hours later, Rake and Dunlow sank into their chairs at the Hotbox, a diner two blocks from Terminal Station. It catered mostly to rail yard workers but became a de facto police cafeteria in these post-midnight hours, as it was one of the few places in the city legally allowed to stay open all night.

"If it isn't Grits Rakestraw!" Brian Helton's voice called out.

Laughter from all over the dining room. Rake willed that his cheeks not turn red, though they probably did, as Helton and his partner, Bo Peterson, walked in.

Rake had been hearing a lot of the "Grits" line. Officers in his presence made a point of discussing what they'd eaten for breakfast, as if this was the funniest damn thing they'd ever heard.

"They do serve grits here all night, I believe," Helton said. He had short blond hair turning gray and he looked like the sort of fellow who might have once had a lot of promise, longer ago than he cared to admit. Perhaps he'd been skilled at throwing a ball of some kind and had married a cheerleader who was still distraught over the fact that they couldn't afford to live in a better neighborhood.

"Flavored with niggers' tears," Peterson added. With their similar manners and surnames, Rake saw Helton and Peterson as basically the same person, divided in half by some horrible accident. Though he changed his mind about which was which. Peterson had darker hair and a rounder face, but otherwise their differences appeared minor.

They dragged another table over to join Rake and Dunlow for "lunch," which Rake still thought was a strange thing to call a meal you ate at midnight when you worked the night shift.

"They're saying Henry Wallace is gonna try to give a speech here next month," Peterson said.

"I don't care to discuss politics at work," Dunlow said. Dunlow still had fading bruises on his face from his tussle with Triple James. "Nor anywhere else." He belched.

"Well, our esteemed former VP has made it his own personal policy not to give any talks before segregated audiences," Helton explained. "So if he gives a talk here, that means some of us will have the honor of arresting him."

Wallace had served as vice president under FDR, one of the most hated men in the South, for one term before being unceremoniously dumped in favor of Truman in '44. Now he was running, against the man who had supplanted him, as a third-party agitator. Wallace had gone hard left during his time in the political wilderness, attracting all manner of Communists and socialists, railing against segregation and doing what he could to cause trouble in the South.

"They won't let us arrest the ex-VP, you idiot," Peterson said. "We'd just have to shut it down."

"Where's it happening?" Rake asked.

"Haven't said yet. They'll likely announce it as last-minute as possible."

After they'd eaten and the waitress had cleared all but their coffee mugs, Helton asked, "Y'all hear the latest on Nigger Bayle? He's gonna be reinstated."

"Bullshit," Dunlow said.

"It's bull but it's happening."

Dunlow was the one who'd reported Negro Officer Bayle for consumption of alcohol. He claimed that he'd seen Bayle among a trio of Negroes drinking from flasks outside a bar. Rake had learned over the ensuing days that things hadn't quite happened that way—it was actually one of Dunlow's Negro informants who'd seen it, supposedly.

"Next time you want to get a nigra suspended," Helton said to Dunlow, "say you saw him doing something more lurid."

"Bad enough we got coloreds wearing the same badge as us," Dunlow said, "but some of them are drinkers, too."

Though Rake was officially Dunlow's partner, he had worked a handful of shifts with Peterson and Helton in his first few weeks, as the Department liked the rookies to learn from as many veterans as possible. Rake swiftly determined that he had little to learn from them. Like Dunlow, they were on the wrong side of forty for beat cops, and they were far more interested in getting cuts from gamblers and moonshiners than in enforcing the law.

The first time Rake had met Peterson, the older cop had extended his left hand, saying, "I have a friend in Black Rock." Rake had extended his right, puzzling over the comment. Their two opposite hands had hovered there like a couple of mismatched shoes. Peterson had repeated his comment and kept his left hand dangling. *Who the hell shakes hands with his left?* Rake had thought. Then Peterson had pulled his hand back and walked away without another word. It wasn't until Rake saw Peterson have a similar encounter with another rookie cop that Rake put a few things together. That time, Peterson and the other cop shook with their left hands, the fingers loose, almost like two fish flopping against each other. They'd noticed Rake watching them then, and had glanced at each other, which was when Rake realized that the left-hand thing was a secret Kluxer greeting.

And the first time he'd walked with Helton, they had arrested an old Negro who had simply been walking home along Juniper Street at midnight. Helton had demanded the Negro's work papers, wanting proof that he was employed at a night job and therefore had reason to be out so late. There was no official curfew in Atlanta, yet most of the cops enforced one on the colored population. Helton had made such arrests in Rake's presence three times now, and every time it happened, Rake silently vowed that next time he would protest, insist that this was ridiculous, or at least refuse to go to the call box. Yet every time it happened, he went along with it, reluctant to win himself a new enemy.

"Your informant may have actually been wrong about Bayle," Rake said to Dunlow.

"Really, now?"

"Rookie doesn't seem to understand how valuable it is to have friendships," Helton said.

Rake took his time finishing his coffee, then put the mug down. "Don't call me rookie, Helton. I got four years' combat experience while you were over here arresting elderly Negroes for illegal-pedestrianism-after-curfew."

After a second of silence, Peterson laughed. "Kid's got sand, Dunlow."

"Damn right he does," Dunlow vouched. "Had my back at Triple James's while you two and everyone else was trying to find him on the wrong side of town."

"I would like to hear him further explain his opinion on Nigger Bayle," Helton said, seething from Rake's comment. "Seemed to me there that he was supporting Bayle over Dunlow. That doesn't sound like having your partner's back."

Rake realized he was wading deep into waters he'd been trying to avoid. Lord only knew where the sudden drop was.

"The city isn't going to change its mind," he told them. "The Negro cops are here to stay. I'm not saying you have to like it, but I am saying, if we want to keep from driving ourselves crazy, we'll learn to deal with it."

"Oh, we are going to deal with it," Dunlow said. "Make no mistake on that."

"I just mean y'all are looking at this the wrong way."

"Enlighten us, Officer Rakestraw," Peterson said. "Share with us your higher worldview."

"Look, you two patrol over in Kirkwood, so what do you care about colored cops? They're miles away from you. But me and Dunlow are in downtown, just blocks from Darktown every night." He decided not to add the fact that Dunlow made a point of going into Darktown *every damn night* to reassert his ownership. "Right now, sure, it's awkward with us being so close to them. But once they're up to speed, once they've proven themselves decent cops, or close enough, the city'll hire a few more—"

"The devil you say," Peterson nearly spat.

"—and then they'll have the manpower to police their part of town by themselves. Which means us white cops can police the white neighborhoods, and we won't need to spend another moment down near Auburn Avenue or Decatur Street or the West Side." He paused a moment for them to get the point. "Isn't that what you want? You're so huffy about seeing a Negro in a uniform that you can't see this for what it is: a better kind of segregation. Give the colored cops the colored neighborhoods, and we'll never have to set foot in there again. They'll handle their affairs, and we'll handle ours."

Dunlow was watching Rake with a kind of stony silence. The others looked like they were either having trouble following his argument or were wondering if he was deranged.

"Lord have mercy," Helton finally said with a shake of his head. He waved to the waitress for a refill. "A white cop saying that what we need is more black cops. Guess you got a little shell shock over there in France, boy. A little weary of fighting."

"That's a mighty nice story, Rakestraw," Peterson said. "But there are only two ways this little experiment might end. One is them niggers running through burning streets, firing rifles into the air as the whole damned city turns to chaos. The other is us shoving those badges so far down their throats, we'll be able to cut their balls off with 'em."

Rake and Dunlow had been barely driving a minute when Dispatch called in with a report of an assault in Darktown. An old colored woman who lived on Fitzgerald had seen "four or five" men in a fight, some of whom she thought might have been colored officers.

"This sounds good," Dunlow said to Rake after telling Dispatch they were on their way.

It was a side street five blocks south of Auburn, Dunlow driving so fast he nearly drove over the scrum of Negroes in the center of the road, braking just in time. Rake wondered if maybe he'd been toying with hitting them on purpose.

Negro Officer Little was cuffing one of two Negroes who were lying facedown on the sidewalk. The other was already cuffed, his hands slick with red.

Negro Officer Boggs was a few feet away, on one knee, a blue handkerchief held to his forehead.

"What these niggers do?" Dunlow barked.

Little looked up after cuffing the second man, eyes livid. He and Boggs were both out of breath.

"This one stabbed that one," Little said. Rake didn't know much about Little, who was black as pitch and wiry thin, other than the fact that his uncle ran the local Negro paper. "And when we tried to break it up, the one who'd been stabbed threw a bottle at Officer Boggs."

One of the men on the ground wasn't so much out of breath, Rake realized, as moaning in pain.

"Well, well," Dunlow laughed. "That's why I always let niggers fight it out amongst themselves before getting involved."

"There were two children and a woman with them, so we didn't think that was a good idea."

Boggs's eyes looked dizzy. A streak of blood ran down his forehead and the handkerchief wasn't doing a good job sopping it all. He did not appear to be in a rush to stand all the way up. He managed to say, "Call an ambulance, please."

Dunlow laughed. Rake realized one of his own hands was clasped around the handle of his billy club.

"What you think you were doing, boy, throwing a bottle at an officer of the law?" Dunlow demanded. "Or maybe you don't think they're *real* officers of the law, do you?"

The Negro had fallen onto his side and was gasping for air, the act of breathing too painful now.

"And you know what?" Dunlow said. "You're right."

Dunlow loomed over the Negro. Rake was still gripping his billy club. The two Negro officers were standing exactly where they'd been before but they both seemed crouched, bracing for what might come next.

"Because, boy, if you *did* throw a bottle at a *white* officer, you'd damn well be a dead nigger right now."

"Why are you even here, Dunlow?" Boggs asked. "We didn't call for help."

"I'm here because this is my city, boy. I'm here because the good nigra citizens of the area called the police asking for help. That's why I'm here. The better goddamn question is why *you're* here."

Then Dunlow pulled at his belt buckle, as the kicking had caused it to slide a bit beneath his gut. "You want an ambulance for the nigger, you can call it your damn self."

Rake followed Dunlow back to their car, then he said, quietly, "Dunlow, they need an ambulance."

Dunlow stared at him. "You ain't calling one from *my* radio."

Rake stood there, thinking of what he could do.

Dunlow asked, "What's your damn problem, son?" He was just quiet enough so that the Negroes couldn't hear this dispute among white men. "You want to help the niggers so bad? What about your 'better kind of segregation'?"

Rake had no answer.

Dunlow opened the driver's door and got in. "There's a call box a block away. Call it your damn self."

He slammed his door and drove off, nearly driving over one of the fallen Negroes.

Rake felt he had crossed a line he had meant only to toe, and now he'd been abandoned.

"Ah, you look all right," Dunlow said. "Better work on you
though."

"Not for me. For him."

Boggs, with the elbow that was attached to the hand
pressure to his own wound, indicated one of the two men lyi
ground.

"Gut stabbed," Little explained. "Pretty bad."

Dunlow kicked at the gut-stabbed one. "Roll over, nigger.'

Rake felt he should go into the squad car and call the ambu
Dunlow himself hadn't moved to do so. The door was open,
only a few feet away.

The stabbed Negro could not roll over on his own. So
kicked him in the ribs.

Little backed up, outraged. "He can't roll over, Dunlow, he's

Dunlow kicked the Negro again. The Negro howled in pai

Boggs stood up. "Call the ambulance."

Dunlow ignored him. Rake considered making the call him
didn't move.

Little carefully pulled the stabbed man to his knees, then tur
so he was leaning against a telephone pole. The car's blue lights
the scene. The man's howl had gone back down to a moan. H
a white sleeveless T-shirt and the lower left-hand side was bla
blood, glistening.

"Yeah, he did get you pretty good." Dunlow whistled. He stil
making a move for his car radio, clearly enjoying how he cou
this out. "Why you throw a bottle at an officer of the law come
you, boy?"

Judging from the Negro's scrunched eyes and locked jaw, he
too much pain to talk.

Boggs took a ginger step and said, "*I'll* call the ambulance."

"Don't you go near my car, boy," Dunlow warned.

They stared each other down. Rake was behind Dunlow a
could see the look on Boggs's face, the anger there. Pain and the
seemed to have washed a certain veneer from the preacher's son.

Then Dunlow kicked the stabbed Negro directly in his woun

The man screamed and at least one of the Negro cops yelled

Neither of the Negro officers were looking at him when he told them he'd call for an ambulance and a wagon. He ran to the call box as fast as he could.

For twenty minutes Little applied pressure to the man's wound while Boggs sat on the sidewalk denying that he needed medical treatment. Rake, after making the call, knew he should seek out the witnesses the officers had referred to, a woman and some kids, but this situation before him seemed plenty volatile enough and he felt the need to stay. He hadn't been able to stop Dunlow from attacking the man. Yet he needed to believe that, if something like that were to happen again, he would stop it. He would not let events outrace him like that, like they always did.

Other than the nonstabbed Negro, who occasionally chimed in with claims of his innocence and mistaken identity and this just being a spat among kin that really ought not trouble officers of the law, no one spoke for a while.

Finally the ambulance came and the three officers helped the orderlies load the injured man, whose moaning had become distressingly quieter. Rake and Little tried to talk Boggs into going in for treatment, too, but he refused.

"I don't feel like spending three hours at Grady waiting for a stitch or two. I'm fine."

So Little climbed in as the police escort.

After the ambulance pulled away, Rake indicated the other Negro and told Boggs, "I can wait on the wagon with him if you want to get back."

"I'm fine. You can go."

But Boggs hardly seemed in condition to be left alone, even with his suspect handcuffed, so Rake lingered. They waited a while.

Eventually Boggs started pacing, tentatively testing out his legs. His forehead had stopped bleeding so he'd ditched the handkerchief. He looked like hell, though. Rake started pacing, too, and when they were far enough away from the cuffed Negro, Rake decided the silence was too damned awkward.

"Your first on-the-job injury?"

"First one that'll leave a scar."

He wanted to apologize for his partner, but why was Dunlow his responsibility? What would such a gesture be worth? And what consequences would come from not vouching for his partner before a Negro he barely knew?

"It'll make you look rugged. Girls'll love it."

Boggs's initial response was a hard look. As if he was offended and was ready to fight over it. Then he looked away.

Jesus, Rake had only meant it as a harmless tease, like he would have said to any other cop performing a thankless task. That was the thing with these Negroes; either they were jesters who wanted to make light all the time or they were so damned serious, deeply insulted by any perceived grievance. Perhaps humor had been the wrong approach.

"I wanted to ask you about that body you found," Rake said. "Report says you searched through the trash?"

"It wasn't my favorite shift. Do you know who's working the case?"

"No."

"News travels slow to the Butler Street Y."

"I'll let you know if I hear anything."

"Thank you." Boggs seemed to mull something over for a moment. "I wonder if they've talked to Underhill yet."

"Who?"

"Brian Underhill. The last man she was seen alive with."

It took Rake a second, but then he remembered the fellow who'd hit the pole on Auburn. He recalled Boggs and Smith claiming that the man had had a Negress in the car with him earlier.

"I didn't realize it was the same girl."

"I put it in my report."

"No, you didn't."

"Excuse me?"

Again Rake seemed to have set off some alarm in this fellow. He couldn't tell if Boggs was always this jumpy or if it was the knock on the head or, more likely, the recent exposure to Dunlow. Rake himself was unfortunately used to that.

"I read the murder report, Boggs. There was nothing about Underhill in it. Nothing about that traffic stop at all."

Boggs was staring. "You're sure you read the whole report?"

"Yes, I'm sure I read the whole report." Now Rake was the one getting irritated. "All three pages. I read it tonight, and there was nothing about Underhill."

Boggs looked away, then turned completely around, as if he was searching for something. They stood like that for long enough that it started to feel rather strange.

"What?" Rake finally asked.

"Nothing." Boggs turned back around. "I thought I put it in there. I . . . must have forgotten."

That's sloppy work, Rake nearly said. Boggs wasn't the most likable fellow in the world, but he projected a professional air, as though being a good cop was the most important thing in the world. Rake respected that. The son of a reverend, never dropping his g's, his uniform pristine and the brass always shining, his posture military perfect. Hearing him admit such a mistake took some of the shine off him.

"You should refile it," Rake said. "I don't think they have any leads."

"You mean, you don't think anyone is working it at all."

Boggs said that as if he held Rake personally responsible for the stonewalling of other whites.

"I guess that is what I mean. But a person of interest's name in your report would change that."

Another uncomfortable silence from Boggs, who finally said, "I don't think it would."

6

ONLY HOURS AFTER that awful night, Boggs and Smith were needed at the courthouse for a morning trial. Boggs had expected testifying to be one of his favorite experiences, yet it had proven to be the worst. Not least because of the timing: always in the morning, after their night shifts, and they were denied overtime pay—they made $196 a month, far less than the white cops. Between last night and the previous night finding the body, Boggs had enjoyed maybe five hours' sleep the last two days combined.

The first time Negro officers had been needed in a courtroom, the judge had refused to let them enter in uniform, demanding that they enter as *typical nigras.* That had not gone over well at the Y—the officers complained to McInnis for weeks. Only after much back-channel maneuvering by the very reluctant sergeant and after another judge's vouching for their continued "good behavior" (as if they were dogs whose ability to control their bladders was worthy of compliments), they had recently won a concession: they could now wear their uniforms at trial.

But they still couldn't wear them *on the way to or from the courthouse,* just as they weren't allowed to wear them to or from the Y. The latest policy stated that they could carry their uniforms in garment bags to the courthouse, which they would enter via the colored entrance. Then, in an old custodial closet next to the colored restrooms, they could change into their uniforms. They'd been given keys to the closet, which, though it was no longer in use, maintained the smell of mildewed mops and disinfectant. At least it smelled better than the colored restrooms.

So many of their interactions were fraught, perplexing, dangerous. There was no precedent to follow, no *Jim Crow Guide to Colored Polic-*

ing. They had each survived into adulthood by proceeding warily, yet now they were expected to walk with a heavy step and newfound power through their neighborhoods. In every other part of the city, however, they were still expected to vanish, or worse.

➤

"Your Honor," the city prosecutor said, "the city would like to call, ah, to call . . ." and some papers spilled onto the floor. The young attorney looked like an actor in a high school play, complete with an unruly cowlick. He was someone important's nephew, surely, doing a year or two of city work to gain insight into the darkness of the human soul before settling into the family firm. "Ah, yes, here it is, the city would like to call Negro Officer Lucius Boggs."

"If you must," said His Honor, the troll-like and perpetually grumpy Judge Gillespie.

Boggs took the stand at the downtown courthouse and waited while a clerk found the colored Bible suitable for Boggs's hand. Boggs was asked if he would tell the truth etc., and he said he would.

He had a bandage on his forehead and three stitches that he'd received earlier that morning after visiting a Negro doctor and family friend. *Shoulda gone to Grady last night,* the physician had said, whistling when he'd seen the wound. *Lucky this isn't infected yet.* Boggs hadn't bothered to explain that the last thing he wanted to do was go to the colored hospital's emergency room, where he would have had to wait hours while surrounded by many of the people he had likely arrested or tried to arrest over the past few months.

Now he looked like a fool, half his forehead covered in white, and still dealing with a headache that the doctor assured him would pass "in a day or two." The doctor said the scar shouldn't look too bad. *Give your face some character.*

On trial was one Chandler Poe, a lanky Negro in his late forties, with reddish hair growing in mangy tufts from his narrow head, and a long nose that betrayed Cherokee heritage.

Boggs and Smith had already noticed that the white detectives who had been assigned the case did not seem to be in attendance. Also disconcerting was the presence of a dozen white civilians, all of them well dressed.

"Now, Boggs," the kid attorney asked in his genteel Sewanee voice, "according to your report here, you and another officer arrested Poe as he was leaving his residence with several barrels of corn liquor in his possession?"

"Yes, Officer Smith and I made that arrest on June third. Mr. Poe at first denied knowing what was in the barrels, but as we waited for a wagon to arrive he admitted what he was doing."

Judge Gillespie was a loud breather, Boggs had noticed. Each time Boggs put a "Mr." in front of Poe's name or an "Officer" in front of Smith's, he could hear the judge's breathing grow louder.

"And what exactly did Poe admit?"

Electric fans blared and windows were open but there wasn't a shirt that hadn't been sweated through. The room was slated for air-conditioning next year.

"Mr. Poe said he was in the business of paying wholesalers for corn liquor and then selling it to several drinking parlors."

Boggs was bothered by the many mysterious white faces in the gallery. Even the Negro *Daily Times* reporter in the third row, busily taking notes for the next installment of his ongoing journalistic recording of the life and times of the colored cops, felt hostile somehow.

"Did Poe name any of these wholesalers?" the prosecutor asked.

"No, Mr. Poe kept that information to himself."

Much sooner than Boggs had been expecting, the prosecutor told the judge he had no further questions. The kid had mentioned a fraction of the reams of evidence Boggs and Smith had gathered.

"Hmmpf?" Judge Gillespie said. He'd stopped paying attention a while ago and had been filling out some municipal paperwork. "Oh, yes. Ah, would the defense like to cross-examine?"

"No, we certainly do not," replied Poe's attorney, a tall older man wearing a smart blue suit and wingtips, altogether too well dressed to be a public defender.

Boggs was dismissed, and with the prosecution prematurely resting its case, the defense attorney called a Mr. Henry Jefferson. An older white man with a shock of colorless hair falling across his forehead took the stand.

Under questioning, Mr. Jefferson explained that "Chandler" was a docile handyman who worked a number of jobs for the family. And quite a good banjo player to boot. In fact, ol' Chandler had recently performed at a particularly grand family reunion that the Jefferson clan had held a few months ago, entertaining nearly a hundred people.

"He's a good boy," Mr. Jefferson told the judge. "Now, I'm sure he's liable to get himself into trouble now and again, and we've talked to him about that. But he means well."

The defense attorney thanked Mr. Jefferson for taking time from his busy schedule as vice president of the Marshall & Sons Textile Mill to come out here and offer his testimony.

"That's all right," Jefferson said, "but I wanted to make sure Chandler wasn't punished unnecessarily for a momentary lapse in judgment. He's a good nigra and it's a shame to see the city wasting resources on a hearing like this for what's clearly just a misunderstanding between the coloreds."

Boggs was clenching his jaw. Smith made fists in his lap.

Mr. Jefferson turned out to be but the first in a parade of character witnesses, all of them concurring in the benign nature of the accused, all of them agreeing that he posed no threat to society so long as he had a stern white hand to guide him, and all noting that the city would be much the poorer if it was deprived of his musical skills. The fact that the prosecutor cross-examined the white citizens into admitting that they could not dispute any of Boggs's evidence hardly mattered.

After the last witnesses, the judge got on with his ruling. He portentously informed Poe that he should tread lightly from here on out. Then he acquitted Poe of the charges, and down came the gavel.

Poe made eye contact with the Negro officers and, though he didn't actually wink or smile, something about the roundness of his eyes and the angle of his head managed to convey it all the same, an invisible wink. Then the bootlegger filed out.

Boggs and Smith approached the young prosecutor as he gathered his papers.

"First time in a courtroom?" Smith asked.

"You think I enjoyed that? I spent *hours* on this case." His voice had far more authority and conviction than he'd managed before the judge. "I don't appreciate my record being besmirched by shoddy paperwork, let alone having the deck stacked against me."

He had spent *hours* on the case? Perhaps eight or nine? Boggs and Smith had followed Poe for two months, on and off duty. Weeks of their lives had just vanished with that gavel bang, for nothing.

"Sorry we besmirched you," was all Boggs could get out.

The young lawyer looked at the officers as if for the first time, finally seeming to realize he'd insulted them. There was a glimmer in the kid's eyes of something that Boggs realized, to his surprise, he did not hate. Some morsel of humanity, some shame at his failure, perhaps a sense that he had let down these hardworking, if inferior, police officers.

"You really want to be helpful?" the lawyer said. "Next time y'all want charges to stick on someone, make sure your Department sends in *white* officers to testify against him."

"So what happened in there, fellows?" Jeremy Toon asked them in the hallway. He had been two years ahead of Boggs at Booker T. Washington, Atlanta's sole high school for Negroes. He'd been skinny then and he was skinny still. His fingers clutched a notebook and pencil, which is exactly how Boggs had always remembered him.

"You're a smart man," Smith said. "Figure it out."

"C'mon, now." Toon was a reporter for the *Atlanta Daily Times.* He was a good, decent, ambitious person, and neither Boggs nor Smith could stand him. "Need some comment from you two."

"You know we aren't supposed to be talking," Boggs said, keeping his voice down, very aware of the lawyers and bureaucrats walking past. In a louder but polite voice, he said, "Go to our commanding officer if you need a comment."

The scribe lowered his notebook. He was wearing a brown tweed coat that didn't match his thick black tie. "You know they don't talk to us. Look, I've been covering this since you filed your first report. Y'all had tons of evidence the prosecutor didn't use, and all the judge wanted to hear about was banjos? What do you want our readers to think?"

Smith took one step toward the reporter, halving the gap between them. "Are you asking us to call out our prosecutor in your paper? Or complain about our superior officers? Or maybe you have a pink slip in that notebook, and we can just sign our jobs away and be done with it? That'd be easier, wouldn't it?"

One of the many complications the Negro officers faced was the fact that one of them, Xavier Little, happened to be nephew of the owner of the *Daily Times*. After the officers were sworn in, the *Times* ran an extensive interview with him. As far as Boggs could tell, Little said nothing remotely controversial in the story, yet the day after it hit the stands, McInnis excoriated them all. *Do not talk to the newspapers again, ever. You are not spokesmen for your people. You are goddamn beat cops, and that's all you will be, or you will be unemployed.* The fact that the paper had been an early champion of the push for colored officers, and was eager to chronicle their every move, made this an especially delicate dance for the eight of them.

Toon held out his hands. "I'm on *your* side here, gentlemen."

"Whose side?" Smith looked in every direction. "Which side? How's that work again?"

Boggs's head was pounding and he desperately needed sleep. He was not thinking clearly. Surely that explained why he then said, "You really want to be helpful? I've got something for your paper, but you *didn't* get it from me. Understood?"

"What is it?"

"We have a body," Boggs said, "a colored girl, teens or maybe early twenties. Found dead, shot in the chest. No ID or anything." Smith paced a few steps away, loudly sucking in his breath, all but yelling *Mistake, mistake, mistake.* If McInnis knew Boggs was saying this, they'd be in serious trouble. But Boggs was livid at the judge, livid at Dunlow from last night, livid about the fact that white investigators had done nothing to look into the murder. "All she had was a yellow dress and a heart-shaped locket. We could wait around until someone thinks their daughter or wife is missing, but if you put a note in the paper somewhere . . ."

"What else?"

"That's all we know." He didn't want to tell Toon they found her in garbage. If a husband or parent had to learn that, they should hear it from an officer, in person.

Toon had an impressive stare. "There's something you're not telling me."

It was a mistake to have said this much. But Boggs felt such rage, he hadn't been able to hold himself back. White cops had just let his case against Poe die. Dunlow had beaten a man in front of him the other night. And apparently someone, most likely his own superior officer, had retyped his report on the colored Jane Doe. Falsified it by deleting the reference to Brian Underhill, the last known person seen with the victim, probably to protect the ex-cop. People were undercutting Boggs at every turn, making him look stupid and helpless. He refused to be helpless.

"The last known person to be with her was a middle-aged white man," he said. "Do *not* disclose that."

Toon nodded slowly. "Okay, I'll run something. Call me when you have more."

This was hardly the first time they had been humiliated in court, but that didn't make it any easier. In fact, they'd spent *so much time* preparing for this case because they'd thought that their efforts would finally overwhelm the hard-breathing judge's bias. They had thought that what they did mattered.

"I thought you locked it?" Smith said, opening the former custodial closet's door.

"I did."

Smith hit the switch as Boggs closed the door behind him. Their civilian clothes, which they had hung on pegs, were strewn on the floor.

"For God's sake." Smith picked up his shirt and his slacks, shaking the dust bunnies from them.

Boggs did the same with his shirt. He looked around for his pants. "You're kidding."

He checked the shelves, which were half-stocked with old containers of cleaning solutions and boxes of what appeared to be years-old newspapers and legal transcripts. His pants were gone.

They stood there in silence for a moment, then Smith swung and batted a box of moth balls from a shelf. Little toxic spheres ping-ponged in every direction.

Boggs closed his eyes for a moment. He wanted to hit something, too. Yet he held it in.

"Easy," he said, to himself as much as to his partner.

"*Easy?* You're the one with no britches."

"Which is why you should be cooling down. You're the one who's going to have to fetch me some slacks."

"You're going to hide in here?"

"I am going to *wait* in here for you to get them, yes."

"The hell with that. Let's both go to the Y, in our uniforms. Hell with their rules."

"No. I'm not getting written up for something like that. Not after what just happened."

"Five dollars says your britches are in the judge's chambers."

"He can have them." Boggs reached into his pocket and dug out a key. "I have an extra pair in my locker. Hurry up and we can get some sleep before next shift."

Smith leaned against one of the shelves. He stared at his feet.

"Remind me why we're doing this."

Boggs breathed. "To be upstanding citizens and paragons of our race," he said, his voice gently mocking the mayor's speech from their first day.

"Give me a better reason."

"To provide a good example for colored kids."

A phone rang from an unseen office.

"A better reason."

"There aren't any better jobs."

Smith closed his eyes. "A better reason."

Boggs thought for a moment, then said, "Maceo Snipes." Shot in the back for being the first Negro voter in Taylor County. "Isaac Woodard." War veteran, blinded two years ago by South Carolina cops for daring to wear his army uniform. "The Malcolms and Dorseys." Two married couples, including another veteran and a pregnant woman, ambushed and murdered on a bridge over the Apalachee River.

Smith opened his eyes. "Give me those keys."

7

RAKE WAS FLIPPING burgers at the grill when his nephews, Brooks and Dale Jr., cautiously approached. The fact that they held their hands behind their back meant either that they were about to throw something at him or that they were trying to impersonate harmless children with an innocent question.

"Uncle Denny?" Dale Jr., the six-year-old, asked.

Rake took a pull on his Coke. "Yes?"

"Is it true you were a Boy Scout in the war?"

"Where'd you hear that?"

"Mother and Father said you were a Boy Scout," said Brooks, the freckled four-year-old.

"I was a *scout*. But yes, I suppose you could say it was like being a Boy Scout." It was not remotely like being a Boy Scout. "It was more like I was a tour guide." That was actually true, at the end.

Sunday cookout at the Rakestraws. Rake and his wife, Cassie, playing the hosts, as they usually did. Cassie was inside with baby Margaret and two-year-old Dennis Jr., as well as Rake's sister, Sue Ellen, and his brother-in-law, Dale, who was on his third or eighth beer.

Rake looked through the window into the kitchen and caught Cassie's eye. She winked at him. He wished these next two hours could vanish. It was a rare night off for him, meaning he was roughly on the same schedule as she was, and the baby was finally giving them some time to themselves.

Through another window he could see his old man, Colson, playing with Dennis Jr. and doing a reasonably good impression of a happy granddad.

The boys had been cagey, asking Rake about the war when their grandfather was not in earshot. Rake seldom discussed it, especially when Colson was present. Funny how even marauding brats like these picked up on that.

"Did you kill people?" Brooks asked.

"Brooks!" Dale Jr. popped his younger brother behind the head, then promptly gave Rake the kind of extremely attentive look that showed he was actually thrilled the question had been asked and could not wait to hear the answer.

"Ask me something else."

Dale Jr. seemed deeply disappointed. Borderline crushed. It took him a moment to think of a new question. How many days or weeks or years had they been wondering these things?

"What does a scout do?"

"Well, your grandmother, who you never knew because she passed before you were born, she was born in Germany, and moved here when she was a teenager. So she spoke German, and taught it to me when I was not much older than you. I kept with my studies to the point where I could speak it like a native. When the war came, there was a need for fellows like me who could get by over there."

And, years later, after the surrender, he'd been a tour guide. Stationed at the concentration camp in Dachau, he was tasked with ensuring that every civilian in the surrounding towns visited the camp. *This is where some of them were incinerated. This is where some of them were gassed. These are the cages they were kept in.* For two months. *We had no idea,* the "tourists" always claimed. *We didn't know.* And the tour guides like Rake had replied, *This is why we are here. This is why we have taken over your country. This is what your government was doing. We are here to save you from them.*

Rake opened the grill and flipped the burgers again, though they didn't need it. His wife liked the things damn near scorched.

"Did Uncle Curtis speak German?"

He closed the lid.

"No. Uncle Curtis had never been much for his studies."

The boys pondered this for a moment, amazed that their mythical, deceased uncle was being discussed. He'd survived two years in the Pacific. It was doubtful even the older of these boys had much memory of him.

Then Rake noticed that his nephews were holding hands.

"Uncle Dennis?" the littler one asked.

"Yes?"

"If there's another war, does that mean one of us will die?"

Dale Jr. added, "The one of us that isn't as good at studies?"

Rake crouched down so they were more or less eye level.

"We fought that war so that there won't be any other ones. Don't you worry. Now go inside and bother your parents and don't talk about this anymore."

They "Yes, sir"ed in chorus and wandered over to the door. They'd almost opened it when Rake called after them. "Dale Jr., you start your schooling next fall?"

"Yes, sir."

"Study hard."

⚡

After dinner, Rake walked Dale and the family back to their place, helping them carry home some extra Cokes for the boys and half a watermelon. Dessert had gone late and lightning bugs lit up the hydrangeas as Dale Jr. and Brooks darted ahead on the sidewalk-less road despite their mother's warnings of imminent vehicular dangers.

The two families lived only six blocks apart in Hanford Park, a quiet neighborhood west of the city. Nearly every house here was a bungalow, and even if they'd had second stories, those would have been swallowed up by the low, thick boughs of poplars, tupelos, and white oaks. The canopy was so thick the middle of the roads were in shadow even at midday. It wasn't a moneyed area like Buckhead to the north of downtown, or Ansley Park and Inman Park to the east, but it had what they needed: decent schools, a nearby park, and reliable buses and streetcars for Cassie to get to the downtown stores on days Rake needed to take the car to the station. Neighbors smiled and waved as they tended their gardens or sat on their porches as the setting sun tinted the sky pink.

Several other cops lived in the area, including his damned partner.

When they made it to Dale's, Rake was ready to shake his hand and say good-night, and indeed Sue Ellen had already chased the two rascals inside, but then Dale said, "Hang on a minute. I want to show you something." Dale walked down the block, Rake following. "That's the one over there."

Dale seemed to be indicating a new house half a block from where they stood. The wood was not yet painted, and the front yard was nothing but bare red soil, having been turned over to lay a foundation. Some of the windows were so new they still bore tape from the factory.

"What about it?" Rake asked. He rearranged the items into one hand so he could slap a mosquito from his neck with the other.

"It's the one I told you about. Nigger put it up last week."

Rake's mother had never permitted *that word* to be spoken in their house when he'd been growing up. The Rakestraw children had been brought up to respect everyone, no matter their color. It was years before Rake put a few things together and realized that part of her awareness of the evils of race hate could be traced back to the first war, when she was a German immigrant here and her family had been ostracized as bloodthirsty, baby-killing, nun-raping "Huns." Rake didn't think his mother had ever been friends with any Negroes, but after having words used as weapons against her, in the delicate teenage years no less, she'd no patience for those who employed similar tactics. Rake's father had always backed her up on that—Rake recalled Curtis being whupped for cussing and getting in scrapes with colored children in his rebellious years—and Rake had only heard his father use the word a few times, when it was just men sitting on a porch or watching a Crackers game, far from the missus's ear.

Rake's brother-in-law, however, was a big fan of the word.

"I don't think it's anything you need to trouble yourself with," Rake said.

"Trouble myself? I ain't troubled, Denny. I aim to *do* something about it. I was wondering if you wanted to help out."

The half watermelon was sweating through Rake's shirt. The houses that they had passed on this short walk did not appear any smaller than the ones on Rake's block, and the trees seemed no more prone to disease or drought, and Rake didn't see any more rubbish on the sides of the road. Yet Dale's house was a mere two blocks from the unofficial border with the colored section of town. This particular Negro had built his new house on the wrong side of that border.

"This nigger's put up his house *one block* from mine," Dale said. "I'm sure you're all nice and cozy in your new place, but what's gonna happen to your sweet little spot if this block goes, and the next two? I'm your first line of defense. I'd think you'd want to help out here, before the problem's on *your* doorstep. It's like a damned military operation they have, you know? Trying to flank us over here and outflank us down off North Street."

The war analogies grated. Dale had terrible vision, disqualifying him from service in the army. It was a sore subject with him—he felt his manhood and not his irises had been called into question, according to Sue Ellen.

Rake shifted the watermelon from one side to the other like a half-back bracing for tacklers.

"I didn't say I'm not concerned about the neighborhood, Dale. But I think you should maybe wait and see who this fellow is before you get up in arms about it."

"Who he is, is a nigger. I'd think with what all you've been seeing of 'em in Darktown, you'd know enough not to let them come over *here*. How you like your own habitation to turn out like the place you patrol all night?"

"That's not going to happen."

"Damn right it's not, because we're not gonna let it."

Rake gazed back at the new house again, worried that the home-owner in question might emerge from the building, prompting Dale to do God knew what. At the same time, Rake wasn't exactly thrilled by the idea of Negroes moving in. He'd only been able to buy the house thanks to GI Bill financing, and he couldn't afford to find himself suddenly staring down the barrel of a mortgage gone way out of whack with the value of a property surrounded by Negroes.

Dale stepped closer and lowered his voice. "Me and some buddies have a few ideas we're kicking around, if you know what I mean. We thought someone like you would be able to help us out."

Christ. Rake was angry at himself for letting this go so far. He didn't want to get in a fight with his brother-in-law either, so he tried to tamp down his emotions.

"I advise against you breaking any laws."

Dale smiled, as if to say, *Ha, good one, I get it.* But his smile faded as he saw that Rake wasn't smiling back.

"Well, yeah, sure. I understand you got to say that on account of your job and all, but," and Dale lowered his voice still, "as *family,* as *kin.* As blood to my two sons. Are you going to help out?"

There was another mosquito at Rake's neck but he let it suck away rather than break his stare.

He repeated, "I advise against you breaking any laws."

Dale was just drunk, Rake told himself. His memories of this conversation would not be clear. He would not feel offended by his cop brother-in-law. So Rake hoped.

He handed the watermelon to Dale, who took it and stared for a moment like he had no clue what it was. Birdsong filled the air the way it tends to at dusk, which always made Rake wonder if they were frantically warning one another to hide from the night or if in fact they'd been that loud all day and he'd been too busy to notice.

The next night, Rake and Dunlow returned to their car after taking down a report on an armed robbery at a grocer on Ponce de Leon and Boulevard. The sky above them was swirled in a restless palette of grays and pinks. The sun had just set, and either storms were imminent or God just felt like doing some wild painting that night.

Minutes later, they were driving slowly down Decatur Street when Dunlow spied something.

"Well looky here," he said at a tall form loping along the sidewalk. As they passed him, the man cut north into an alley. Dunlow made a three-point turn and drove into the alley. The man stopped and turned when he felt the headlights on him. He froze, raising his hands in surrender.

Dunlow turned off the engine and got out first, Rake following.

"Chandler, my boy. How's life on the outside?"

"Much better, Officer Dunlow." The tall Negro looked somewhat relieved to see that it was Dunlow he was dealing with. Rake was not used to seeing that reaction—usually people felt the opposite way about his partner. "Much better indeed."

Chandler Poe had already treated himself to a fine shave and a haircut since his release from jail. His usually unkempt reddish hair was pomaded and combed.

"Glad to hear they let you out," Dunlow said. He stood a bit more closely to Chandler than he would to most white men. The old Southern maxim recommended you keep Negroes close so they wouldn't get too high, and Dunlow seemed to take it literally. "You must be feeling awful grateful right now."

"Yes, sir, Officer Dunlow. Most very grateful."

The bootlegger cut his eyes at Rake, at which point Dunlow laughed. "Officer Rakestraw is with me, boy, so you don't need to worry 'bout that."

"It's just that, Officer Dunlow, I only been out a day. I ain't yet been able to—"

He stopped talking when Dunlow's left hand appeared on his shoulder. Chandler was as tall as Dunlow, but a lesser weight class entirely. The hand looked as though it could have snapped the Negro's clavicle like a wishbone.

"Well, opportunity is knocking, boy. There's a whole town full of nigras that've been deprived of your talents the last few weeks. Best get on that."

"Yes, sir."

The hand lingered on Chandler for another moment. Rake realized his own stomach was taut as he braced for what was next. But Dunlow merely lifted his giant hand and brought it down again. A friendly pat, perhaps with a bit more force than necessary, but that was all. For now.

8

LUCIUS REALIZED TOO late what a mistake he'd made in coming to the funeral.

It wasn't like he attended every funeral his father presided over, but this one was special. He knew the church would be packed, knew that people were upset, angry, and in need of what his father alone could provide. He was here to be a part of his community, even though with each passing moment he was reminded that he was no longer a part of it the way he'd once been.

He felt eyes on him from the beginning. He was used to receiving attention at his father's church, but these were not looks of love or respect. No, the funeral of James James Jameson was proving to be a very different experience indeed.

He sat beside his brothers, Reginald and William. William, who was still at Morehouse, was the son most likely to follow in their father's footsteps. Reginald had always appreciated life's nonspiritual splendors a bit too much. Lucius himself had considered the pulpit, had felt the weight of his father's expectation that he one day lead this church, had even practiced writing a few sermons in his teens. But something hadn't clicked. He had expected to hear a voice, see some sign. What he got instead was a draft card.

Lucius watched the reverend and was impressed, as he always was, by the man's command of the crowd. Reverend Boggs was the same height as Lucius and a good deal wider. He often teased his son that Lucius, too, would have that physique one day, though Lucius felt the girth had less to do with genetics and more to do with the minister's prerogative to take a heaping helping of whatever was served by families he visited to celebrate with or console. He was a busy man indeed, and there were days on which the reverend had three different dinners across town, a gastronomic sacrifice but one he managed to make for the Lord. In front of a crowd, though, that size became commanding.

Reverend Boggs told his congregation that he knew they were angry because he was, too. He knew there were times when they wanted to cry out and accuse God of turning his back on them, because he, too, felt abandoned sometimes, he, too, wanted to know what the Big Man would say in response. Every sentence he spoke got heads nodding, the *mmm hmms* coming steady now like the inhalation and exhalation of a single body. But every sentence, whether the reverend meant it or not, seemed to give voice to what Lucius feared they were thinking: *Why did the cops kill another one of us? When will they stop? And why didn't your own son, Reverend Boggs, why didn't he do anything about it?*

Lucius had met Jameson once, years ago, at a church social. He'd not had the highest impression of the fellow, but he realized that might have been snobbery talking. Jameson was uneducated, as was his mother and his siblings; his family had only recently joined the church. Perhaps Jameson had felt out of place in his ill-fitting button-up shirt and too-loose slacks and dragging vowels; maybe he'd been making so many bad jokes because he didn't know what else to talk about around Negroes like these.

"Triple James" was later arrested for the savage, near-fatal assault of a sixteen-year-old white boy (who survived, but in the kind of permanently damaged state that made many wish God had been more merciful and finished the job). At the highly publicized trial, some of the police officers seemed to make things up as they went along, but the jury (all-white by law) clearly had not been troubled by things like evidence or fairness, deliberating a mere ten minutes. A white boy had been viciously beaten outside a club in a colored part of town, and that was all that mattered. How this white boy had gotten to that part of town, and what exactly he'd been planning to do there—these matters had not been discussed, as they would have been disrespectful to the victim. Jameson had lived near the club and had recently been booked for another assault, so he had "a violent history," according to the prosecution. (That assault charge had stemmed from a fight he and two other Negro teenagers had gotten into, instigated when one of them had insulted the other's sister, and umbrage was taken, and things went a tad too far, and, though no one had been seriously hurt in the tussle, a squad car had arrived while the fight was still ongoing, and all three had been given a week in jail.) He was a black boy with a record, so the dots had not been difficult for white jurors to connect.

Boggs felt aware of his own posture as his father preached. *Please stop talking about the police and the unfairness,* Boggs thought. *Please get to the "Let's all rally together" part.* It wasn't like him to question his father's decisions in church like this, but he felt further from the reverend than usual. He was not in uniform, but he may as well have been.

Then Reverend Boggs segued away from the murder for a moment and started another story, one his son knew so well that he saw what was coming as soon as he heard the word "train."

He's going to tell the Uncle Richard story. Lucius didn't even need to listen, he'd heard it so many times.

Back in 1904, Reverend Boggs had been little Daniel Boggs, the son of a postman who'd proudly been wearing his uniform and making deliveries downtown for years, keeping his three sons fed and well clothed, living in a house he had bought with his own money after years of careful saving.

And then there was that week when the hysterical white papers reported about rapes and attacks by Negroes, warning their readers that the darker race was getting more emboldened with every day that white men did not stand up for themselves. No one in the colored community quite knew where these stories had come from, or why they so suddenly seized the white people's imagination. It was as though all the whites were possessed by something at once, a virus, and all you could do was wait for it to pass. Except that when white people caught the virus, it was other folks who got killed.

Little Daniel Boggs had been only four, born in the first month of the new century, and he hadn't known anything about the white people virus, hadn't known that his father had been warned not to go out that day, that the virus was spreading, making some white people speak in tongues, beat their breasts, arm themselves with pistols and rifles and spades and butcher knives. Yet Mr. Boggs, the trusty postal carrier, walked to work nonetheless, and he even made a few deliveries until he saw the crowds, heard the yelling.

All that little Daniel knew was that suddenly his father was home, in the middle of the day, out of breath. Then the curtains were drawn, the lights were shut off, and the doors were locked. Throughout the day the back door would be periodically unlocked when friends and relations, in need of shelter, rapped on it, knowing well enough not to let themselves be seen at the front door.

Soon Uncle Richard showed up, a gash where his right ear met his head, another just below his hairline, redness covering half his face. Daniel had never seen anything like it before, all that red, his favorite uncle transformed into some ghoul. Daniel ran screaming. His mother had to chase him down in the boys' bedroom, grabbing him by the ear and hissing into it that the boy must be silent immediately. The Boggs family couldn't let *them* know anyone was here.

So Daniel sat on his bed crying as quietly as he could while the adults tended to Richard.

Now and again he could hear *them,* hear how the virus was making *them* roam through the city.

He heard the adults talking about fire and smoke, he heard popping sounds that apparently were gunshots, according to the expert opinion of his older brothers, who stopped into the bedroom to tell him so before going back into the parlor with the adults. The virus was tearing through different neighborhoods and there was no telling when it would hit theirs.

It sounded close.

It was a few hours later when Uncle Richard visited him. A faint amount of twilight through the curtains kept the room from pitch darkness. The virus continued to make strange sounds from outside, yelling and hollering and fireworks and noisemakers, even some singing.

Richard was bandaged up, one along his ear and another on his forehead, looking like pictures of Civil War soldiers Daniel had seen in books. Richard smiled at the boy, asked if he was all right, asked if Daniel had run crying from his favorite uncle. *You weren't scared of me, were you?* And Daniel had felt so badly then, so afraid to hurt his uncle's feelings, that, even at the age of four, he lied and claimed the reason he'd been crying was because he'd broken his favorite toy train.

He would always wonder what made him say that. It was true that the axle of one of his wooden trains had broken a few days ago, but he hadn't been all that torn up about it. Yet he said it, and Uncle Richard smiled. *Well, let's see what Uncle Richard can do about that. Where is it?*

Finding one broken train in a room of three boys, in almost complete darkness, was not easy. Yet they found it, and then a screwdriver appeared in Richard's hand. Richard was a carpenter and had been at work when the virus had taken the white people. He'd run here directly, his pockets crammed with tools. Only after years of retelling the story would Daniel wonder if Richard always had so many screwdrivers in his overalls or had he perhaps loaded up on sharp instruments as protection before fleeing. Uncle Richard assessed the toy and spun the wheel on the busted axle and reached into another pocket and took out a small wooden dowel. It would not have amazed Daniel any more had Uncle Richard taken a white rabbit or a dove from one of those pockets. The dowel proved too thick, but ah-ha, here in this other pocket he had one that fit better. Lord only knew what project the man had been working on, but he was perfectly equipped for repairing toys that day, as if he'd come direct from the North Pole.

Within minutes, thanks also to some wood glue from another pocket, the train was good as new. Uncle Richard had been leaning against the wall, and he rolled the train across the wood floor to his admiring nephew, who smiled and rolled it back. So Richard rolled it to him again, and they went like that for a while, Daniel laughing (and Richard gently reminding him not to laugh too loudly) and not quite noticing anymore the giant bandages on his uncle's head.

Then the virus got louder.

Daniel sent the train back to Uncle Richard, whose great big hand covered the entire toy. He did not send it back. He picked it up, slowly stood, and slightly parted the curtained window, putting a finger from his other hand to his lips.

The virus was making the white people sing "Dixie," and they were close enough for Daniel to make out all the words.

Daniel wished his uncle would push the train again but he knew something important was happening. Uncle Richard was here, so nothing could possibly go wrong, yet he felt scared.

The virus was making glass break. Then another popping sound, then another. More glass.

Someone screamed. Then footsteps and hollers, as if the person who'd screamed was being chased. It was a game, Richard explained in a whisper, just a strange game people are playing. But don't talk anymore tonight.

Later, in the middle of the night, Daniel would need to use the toilet, would walk into the hallway and see many of his uncles and cousins gathered there in the parlor and the foyer, the light dim and his brain muddy and his mother shooing him. He would wonder for a while whether he was only dreaming the fact that his father and uncle were holding rifles.

Two days later, after the white people's virus had passed, people slowly dared to leave their houses. Daniel's father returned to work after conferring with friends, and Daniel and his mother and two brothers went out again, hoping to find a grocer's that was open, as their pantry had gone bare.

As they walked, Daniel noticed that many of the street poles were wearing hats. The sign at the corner of Juniper and Pierce wore a gray derby. A bus stop sign a block away wore a plaid driver's cap. A black fedora was perched atop Courtland and Ellis.

And there on Peachtree and Auburn sat a blue mailman's cap, as unmistakable as his father's laugh. Daniel tugged on his mother's sleeve and pointed it out, *Look, Daddy's cap!* and did not understand why her face turned stone blank when she saw it, did not understand why she gripped his hand more tightly then and hurried the boys along and told them with a harsher tone than usual to hush up.

Daniel would remember those hats for years, recalling them when, as an older boy, he learned they were there because they had belonged to Negroes who'd been killed or beaten by the mob, the headwear tossed up like trophies. One slight remove away from the tribal peoples who'd placed their enemies' heads on stakes for vultures to pick at. It had not been his father's hat, but it could have been.

"It could have been any of our hats," the reverend told his congregation. "But this time, it was James."

In truth, Lucius was so upset by the stares and comments that he wasn't able to listen to all that his father was saying, never got to hear how the old man drew a parallel between that tragedy and this one. What lesson he was trying to impart, what the train was supposed to be a metaphor for. Whether Uncle Richard, who would also die young, was symbolic of Jameson or someone else, what the point of the story was at all. He'd heard it so many times and it always had a different point, the basic gist being that life might seem terribly unfair and unjust but it wasn't, not really, because there was a plan behind it. Even if the plan seemed a very poorly written one indeed, and in need of profound revisions.

After the service ended, Lucius told his brothers he couldn't join them at the burial. He had to get to the precinct. They all nodded, seeing through the lie and not seeming to blame him.

Soon he was outside, walking through the crowd, the hats and the suits and clusters of family members. Many of those heads seeming to twitch in his direction. Then someone did more than twitch: a man with gray hair and a thick mustache stopped in front of Boggs, closer than was polite.

"You're one of the policemen, aren't you?" His eyes were red, not like he'd been crying in church but like he hadn't been sleeping much lately, and had perhaps been crying a lot, just not in the last couple of hours.

"Yes, sir."

Lucius didn't recognize him; he wasn't a part of this congregation. He knew everyone in the crowd was staring, registering each word and gesture.

"I thought you were supposed to do something about this," the man said. "My son's in jail and my daughter-in-law's in there, too, and what are you doing about it?"

Freddie's father and Belle's father-in-law, then. Boggs had heard she'd married well, and this gentleman's suit seemed to prove it.

"I'm very sorry about what's happened, sir, and—"

"They tortured her. You know that, don't you? Poured hot grits on her head! And what did she do? What did she do? Trying to protect her brother from them."

Boggs felt the blood rushing to his face. He couldn't tell if the people crowding around them were closer than before or if it only felt that way because everyone had become utterly silent.

A woman materialized beside the man—she was short and her face was barely visible through the black veil that cascaded from a wide-brimmed hat. Yet the hatred in her eyes burned through.

The man pressed a finger into Boggs's chest. "I thought you were supposed to stop this!"

Lucius looked down at the finger for an extra beat. "We're doing what we can to make things better, sir."

"They shot him in the street like a dog," the woman said.

"My brother works very hard for all of us," William said. Boggs had forgotten his kid brother was there. "I know this is a very difficult time, but pointing fingers at each other will not help."

The man's finger seemed to melt away. The couple's eyes were on William now, that beautiful unlined face that had soothed tempers and allayed jealousies all his life. Anger did not seem to exist in rooms where William was present. He'd possessed magic as a boy; he was a man now, twenty and with one more year of schooling to go, and his powers were only stronger.

Boggs stood there and felt cooled by the vast shadow that his younger brother seemed to cast.

"My son hasn't seen a lawyer yet." The man was speaking more to William now, his voice already going from accusatory to plaintive. "I don't even know if my boy's *alive!*"

The tears returned. His wife's hands were gripping his left forearm, as if the crowd were trying to tear them apart rather than support them.

William touched the man's other forearm. "My father was hoping to get a chance to talk to you, Mr. Simmons. Why don't we go over and get him now?" With his free hand he motioned back to the church. "Ma'am?"

Mrs. Simmons nodded, and William calmly yet assuredly led them off. Twenty years old! Boggs watched as his brother's two hands rested atop the outer shoulders of the grieving couple, and the crowd parted and allowed them to pass, and all those black dresses and hats and somber suits made a point of turning to face each other again, as though they had not been watching.

Boggs descended the church steps. Trying not to walk too fast. But wishing he could.

"Hey," Reginald said from a step behind. "Come on, let's drop by my office. I got a bottle of whiskey you could use right now."

"You know I can't do that anymore."

Reginald laughed. "Oh yeah, sorry. But come on, let's go cool off someplace. You need it."

"I need to be alone."

Reginald's footsteps stopped as Lucius walked off.

"Brother, you are precisely that."

That night at the Y, he received a call from Toon at the *Daily Times*.

"We got word on your Jane Doe. Farmer from Peacedale called saying it might be his daughter."

"He leave a name and number?"

"Otis Ellsworth, and he doesn't own a phone. He was using a pay phone on some small-town Main Street or something. Said he'd come by tomorrow to see the body."

"He sound sure of himself?"

"Said she didn't own a dress like that, that he knew of, but she'd been living in Atlanta a few months and probably got some new clothes. Said she had that birthmark on her shoulder, and they hadn't heard from her in a couple of weeks like they usually do."

The body was at the morgue, which was at the main headquarters. Neither Boggs nor any of the colored officers were supposed to be there. Ever. "When did he say he was coming?"

"There's a train that gets in to Terminal Station at half past noon," Toon said. "He'll be on it."

Someone falsified Boggs's report, deleting Brian Underhill, protecting an ex-cop who by all rights should be the principal subject of an investigation. Why? Like at Jameson's funeral, he felt the wrathful eyes of his neighbors on him, judging him a failure, unworthy. There was nothing Boggs could do about the Jameson case. But the Jane Doe case was different.

Boggs vowed that, when Mr. Ellsworth showed up at the station, he would be there to meet him.

9

AT NOON THE sky above the police headquarters was cloudless, so Boggs hid in the scant shade offered by the colored entrance's awning. He knew the white cops would be incensed to see him at the headquarters, where his presence was forbidden. Hopefully, this alley-facing door was the one place where he was least likely to encounter any whites.

His adherence to the white cops' ridiculous rules had cost the girl her life—he should have run after her that night, but he and Smith had chosen to follow the white driver, Underhill, instead. At the very least, Boggs would make sure she was identified, and that the father wouldn't have to do the deed beside some insipid cracker.

So he waited.

When he'd first signed on for the job, he had been focused on the momentousness of the occasion, the responsibility and the uniform and the gun and the awesome weight of things he might be called upon to do. The colored eight's first day had been much-ballyhooed across town, complete with the mayor offering a speech to an overflow crowd. Their first shift practically turned into a neighborhood parade, everyone along Auburn Avenue following their every move, taking photos, writing poems. It seemed so long ago already.

Boggs had been perhaps too enamored with the romanticism of the moment, not thinking enough about how he would be arresting people for things like gambling and drinking that they felt were their God-given right, intervening in marital disputes that had no true solution, and staring up close at horrific societal problems that seemed almost cocky in their intractability. He'd known what he was getting into, he just hadn't braced himself for the accumulated weight of doing it hour after hour, night after night. And it had barely been four months.

He had needed purpose. He had just completed his degree when he'd been drafted for the war, and he had perhaps naïvely believed that the great fight against totalitarianism would be the perfect place for him to put all those Morehouse ideals into action. Yet his time in the army had been torture. He never progressed beyond a South Carolina training camp during those long years, despite his constant appeals to see action. He eventually learned he had been branded a "Premature Anti-Fascist" by his commanding officers. He and his prominent family members had spoken out about the menace of Mussolini ravaging Ethiopia years before Pearl Harbor had convinced the rest of America that the Axis needed to be stopped (his father had written a widely read essay, and Lucius had penned some pieces in the Morehouse newspaper). Because they had dared to be right about the evil that their fellow Americans had been slow to acknowledge, they were considered untrustworthy, their motives suspect. His superior officers had done whatever was necessary to keep him and his fellow PAFs very far away from any battlefields or loaded weapons.

After he'd returned to Atlanta, the push to register Negro voters had felt like a calling, something to help take his mind off the boring numbers counting that constituted his job at the insurance company where Reginald worked. At his crammed little desk he'd tabulated how long each Negro in a given neighborhood might live based on current age, schooling, past diseases, wars fought, crimes committed. Reginald insisted this was important work, that colored people deserved insurance just like white folks did, but to Lucius it was like being some clerical mercenary.

He had always felt marked for something bigger. That was the curse of being raised by a reverend. Even if you decide not to follow him to the pulpit, you have been raised by a man who constantly drilled into you the fact that you are special, that you will lead your people some-how, that there is some crucial victory waiting to be won.

So when the successful voter registration drive finally led the mayor to post eight job openings on the police force, things suddenly seemed to make a strange kind of sense.

Still he waited for Mr. Ellsworth.

Occasionally people walked through the police station's colored entrance, but one glance and Boggs could tell they weren't farmers from Peacedale. Maybe they were janitors, or errand boys, or they were here to inquire about their recently arrested son or father. It bothered Boggs that they had to come to this back door to be insulted by white cops and clerks. Boggs and his colleagues would be allowed in the station "eventually," McInnis had said a few times, but when was "eventually"? Next year, or when Boggs was forty? Had they made it to the double-*l* in "eventually" yet, or were they still on the first *e?*

It was a scorching day, and his shade was shrinking. Air conditioners hummed above him, condensation dripping on either side. He was not in uniform, instead wearing khaki pants and a crisp white shirt. His pants pocket hid his badge. He still wasn't used to the bandage on his face and couldn't wait until his return visit to the doctor to have the stitches removed.

Finally he saw a man who looked the part hesitantly approach the old wooden steps. The wooden steps that were warped on the sides because they hadn't been sealed right, so warped that Boggs was tempted to ask the station to rebuild them, though he wasn't sure if it was worth the effort. (To repair them would be to acknowledge that a separate colored entrance was necessary.) The wooden steps that audibly creaked as the man in jean overalls and an off-white work shirt with red clay stains at the elbows and thick, clay-caked boots rose upon them.

"Mr. Ellsworth?" Boggs would have guessed the man was not yet forty, but a very old kind of not-yet-forty. Thin but not gaunt, with lines spiderwebbing the dark skin around his light brown eyes.

"Yeah?"

Boggs took his badge out of his pocket and held it there a moment. "I'm Officer Lucius Boggs. Thank you for coming in."

Ellsworth's eyes seemed hollow, not all there. He didn't reply. There was no adequate response to being thanked for coming in to identify the body of your daughter.

Sensing this, Boggs dispensed with any small talk and said, "Why don't you follow me."

Ellsworth had been wearing a brown driver's cap, but he removed it now and held it awkwardly at his breast, as if hearing the national anthem or watching a casket pass. Two inches above his left ear a thin scar curved hairlessly like an upside-down smile.

Boggs opened the door and the air felt cooler immediately. He led Ellsworth down the hallway, passing the white clerk, a white-haired old man who kept to himself his objections to this colored officer entering the inner sanctum. Too shocked to speak, perhaps.

The door to the basement was about ten yards away. The hallway was narrow, with occasional head-high windows offering views into the bullpens, through which, surely, some cops at their desks could see him. He would not look. He didn't hear any cries or curses as he continued, didn't hear his name called out or anything worse.

He reached the basement door and opened it. He exhaled a little more deeply.

When they reached the bottom of the stairs, Boggs faced Ellsworth again. The farmer's head had been on a swivel before, turning this way and that, taking in all the sights, but now it seemed that his neck had contracted, his shoulders protectively high.

"Are you all right?"

"Yeah. First time in a police station is all."

Boggs had only dealt with a few grieving parents at this point in his career, but still, something in Ellsworth's manner seemed off. Boggs had seen other fathers turn inward, silent and stony, but even then there was always some telltale evidence of misery and dread on their faces, some sign that this rocklike facade was being held up only by extreme effort. Ellsworth seemed not so much devastated as down.

Boggs pushed open the metal double doors, revealing a narrow hallway: cement floor and cement wall and a few lightbulbs dangling overhead. Boggs knew the way because he'd spoken to a few civilians who had made this walk before. They came to another set of double doors, and beyond that was the morgue, at the front of which sat an old white mortician who looked confused by his dark visitors.

Boggs held out his badge, realizing that he was pushing deeper into forbidden territory. "We're here to identify the colored Jane Doe."

The man raised his right eyebrow. "You aren't a detective."

"That's correct, sir. My name is Officer Lucius Boggs."

"You know the rules, boy."

"This gentleman is here to identify his daughter."

The ID of a body whose murderer had not yet been identified was supposed to be conducted by a detective. But Boggs wanted to be there when Ellsworth saw her, wanted to be able to read the man's expression and glean whatever information was available at that awful, visceral moment. He had hoped the mortician would see that a colored cop was best for a colored Jane Doe. And he had hoped that even in a bigot's heart, some inner humanity would respect the sight of a grieving father. He had been wrong about both.

The mortician picked up a phone and dialed one number. "I need a detective in the morgue immediately. Preferably two."

Attempting to save face, Boggs turned to Ellsworth. "It will be just a minute, sir. A detective needs to be present."

The mortician rose and walked to one of his file cabinets, removing the paperwork on colored Jane Doe. Then he stood at his desk and waited. Boggs did not make eye contact with him. Ellsworth shifted on his feet, and Boggs felt an additional bit of guilt for drawing out his experience.

They heard footsteps in the hallway, approaching the double doors. Ellsworth's face was blank. Boggs wondered what this tiller of the land would usually be doing now, harvesting cotton or spreading cow shit over someone else's property. He'd noticed Ellsworth's fingers, how long they were, lined with scars and old wounds and age and hard, painful use.

Two white detectives entered, one of them with gray hair, wearing a crisp blue suit like some insurance salesman, and the other in his thirties, dark hair parted like Superman and a chest just as imposing. They passed Boggs without acknowledging his presence. Which was a better reaction than he'd been expecting. The insurance-salesman detective took the folder from the mortician and flipped through it. Boggs could tell these men knew nothing about the case and had simply been sent down because they were the only ones available at the moment.

Superman finally said, "We'll take it from here."

Boggs took one step back, as if to leave, but no more. Meanwhile, the salesman detective brusquely asked Ellsworth's name and address. After getting the answers, he asked, "And what leads you to believe you might know the deceased, Otis?"

Ellsworth's voice was even smaller than before. "Our daughter moved out to Atlanta a few months ago, sir. Haven't gotten a letter from her in a while. We saw the note in the newspaper, sir, and wondered if it could be her."

"Note in a newspaper?"

Boggs broke in, "The *Atlanta Daily Times* ran a sidebar asking if anyone might have information about a missing woman, Detective."

The detective looked vaguely insulted to have been addressed by the colored cop. He said, "Let's have a look, uncle."

The mortician and the detectives walked into the morgue, Ellsworth a step behind. Then Boggs followed Ellsworth.

The older detective—Boggs wished he was surprised that they hadn't bothered to identify themselves—was standing next to the mortician as the proper cooling board was identified, on the left-hand side, where the colored bodies were kept away from the white ones. Superman had taken up the fainting-prevention position, standing closer to Ellsworth than either man was probably comfortable with. The mortician reached underneath the corner of the blanket, pulling out the toe tag and double-checking the number.

Boggs slowly moved to his left, circumnavigating the scene until he was in position to see Ellsworth's reaction. He stopped when he was in a good spot, the mortician now pulling the cooling board all the way out, the various bumps and ridges of the blanket like some topographic map of pain.

"There will be severe discoloration and bloating, especially of the face," the mortician said, "so if possible you should look to birthmarks or scars."

Only now did the younger detective seem to notice that Boggs was still there. They made eye contact, and Boggs could sense the man's rebuke, but Boggs looked away without acknowledging it. If they wanted him to leave, he would at least make them say it out loud. If nothing else, his time with the police had taught him that the best way to be allowed to do something was to do it with authority and put the onus on someone to stop you. Momentum had a way of swaying lazy minds.

Like a horrible magician, the mortician pulled back the blanket.

For many reasons, Boggs kept his eyes on Ellsworth and tried to ignore the grayness at the bottom of his vision. Ellsworth was looking down, and the air seemed to leave him for a moment. The point at which he would normally inhale again came and went, and seemed never to return.

He said, very quietly, "That's our Lily."

The white detectives told Ellsworth they needed to ask him a few more questions upstairs. The younger detective walked first, the farmer next, and the older detective behind. Boggs followed as they walked down the hall.

"Whose case is this?" he asked the older detective.

"Why are you shadowing us?" the detective replied, stopping to face Boggs while the other two continued on. "Why are you even in this building?"

"I thought it would be wise to have a colored officer present. I thought he might betray something if he felt more comfortable."

"Betray something? Fascinating. And what did he betray?"

"I'm not . . . I'm still putting things together."

At the other end of the hallway, the younger cop and the farmer had stopped at the next set of double doors, watching them.

"Well, us real cops will take it from here. Run along now, boy."

"What are you going to do with him?"

The detective smiled. "We're going to ask questions, and he's going to answer them."

Then the white men led the farmer through the double doors, and Boggs was alone in the hallway.

Or so he thought. A moment later, the mortician's voice came from a ways behind him. "Nigger, you'd best get out of this station fast or I'm gonna have a new body to treat."

In the sixty seconds it took to exit the station, Boggs passed the hostile eyes of dozens of cops. His presence there had been broadcast, either by the mortician or the detectives. He heard epithets and threats, some whispered and some not, and in the background some primate hooting and hollering as he made his way to the colored door. Sweat ran down his back despite the air-conditioning.

Outside again, a new reason to sweat as the heat slapped him in the face, leaned on his shoulders. He walked around the building, still unsure of his next move. *Calm down, calm down.*

He was in front of the building when he heard his name.

"Hey there, Boggs." It was Rakestraw, walking toward the building. Boggs still had no read on this fellow. Rakestraw had not taken part in Dunlow's beating of the stabbed man the other night, but he hadn't done anything to stop it either. There were plenty of white folks like that, happy to define themselves as not-quite-as-bad-as-some, conveniently surrounding themselves with awful people in contrast to whom they looked good. He wore a benign expression, almost smiling, as he asked, "What brings you here?"

"The colored Jane Doe's been identified. Lily Ellsworth, formerly of Peacedale. Her father's in an interrogation room, I think."

"Who with?"

"Two detectives. Didn't share their names."

"They think he did it?"

"I don't know," Boggs said as he walked away. "But he didn't."

10

RAKE STEPPED INTO the observation room. Because of the dim light, the first thing his eyes could make out was Otis Ellsworth, on the other side of the glass in the interrogation room, sitting at a bare table. Rake had seen several people in that room over the last few months, and none of them necessarily looked any more alone than another. Aloneness wasn't something you could compare or even quantify. But the gaunt Negro was certainly alone.

Then Rake's eyes adjusted and he saw, here in the observation room with him, two other cops.

"Here to watch the fireworks?" Rake recognized the voice of Dunlow's friend, Brian Helton, though he couldn't make out the face, as Helton was sitting in front of the two-way mirror.

"Here to see a case get closed, hopefully."

"Oh, it'll be closed." That was spoken by an older plainclothes cop. Big nose, red cheeks, black suit. "You are?"

"Denny Rakestraw, sir. I'm partnered with Officer Dunlow."

"Have a seat and watch how an interrogation's really done. Sharpe's great at getting confessions. Especially when he's got Clayton with him."

"Clayton played for the Dogs, didn't he?" asked Helton.

"Middle linebacker," the big-nosed cop said. "I remember seeing him play. Hell of a hitter."

There were three metal chairs in the room, so Rake took the empty one.

"Peacedale PD says he doesn't have a record but that he's an odd duck," Big Nose said.

"Good-looking girl, I heard," Helton replied.

Where had he heard she was good-looking? Rake wondered. *From whom? She sure as hell didn't look good* now. *Only Boggs and Smith had seen her the night she'd died.*

"I say he talks before they lay a finger on him," Helton wagered.

"Not when it's kin. He'll deny it for a while."

A moment later, the door to the interrogation room opened and the two detectives, Sharpe and Clayton, entered. Ellsworth sat up straighter.

"Keep your hands on the table," Clayton, the linebacker, commanded. Ellsworth obeyed.

"Tell us about your daughter, Otis," Sharpe said.

Ellsworth stared straight ahead, avoiding eye contact. "What . . . What would you like to know, sir?" His voice so quiet Rake could barely hear him over the mike.

"When did she come to Atlanta?"

"Believe it was February, sir."

"Why'd she leave home?"

"Well, sir, she . . . wanted something new, you could say. I think she'd heard too many stories about life in the city, sir."

"Lots of your people have been coming here, that's true. Running out of places to put you all."

"The irony is that they often wind up on the chain gangs," Clayton added, "which operate outside the city limits. So, in a way, they come here only to get sent out again."

"But you don't get a chain gang for murder, you get hung for that."

Rake could see the sweat running down Ellsworth's cheeks. He was sitting in the hottest room in the building.

Sharpe leaned forward. "Now let me explain something straight off, Otis. I don't know what kind of police you're used to dealing with out there in Peacedale, but we see a lot of murders here. We see these sordid things quite a bit. I've seen so many things I wish I hadn't. And there ain't a colored boy gonna pull one over on me in my own station, understand?"

"Yes, sir."

"All right." Sharpe stood up straight again. "What was she doing in Atlanta?"

"She was a maid, sir."

"And she learned how to do such things on your farm?"

"No, sir. I mean, she helped at the farm as a little thing, but as soon as she got to be a bit older she took work as a maid at some white people's houses in Peacedale. Did that four, five years. They weren't happy when she left."

"And how about you, Otis? How did you feel when your girl left?"

Ellsworth paused. "I was worried for her, sir."

"Why's that, Otis?"

"She wasn't learned in city ways. We were very worried for her."

"But you let her come out here anyway, all by her lonesome?"

"No, sir, my wife has an aunt here. She helped Lily find a rooming house run by good people, and she said she could help her find work. But, ah, I believe she moved out at one point."

"And then you came to take her back, didn't you, Otis?"

"You didn't like your daughter running off and making her own money and not helping the family back home, did you?" Clayton added.

"That's not so, sir. This is the first time I been in Atlanta in about two years."

Clayton slapped the back of Ellsworth's head, hard enough for it to snap forward. The farmer kept his head lowered for a moment, expecting another blow.

Sharpe exhaled with theatrical impatience. "Don't try to be clever, Otis. We can double-check these things, you know. Police in Peacedale been keeping an eye on you."

Ellsworth wiped the sweat from his brow, his hand shaking. Then he wiped his hand on his pant leg before seeming to remember the cops' instruction to keep his hands in view.

"You can ask Mr. Timley, sir. He's the white man owns the land we work. He'll know I never left town 'til today."

"Oh, you got friends in high places, that right?" Clayton mocked.

"Let me cut right to it, Otis," Sharpe said. "We know you did it. We *know* you did. It couldn't be more obvious. You haven't shed a tear since you got here, not even after seeing that bloated, awful, smelly body down there. I know it when I've seen someone grieving, Otis. Especially nigras, my *good*ness you people are demonstrative! And you ain't grieving, uncle. Not one bit. You're sad, I'll give you that. Sad you got caught, maybe a bit regretful, too. But you ain't grieving."

"Are you regretful, Otis?" Clayton asked.

Ellsworth seemed to be trying to swallow saliva, or maybe blood if he'd bit his tongue when he'd been hit in the head. It took him a moment to say, "I regret a lot of things, sir."

Ellsworth's fingers seemed to be clawing at the wooden table. They looked strong enough that Rake wouldn't have been surprised if he peeled off a layer of oak with a fingernail. Rake realized his own stomach muscles were tense, and he, too, was sweating.

"Lily and me never got on too well, and I'm regretful for that." Ellsworth had dropped his *sirs* and his eyes were watering and his throat was thick. "But mostly I feel broke up for my wife. This is gonna kill her."

"But not you?" Clayton asked. "You ain't all that broke up for yourself, after your own daughter got killed like that?"

"Maybe I would be more, if she was my own blood. She's my wife's by another man."

"Ah-ha!" called out Helton, here in the observation room. "*There's* the bull's-eye."

"Horny devil, you," Big Nose said, wagging his finger at the glass.

The two detectives in the interrogation room were only slightly less excited to hear this news. They made eye contact with each other, relishing this, and then Clayton deferred to Sharpe.

"*Well* now, that certainly is an interesting piece of information, Otis. *Very* interesting. And rather disappointing that you kept it from us so long."

"We told you not to act clever."

"Oh, I'm sure it'll be hard for her," Sharpe said. "But not much harder than it's always been for her to see the way you looked at her daughter. Must have been very hard on your wife to see your eye wander, in her own home to boot."

Ellsworth had closed his eyes to fight back the tears, and now he seemed to realize where the cops were going. He opened his eyes again, red and streaky.

"No, no, sir, that ain't the case."

"How old was she when you and your wife got together, Otis? Old enough for you to catch her scent, or did that take a few years?"

"I never touched that girl." He sat up straight now, his head moving to one side and then the other, the colored approximation of eye contact, safely aimed at the white men's chests. "I helped raise her like my own."

"I told you we've seen it all, Otis. Loose woman has a child out of wedlock, she brings in a new buck to help her out, but that buck can't keep his eyes off the little girl. Things happen."

Rake knew he was no genius at police work, but he found it hard to imagine that Ellsworth was lying. Maybe it was from his unfortunate tendency to side with the bullied. Maybe it was because the lack of professionalism from the two interrogators galled him. *Why aren't you asking about Underhill, the last man seen in her presence?* he wondered. *Do you even know his name?* He wasn't sure if he was surrounded by shoddy police work or something worse.

"We heard she was a *very* good-looking girl, Otis."

"And you left her out with the garbage."

"Haven't even asked us how she died. Innocent parents usually ask that."

If Rake's mouth was dry, Ellsworth's was no doubt parched. The farmer again seemed to stammer before he could say, "I saw the bullet hole."

"You know bullet holes?"

"I hunt."

"So you own a firearm?"

"I have a hunting rifle."

"You a good shot?"

Ellsworth turned his head and, for the first time, looked Sharpe in the eye. "I did not hurt her."

From the other side, Clayton lowered his body and drove a fist into Ellsworth's rib cage. Had the farmer seen it coming, pride might have clamped his jaw shut, but because he was turned the other way he cried out.

"Shoulda squared him up for a solar plexus shot," Helton critiqued from the observation room.

"Then they can't talk," Big Nose corrected him. "Can't even *breathe* after that. The point is to get a confession, dummy, so he needs to be able to speak."

"Still."

"They'll resort to that if they have to."

Ellsworth seemed to be having trouble breathing nonetheless. His palms were still flat on the table but had gone slack, and his face hung too low for Rake to see his expression.

"You forgetting yourself, Otis? That happens in cases like this, when you realize you're out of options. Normally a nigra knows how to behave, but when you've done as wrong as you have, you start feeling those things don't apply to you, am I right?"

It took a few seconds for him to say, "It wasn't me, sir."

Clayton slapped him in the face. Just hard enough to be insulting. And to inform him that his face would not be off limits.

"She was running from you, wasn't she?" Sharpe asked. "She'd seen you looking at her. She knew what was coming."

Ellsworth shaking his head.

Clayton, who had walked around Ellsworth's chair to trade places with his partner, delivered a mirror-image blow on the other side of the man's ribs.

Rake wished he hadn't come. He did not enjoy watching this. Yet Helton and Big Nose sure seemed to. He stood and took two steps and reached for the doorknob.

Helton said to Big Nose, "Yeah, *now* he's leaving."

Rake's hand lingered on the knob. He asked, "When are they going to ask about Underhill?"

"Who?" Helton asked.

"Brian Underhill. The last man she was seen alive with."

Big Nose had been staring straight ahead, but he turned to Rake. Watching him very carefully.

"I don't expect they're going to ask about him," Big Nose said slowly and clearly, the kind of voice that almost has body language with it even though he didn't move.

"Why not? Maybe the father's aware of some past history between her and Underhill?"

"I can't listen with your yapping," Big Nose said. "Louder'n a hound dog with no bone. Go make yourself useful somewhere."

Rake left. Stung by the remark, he would indeed make himself useful. In the hallway, he knocked on the interrogation room door.

Silence for a few beats. Then the door opened, only a crack. A sliver of Clayton's face, sweatier up close than he'd appeared in the window. Eyes hostile. "What?"

"Ask if he knows the name Underhill."

It took longer than it should have for Clayton to reply. As if the adrenaline in his blood was so thick he couldn't switch back to a less charged encounter. "Excuse me?"

"The last person she was seen alive with was a white man named Brian Underhill. She was in his car, the evening of July ninth, in Darktown."

Clayton blinked a few times, breathing hard. "Says who?"

"A couple of the colored cops. They saw them together."

Clayton shook his head. "*Colored* cops? Fuck you." He closed the door and got back to work.

11

BOGGS WAS LIVID as he made the long walk home. He'd put himself at great risk—he could expect a tongue-lashing from McInnis and possibly a suspension, or worse—and he'd not a thing to show for it. Now white cops were likely interrogating Ellsworth, no doubt violently. Why had he expected anything different?

All those votes he'd helped register, and their number one reason for colored cops was to stop police brutality. Yet their hiring didn't seem to be changing that. It still happened, everywhere, in the station and out on the streets. He'd known what was coming by the way the two detectives had led Ellsworth away. This and Dunlow's beat-down the other night seemed to make it official, as with an APD stamp: Boggs was nothing but a meaningless figurehead.

He never should have told the *Daily Times* reporter. He should have let the family continue in their ignorance, let the mystery of whatever happened to Lily drag on. That would have been hell, too, but a different kind. He'd merely swapped their hells. That's all that Officer Lucius Boggs had the power to do for his fellow Negro citizens: give them a slightly different hell.

The only way to salvage the day would be to do something that would again put him at risk. Was he that stupid? Was he about to get himself fired? Was this one farmer and his dead daughter worth it?

He stopped and walked back to the station.

Atlantans did not often see colored men loitering outside the police headquarters, yet that's what Boggs was doing. He stood at the corner across the street, near a light pole marked with red tape denoting it a bus stop. *Atlanta Constitution* in his hand, though he wasn't really reading it. He skimmed the occasional story but mainly kept his eyes on the station.

The white detectives had steered Ellsworth toward the interrogation room about an hour and a half ago. For all Boggs knew, the man had already been released. Or perhaps he'd been booked. Boggs hoped not. His goal was to talk to the man, but he wasn't sure what his exact plan was, how long he'd allow himself to stand here.

He was a cop staking out a police station.

He'd been there ten minutes when two white cops, emerging from the station, saw him, muttered to each other, and stood watching him from across the street.

Boggs cursed under his breath as they jaywalked toward him. He didn't recognize them, but he wondered if they knew him. It would no doubt take him years to know all the faces of the dozens of white cops, but how long until every cop had memorized the eight colored faces among them?

"What are you doing here, boy?"

"Waiting," he said, looking up from his paper. The two cops both seemed younger than him, high school a very recent memory, maybe a year or two of odd jobs before deciding to take the police test. Boggs knew he was going to have to get better at identifying and describing faces, but right then the only way he could describe them was young, white, angry. Might as well have been identical.

"You're loitering," the other one said, "so you'd best move along *now*."

The other one glanced at Boggs's bandage. "Looks like you've been beaten up already, be a shame to have it happen again and—"

"My name is Officer Lucius Boggs and I'm waiting on someone."

The white cops looked at each other. "Ah hell," one of them said.

The other stepped more closely to him. "You don't belong here. Get back with your kind."

"I'm waiting on someone." He tried to keep his face relaxed. He had been trained for years to avoid exactly the sort of confrontations that he now found himself having, repeatedly. After three months, it hadn't become any less disorienting. "I'll be gone once he's arrived."

"Who are you waiting on?"

He wanted to say, *That's my business, and mind yours.* He wanted to ask them if they had a beat they should be walking. He sorely wanted to mouth off, and right then he didn't even mind being outnumbered two to one. But they had thousands at their backs.

So he tried to look friendly. Even smiled. Hating himself for it. "How long have you been on the force, three months like me? Is this how you want to start off?"

The bluff didn't work. "You have any idea how much money we'd make if we knocked you down to size? There's a big pool on your head."

"I've heard that." Boggs's adrenaline was spiking and he could feel a tremor rise in his chest. He was afraid he'd start shaking from the energy and look scared. Or he'd have to unleash that energy by hitting one of them. He wasn't sure which would be worse. "It was seventy-five dollars a couple of weeks ago, wasn't it? It reach a hundred yet? Didn't know a Negro could be worth so much after slavery."

One of the cops smiled. But the other leaned closer to Boggs and said, "You ain't worth *shit*." Staying in Boggs's space for a moment. Then he backed off and the two white cops walked away.

They looked over their shoulder at him twice in the time it took them to walk a block, until they were out of view.

Boggs's heart was still pounding and he had to pace off the high. *Lord almighty.* He wanted to hit something. He tried to calm himself down, realizing he was only going to attract more attention by pacing like a strung-out junkie.

Twenty minutes later, Ellsworth emerged from headquarters. He was walking even more slowly than he had been that morning. Before, it had been fear. Now, it was pain: Boggs could pick up the clenched teeth by the set of the man's jaw, could see the limp from across the street.

"Mr. Ellsworth," Boggs called out as he crossed. Ellsworth flinched, stepping back. The quick movement made him suck in his breath and put a hand to the left side of his rib cage. His face appeared unmarked, but the detectives had known to aim low. Also his hat was gone. "I was hoping we could talk for a bit."

"Done enough talking." His voice tiny.

"Please, sir. I'd just like to ask you a few questions about your daughter."

"Your white men already did that."

Ellsworth started to shuffle away. Boggs held up his palms. "I don't ask the way they do."

Ellsworth ignored him. Boggs let him pass. He watched as Ellsworth stopped for a moment, as if to gather himself, and take another few steps. The man could barely walk.

"How long do you think it's going to take for you to get to the station like that? Two hours?"

No reply. One more step, then another. Then stop.

Boggs walked over to him. "Let me get you a cab and we'll ride over together. There's a spot near the station where I can get you some lunch. You could use some water, I bet."

Ellsworth glared. "What do you want?"

"The white officers don't care what happened to your daughter, sir. I do. Will you let me help you?"

Ellsworth gazed up the street. Boggs wondered how many rows this farmer had hoed in his many years and he realized that, to Ellsworth, walking a mile on smooth sidewalks with broken ribs might not rank near the top of his hardest days. He wasn't sure if Ellsworth was calculating the distance or trying to remember train schedules, seeing flashes of whatever the detectives had done to him or trying to remember the last time he'd seen his daughter alive.

The farmer sounded deeply resigned as he said, "I'll let you try."

⚡

It took a few minutes to hail a cab that would transport Negroes, but finally they were on their way. The fare was an extravagance Boggs normally would not permit himself.

They'd been in the cab only a few seconds when Boggs realized that Ellsworth smelled of urine. The farmer's shirttails were hanging out, though they'd been tucked in when he'd arrived at the station. Shame had compelled him to cover the evidence.

They were silent as they rode through downtown. They passed restaurants that would not have served them, some of whose waiters or chefs would attack Boggs if he dared walk in—an eighteen-year-old visitor from New York had been so treated a few weeks ago, Boggs had read in the *Daily Times*. He passed office towers that only granted admittance to Negroes who shined shoes or cleaned bathrooms. He passed white women who would no doubt scream if he made eye contact with them. "Reckless eyeballing" was the official charge police filed in such cases; since becoming a cop, he had looked up the statute to make sure it existed. It did.

They passed hotels that would not admit him, and passed the ridiculously costumed Negro bellhops who were those establishments' only colored employees. During the Depression, hotel managers had been accused by the Silver Shirts and the Brown Shirts and other Fascist groups of betraying their white race by hiring Negroes at a time when so many whites were starving. One of Boggs's cousins had been fired back then, laid off like most of the Negro bellhops when the hotel managers had seen the logic of the Fascists' argument after a parade of uniformed goose-steppers marched down Peachtree Street. Now that the Depression was a memory, some of those white bellhops had moved on to better work, and Boggs's cousin once again had the honor of carrying white people's baggage.

Boggs paid the fare at Terminal Station. Across the street was a café at whose window Negroes were permitted to purchase food to be eaten elsewhere. Ellsworth insisted he wasn't hungry, however, so they skipped it and entered the station. The wide doors gaped open to allow some air flow, and they walked in and saw the high arched ceilings above, the marble floor shining despite being trod upon by thousands already that day. They walked to their left and entered the cramped colored waiting room, where there was no air flow and hardly any room to sit. The end of one bench had just enough room for Ellsworth's narrow frame. Boggs stood in front of him.

"I'm very sorry for your loss," Boggs said, feeling badly that he hadn't the opportunity before. He kept his voice low, though surely others could hear them. This was hardly the ideal spot for an interview, but it was all he had.

Ellsworth was looking away. His eyes not really there.

Boggs felt coldly professional as he took the small notebook out of his pocket. He asked for Lily's full name and age, then asked, "Could you tell me why she was in Atlanta?"

"I don't know. She stubborn."

"What do you mean?"

"Think she do better out here, I guess."

"How?"

"Search me. But she never was one for hard labor, you know. She no farmer's wife."

"You work your own land?"

"No. But I get by."

"So she came here to be a maid somewhere?" It was unlikely that a colored girl from the country could find better work than as domestic help; the few textile jobs open to colored women would have been taken by native Atlantans, and since the war had ended such openings had become scarce. "Why couldn't she do that somewhere closer to Peacedale?"

Ellsworth shook his head and made a face like *If you had daughters, you would not ask such logical questions about them.*

"Why Atlanta?"

"She had a fight with my wife. They weren't getting on so well."

"She a hard girl to raise?"

"They got on fine, most times. Things happen here and there. I don't ask about that, you know? They just need to get on well enough to get that food on the table, keep the little ones in line. All I ask about. They having some fight or lip or whatnot, I only step in if it happens in front of me."

"Do you know where she was when she got here, where she was living or working?"

"Yeah, she wrote us some letters. Had return addresses on 'em."

"Do you still have them?"

"Wife does."

"I'd very much like to see them."

"Well, you have to come out and look for 'em, then. I ain't coming back."

"I'd be happy to." He asked for Ellsworth's address and wrote it down.

"You come during the day, I be out in the fields. And if you come at night, well, you don't want to be doing that."

"I'll be fine, sir."

Ellsworth watched him, his face unreadable as a stone that hasn't been engraved yet. "Yeah."

"Was there anything in her letters, Mr. Ellsworth, that made you fear for her safety?"

"Didn't like the idea her being here, that what you mean."

"But did she ever write anything specifically that struck you as—"

Ellsworth shaking his head was enough to get Boggs to stop.

"Did she ever mention the name Brian Underhill?"

"No. Who that?"

"Just someone we've been keeping our eye on. How about Lionel Dunlow or Denny Rakestraw?"

More head shakes. "Don't recall any names being mentioned. 'Cept that one, the senator."

"The senator?"

"She got a job working as a maid to a senator. Senator's wife, that is. Senator wasn't around."

Boggs tried not to look shocked. "Which one?"

"Don't recall."

Boggs could not believe that the man would not know the name of a senator his daughter was working for. But at the same time, he could. "When was that?"

"May. Strawberry season. I was looking at the letter, and when my wife had her turn, she scolded me, said I got sweat on it. Smeared some of the words." A tiny smile, easily slain.

"Did you mention any of this to the police in the station?"

"Didn't ask about that. Only want to ask about me. They hinted disgusting things. I'm a man of God. I read the Good Book. Lily taught me to, matter of fact. And I'm in there every Sunday and some other days besides. Those police, they hinted disgusting things."

"I'm sorry about that, Mr. Ellsworth."

"Why you keep calling me Mr. Ellsworth?"

"It's your name, sir."

Ellsworth shook his head and his eyes looked angry, like he couldn't understand why this odd city man was talking in code. "It's Otis."

"All right, Otis. But I'm not like those cops."

"No kiddin'. How you even a cop?"

"We do strange things here in Atlanta."

"Yes, you do. I ain't been here in years. Not coming back for years, neither. Maybe not ever."

"In that letter, the one when she was working for the senator, did she say anything about him or his wife? Or their house or the job?"

"Not much to say about domestic work." An empty laugh. "She didn't write us about dusting and whatnot. You know, just saying hello and asking after the crops and the family and such."

Ellsworth clearly thought Boggs's questions were ridiculous. Boggs was dying to know more about her job, but he decided to drop this angle and pursue it by reading the letters when he got them.

"Did she sound happy?"

"Lily?" The farmer's eyes were glassy now, like he'd drifted away again. The sound of his girl's name on his own lips had cast a spell.

"Yes, sir. Anything in the letters about being worried or scared, or the opposite, was there some event she was looking forward to?"

"She put on a brave face. Letters were always, 'the city's so great, the food is great, the clothes are great, the music great.' I know her, I know she probably be lonely and confused and maybe scared, but she ain't gonna say that in no letter, don't want to let her momma know she was right all along."

"Her mother didn't want her to come to Atlanta?"

"She always say cities aren't good for young women. I'd say she right about that."

"Why didn't your wife come in today?"

Ellsworth looked at his hands. "Too hard. Too hard on her. I don't . . . I don't know how I'm gonna tell her."

There was something that didn't sound right to Boggs, but he couldn't place what it was.

"When you saw the newspaper story, what made you think it might be Lily?"

"Friend of mine told me. Saw the story. He knew we were worried on Lily, and the story mentioned that locket. Wife gave it to her long while ago."

A baby cried out as a mother surrounded by luggage searched through her bags for something. It was easily ninety degrees in there.

"To work at the house of a senator, your daughter must have had impeccable manners."

"We raise her right."

"And she taught you to read, so she had schooling?"

"Good teacher out there. Only takes the one, get 'em started. He gave her the learning, she and all her friends. Too much learning, probably."

"How so?"

"Head got too big."

"What do you mean?"

"She on us to *vote.*" The searching look in his eyes told Boggs this had been an unreasonable request, and that Boggs was expected to nod along in sympathy. "Brought it up so many times I finally have to forbid her talking 'bout it no more. They beat a colored man two counties over who tried to register. Beat him to death. Policeman did it." Boggs knew that murder well. It hadn't made the white papers but had been covered heavily by the *Daily Times,* and his father had tried to help the slain man's family hire an attorney. They had chosen to flee north instead. "And Lily wanted *us* to try the same thing."

"So it was important to her."

"That teacher was giving her ideas. We do our best to protect her, you know? We try and tell her the kind of trouble she could get us in."

The effort to register black voters in Atlanta had been a success, but Boggs knew it had been a different story in the country. Signs had been plastered in small towns warning of retribution if any Negroes tried to vote, and that particular murder had been only one example of what befell some of the tenant farmers who dared step forward. Boggs and Ellsworth lived in different worlds.

He took down the teacher's name and school, thinking it might be worth paying him a visit.

"Did she talk about that sort of thing in public?" Boggs asked.

"I hope not. We warned her, we told her to watch herself. We try to protect her." His eyes began to water, and then the announcer's tinny voice called out that the local to Macon was arriving.

"I didn't have to come in like this, you know," Ellsworth said as they walked to the track. "On a train and walking. I coulda driven my own truck, that's right."

"You have a truck?"

"Yes, sir. It's a little beat up but it works just fine. Got it off another farmer just a few weeks ago, gets me where I need. I got me some money, you know."

"You've been saving a long time?"

Ellsworth looked out at the small crowd queuing up to the track, and the verbal momentum he'd had before, the fluid bragging, was gone. As if realizing he'd said too much. "I manage."

"Surprised Lily would want to run off if you had money."

"We get by, that's all. We get by. But we on to better things. Going off to Chicago. Yes, sir. Living better up there."

"When do you leave?"

"Springtime. After one more harvest, then have to wait out those winters they have. But now that I got enough saved, we can do it. Enough to ride in one of the fancy train cars, too. But I think we'll drive, drive my new truck, see the country on the way. That's how to do it."

There was much here that didn't make sense. Did Ellsworth really have any money, or was he just trying to talk big to regain his manhood? He was a sharecropper, not a landowner. What Boggs knew about life on Georgia tenant farms told him it would be noteworthy for the man to have saved anything at all. Where had the money come from, some rare bumper crop—which was unlikely, especially with all the rain this year and the stories of produce rotting in the ground—or something else?

The train was approaching.

"Did Lily ever send anything home? Souvenirs from the city, some nice clothes for her sisters?"

"She don't have no sisters, just two brothers. They don't need no nice clothes." He laughed at that, too hard. It wasn't funny, and he wasn't looking at Boggs anymore. He was staring at that train, all but waving for it to hurry up so he wouldn't have to answer any more questions.

The train stopped and sighed, the cars for white passengers in back with their windows shut to keep in the cooler air, the Negro cars up front with windows open, those passengers inside who were not disembarking fanning themselves in the now-still air. Off came the porters, and people were moving in all directions, so much so that Boggs put a hand at one of the farmer's forearms because he was afraid the injured man might get knocked down. The arm was thin but solid as an iron bar.

"I'll be by as soon as I can to pick up those letters. And maybe talk to your wife."

"You don't need to trouble yourself. We just got to mourn and make our way."

Was Ellsworth hiding something, or was he just so used to his place at the bottom of life's pecking order that he was acting awkwardly when presented with someone who actually wanted to help him? Boggs explained that it was no trouble at all, but the expression on the farmer's face was not gratitude, just a kind of dire acceptance that triggered something deep in Boggs's gut. As if it were easier for Ellsworth to meekly accept the latest plague the Lord had unleashed than to scream into the dark maw of life, demanding explanations.

Lily's father limped up the stairs, his fingers gripping the rail with each step.

Once Ellsworth was off, Boggs walked out of the station, tapping his notebook on his thigh. He needed to talk to Smith and figure out his next move, carefully. As a Negro officer, there were many duties he was now authorized to perform, but conducting investigations was not one of them.

He had broken plenty of rules today. If he wasn't fired for it, he would break a few more.

12

PAST MIDNIGHT AND Rake walked slowly through his own neighborhood, clad in jeans and a T-shirt. It was warmer outside than in his bedroom but at least he wasn't sweating anymore—he had woken from a bad dream absolutely drenched. So he had come out for some air, some space, some new thoughts to dispel whatever had been plaguing his subconscious. He had become such an odd night crawler. In a way, perhaps the war had been training for his new vocation, as there had been weeks in Europe when it was only safe for him to move at night, and he'd slept in barns and attics by day.

He forgot the dreams almost the moment he woke up, every time.

They came maybe once a week. There seemed no rhyme or reason to why they visited when they did. When he first opened his eyes, he would see a shard of that other world, the mud in France or a certain house in Germany, or sometimes it would be a sound that had woken him, the canons and guns and screams and whines, but then they vanished. He told himself it was better that way, but their very unknowingness made them all the more disquieting.

A dog barked a few times, too far away for it to be directed at him. Owls cooed from invisible branches. The locusts sounded even louder in his neighborhood than they did over in Darktown, which made some sense since there were more trees here. Boughs heavy with wide summer leaves hung low over the sidewalks.

He'd been out ten minutes when he heard the sound of broken glass. Not glass breaking, but already broken glass being dropped, or poured.

He looked to his left. There was a figure crouched outside a house, beside a trash can. Something long and thin there, and for a moment Rake froze, taking it for a rifle. Then he realized it wasn't a firearm but the handle of a broom. Someone was *sweeping a yard*. At midnight.

Then the man stood up, and where before Rake had seen only a hunched back and the broom, now he saw a man standing to dump a dustpan full of glass shards into a trash can. Because he was standing just beside an illuminated window, it was hard to make out much more than his basic shape. Only after Rake's eyes adjusted to the trick of the light did he notice the funny outline around the man's head, a fuzziness that he'd at first attributed to his own eyes and now realized was the hair of a Negro.

Rake put a few things together then. This was the new neighbor, the Negro who had somehow bought an empty lot and built a house on it, a few blocks on the wrong side of the unofficial color line.

Three of the windows in the man's house were illuminated. The light that poured out through one of them did so through a series of jagged lines.

No other house had any lights on, and Rake hadn't seen or even heard a single car drive by since he'd been out.

The man probably hadn't noticed him yet. Rake could just walk away, go home, get back in bed. Such an act, he realized, would be an expression of weakness. He crossed the street. Keeping his voice quiet enough not to wake any neighbors but loud enough for the man to hear him, he asked, "Are you all right, there?"

The man had been crouched down, but now he looked up. He had a beard, and his forehead was shiny with sweat.

"I'm fine, sir." The Negro kept watching Rake.

"I'm a police officer, sir. I live nearby, just happened to be out for a walk. Do you need anything?"

The man carefully assessed him. "I'm all right, Officer."

Though he had not been invited, Rake stepped onto the man's property. He felt it would be seen as a sign of neighborliness.

"Careful where you step, I don't think I've gotten it all." The man was down on his knees, feeling around for glass. There was a flashlight beside him.

"When did this happen?"

"I don't know. I came home from work about twenty minutes ago and this is how it was. This and the other ones."

"What other ones?"

"One on the other side, and one in the back."

Rake wondered if it would have been one person or a group, timing it just right. He thought of teenagers having fun, of lintheads after a few drinks, of his brother-in-law, Dale. He felt various kinds of disappointment at the last thought.

"My wife had taken the kids to her sister's for the night. Thank God, too, because a brick landed in my little boy's bed."

The Negro neighbor let Rake borrow his flashlight to inspect the periphery of the house. Rake didn't find anything suspicious or incriminating, no bottles or cigarette butts, though the latter would have been difficult to spot without sunlight.

The neighbor explained that he'd already picked up the glass from the other two windows. And anyway, most of the glass had fallen *in* the house.

Rake asked the man's name.

"James Calvin." He looked forty, Rake guessed. A green Plymouth pickup was parked in the driveway. He was an inch shorter than Rake and slimmer, though his T-shirt showed arms sculpted by hard work.

"Do you mind if I asked you how you came to own this land, Mr. Calvin?"

Rake had been calling him "sir" and he hoped that and the "Mr." showed that he took this man seriously, that he was not like some of the others. Mr. Calvin did not seem to be in the mood to thank him for it, however.

"The land was left to me. The house I built with my own money, saved over many years."

"Who left it to you?"

"Mr. Red Westerly."

Rake knew the name. Westerly was one of the cousins of the heirs to the Coke fortune and had owned much of the real estate in this area. "You did work with him?"

"I helped build about two dozen of his houses, yes, sir. There were times, when his business wasn't doing so well, that he couldn't pay me what he'd said he would, but he always promised to make good on it. When he passed last year, he'd willed me this plot, and two others I'm renting out in Summerhill."

Rake hadn't even noticed that there had been an empty plot on a corner, at least not until the day people were clearing out the bushes and laying the foundation that became this house. He was surprised to hear Westerly would leave any land to a Negro, and more surprised to hear that a probate judge hadn't moved to stop it somehow.

Most real estate agents knew enough not to try selling property in a white neighborhood to a Negro. Having land willed to you by an eccentric benefactor was a novel way to dodge that problem.

"You're a carpenter?"

"Started as a mason. Had occasion to pick up pretty much everything else as I went along. Can build the whole house myself these days."

Rake motioned to the broken window. "Would you like me to take a look inside?"

They were standing just outside the first window. Rake had glanced around the neighborhood a few times now, and no other lights had turned on. Of course, if someone was watching them, they'd be doing so from an unlit room for a better view.

"What for?"

"Just to . . . look for anything."

"Nothing to see. Just three bricks and a lot of glass. You sure you didn't hear or see anything before you got here?"

"No, sir."

"Midnight's a strange time to be out for a stroll." He said this with a slight smile, and without looking at Rake, as if to make extra sure it didn't sound like an accusation.

"It is. Trouble sleeping. Plus, I walk around at night for a living. So I suppose it isn't so strange to me."

But Rake felt tired now, as if his body was finally remembering that it had been sleeping a little while ago and would very much like to get back to it.

"Would you like to file a report, Mr. Calvin?"

"To you?"

"No, it would be other officers who'd take the report. I don't patrol this neighborhood."

"Where do you patrol?"

He was about to say "near Darktown" when he caught himself. "Downtown, and near Auburn Avenue."

"So they'll write me up a report and, what, they'll try to find who did this? You think that would happen?"

"No, sir. I honestly don't."

"Then I won't make them waste their time."

Rake nodded. "I think I'll head home then."

"All right."

"I'm sorry that this happened, sir. I'm glad your kids are okay."

Rake realized that Calvin had never asked his name. Perhaps he'd expected Rake to volunteer it and found it odd that he hadn't. The omission had not been deliberate, but now that Rake realized it, he decided he'd keep it to himself.

Instead of a name, Calvin asked, "Whereabouts do you live?"

"On Prospect, three blocks that way."

"You like it?"

"I do. It's a good community. Nice place for kids."

"Glad to hear that. That's what I want. My wife and I, that's all we want."

He was looking at Rake more intently than before.

"Aren't there other good neighborhoods?" Rake asked.

"What do you mean?"

"It just seems to me, sir, that you might be needlessly provoking people."

"This is the property that was left to me."

True, Rake thought, *but you could always sell it and buy a house more appropriately located.* He was too tired to make this argument, too anxious to end the conversation.

Calvin said, "I'm not breaking any laws by being here."

"I understand that."

"The people that threw those bricks are the ones broke the laws."

Calvin was getting angrier now, as if he'd watched Rake long enough to decide that he could reveal more of himself to the white man, as if Calvin was now free to say things to this stranger that he perhaps should not.

"I understand, sir," Rake said. It was so difficult to walk this line. To let colored people know that just because you were the same color as fire-breathing racists didn't mean you agreed with them. And at the same time, just because you were talking to a colored person and desperately trying to impart some wisdom and necessary advice, that didn't mean that you agreed with what Calvin was doing to his wife and kids, or to your own neighborhood.

"All I'm doing is living," Calvin said. "Working my job and sleeping at night. That's all I ask and all I expect."

A car approached. Going the usual speed, and as it neared Rake felt himself stiffening. He turned to watch it pass, and pass it did, the form at the wheel too nebulous to make out. He didn't bother memorizing the tags, as it pulled into a house three doors down, and Rake heard the car door open, shuffling footsteps, keys jingling.

Rake bade Mr. Calvin good-night, then walked home, feeling small beneath the stars.

13

IT WAS NINE and not yet abysmally hot as the bus climbed up Monroe. It passed Piedmont Park, where white ladies leisurely strolled through the greenery, clutching parasols or pushing prams, getting some air before that air grew stifling. Dew still clung to the grass and dazed squirrels hid in the shade at the base of hickories and red oaks.

Boggs rarely rode the bus. Sweet Auburn had what he needed, and when he did require something farther off, he had his father's car. But today's errand was a unique one, requiring him to make like the majority of Negroes in his city, and thus he subjected himself to the back of the bus. He subjected himself to the white driver's occasional comments about Negroes, which he made to some white men who sat in front. He subjected himself to the fact that the very road he was on changed names from Boulevard to Monroe not because the road itself changed but because the southern length of it was a colored neighborhood and the northern length was white and therefore the people who lived on it should put different words on their return addresses.

He got off at the intersection of Piedmont. The houses here were close to the street but set up high on brick steps and wide porches, some of them surrounded by giant azaleas that rose to the houses' second stories. Ansley Park was one of the wealthier neighborhoods in the city; Boggs had certainly never walked here before, and he felt those looming Tudors and Queen Annes observing him, their porches like noses held high in disdain.

He was here to pay a visit to Lily Ellsworth's former employer.

He was wearing a white button-up shirt tucked into tan trousers. He was clean but had deliberately not ironed his clothes, as he'd been afraid of looking *too* together. From what he'd observed from Otis

Ellsworth, he needed to be at least slightly shabby to pass for the man's son.

The previous day, the farmer had called police headquarters and left a detailed message for Boggs, listing the return address of all his daughter's letters from Atlanta, as well as the name of the "senator" she'd worked for. Boggs had since looked up the addresses and checked them against the few records in the Negro precinct's files: the first two addresses were boardinghouses. The third was Mama Dove's, a brothel.

Perhaps that was why Ellsworth didn't seem to want Boggs to come out to Peacedale and see the letters? Did Ellsworth know his daughter had fallen that low? The call may have been a way for Ellsworth to forestall the visit. It certainly played to Boggs's own fears: as much as he knew he should go out there—to see if any other information had occurred to Ellsworth now that the initial shock had passed, and to talk to the rest of Lily's family and learn more about the "argument" between mother and daughter—he was wary of it. McInnis would fire him immediately if word got out that Boggs was traveling the state to investigate a murder. Worse, Peacedale was very far away indeed from the protections Boggs enjoyed in Atlanta. The thought of going that deep into the country chilled him.

Instead, he had read the file on Lily's murder, which had not taken long at all. The white detectives had noted that Otis Ellsworth admitted he wasn't her biological father, something he'd failed to mention to Boggs. The report noted the detectives' theory that Ellsworth may have killed her, a claim Boggs thought absurd, and apparently they realized it was a flimsy idea, as they offered no evidence and had not charged the man. Forensics had done little work on her body. The white detectives seemed to assume she had been killed in the alley and left there, but Boggs hadn't found any blood on the ground. It seemed obvious to him she had been killed elsewhere and then moved.

So today Boggs was walking toward the home not of a senator, as Ellsworth had incorrectly recalled, but a congressman: Billy Prescott, U.S. Representative. He was a longtime officeholder, notoriously sly deal-maker, and one of the few elected officials Boggs had actually met.

Prescott had been in power since '32. He was a Democrat, of course,

as were pretty much all the elected officials from Georgia and the surrounding states of the old Confederacy (Republicans were the party of
Lincoln, emancipator of the slaves, and therefore were considered by
white Southerners to be barely better than Negroes, Jews, and Communists). Atlanta politicians weren't typically the pitchfork-wielding
demagogues like the state's senators and rural congressmen were, however, and Prescott had been rather quiet on racial matters during his first
years in office. Like the rest of his delegation, he opposed antilynching
legislation, and he'd avoided any civic events that might involve leaders
of the colored community. But his wary stance toward what white folks
called "the Negro question" had seemed to change over the last few
years, either because he was more comfortable in his long incumbency
or because he could see how the Negro vote was shifting the balance of
power in his urban district. Two years ago he had sat alongside Mayor
Hartsfield in a meeting with Reverend Boggs and other colored leaders
to discuss their concerns, chief of which was hiring Negro officers.
Weeks after that meeting, he'd even agreed to speak at a conference on
Negro rights at Morehouse—an unprecedented move for a Georgia
congressman—so long as his presence wasn't advertised in advance.
Boggs had attended the conference with his father, and had been one of
a few alumni war veterans who'd been invited to share a brief audience
with Prescott beforehand. In those few minutes, Prescott had struck
Boggs as intelligent and, if not exactly striving for racial fairness, at
least curious to learn more about the overlooked corners of his district.
Months later, Hartsfield's decision to hire Negro cops sent most Georgia legislators into seizures, one group even drafting a state bill that
would have banned Negro police. But Prescott (according to Reverend
Boggs, who said he'd heard from friends at City Hall) had threatened
to tie up farm subsidies of influential farmers in their districts if they
followed through, and the law died in conference. Ever since, Boggs's
father had spoken of the man as an ally, if one he didn't know well.

This being late July, Congress was still in session and Representative Prescott was busy with his legislating up north. Though he lived
in Washington most of the year, his home in Atlanta left little to be
desired. A white Tudor, it had a wide porch set behind twin magnolias
and a perfectly maintained lawn unmarred by a single magnolia pod

or stray leaf. Black-eyed Susans dotted the garden, and two lavender chaste trees flanked the driveway, their branches adorned with long, spiky purple flowers like some strange new hairdo. The house looked like the sort of place that should have a gate around it, and it probably would before long.

Boggs had not yet sweated through his shirt, but the small of his back was damp. Traffic passed intermittently behind him.

The door to the house seemed wider than it needed to be. Its knocker was made of brass. Boggs imagined it would issue quite an authoritative knock.

He did not consider using it.

He instead walked past the entrance, his shoes crunching on the stones of the semicircular driveway. Having swallowed his pride, he followed a dirt walkway around the side of the building, searching for the back door. He was careful not to peer into any of the side windows. The holly bushes were well manicured, their dry leaves no doubt sharp enough to draw blood. He found the much-less-impressive back door, walked up the three wooden steps, and knocked.

The steps had creaked when he walked up them and they were pocked with holes from carpenter bees. Behind him were three fig trees, a hummingbird darting past. He'd been waiting long enough to consider a second knock when the door opened a few inches and he saw the face of a maid. She was young, maybe twenty, pretty, and annoyed.

"What do you want?"

"I was hoping to speak with Mrs. Prescott."

She eyed the bandage on his forehead. Everyone did. "What is this regarding?" She looked a few years younger than Boggs, yet she spoke to him as if he were simple. "Because unless what you've come to talk about is real *mighty* important, you'd best not trouble her with it."

"I'm looking for my sister, who used to work here. I was hoping Mrs. Prescott might know where she moved on to. Please, miss."

She watched him for a second. She seemed interested in the mention of her predecessor. And that interested him.

"Which girl?" she asked, but the question seemed fake to him, like she was asking only to cover up her initial reaction.

"Lily Ellsworth. I'm her brother, Lucius. We haven't heard from her in a while."

She looked down for a moment. "I'll go see if she's available."

She was backing up and closing the door when Boggs reached out and held it open.

"I know you, don't I? Or at least your people? They worship at Wheat Street, don't they? The Joneses?"

He was lying, but it worked, because she replied, "No, Ebenezer Baptist. We're the Cannons. I'm Julie."

"I'm sorry, my mistake. You just looked familiar."

He dedicated *Julie Cannon* to memory while he waited, studying his surroundings. He wondered if any white detective had come knocking on the Prescotts' door yet. Had she been a *white* former maid to a congressman, a detective would have at least asked a few questions, albeit discreetly. But Southern discretion was so strong that a full-bore investigation would have been unlikely even for a white girl. Because Lily was only a Negro, the case had not been judged important enough to bother such an esteemed household. The suggestion of any sexual improprieties (had the wife fired her because the congressman had taken advantage and the wife was jealous?) would never be made. Boggs was willing to bet he was the first cop to come here since Lily's murder. The household might not even know she was dead.

He heard footsteps. He made sure he was standing straight but not too straight, hands at his sides.

Caroline Prescott—he had looked up her name in the Auburn Avenue library the day before—was exceptionally thin, the cords of her neck too prominent. The severe way in which her hair was pulled back made her light blue eyes seem to bulge. She stood without a cane but he wondered if she used one when she was outside her home.

"Yes, what is it today?" she asked in the kind of tea-soaked tone certain white ladies use when addressing Negroes.

"Yes, ma'am, my name is Lucius Ellsworth and I understand my sister Lily works here?" He did not look her in the eye. He imitated Otis Ellsworth's accent, though a few degrees less country. Given that Otis had described his daughter as educated, Boggs figured she would have sounded different from her stepfather. "We haven't heard from her in some time, and my folks asked me to come—"

"Lily no longer works here."

"Oh. I'm sorry, ma'am, I didn't know that. About how long ago—"

She seemed irritated to be bothered with such a trifle. "I can't recall, a month or two ago."

"Did she by chance leave a forwarding address, or maybe a—"

"I haven't the faintest idea where she might be. It did not work out for her here, I'm afraid. I hope she found her way to something more suited to her talents."

He couldn't tell if she spoke so coldly to every colored person or if this particular subject had caused her claws to come out.

"All right. Thank you, ma'am."

Over her shoulder he could also see, a good ten feet away, the new maid, Miss Julie Cannon, observing the scene with a furrowed brow. She could hear that he was speaking differently than before.

He took a step back, as if to go, but first he added, "She spoke very well of this place, ma'am. Really enjoyed working here."

"I'm sure she did." If Mrs. Prescott's voice had been cold before, now it was bloodless. Yet she did not slam the door, as that would have been unladylike. She didn't even close it. She simply vacated the area, and in her absence Julie appeared, as closing doors was part of her job.

Julie watched him carefully. He winked at her without smiling, then walked away.

The night before, Boggs had returned home after another long shift and sat in his parents' study, a lone lamp keeping him company. Most nights, no matter how tired he was, he needed this brief moment, maybe only ten minutes, to sit and rest and let all he'd seen bleed from his mind. A glass of water carefully placed on a coaster beside him, window open to the sound of locusts, he read the Bible.

He had memorized several verses about perseverance to help himself through the awful months of the South Carolina army camp. Despite knowing them by heart, he read them now from an old family Bible— the very same one that his great-grandmother, born a slave, had learned to read from. As if seeing the words on paper rather than in his mind would make them more real.

Galatians 6:9—"Let us not become weary in doing good, for at the proper time we will reap a harvest if we do not give up."

James 1:12—"Blessed is the man who perseveres under trial, because when he has stood the test, he will receive the crown of life that God has promised to those who love him."

Somewhat more ominously, Revelation 2:10—"Do not be afraid of what you are about to suffer. I tell you, the devil will put some of you in prison to test you, and you will suffer persecution for ten days. Be faithful, even to the point of death, and I will give you the crown of life."

Sometimes it was helpful to be reminded that others had felt the same way he did, people going back centuries, all over the globe. Others had endured so much more. Surely he, a man with a salary and a roof over his head and a loving family, could withstand that which plagued him.

Other times, the words grated. So much about suffering and enduring. So much about the nobleness of feeling the pain inflicted by others. It was then that the words on the page felt as dead as those who had written them, and Boggs shelved the book and went to sleep.

Boggs and Smith walked south toward the Decatur Street clubs, the roughest part of town, just across the street from the railroad tracks. Women in lurid and revealing dresses had a habit of slowly walking the sidewalks alone here, empty bottles magically rolled across the street, knives found a way to lodge themselves into people's backs. It was another thick night, and as they approached the neon sign of Early's Late Place, they heard the scuffling of shoes and the hollers. They picked up their pace and were running by the time they saw the scrum of men spilling into the street.

"Police!" Smith yelled. "Break it up!"

Men were falling down and getting up and being pulled back down again. A circle of men, widening and spinning and out of control. Boggs thought he counted five men, but there might have been a sixth in there somewhere. He realized he was lingering at the periphery only when he saw his partner launch into the mess.

"I said *Break it up!*" Smith hollered, pushing past one man who'd already been falling anyway.

Another man pulled back his arm to throw a punch, and in so doing his elbow brushed against the bill of Smith's cap, knocking it off. Smith took out his billy club and struck the man's right shoulder. The man dropped, his unthrown punch a memory of things that never happened. Whoever he'd been trying to hit now stood up and saw before him the figure of a capless Officer Smith with a billy club pulled back a second time, eyes searching for a new target.

"Awright, awright!" The man submitted, palms out.

Smith kept his baton in position and pointed behind him with his other hand. "On the sidewalk, on your ass. Now."

Two other men were tangled together and rolling on the ground, their bodies like the interlocked fingers of two hands desperately trying to become fists. Each time one of them was on top, he'd try to pull one of his arms loose to throw a punch, but then his opponent would flip him, an endless seesaw of futile anger.

"Break it up!" Boggs yelled at them, trying to pull off whichever one was on top. Then they rolled again, nearly taking out his legs in the process. He backed up and was about to try again when he heard a blow land somewhere behind him, and a body knocked into him from behind.

He turned around in time to see that body fall, and then Smith stepped forward to club another man down.

Smith looked disgusted at his partner. "For God's sake, subdue them!"

Boggs yelled at the two wrestlers to stop, but Smith clubbed whichever unlucky one of them happened to be on top at the moment. One blow is all it took, between the shoulder blades. The cops heard a grunt and before they could even see the man go limp, his opponent took advantage by flipping him over triumphantly.

So Smith clubbed that fellow, too, over the head.

A moment later the subjects were lined up on the sidewalk. The cops had dragged those who weren't in any condition to make it that far themselves. Turned out there were actually seven of them, two of them unconscious.

From out of the club walked a tall man whose white apron and large belly marked him the chef or owner or both. The glorious scent of smoked meat pervaded the whole neighborhood, and his person particularly.

"We had things under control," he said. "Didn't need no police out here."

Boggs spoke first, needing to recover some authority after seeing that look in his partner's eyes. It didn't escape his notice the other night, with Little, he'd nearly been brained, but tonight, with Smith, they'd controlled a whole group of belligerents. No thanks to him, as his untouched billy club still was safely nestled in its strap. "Yes, things appeared very under control when we arrived."

"We have better things to do than clean up your messes." Smith's voice was much louder than his partner's. "Now get your ass inside unless you want to join them."

"I run a clean business, Officers. I just seem to be attracting some bad elements now and again."

"Funny how that happens," Boggs said. Sweat from his forehead was making the sewn-up wound sting beneath its bandage. Even with his cap on, others could still see an inch or two of the white gauze. His fellow officers had assured him otherwise, but he knew he looked ridiculous.

One of the men who'd been clubbed was rubbing the back of his neck. "Y'all are supposed to yell 'Police' when you come up behind a man. Even the white cops know that."

"We *did* yell 'Police,'" Boggs said. "You might not've heard it because you had that fellow's arm wrapped around your head, but we said it."

Some of them, or perhaps all, smelled of drink.

"You got your partners in there pouring it all down the drain, don't you?" Boggs asked the cook.

"Why you all troubling us like this?" the cook asked. "Fellows need a place where they can relax, and I provide it. I hardly ever have any trouble, and when I do, I make 'em take it outside."

One of the men started to snore.

The chef leaned closer to Smith and whispered, "I done taken care of your boys."

Smith's expression told the cook that getting this close was a mistake. As was his comment.

"'My boys'? Didn't know I *had* any boys."

So the cook had paid off some white cops. At least, that's what Smith and Boggs assumed. Surely none of the other Negro cops would have taken a cent from this man. Right?

"You need something, just ask," the cook said, looking sheepish now. "That's how it works."

"I need you to go inside, sir," Smith said. "Before one of us does something you'll regret."

The cook finally obeyed, shaking his head.

"Maybe I should go to college, too," said the youngest of the fighters, his cheeks not just unshaven but probably never-been-shaven. "Then I can be a cop and boss other colored folk around."

Smith stepped closer and bent down in search of the kid's eyes. "It's always the one that ain't been clubbed yet who's still talking."

One of the men who *had* been clubbed muttered for the kid to shut his barn door.

"How old *are* you, kid?" Boggs asked. "Y'all are getting a schoolboy drunk?"

"He ain't no schoolboy."

"Truancy, too, then," Smith said. No one bothered to reply.

"I'll go to the call box," Boggs said.

Sighs and mutters and very quiet curses. They knew the call box meant the wagon, which meant arrest, which meant a night in the station, which meant white cops.

"C'mon, man," one of them whined. "Just let us go home."

"Call him 'officer,'" another one recommended. "They like that."

"We also like it when the men of this neighborhood act like men and not a bunch of fools," Boggs said. "It's a Wednesday night, for God's sake."

"Make the call," Smith said.

Neither of them wanted to involve any white cops tonight, especially after the stunt Dunlow had pulled the other night, but they needed a wagon to get this many men in jail. Boggs headed down the street—the nearest call box was a block away.

More mutters and curses. One of them said, "Y'all ain't no different from the white ones."

That such a remark could come only moments after they had demonstrated just how different they were—no bribes, no thank you, no way—enraged Smith. He held his club across his body, left hand gripping the end, and said, "Next one to open his mouth is gonna wake up in Grady with no teeth."

At least two of them were snoring now. The ones who were still awake stared at their shoes.

Boggs and Smith stood for a full hour before the wagon finally appeared. Only two of the men they'd arrested were awake. As the wagon pulled up to the curb, Boggs spied a head in the back.

The wagon didn't turn off its engine, and the driver didn't open his door. Boggs stood guard, annoyed to realize what was happening, while Smith walked over to the driver.

"Sorry, boys," the driver said. "Gonna have to wait on me to process this one."

In the back of the wagon was a white woman, long dark hair, late thirties. Drunk by the look of her dizzy eyes and unfortunate hair. She glanced at Smith and then back out the other window.

Arrested black men could not be put in the same wagon as arrested white women. The law. Smith bit back what he wanted to say and merely nodded.

"I'll call in another one for you," the driver said. Smith wasn't sure if he believed him.

The wagon drove off.

"This mean we're free men?" one of the waiting-to-be-jailed asked.

Another said, "Ain't no free men around here," and someone else laughed.

A minute of silence, Smith pacing angrily, Boggs stonily still.

Then the young one informed the officers that he needed to use a bathroom, please.

Another ninety minutes. All the fighters dead asleep.

Boggs and Smith felt it like a dare from the white cops. *Is it really worth your time? Wouldn't it have been easier to let them just go home? Why bother?* They felt that last unspoken line echoing in their heads. *Why bother with any of this?*

Each passing minute made it harder for them to stand there. And each passing minute made them less likely to give in. Their shift would end in another hour, and neither wanted to think about what would happen if the wagon still hadn't come. They'd endured long waits before, had been forced to stay hours past shift's end more than once. They would do it again if they had to.

Just that afternoon Boggs had given a pep talk to Xavier Little. *I don't know if I can take much more of this,* Little had confessed. Seeing Dunlow kick that stabbed man the other night, playing with the man's life so casually, had chilled him. *The white cops keep doing things like that in front of me, daring me to stop them. What Dunlow did isn't even the worst thing I've seen. Just the latest. Just the one I have on my mind right now.*

Boggs had resisted asking Little what the worst thing was. He'd told the fellow to buck up, stay strong, pray on it, all those clichés he hated voicing because he didn't know what else to say. Many of them had confided in each other their fears, their second thoughts that perhaps this occupation wasn't such a great idea after all. In such moments it was the other fellow's role to remind his colleague that they were doing this for a reason, that they couldn't afford to back down, that they would collectively lose so much if any of them put individual concerns first by quitting. Little was a bookish fellow, seemed more suited to working for his uncle's newspaper. Boggs was worried he'd be the first to fold.

And now it was Boggs whose spirits needed lifting. He stood in front of these fools he'd arrested and wondered if this was worthwhile.

Two hours after he had called for a wagon, the thunder started. As if the rain had been awaiting the thunder's permission, the skies opened, the shower pelting them hard enough that the unconscious men woke up, with no idea where they were.

A full *three hours* after Boggs had made the call, another wagon finally arrived.

The officers woke the men up, all of whom had fallen back asleep.

Groggy and sore, some of them looked resigned to their fate, and some looked like they had only the vaguest understanding of what was happening. Then the wagon pulled away and the officers walked north.

The rain had been intense but brief, gone in twenty minutes. Even with their ponchos, they were drenched. Boggs's cut forehead was stinging worse than before. Every time they took a step they heard their soaked socks sloshing. They would have blisters in the morning, they knew from experience.

All Boggs wanted to do was walk. Run, really, but he'd settle for walking. Walk across the entire city, exhaust himself, feel the sweat coat his body. Push himself to new limits, walk 'til he collapsed. Civil war soldiers on both sides had walked miles a day for weeks on end. Slaves walked even farther, no doubt, though usually not in a straight line but the same rows, over and over, endlessly. How far had his forbears walked? Could he make it to any state lines if he started now? But again, *Why bother?* As if things were any different in Alabama or North Carolina. Things were as good as they could be for a Southern Negro here, in Atlanta, blocks from Auburn Avenue. At least, that's what he'd always been told.

How long would it take to walk to Chicago, where so many people had ventured in search of a better life?

He worried that maybe he was just weak. When he'd returned from the war, bitter and angry from his meaningless time spent at that army camp, soul afire from all the insults his white superiors had leveled at him, his father had told him that maybe Lucius's relatively comfortable upbringing in the Sweet Auburn community had insulated him from the hatred the reverend had grown up with. Those sage words hadn't been what Lucius wanted to hear, but he feared his father was right.

Boggs and Smith walked on. The city had been so quiet before the storm but now it was like someone had adjusted the volume, water gushing from downspouts, water dripping from eaves, the random explosions of cars driving into puddles, the secondary showers of rainwater falling from heavy boughs.

Then they heard new sounds: laughter, and the breaking of a bottle.

"Wait," Smith said.

More laughter, and Smith turned into an alley. Boggs didn't want to follow, wanted to just walk and walk. But follow he did.

The alley snaked between two squat brick buildings that, by the looks of them, had been planned as housing for a nearby mill expansion that had never happened. It was home to an odd-jobs Negro named Andrews who they'd seen a few times while monitoring Chandler Poe, the bootlegger that Judge Gillespie had let off. Smith crept up to an open window and looked inside, Boggs just behind him.

Three men sitting at a table, playing cards, chips and coins scattered between them. Glasses of yellowish liquid standing sentry by each pile. They saw Andrews, Poe, and a portly, balding man Boggs didn't recognize.

Smith saw a bottle near his feet. He picked it up and, without warning his partner, tossed it against the side of the building. A pop, glass shards chinking all over. Boggs jumped back.

The laughter from inside stopped. Smith ducked his head below the window and crept farther into the back. Boggs flattened himself against the wall.

From inside the voices were asking each other what it was and who was there, each of them sounding drunker and more confused than the one before him. One of them said they should check it out, exactly the bit of stupid bravery Smith had been counting on.

The men stumbled out, down the three wooden steps and into the alley, nothing but silhouettes until they were close enough for their faces to be caught in the lamplight that shone through a window. None of them had thought to bring a flashlight or even a candle, and none of their eyes were as adjusted to the dark as the two cops' they still couldn't see.

Smith wanted to use his fists, would have greatly preferred the sensation in his knuckles and up through his arm and shoulder, but he didn't care to leave such evidence on his flesh. So it was with his billy club that he swung crosswise against Poe's left cheek. The cracking bone was the only sound as the bootlegger fell.

This is dumb, dumb, dumb, Boggs was thinking as Smith drove the butt of his club into Andrews's stomach, doubling him over.

Andrews was vomiting and hadn't even fallen yet when Smith turned his attention to the third man, who was backing up as quickly as a drunk man could. "No no no, c'mon," the man said, and he got his wish, as Smith chose to ignore him and instead picked Poe up off the ground.

"Police!" Boggs shouted at the bald man. "This your house?"

"No! No, sir!" the man said, backing up again until he'd tripped over the wooden steps.

"Then get yourself back home."

The man ran off. A second later Boggs could hear him trip and fall again, then keep running.

Poe was trying to break free of Smith, who pressed him against the wall and then jabbed his club into the bootlegger's ribs. Poe wailed.

Boggs kicked, not too hard, at the fallen Andrews. "Back in your house, now!"

Andrews seemed only too happy to obey, moving faster than Boggs would have thought possible.

Smith let Poe fall to the ground. He swung at the bootlegger again, and again.

"Take your *god*damn *low*-life self out of my *god*damn *neigh*borhood!" Each of Smith's curses was accompanied by another swing. Poe enclosed his head in a protective ball of arms and hands, not that it helped.

"Where your white boy at now, huh? Where's your cracker cop now?" Again with the club, breaking fingers. "How much you paying him, you son of a bitch?"

Boggs turned and looked out of the alley, hoping not to see any bedroom lights flicker on.

"I'll pay you more, I'll pay you more!"

Wrong answer. Smith swung again, harder than before. Saliva hanging from his chin.

"This ain't Dunlow's neighborhood no more, you understand? It's mine! It's my goddamn neighborhood! Take your goddamn booze somewhere else!"

"Okay!" Poe pleaded. "Okay!"

Smith crouched down closer. "Oh, you're so damned smart, ain't you? You got the white cops and the judges behind you, huh? Well, you don't have me, got it? You do not have me, and if I see you in this neighborhood again, this will all seem like a goddamn slap on the wrist, got it?"

"I got it, I got it!"

Smith stood again, the tension in his shoulders seeming to predict yet another swing, so Boggs stepped forward and clamped his hand on it. "Enough."

Smith didn't reply, didn't even move his head to acknowledge that, but he didn't swing again either. Just stood there, recovering. He hoped Poe would be stupid enough to say something more, but Poe wasn't.

In twenty minutes their shift would be over, Boggs told himself. In sixty minutes he would try to forget this as he laid down his weary bones. Even though he knew he would never forget it, and he sensed like an added weight on his shoulders that this evening would haunt him and his partner in more ways than one.

14

MORE THAN ONCE Rake had imagined himself accidentally shooting his partner. Just imagined it. Not actually planned it. Not actually sketched it out or hidden a drop weapon. Not actually asked some random ex-con to do the job for him in exchange for lenience next time. Things weren't *quite* that bad. But he had certainly imagined how nice it would be if his partner, by chance, accidentally died. Perhaps Dunlow might have a heart attack soon. Perhaps he would start bullying the wrong Negro, would pick on some strapping lad who had a nasty grudge and a weapon in his back pocket. Perhaps, if that happened, Rake would deliberately wait an extra second or two before intervening, just to make sure Dunlow was dead first.

Dunlow had been a beat cop for twenty years, and though he seemed to think this made him a better beat cop, superior somehow, what it really meant was that he'd never been promoted. Given the increasing number of beatings and shakedowns Rake had seen the man perform in their first few weeks together, Rake couldn't help but wonder what Dunlow might be holding back for later. What greater misdeeds he was concealing from Rake's view. Was Dunlow testing Rake, hoping to see how far he would go to do things Dunlow's way? Had Rake failed a test when he hadn't taken part in a bribe? Had he failed by calling the ambulance and wagon the night Boggs had been injured?

And what, if anything, did Dunlow have to do with the death of the Ellsworth girl?

"Anybody looking into who killed that girl in the trash?" he asked from the passenger seat, the night after his midnight talk with Mr. Calvin.

"I heard it was her old man."

"Didn't he live out in the country somewhere?"

"Yes, but they do have trains. I'm hearing he came back into the city and got in a fight with her, shot her dead."

That a father might shoot his daughter after a heated argument wasn't as unlikely as some would prefer to believe, Rake knew. If you're going to be killed, you probably know the person who's going to do it, and you may even be related to them. Love and lust, pride and insult, heat of the moment, things instantly regretted. But to then throw your daughter's corpse out like garbage? For Rake, that stretched the bounds of credulity, but for Dunlow, Negroes were capable of any atrocity.

"Fight over what?"

"She was sleeping with white men."

"Where'd you hear that?"

"Around. Some of us actually talk to people when we walk our beat, rookie. Some of us actually get dirty, immerse ourselves in the life of the neighborhood. You'd be wise to do more of that yourself."

"What do you know about that fellow we pulled over a couple of weeks ago," Rake asked, trying to sound casual. "Brian Underhill?"

"Why do you ask?"

"That girl in the trash, Boggs says she was the girl they saw in Underhill's car that night. Said he hit her, then she got out and ran." *And then you let the man go.*

"*Boggs says?!*" The car swerved from Dunlow's reaction. He stared at his partner. Gritted teeth. If eyes could be gritted, they would have been, too. "You're getting tips from the nigger cops? Are you goddamn crazy?"

He pulled onto the side of the road. Rake stared out the front window for a moment to escape the heat radiating from his partner's face.

"What the fuck do you think you're doing, consorting with them?"

"Dunlow, Jesus, Boggs mentioned something about her that time he and I were waiting on an ambulance. That's hardly *consorting.*" Later he would regret how quickly he had disavowed his talk with Boggs. But the force of Dunlow's reaction had startled him, and he could sense his partner busily erecting mental barriers to the other questions Rake had wanted to ask.

Dunlow nodded, realizing he'd gotten too worked up. He pulled them back onto the road.

"What I know of Brian Underhill is that he is not a murderer." A freight train blew its lonesome wail. "He's a former cop. Worked fifteen, sixteen years or so."

Rake knew this part already—he'd looked the man up. Wanting to know a few of the answers before Dunlow offered any, so he could note discrepancies. "What happened?"

"Damned lottery sting."

Four years ago, a state-led investigation of the city's sundry lottery schemes had turned up plentiful examples of police corruption. Numbers running was one of the biggest businesses in Atlanta—some journalists figured it was possibly third only to trains and textiles. The not-so-little, not-so-secret dirty little secret was that Atlanta's finest were often involved, protecting the numbers runners, taking orders, receiving their cut.

Nine cops were fired after the investigation was splashed all over the *Journal's* and the *Constitution's* front pages, no doubt furthering the career of some district attorney or other. From the police's perspective, those nine cops were scapegoats taking the fall for senior officers. Rake had been in Europe then, but he still heard enough stories about the sting from aggrieved cops who complained about it the way they griped about a similar operation against the Kluxers a few years back.

"You know him?" Rake asked.

"Well enough. He was a detective on Homicide, and I'd occasion to work with him a few times. Didn't make all that much of an impression, tell you the truth."

"He made enough of one for you to say pretty certainly that he isn't a murderer."

"Are you interrogating me, Officer Rakestraw?"

Rake tried to use a sincerely surprised tone, which he realized he wasn't very good at. "I'm just asking a few questions. He's the last person to be seen with this girl, and he's—"

"According to the monkeys."

"—the only lead anyone's got, so it seems worth pursuing."

"And why is that? Educate me on your thought process."

"Well, you yourself just said there's reason to believe she was sleeping with a white man. Maybe it was Underhill. Maybe they had a spat, or he thought she was cheating."

"Best not to let a fellow like him hear you say that."

"Why not? Because he's the kind of fellow who might shoot some-one and throw the body out like garbage?"

"You think you're very clever."

"Just trying to figure a few things out."

"The report—which, by the way, you aren't the only person in this car that's read it—says she was shot with a .22. People may say some bad things about Underhill, but him carrying a little .22 ain't one of them."

"What are some of the bad things people say about him?"

Dunlow shook his head. "Giving me a goddamn headache."

At ten o'clock the next morning, Rake staked out the last known address of Brian Underhill, a four-story brick apartment building in Mechanicsville, south of downtown. The neighborhood had become overcrowded during the war, with so many men needed at the rail yards, and had remained overcrowded afterward. There was just enough foot traffic for Rake to feel slightly conspicuous there in his parked car but not so much so that he gave up.

He needed to know what this man's story was. The fact that Dunlow had all but warned him off only made this more necessary. Some basic research had revealed Underhill's address, a copy of his photograph (four years old now, but good enough), and a brief outline of his trun-cated career. If Rake had been a detective in Homicide, he would have had more resources at his disposal, and a legitimately helpful partner. But he was just a beat cop, and besides, it was clear now that Lily Ells-worth's murder would never be investigated. Eventually some Negro arrested for some other murder would "confess" to hers as well, and presto, the crime would be solved. No one would ever know, or care, who killed Lily.

Did Rake care? Yes, he did. He didn't think a girl of any color should be killed, dropped in an alley, and forgotten. He took his responsibility to enforce the law seriously, even if others did not.

Not that he was motivated solely by pure intentions. What moti-vated him was this: the inkling, the strong hint, the tingle on the back of his neck that his partner knew far more about the murder than he was letting on. His partner, who had already tried to get one of the colored cops fired for drinking based on zero evidence and who delighted in provoking them. Rake had never asked to be assigned to a corrupt cop, and he'd hoped he would eventually be reassigned. But waiting around for a transfer felt like a luxury he could no longer afford.

So he sat in the car and waited. He had lied to his wife and told her his shift was earlier than it was, all so he'd have two precious hours to follow Underhill before roll call.

The car radio on, he listened to the latest from the Democratic National Convention in Philadelphia, where delegates had narrowly approved a civil rights plank, no doubt encouraged by Truman's surprising decisions to desegregate the armed forces and set up a federal Committee on Civil Rights. The vote outraged Southern Democrats; now the Mississippi and Alabama delegates had stormed out of the convention hall and were said to be forming their own States Rights Democratic Party, with Strom Thurmond their nominee. Some were dubbing them the "Dixiecrats" and said this splintering would all but hand the election to Dewey. Rake turned off the radio.

Sitting there in the hot car, nothing to occupy his mind, he found himself thinking about his brother. Curtis had been the joker in the family, the schemer. The one convinced they could make a fortune selling lemonade on the sidewalk, or by digging for treasure. One of his favorite tricks was to tackle his younger brother from behind, preferably when other people were around to see it. Rake's head was on a swivel from a young age, always aware that an ambush was possible, yet always surprised when it happened. Curtis's ability to plan an entire day around being in the right place at the right time was uncanny. The ambush/tackling phase had faded by the time Curtis was old enough to drive, and cause worse trouble. Curtis no doubt would have loved being a cop on a stakeout, waiting patiently for the subject to emerge, so long as there was someone beside him to tell jokes to for hour after hour. The realization made Rake miss him all the more.

Underhill did nothing of interest that first day, other than walking five blocks to a diner, eating a very late breakfast, and then walking home.

He did nothing of interest the following day, either. Yet Rake kept at it.

The third time Rake kept watch was at night, three in the morning, after his shift ended. He had expected Underhill would be asleep, but the lights were on. He had slid into a parking space, a block away from the building, when he recognized one of the cars parked on the other side of the street.

Dunlow's.

Rake got out of the car, closing the door silently. Dodging puddles from an earlier shower and walking on the grassy strip between road and sidewalk to be as quiet as possible.

From the car Rake had been able to see that the blinds were down in Underhill's second-floor apartment, the windows cracked open for some air. He squeezed between two holly bushes as he positioned himself along the side of the building, leaning on the damp wall beside a window.

This part of the city was remarkably quiet at night, other than the locusts. At first all he could hear was someone snoring in the first-floor apartment. Then he heard men's voices, just short of intelligible. Dunlow's voice. Another voice, which must be Underhill's. Was there a third? No, he didn't think so.

Then the voices got louder. He heard Underhill say, "This isn't your goddamn problem," but Dunlow's response wasn't as clear, though he caught the word "problem" again. Dunlow must have been farther from the window, or had his back to it.

"Smartest damn thing you've ever done," Underhill said. The next exchange he couldn't make out. Then Dunlow said something including "inside man." The voices ranged in and out of clarity, though a few times Rake thought he heard them refer to "the Trust Division," whatever that was.

"Because I want more," he heard Underhill say. "I'm tired of taking the bones they toss. Got something worth a whole lot more now."

Then quiet again. Rake felt less tired now, charged to be on the verge of discovering something.

Lügen haben kurze Beine, Rake thought. *Lies have short legs.* Dunlow had acted—twice now—like he barely knew Underhill, yet clearly that wasn't the case.

He'd lost track of how long it had been quiet when he heard the front door open. *Shit*. Dunlow was leaving already. The holly bushes on either side of Rake were taller than he was, and the nearest streetlight wasn't enough to reveal him. He squatted down all the same. After a few seconds, he could see Dunlow sauntering toward his old Dodge, opening the door, getting in. Driving away.

Whether Dunlow noticed Rake's car just across the street from his own was something Rake would have to wonder about.

15

TOMMY SMITH SAT at the back corner table of Ruffin's Royal Hideaway. On the table before him was a loaded gun, and just beyond it, the two wide eyes of a man he'd very much like to give a third eye.

The music from the trumpet and bass and drums was making everything seem dizzy, every now and again a cymbal crashed and the floor would shake, the gun bouncing a bit on the table, bouncing ever so closer to the long-fingered but folded hands of Alonzo, who, *yes, damn well* yes *he deserved a bullet in the head,* Smith thought. *Yes.*

How had Tommy gotten here?

Things tended to happen this way with him. He tended to make decisions *after* he'd made decisions, if that made any sense. His uncle had long commented on this trait, the impulsive way Tommy got himself into fixes and only later tried to invent explanations as to how and why. Sometimes those fixes turned out to be good things, like the day he walked up to City Hall and filled out an application to be a police officer despite the fact that he'd scarcely given thought to the occupation until that very moment. Sometimes those fixes were not terribly good at all, like when he'd beaten Chandler Poe half to death in that alley.

And here, now, the gun on the table. Was this really the smartest thing he could be doing?

It had started with him deciding to go hear some music. Innocent enough. He lived an easy stroll from Ruffin's Royal, a dimly lit second-floor nightclub that sat over a hardware store. It absorbed the spillover crowds who couldn't get into the Top Hat or Shim Sham a block away. Tommy had needed an escape, from the job and his troubles and even his partner. He liked Boggs well enough, but the man was so damned proper. Almost emotionless. A bit too skilled at retreating beneath his shell. Smith had a shell, too—what Negro in the Jim Crow South did not?—but he came out of it when he needed to. Men like Boggs, though, either *became* the shell—hollowed out, lacking a heart, reducing themselves to a performance for white folks—or got so bottled up by the pressure that they would one day explode. And that was a risky thing to be around.

Tommy sat at the bar, exchanging some friendly words with Ruffin, the owner and barkeep, a man who seemed pleased with Smith's efforts to put away all the moonshiners. Legal providers of alcohol, like Ruffin, were no fans of the way moonshiners from the North Georgia mountains drove the hundred miles south with barrels of illegal and often dangerous concoctions that working men could buy at random houses, the buyers never needing to walk into a tax-paying establishment like this. Ruffin had shook Smith's hand and thanked him for stopping by, as if Smith were some politician and not just a fellow who needed to hear some music. Ruffin told Smith that the first drink was on the house, but Smith graciously refused, opting instead to pay for his Co-Cola.

Over the last few days, Smith had asked Ruffin and nearly every bartender near Auburn Avenue if they'd ever seen a girl matching Lily Ellsworth's description. But with no photo—Otis still hadn't provided them with one—he'd gotten no leads.

Smith had sought out Ruffin's because the joint had air-conditioning. This being Wednesday, Smith hadn't thought it would be crowded, but he figured wrong. Every table was packed and clusters of people danced before the band, delighted to be someplace where they could move like that and not drop dead from heat exhaustion.

He was wearing his lightest gray jacket over a blue shirt, the sleeves rolled up, a gray tie loosely knotted. He felt a fat drop of sweat roll down his back as he glanced across the room and saw three women sitting in one of the booths. He recognized one from high school, Delia Something. Friendly, he'd remembered, and pleasant enough to look at, but whoever was sitting to her left demanded attention.

She had a thin, narrow face, like some Egyptian princess, eyes small and jewellike against that smooth skin. Her hair was pulled back in a ponytail and she wore a sky-blue blouse that matched his shirt, a thin gold necklace two inches above her heart.

The air-conditioning and music and Coke were nice, but it was company he had ventured out for. He'd caught her eye twice by the time he found himself wandering over to their table.

Delia smiled warily, having seen him from the moment he'd left his stool, his casual jaguar gait not disguised in the slightest.

"Delia," Smith asked, one hand casually in the pocket of his high-waisted pants, "how is it that you always surround yourself with such beautiful friends?"

"This is Tommy Smith, ladies. One of Atlanta's new police officers. So hide that contraband in your purses."

He hadn't spoken to Delia in more than a year, he figured, yet she knew what he did these days. Everyone seemed to.

"I'm here in an unofficial capacity." Turning to the girl on the left, he extended a hand and asked, "And you are . . . ?"

"Susanna Jones," and she let him take her hand, which was cool and clammy from clasping her drink. He lifted her hand to his lips. He ignored Delia's rolling eyes, and he hoped it wasn't too rude how he was ignoring the third girl. If she was Susanna's friend, she was no doubt used to being ignored.

"I would be delighted to share a dance with you."

"It's rather warm for dancing," Susanna replied, her head held at the slightest angle to the right, her left eyebrow raised.

"It sounds to me like they're getting ready for a slower number."

"Really? You can just feel that?"

"I have finely honed senses of perception."

"Girl," Delia said, "just go and dance so we don't need to hear no more of his lines."

His sense of perception had proven correct, for he and Susanna had barely found a spot on the floor when the band slowed down with a bluesy number that honestly wasn't so great for dancing, but they were together, and there was music, and it was Wednesday night and even though he wasn't drinking he had managed, for a moment, to forget everything he'd wanted to forget.

She was a teacher, she told him.

"I don't go out to places like this usually, and I certainly can't do something like this during the school year."

"Parents keep watch?"

"We need to keep up a respectable image."

"This place is perfectly respectable."

She'd responded only with an "mmm hmm," so low he didn't hear it so much as feel it.

The trumpeter, horn at his side, was singing something to the effect of his woman having a backside so firm he could bounce a penny off it.

"How do you like being a policeman?" she asked a few bars later.

"I'm rather fond of the uniform."

"And that's a good reason to take a job that puts your life in danger?"

"It's not that dangerous. And it really is a smashing uniform."

"You can model it for me next time I'm arrested."

"You would have to fall a very long way for that to happen, Miss Schoolteacher."

"Sometimes I *do* want to murder some of those children."

The next song was not a slow one, not by any stretch of the imagination, nor was the one after that, or the next one, and right around there Smith lost count. The girl could dance, better than him even, which was impressive, as Tommy Smith was a man who knew his steps.

Later, he was at the bar, ordering another Coke for himself and a gin and tonic for her, when the evening managed to nearly get ruined.

He hadn't noticed Alonzo come in because he'd been so busy dancing. Yet there the man was, Alonzo Keller, cardsharp and flimflam man, known to his low-life associates as Zo. A man guilty of an offense that Smith could not forgive. Zo was walking toward the bar, having not noticed Smith.

"Thought I smelled something funny," Smith said.

Zo was tall, had a couple of inches on Smith, but he was thin and certainly didn't carry himself like someone worth fearing. His kind was all about outsmarting others, and being just smart enough to find the right kind of stupid people to cheat money from.

His retort was disappointing. "Hey there, Officer."

"That's all you got for me?"

Zo had a friend beside him, shorter but thicker. Both were light-skinned and wore white shirts with their sleeves rolled up, Zo's tie striped red and green and the other's tie nonexistent.

"I'm not looking for no trouble," Zo said as he slunk off. His friend was a step slower, so when Zo walked away, the friend was suddenly right there in Smith's line of sight.

The friend stared back and then some. "You got a problem, pretty boy?" he asked.

Then Ruffin appeared, two drinks for Smith in his hand. Tommy dropped bills on the bar without looking at the barkeep. This would have been an ideal opportunity to turn this into a very different evening, Smith realized. Yet he managed to hold himself back. For now.

"No problem at all," he said with a smile.

He was wrong, though: it *was* a very different evening now. He had seen Zo and not done what he had wanted to do, what he *should* have done. So when he returned to the booth with a drink for Susanna and one for himself, talking with her and Delia and the other girl whose name he'd never caught, he was not his charming self. He tried—Lord, he tried, because Susanna's jewellike eyes were sparkling at him in the way he had *hoped* they might when he'd first seen her—but he was too angry now, lost in thought about Zo and the other fellow, that he missed a few of the girls' jokes, and he seemed to register too late that a certain spark at their table was being extinguished.

He asked Susanna to dance with him again, hoping that might help. Halfway through the next song, she batted away one of his hands that had perhaps wandered too far south. They started again, and later when he tried to kiss her neck she arched away from him. He shook his head, annoyed. They stood there, looking at each other, a desert island surrounded by spinning cyclones of happier couples.

"I'm not looking to move so quickly there, Cyrano."

"I'm just trying to have a good time, girl."

She shook her head and muttered something he didn't catch. He watched her return to the booth, saying something to Delia. Whatever she said must have been something very bad indeed, because her two friends glared at him with murderous intentions.

Damn. It could have been such a wonderful evening, Susanna. He walked back to the bar.

Zo and his partner were sitting at a table in the far corner, conspiring about something.

Once again, Smith did not recall making a decision to visit their table, yet suddenly he was there. Sitting opposite Zo.

"No one invited you," the other man said.

"I didn't catch your name, friend," Smith said. "And you know what? That's a very good thing for you. Because you wouldn't want me to know who you are or where you live. You can skedaddle while I have a word with Zo here."

"He for real?" the man asked Zo.

"It's all right, man," Zo said. "I'll be by."

The man left his drink behind, as if he believed he would soon be back.

The trumpeter was singing into the microphone about how his woman had sold all his dogs.

Delia appeared behind Smith, berating him with, "You got some nerve, Tommy Smith. After I vouch for you to one of my friends, you treat her like that? You should be ashamed of yourself."

Zo laughed, only too delighted to see the hated officer taken down a notch.

Tommy turned to face her, annoyed that she'd ruined his entrance. "I am ashamed, Delia. And I'm sorry. Now, to make it up to you, I'm gonna tell you a little story about my friend Zo here."

"I don't want to hear no story." She was about to back up but he grabbed her wrist with his right hand. With his other hand he removed his revolver from where it had been rather precariously nestled at the small of his back. The left hand and gun were now resting on the table, and Zo leaned back at the sight of it. Delia's eyes were saucers.

"That's all right, that's all right," Smith said to her, keeping his eyes only on her, as if completely unconcerned with what the lowlife opposite him might do next. "This is to make sure my man Alonzo doesn't try to walk away before I finish. Put your hands on the table, Zo."

Palms as flat as his expression, Zo complied.

Delia's face was rigid as he released her hand. Tommy reached forward with his other hand and picked up the glass that Zo's friend had left behind. Booze. He hadn't touched a drop since March. The glass felt cold and magical in his hand. He felt his heart pound, but his decision had been made.

"You watching this, Zo? Be sure and get a good look." He tipped back the glass and swallowed the contents in a single gulp. Rum and something. Fruity and easy to drink but still that illicit warmth he hadn't felt in months.

"Oooh-wee," he said. "Been a while." Then he reached for Zo's drink, the man himself a statue as Smith took it, shook the ice a bit—it looked like straight liquor—and downed it. Bourbon. It burned so he had to stop himself from coughing and ruining the effect. "Whoa, you go for the strong stuff! Goodness, all that liquor in me, there's no telling what I'm liable to do!"

Smith leaned back in his chair now, the gun and his left hand still resting on the table, casually so, as if he were cradling a glass and not a gun with six shots.

"Now, Delia, couple of weeks ago, one of my fellow officers got suspended for no good reason. Lost a lot of pay and a lot of respect. You know how that came about?"

He locked eyes with Zo, whose forehead looked even sweatier than Smith's. "See, there are special rules governing how officers of the law must behave, even when we aren't on the clock. Funny thing is, my fellow Officer Bayle has never had a drink in his life. He's a very religious man. It happens that one night he's reported to have been out drinking and carousing and causing a scene. So he gets suspended. Thing is, he'd been home in bed that night, not that he had an alibi for it, other'n his wife. But that made it awfully difficult to fight the charges."

Delia said, "Tommy, please put that gun away."

"I will directly. But I'm almost to the good part. The man who reported him was a cop, a white one, who claimed he'd been at the club that night. The thing is, the white cop actually *hadn't* been at that club at all. That little fact came out later, when he had to testify under oath to an internal committee investigating the charges. You got that? An internal committee. We take these things *seriously* in the police department. But it makes you wonder, if the white cop hadn't been there, what made him think Officer Bayle had been out drinking?"

Delia's voice quavered, "Tommy, I want to go home."

"You will, Delia, I promise you that. Just hold on. You see, Zo, when you decide to be a rat to the police, there's usually a record of it. Maybe you didn't know that. But it comes out eventually, even to us nigger cops who have to work in the basement of the YMCA. We have ways to see these reports, too, you know, and lo and behold, this white cop, Dunlow's his name, he says that he had it on good information from his boy *Alonzo* that Sherman Bayle was drinking that night."

"I don't know nothing about that," Alonzo said.

Smith smiled. He opened the fingers that had been holding the gun and slowly slid the firearm until it was in the center of the table. Then he pulled his hand back, resting it at the edge of the table. The gun perfectly between that hand and Alonzo's two. Smith's other hand rested on the edge of an empty chair, just a few inches from where Delia stood stock-still.

"I ain't here to be lied to. I'm here because I want you to confess the truth, in front of my old friend Delia here. That you're a goddamn rat, that you're a traitor who'd give up another Negro for a few dollars from a white man." Wailing trumpet in the background. "Tell it, Zo. Admit what you are."

Delia said, "Tommy, come on, I don't need to be no part of this."

"You're right," he agreed, his eyes still on Zo. "I'm sorry, Delia. Good night." He lifted his right hand from the chair to wave her away.

She backed up slowly, and even though she was out of his peripheral vision now he had a sense she had backed up only a couple of steps, as if she didn't believe he'd released her or as if she realized now that she had to see this moment through.

Smith continued: "You lied to Dunlow about seeing Officer Bayle drinking. Because maybe you were sore at Bayle for how he busted your buddy the week before. Or maybe the whole story was Dunlow's, and he just needed a spineless nigger to sign off as witness, and you raised your little hand."

Applause as one song ended and the next began. If anyone else in the joint had noticed there was a loaded revolver sitting in the middle of a table like some lethal napkin dispenser, they hadn't run screaming or dived beneath any chairs.

"Because, the thing is, you ain't that different from a lot of people who just cannot abide seeing a black man in uniform. I know a lot about that, matter of fact. I served in the war, Zo, not that you did.

You were in jail at the time, if I remember right. But some of us did our duty."

"It wasn't me."

"People just can't abide a black man in uniform. I've known that a long time. My father, he served in the First World War. Did yours?"

"I wouldn't know."

"I never knew my father, either. Reason I didn't know mine is *because* he served, and he survived the trenches and the mustard gas and all that, yes he did. Glory be and all that doughboy shit. Then he came back to Georgia and his little infant son Tommy and his pretty wife, and you know what happened? Just a few months later, when he was marching in a parade with some other proud veterans? Got himself lynched. Beat to a pulp and hung from a tree. Because the white man, no, he cannot *stand* the sight of an uppity Negro in a nice uniform like that. It is the last thing he wants to see. Or the second-to-last."

"Sorry to hear that."

"Hey, I wasn't but seven or eight months when it happened. Sad thing is how many people seemed to forget about all that, you know? Those were some bad years, lotta black veterans strung up when they came back home, but everybody wants to forget. Thing is, I can't forget, because it's who I am. I'm a goddamn antiamnesia medication. And it's happened again, hasn't it? Just a few years ago, black men coming back in uniform and strung from trees. Shot dead or strung up or both. That's bad enough without us realizing that other colored folks don't like to see us in uniform, either. Low-down good-for-nothing folk like you."

They stared at each other a while then, and now was the part of the song where the cymbals started crashing, and with each impact the revolver bounced a bit on the table. Sliding ever so closer to Zo.

"Come on now, Zo. You tried to get Bayle fired, and now you can do even *better* than getting a colored cop fired. You can shoot one down. Because here's a cop being drunk and disorderly and irresponsible with a loaded weapon."

Zo stared him down.

"Pick that gun up," Smith said. "Show everybody how you feel about niggers in uniform."

The music seemed to have stopped. People were standing still, as this was no longer a private concern.

"I don't want no trouble," Zo finally said. "I'm going home now."

"Not. Until. You. Say. It."

Zo's nostrils flared. "Fine. Dunlow leaned on me, so I signed it. Happy? Big cracker's been throwing his weight so long, he knows how and when to lean on someone. And now you're here to take his place, ain't you? Doing a fine job so far."

"I ain't no Dunlow."

Zo stood. Very, very slowly. "I don't know what the hell you are."

Smith watched as Zo moved past the table, just in case he decided to reach for the gun, but he did not.

When Zo was gone, Smith pocketed the piece. Not sure if he was relieved or disappointed, knowing only that the rush was fading, the moment gone already.

"Tommy Smith," Delia said, "you are plain crazy."

"Only sometimes."

"I think you ought to head home."

He stood and noticed that her friends were gone. He offered to escort Delia to her place, as a woman shouldn't be out alone at night. She looked like she wasn't sure if this was a good or horrible idea. The music started again and people were averting their eyes.

He was nearly out the door, trailing Delia—realizing, now that he thought of it, that she wasn't all that bad-looking, had a fun body on her, and this evening might be salvaged after all—when he saw that Ruffin was standing at the doorway, far from his station at the bar, a hand extended. Smith reached out and clasped it.

Tommy Smith was a strong man. Yet the hand that clasped his nearly broke his wrist.

Before Smith could pull his hand away, Ruffin had clamped his other hand on Smith's elbow, and that grip was even tighter. Ruffin leaned in close, looked Smith in the eyes, and, in a voice just quiet enough that no one save Smith would be able to hear, commanded, "Don't you disgrace us, now."

His voice angry, stern, paternal.

"No, sir."

"There is a lot riding on you, son. And I expect you to bear that in mind day and night."

"I do."

"Don't you go bring no shame on us."

"I won't, sir."

Delia was a few paces away. She'd turned to look back at them, wondering what was taking so long. *Men doing their talking.* From that far away she couldn't see the look in Smith's eyes, but if she had, what would she have seen? Shame? Embarrassment? That anger again—or was it gone, had Ruffin quashed it?

Ruffin released Smith's hand and elbow. He leaned back, a big smile on the barkeep's lips, so any patron who might be watching merely saw the owner thanking the officer for stopping by, another great night in Atlanta, come back soon and bring y'all's friends.

Smith walked out quickly, passing Delia, ignoring her "What's the matter?" and walking straight home.

16

THE BODY LAY in the sort of position no living person would choose no matter how tired he might be. And the blackness around his mouth was not dirt.

It was halfway down a ten-foot slope that led to one of the sewer creeks that had been dug out during the Depression. As this was a colored section on the southern edge of the West Side, the sewer pipes had never been laid. It was nothing more than a nasty, empty creek bed that filled with stagnant water after hard rains. Still, its original purpose was being served all the same, as it smelled like someone had been emptying privies into it.

The body had fallen, or been thrown, headfirst, the boot soles facing up. Those soles looked pretty clean, Rake noticed, so he probably hadn't walked out here. Been carried, then thrown.

Nothing else about the body was remotely clean. His face was missing, chewed up by rats or vultures. Parts of his dark gray fingers appeared to have been gnawed on as well. Rake had picked up on the stench the moment he'd gotten out of his car. This close in and it was overpowering.

Rake and Dunlow had been driving their shift when they'd been called to the scene, even though it was far from their beat.

Two other cops and a plainclothes detective were standing beside the body. Everyone held handkerchiefs to their faces. By odd chance, each handkerchief was a different color (one red, one white, one blue, one green, one yellow), lending an almost festive air to the proceedings.

"Little boy saw him," one of the beat cops said. "He and his brother were playing hide-and-seek."

The squad cars' headlights illuminated the earth between the road and the body, but still it was hard to tell if there was any spilled blood there, given how dark the earth itself was. Georgia's red clay, Rake's dad liked to say, was just like soil in the rest of America, but with blood mixed in.

"This seems well covered," Dunlow said. "What are we here for?"

"He don't have any ID on him," the other cop said, "but looks to me like that could be your bootlegger. Ain't just any nigger has hair like that."

Dunlow and Rake stepped closer to the body, walking carefully so they wouldn't lose their purchase with the damp earth. Two flashlight beams were already on the corpse's face, but Dunlow added a third. It was horrific to look at, parts of the skull visible, bugs everywhere. But that hair was certainly recognizable.

"Well goddamn. Yeah, that's Chandler Poe."

"Didn't he just get out of lockup?"

"Not much more'n a week ago. Probation."

"It appears that a few months' sentence might have been more merciful."

"I'd say the moonshining market," the detective mused, sifting soil with one of his hands as if searching for gold, "is getting a tad heated."

Normally they would wait for a coroner before disturbing the body, but because it was just a Negro, and a known hoodlum at that, the detective rolled the body over.

"Goodness. That couldn't have been fun."

Poe's shirt and jacket were tar black, and torn patches of cloth were folded back weirdly, pressed by his body's weight and then molded by the clay as if set in plaster. Bolts of cotton were flayed in every direction.

"Multiple stab wounds, with a final coup de grâce," the detective said. He pronounced it "gracey" but no one corrected him. Maybe he was trying to be funny. "Don't see any bullet wounds, but I'll let the coroner tell me for sure."

"Need us for anything else?" Dunlow asked, spitting into the creek.

"I'd say an arrest or two might be a good idea." The detective sounded as if he were on the verge of sleep. "Assuming you know who he's been running with."

Rake didn't know all the details of Dunlow's relationship with Poe, other than the obvious fact that Dunlow took a cut from the boot-legger. Rake had gathered from a few comments that it had been a years-long relationship. The way it typically worked was that boot-leggers in the North Georgia mountains would drive into the city late at night, arriving at a warehouse in an abandoned building or under-neath a bridge to quickly unload their barrels. The local distributors would transfer the stock to a truck and then disappear. Most of the money for the operations came from men with deep pockets, often men who had other, respectable businesses. The fact that Dunlow took his cut from Poe probably meant he did not get a cut from the distributors or the people on top, Rake thought, though he couldn't be sure.

"Think he was killed by the folks he worked for?" Rake asked as Dunlow drove past the spots most likely to be hosting a drinking and gambling session. He wasn't bothering with the usual nightclubs and taverns, opting instead for residences known to host house parties. The kind of men he was looking for weren't the type for the suit-and-music scene.

"Hell no. No point. Man was just arrested and didn't roll over on anyone."

"Maybe he did roll over on someone and we don't know it."

"If he did, we *would* know it. *I* sure as hell would know."

Dunlow stopped in front of a small bungalow that seemed to be sinking into the earth around it, which it probably was. Maybe the roof had been level to the ground when it had been built, but it wasn't anymore, the north side a good two feet higher than the south.

"This is Shane Andrews's place, right?" He was a gambler and petty criminal who'd fed them some information on a burglary a few weeks back.

"That's the man."

Rake reached for the radio to update Dispatch on their location, but Dunlow grabbed his hand.

"They don't need to know where we're at all the time. And we don't need no help on this. Shane and Poe go back. They worked the labor camps outside Charleston together during the war. Card games and flimflam, then bootlegging for whoever needed the help. Eventually rode the rails here to do the same thing."

The house had appeared dark at first, but the longer they sat there they noticed that when the night's breeze parted the curtains in one of the windows, faint light trickled through. No other windows in the neighborhood were illuminated.

Rake slowly crept into the alley. He heard voices. Laughter. The clink of some coins, or maybe chips. That sound alone gave them the right to knock down the doors, at least according to Department policy.

The windows in back were dark. Rake carefully tested the knob, which turned. As he slowly opened the door, which did not squeak, he heard the much louder sound of Dunlow crashing through the front door.

"Police!" Dunlow called out. "Hands up, all of you!"

Rake raced through the kitchenette, pulling his gun from his holster.

He made it through a hallway. He heard men pleading for mercy or forgiveness or pleading simply that this not be happening, then he heard the sound of contact and a groan and then the sound of something hitting the ground. The fear that he might be allowing his partner—loathed though he may be—to get killed on his watch made the finger on his trigger feel suddenly very heavy indeed.

He kicked open a door and found himself in an unfinished living room, or squatting room to be more appropriate. Most of the walls were stripped and there was a large fireplace that wasn't being used in that season but otherwise provided both heat and cooking many months a year, like some ranchers' hut in the wrong geography. It was likely a crash pad for dope fiends, a large empty space to fill with empty people's emptiness. Right now it was full of four Negroes, all of them standing, all of their hands in the air. Two tables were decorated with drinks, cards, chips, and dollars.

Actually, there were five Negroes, as Rake hadn't initially noticed the one who was on the ground at Dunlow's feet. Rake was pointing his gun everywhere he looked, but Dunlow held only his billy club, which apparently had dealt with someone already.

"Hands on the wall, goddammit!" Dunlow ordered. "You boys know how this works."

The four did as they were told. Dunlow smirked at Rake's gun, then nodded toward the lined-up bodies. Rake patted them down and found nothing but a couple of knives and a screwdriver, which he duly collected. From behind, he could tell that one man was thin and nothing to worry about, two were average build, and the fourth was a monster he'd need to watch close.

"Sit your asses back down," Dunlow said when Rake was finished. Rake checked the man on the ground. He had no weapons but he did have a pulse, so Rake left him there.

The four others sat and watched Dunlow like overgrown schoolchildren who were not yet sure which violation they were about to be punished for.

"Let's see here," Dunlow mused. "We got Shane, Alan B., Zo, and Big Moe." He paced in a slow circle around the two tables at which the men sat. "Usually when I find y'all together, Chandler's here, too."

Rake was trying to watch all four to see if any of them betrayed any guilt, or at least knowledge. Shane Andrews was fortyish, pug-nosed, and stout, and he looked mostly just scared. Alan B. was another Rake recognized, a tall thin one who looked like he'd be helpless in a fight. Big Moe must be the enormous fellow, who stood at least six two and even sitting seemed like a force of nature ready to be unleashed. He was young, perhaps Rake's age, but fear furrowed his brow. The fourth, a round-faced Negro who must have been Zo, was a stranger to Rake, and his face was expressionless.

"Where's Poe?" Dunlow bellowed. "Where the hell is Poe?"

Silence. Dunlow circled them.

"I'm surprised at y'all's lack of cooperation. No one ever talks to the police no more, huh? I'm trying to help you out here. I'm trying to find a man that hurt a Negro. If I were to find one of *you* been hurt, I'd be doing the same thing right now."

Silence.

With one hand, Dunlow grabbed Andrews by the neck and pulled him to his feet, pushed him back three steps, and slammed him into a wall. Rake kept his hand near his reholstered firearm and stepped closer to the other three, lest one of them think now was a good time to be stupid.

"Where's Poe, Shane?" Dunlow spat in Shane's face.

"I don't know!" Eyes wide. His old yellowed T-shirt strained against a belly that was rising and falling very, very quickly.

The look in Dunlow's eyes was clear to Rake, who had seen it many times before. Dunlow kept one hand at Shane's clavicle, pinning him against the wall and threatening to move up to his neck. With his other hand he removed his sidearm from its holster. He pointed it at the ceiling and held it no more than three inches from Shane's head.

"I ain't done nothing, Officer Dunlow!"

"When was the last time you saw Poe?"

"Few nights ago. Right here."

"You don't know where Poe is now?"

"No, no, sir."

"So you don't know what he was doing the other night on the West Side?" Dunlow asked.

"No, sir."

Dunlow lightly tapped the side of the Negro's head with the barrel of his gun. If his finger were to accidentally hit the trigger, he would shoot the ceiling, and not the man's skull, Rake told himself. Hoping he was right.

"And you don't know how he got himself stabbed to death out there?"

From Rake's perspective, it was hard to gauge a man's reaction to certain shocking news when he was already terrified.

"Poe dead?" Shane asked.

"Poe dead."

Rake kept scanning the faces of the other Negroes, but their expressions ran from fear to resignation. They had seen this act before.

"You were with him a few nights ago," Rake said to Shane, trying to stay relevant. "As you've already told us."

"I didn't touch him, didn't lay a finger on him! Me and him tight!"

Again Dunlow tapped Shane's head with the gun. "I didn't really think you had the stones to do such a thing."

"That's true, Officer Dunlow, that ain't me."

Dunlow waited a few seconds, drawing it out. "Then who was it? One of your boys here?"

Andrews paused. Dunlow pulled him back from the wall and

slammed his head into it. Fissures opened in the gray plaster, chunks sprinkling onto the floor.

"Now don't be thinking, dammit! Just answer my question!"

Dunlow slammed his head again. Plaster dust grayed the Negro's hair.

"Even if he does know something, he's afraid to tell you," Zo said from his seat. Rake took a step toward him. Zo seemed alarmingly unfrightened.

"Is that a fact, Zo?" Dunlow asked while keeping his eyes on Shane.

"Seems so to me, Officer Dunlow."

"Way I figure it, he should be goddamn afraid *not* to tell me."

Shane himself had his eyes shut now, as if by excusing himself from the conversation he might also disappear from the scene. Yet Dunlow's hold was plenty secure.

"He is," Zo said. "He most definitely is. But he's afraid of them colored cops, too. Maybe more."

"If there's something you're trying to say, you black bastard, you'd best quit with the riddles and say it straight."

"Smith and Boggs killed Poe. That's what Shane's too afraid to tell you."

This time Dunlow turned to face Zo.

"Say again?"

"They came by a few nights ago, when Poe was here. Real late, almost morning. Shane and some boys was all just setting here, not troubling nobody, and then those colored cops took them out back and started beating on Poe."

Dunlow was watching Zo very carefully.

"You were there?"

"No, but Shane told me about it."

Dunlow looked back at Shane and tightened his grip. "Then why the hell ain't Shane telling me himself?"

Shane opened his eyes and nodded. "It's like he say. I told him about it. They just come out and beat on us, mostly on Poe. I ain't seen Poe since."

"And which of the nigger cops was it?"

"The loud one, Smith. And that uppity one he got."

"Boggs?"

"Him's the one."

"They just came over here and beat him for nothing?"

"Yes, sir. They say . . ." Shane's voice trailed off and he looked down again. He did not relish delivering this news.

"They say *what*, goddamn it?"

"They say this ain't your neighborhood no more," Zo again supplied the voice for the terrified Shane. "That it's theirs. They beat on Poe to teach him that lesson."

This was too much for Dunlow to respond to. The old cop was silent.

"Then what?" Rake asked for his partner. "And I want to hear it from the actual witness this time."

"I don't know," Shane said. "They told me to get inside and not say nothing, that's what I did. Got right in this room here. They stopped, by and by."

"You didn't see them take him anywhere?" Rake asked.

"Nossir, Officer." They didn't yet know or fear Rake's name the way they did Dunlow's.

"You hear them drive away?" Dunlow asked. An odd question, since the Negro officers didn't have squad cars. Boggs and Smith were always on foot. How would they have transported Poe to the West Side? Did either of them even own a car?

"I, I don't recall no car. Mighta been one. Just don't know. I went to bed, and when I woke up, Poe was gone."

Shane was staring at Dunlow's gun. Dunlow finally noticed and holstered it. He moved his other hand from Shane's neck, patting him on the shoulder.

Then Dunlow turned back to the table. He grabbed the coins that lay there, as well as a few dollars. "This will pay for Chandler's funeral."

He stuffed them in his pockets. Then he punched Zo square in the nose. The Negro's head snapped back and the rest of his body followed, the chair toppling straight over. The other two backed up, their chair legs scraping against the floor.

"I believe ol' Zo took a bit too much pleasure in delivering that news," Dunlow informed them. "Anybody else need reminding whose neighborhood this is?"

All eyes were on the floor as Officer Dunlow took his leave, his partner a step behind.

17

SERGEANT JOSEPH McINNIS had barely sat in the lonely guest chair of Captain Dodd's office when he was asked what the hell the niggers were up to at "the Butler Street so-called *precinct.*"

Dodd's was a small, cramped office that, judging from the lack of window and the scuff marks on the floor, had once been a storage room of some sort. The shelves had been removed and a thick desk had somehow squeezed its way through the door. Dodd had been captain for ten years, nearly as long as McInnis had been a cop. Dodd had a lot less hair than he'd had ten years ago. McInnis couldn't say that he liked the captain all that much, but he seemed a reasonably fair man to toil under, so long as no one on your team did anything disastrously wrong.

McInnis had a feeling that someone on his team had done something disastrously wrong.

He had been doing his rounds at the main headquarters, checking paperwork and the logs from the *real* cops, and was about to head over to the Butler Street Y, as was his strange and hated custom these last few months. The lone white cop over with the coloreds—with nary another white soul to chat with—the only time he was able to interact with other whites on the job was during these all-too-brief preshift moments and during the times when he was out on the street managing chaos at major arrests, trying to make sure his Negro officers didn't screw up while also trying to keep the white officers from flat-out attacking his "men."

"I had a long conversation with Dunlow this morning," Dodd said.

McInnis didn't know what blanks he should be filling in. He'd read the logs, and nothing had leaped out as being particularly unusual. "Yes?"

"They didn't put this to paper yet, as I told them not to. I don't want it blowing up beyond that which it'll already blow up to. But Dunlow's fingering two of your men for murder."

"Excuse me?"

"Black bootlegger named Chandler Poe got himself beat to hell and stabbed, probably a few nights ago. Coroner said he got worked over and then cut up, dumped at the canal on the West Side." Which is why McInnis hadn't seen it in any of the logs, as that wasn't his ward. "And Dunlow says two of your boys done it: Boggs and Smith."

McInnis was not one to cross his legs. His feet were flat on the floor and his knees were right angles as he asked, "Based on what?"

"Based on one eyewitness so far, and they say they got another. We got investigators on it. So, I ask again, what in the hell have you been teaching those niggers?"

McInnis sorted some things in his head: the recent logs by Boggs and Smith reported no interactions with Poe, not since they'd gone to the courthouse for the trial that had let the man off.

"These eyewitnesses, they claim they saw my officers kill Poe?"

"One witness so far, but yeah."

"Who?"

"Nigger named Shane Andrews."

McInnis laughed. "So we got one dead Negro bootlegger, and then a live Negro bootlegger saying that a *cop* killed the other one. And we're choosing to *believe* him? You know Dunlow. This is the same cop tried to frame one of my boys for drinking."

"You can't say he was trying to *frame* him, Mac. He mighta been right, and just couldn't prove it. Or it mighta been an honest misunderstanding, confusing Negroes."

"Dunlow knows one damned Negro from the other, you can be sure of that. He's out to take my boys down, and you know it."

Dodd shook his head and sighed. "Christ. I don't enjoy this so much either, Mac."

"Well, all due respect, you don't have to deal with it every waking moment like I have to. Now, I like to think I've done beyond an adequate job with the resources I've been given. I've eight Negroes under my command, and you want me to turn them into policemen, and—"

"It's not *me* that wants that."

"All right, blame the mayor, fair enough. Point is, I'm out there on an island doing what I can, and maybe they all ain't the greatest officers the city of Atlanta's ever produced, but I'll be damned if some middle-aged overweight beat cop is going to accuse any of *my* officers of being murderers."

Dodd considered this a moment. He had not expected such a reaction. "I didn't mean to imply this reflected poorly on you. I just wanted to do you the courtesy of explaining everything before you found out some other way. The process is moving along. I got two detectives looking into it, and I imagine they're going to want to talk to Boggs and Smith. When that happens—"

"They cannot talk to my boys."

"Excuse me?"

"If Internal Investigations wants to file a formal complaint about the conduct of my officers, it can do so. Short of that, my officers don't have to answer a detective's questions, and you know that."

Dodd looked like he was choosing between anger and shock.

"What, you're trying to shield your niggers now? You're so sure they didn't do this, but you're shielding them?"

"I'd like to think I'm doing what any other commanding officer would do, sir. My men don't have to be a part of some crazy witch hunt started by a lazy cop who's upset that he just lost one of his most reliable bribes."

Dodd folded his hands across his chest. "Sergeant McInnis. I want to make sure I understand something. And I want to make sure *you* understand it. I got a veteran white cop saying that your nigger rookies done lost their heads and beat a criminal to death. And you are allowing your own pride about training them to blind you into choosing the wrong side."

"*My* nigger rookies, like you said. Anyone that wants to accuse my niggers of murder will go through me. That's protocol."

"I call it damnfool pride."

" 'You say tomato' and all that."

Dodd said, "Look, Mac, I know you didn't want this posting, but—"

"Damn right I didn't." McInnis stood to leave. "I know a suicide mission when I see one."

"Sit your ass back down."

It took much swallowing of pride for Mac to sit his ass back down, but sit it back he did. Just like take the post he did, when Dodd told him to. Just like train the Negroes he did, when Dodd told him to. He had been a sergeant for four years now, the first year spent on an antinumbers investigation that—he'd known the moment he'd been assigned to it—would win him far more enemies on the force than friends. And he'd been proven correct. Yet he'd done the job because it was important, because it was the right thing, and because he'd been ordered to by superiors he'd respected and trusted. Crooked cops had controlled gambling rings across the city, so he'd shut them down. And as thanks? First he'd been sent to an undermanned Homicide squad that was in charge of some of the most forlorn areas of Darktown and Buttermilk Bottom, the kind of post that offered nothing but sad murder after sad murder, his commanding officers not really caring whether the right criminals were punished so long as enough Negroes were put away that the rest of the population took the hint and settled down. The kind of posting that left an enterprising young sergeant with effectively zero chance of impressing anyone. And then, when he thought he'd finally done his time and was deserving of a better post? *Hey, Mac, we're hiring some niggers, and you got a nice new basement office, deep in the jungle.*

Dodd said, "If you think you are deserving of special treatment because you're the only sergeant here that has to deal with nigger officers, you are mistaken. As I believe I've demonstrated over the years, I give no special treatment to anyone. We have jobs to do and we do them. Part of my job is to determine who killed that bootlegger, and if the evidence suggests that one of your boys did it, there will be a reckoning for that."

Which McInnis interpreted as: *You will be to blame, Mac. If one of your boys killed a man and covered it up in his logs, it's on you. This whole damned Negro cop experiment will go down, which the rest of us will be quite thrilled about. But your career will go down with it.*

"If your detectives muster up anything beyond Dunlow's word, I'll listen," McInnis said, standing back up. He grabbed the doorknob. "'Til then, my boys have jobs to do, and so do I, sir."

That afternoon, before roll call, Boggs made his return visit to the doctor to have the stitches removed. When he gazed into a mirror, he was disappointed by the result. Halfway between his right eye and his hairline was a two-inch scar, the skin the slightest bit whiter and redder than the rest, though the doc claimed the coloring would change with time. The scar would still be visible, though.

"It's manly," the doc said, putting Boggs's money in his pocket. "Makes a statement."

Yeah, Boggs thought. It says, *I'm a fellow people throw things at.*

At the Butler Street precinct, after roll call, McInnis invited Boggs into his office.

"Have a seat."

Boggs obeyed, glancing at the two rivulets of water that were running down the wall. It had rained that afternoon, nothing torrential, but it didn't take much to make the walls run. When they'd first started using this basement as their office, they'd put rags and old towels at the base of the walls to prevent the water from spreading on the bad days. But then the rags started to reek of mildew, so they pitched them. They had to choose their battles.

McInnis seemed very interested in some paperwork on his desk. Time passed without a word from the sergeant, and Boggs realized that McInnis was deliberately waiting until the basement was clear of the other officers. When they heard the last pair of footsteps recede up the old wooden steps, McInnis finally looked up. He had small eyes, an icy clear blue that Boggs figured some white girls had once swooned over.

"What would you like to talk to me about, Officer Boggs?" Hands folded neatly on the desk, neck hunched just the slightest bit like he was preparing to pounce.

"I'm . . . I thought *you* called me in here, sir."

"I did. There's something you want to talk to me about."

Lord, Lord. White men and their games. How they loved to draw things out.

"I'm sorry, sir. I don't understand."

"Officer Boggs. You're probably the sharpest one I've got. I see that. And a preacher's son to boot. Not the officer I would expect something like this to be happening to." A pause. "In general I would say that I have, top to bottom, a downright passable octet of officers. But I'm disappointed in you, Officer Boggs."

Boggs had been bracing for a dressing-down about the Poe beating. He'd had time to rehearse his reaction, figure out the most believable lies. He and Smith hadn't conferred as much as they probably should have, hadn't made anything resembling a plan. Nothing beyond their terse conversation, immediately after the beating, that neither would discuss it.

He knew his partner had crossed a line, and surely there would be repercussions. They were both under pressure, yes, and the moments when Boggs considered leaving the force were outnumbering the ones when he felt good about his job, yes, but still—Boggs had never snapped like that. He told himself he never would, that it wasn't his nature, that he was better than that.

He wondered if that was true.

Maybe the beating wasn't such a big deal. Boggs had seen a few white cops administer beat-downs like that. If they were here to be cops, to learn how to do the job and do it well, what was the harm in emulating the veteran cops? Did they want to be better than them, or become them?

But what McInnis asked was, "What in God's name did you think you were doing at the station?"

Boggs relaxed, a bit. He knew he would be in trouble for this, but at least it was an infraction he could tell the truth about. "I'm sorry, sir. I felt that if the deceased's father could see a Negro officer's face, it might have made the process—"

"The rules about your presence in that building could not possibly be clearer." McInnis spoke slowly but he'd upped the volume. "I don't care to hear your flawed reasoning. If you *ever* show your face there again, you will be suspended, at least. And that's if the white officers don't decide to make a lesson of you first. You're lucky that didn't happen already."

"Yes, sir."

McInnis stared him down for a moment. "Now, what else have you done wrong lately? . . . Oh, that's right: Tell me about Chandler Poe."

"What about him, sir?"

"You see him a few nights ago?"

"The last time I saw him he was being acquitted by a judge."

"After all that hard work you and Smith put into building a case against him."

"Yes, sir."

"I never did get a chance to discuss that with you. But I imagine you were rather sore about that."

"Rather sore doesn't begin to describe it, sir."

"And so I'm wondering what might have happened if you and your partner had chanced upon him late one night."

Sweat was running down his back. He hoped it wouldn't trickle down his brow or shine on his forehead. He tended to get a shiny forehead, he knew. He didn't have enough experience at lying to authority figures.

"Hopefully the arrest scared him enough, sir, that he'll move on."

"You haven't seen him?"

"No, sir."

"And you never will see him again. Because he's dead."

Boggs had been trying to appear relaxed, but now he clenched his abdomen, his neck stiffened. All his muscles seizing tighter now, his brows low. "What happened?"

"All I know is he was beaten and stabbed, but I was hoping you would tell me the details."

"Sergeant, I have no idea. I can make a list of his enemies and his acquaintances and we can go from there."

McInnis was watchful. Signs of trust nowhere near that calm, pale face.

"I certainly hope that's true, Officer. For your sake. Your reports for the past few evenings say nothing whatsoever about you coming into contact with Poe. I would hate for them to be anything less than accurate."

Coming into contact with Poe—even with Boggs's nerves firing so wildly, he was impressed by that line. "They're accurate, sir."

McInnis unfolded his hands, drummed some fingers on the desk. "Like I said, Boggs. You're probably the smartest one I got. But you aren't that smart. You understand?"

"I'm sorry, I don't."

"You aren't so smart that you can get away with being incredibly stupid. That clear enough for you? And that reverend daddy of yours will be awfully disappointed if the colored police squad he worked so hard to build falls apart because of something his should-have-known-better son did. Is *that* clear enough?"

"I haven't done anything wrong, sir."

"Or your partner?"

"My partner's a good cop."

"Uh-huh. And you'd stand up for him even if it hurt your own standing?"

"I'm . . . I guess I'm not that smart, sir, because I really don't know what we're talking about."

Silence. McInnis's eyes small and serpent-still. "Go walk your beat, Officer."

Boggs stood up. The fear was already leaving him, and in its wake he felt an anger that surprised him. He had turned toward the door, but now he faced McInnis again.

"Filing an inaccurate report. You've drilled it into our heads, how bad that is."

"I'm so glad it made an impression."

"And I've always assumed it applied not just to beat cops," Boggs said, hoping he wasn't making a mistake, "but to everyone."

"Are you trying to ask me something, Officer?"

He wished he could have done that, yes. Wished he could have said, *Why did you alter my report about Lily Ellsworth's body? Why did you cut out the reference to Underhill? What are you covering up?*

Instead, he said, "No, sir," and took his leave.

Boggs was able to hold the news inside him long enough to walk two blocks with Smith before finally letting it out: "Chandler Poe is dead."

"Dead?" Smith stopped.

"And McInnis thinks we did it."

They had been passing a couple of small storefronts at the corner of Auburn, so they turned up a side street to avoid any pedestrians. It was hot and nearing the dinner hour.

"What happened?" Smith asked.

"I don't know. McInnis said he was stabbed, but that's all I got. So is there anything else you need to tell me?"

"What? I did not stab the man. Hell, you were there."

"I was there when you beat the hell out of him. I wasn't there later on."

Smith's eyes widened, as if he was stunned his partner could believe such a thing. "I did *not* kill him."

Part of Boggs enjoyed seeing how panicked Smith was then. *You and your damned temper is why we're in this mess, so you damn well better be panicked.*

"Well," Boggs said, "someone sure did."

"They're trying to frame us. It's probably Dunlow. First he tries to frame Bayle for drinking, it don't work, so he kicks it up to murder."

"Whoever it is, I was in there lying to McInnis for you."

Smith was having too much trouble thinking through all the angles to bother with a simple thank-you. After a moment, he said, "Wonder why McInnis didn't talk to *me* yet."

"I would expect that's coming. He probably wanted to light a fire under me and see if it would smoke you out."

"You think he knows?"

"That's probably coming. You beat the man in front of two witnesses."

"Two drunks."

"That doesn't matter! To them a drunk nigger's word against a nigger cop's word is just two niggers, and they'll believe the one they *want* to believe. Most of the force has been looking for any excuse to fire us, and you've handed them one on a silver platter!"

Smith stared out at the street as if refusing to even look at this truth.

"It's perfect—this way they get to throw us in jail, too, a lesson to everyone about what happens if you give an ounce of power to a colored man. Thank you so much, Tommy, you've set us back about eighty years."

"Don't," Smith put up a hand. "Don't put this all on me. You may have the goddamn weight of the people on your shoulders, preacher's son, but I'm just trying to do my job. Hell, you were there. You could have stopped me if you'd wanted to."

"What?"

"You got a gun in your holster. You got two fists at the end of your arms. Unless you don't know how to use them? All that mopping and sweeping at Fort Bragg made it kind of hard to learn to fight, huh? You just turned the other cheek and let me do the dirty work that *you* damn well wanted to do yourself. That way you could see it done *and* stand back and judge me at the same time."

Boggs did indeed have two fists at the end of his arms, clenched tight.

"I *did* stop you, and if I hadn't, then you'd have killed him with your bare hands, and we wouldn't be having this discussion unless I was visiting your ass in jail."

If that vision frightened Smith, he had an odd way of showing it: he smiled.

"You want to be rid of me, Lucius? Then go right in there and tell McInnis the truth."

"Oh, I've been tempted. I have been strongly tempted. But at this point, that would be like committing suicide."

An awkward silence passed. A car honked on Auburn and they both realized they were abandoning their post as they bickered.

"We are both going to jail," Lucius said, "unless we start looking out for each other."

"They *all* want us to fail, like you said," Smith said. "Even McInnis. Maybe that's why he altered your report on Ellsworth."

"I've been looking into that, actually." He told Smith about his visit to Representative Prescott's house.

"You acting like you're a detective. You know that ain't our job."

"Which is why I'm not going to put anything I've learned so far into any report that McInnis or anyone else can erase."

Smith smiled. "Ooh, Mr. By-the-Book is flying off the cuff! I like it."

"We both know the white cops aren't investigating it and are just looking for a way to put it on her old man, or any other black man they can find. So *I'm* going to find out who did it, yes. And if I need help, or if I need someone to cover for me, I'm calling on *you,* because you *owe* me."

"Hell, you don't need to blackmail me into it. I'm in. If we're going to get fired anyway, let's have it be for a good reason. What's our next step?"

Boggs took the list of Lily Ellsworth's addresses out of his pocket. "House calls."

18

IF DUNLOW HAD been a problem for Rake before, now he was a crisis. He had despised Boggs's and Smith's very souls from the moment they had taken their oaths, and now he was convinced they'd killed one of his favorite informants.

Rake tried pointing out that he had no evidence and was going solely on the word of two Negro bootleggers who would also testify, if called, that they were drunk that night. Yet Dunlow was not to be reasoned with. He insisted he would find more evidence—finally, the man seemed motivated to do his job—but he also claimed they already had plenty. This wasn't for a criminal trial, after all, it was just to get the Negroes off the force. Once that happened, it wouldn't be Dunlow's problem any longer.

Rake felt his fate becoming ever more tightly entwined with his partner's. He needed to cut himself free now, before things got worse. Which meant closing the case of the former Negro Jane Doe. Determining the link between Dunlow and Underhill. Either finding evidence that Dunlow had been involved in a murder or, at the very least, convincing his superiors to get him a new partner.

So he continued tailing Underhill. Twice in one week he tailed him to Mama Dove's brothel, two blocks from the Decatur Street tracks. It was located farther away from the bars and nightclubs than most of the whorehouses, which seemed part of its allure. It was still in Darktown, but in a slightly more upscale corner of it, so that the white johns didn't feel like they were risking their lives to satiate themselves. The white cops had no problem with a brothel in Darktown, and in fact had a disincentive to shutting her down: Mama Dove paid them off handsomely.

Rake hadn't actually seen her pay Dunlow, but he'd gathered what was happening when it had occurred. It had been a couple of months ago: Rake had been ordered to stay in the car while Dunlow ran inside. Less than ten minutes later, Dunlow was back, and they were driving away. Rake had been tempted to crack a line about how speedy a lover Dunlow was, but he'd thought the better of it.

The third time Dunlow had paid such a visit, he apparently decided Rake was worthy of his trust: he handed Rake a crisp ten-dollar bill, his cut.

Rake had said no thanks.

Dunlow had insisted, deeply insulted.

Rake had said no thanks.

They had not spoken much for the remainder of that shift, and Dunlow had never again paid a visit to Mama Dove's while Rake was with him. Rake had little doubt the visits continued. He told himself his rejection of Dunlow was noble and not stupid, hoping he'd not cost himself far more than ten dollars.

Though Underhill was no longer a cop, his visit to Mama Dove's the other night had been about as brief as Dunlow's were. If he wasn't visiting her to jump in bed with a girl, why *was* he visiting?

Five nights after tailing Underhill to the brothel the first time, Rake had been in the middle of a shift—driving alone, as Dunlow was at the station and Rake was returning after assisting with an arrest—when he happened upon Underhill's Buick at an intersection. They'd been across from each other, heading opposite ways on Ponce. When the light had turned green, Underhill had continued east, so Rake went west for a block, then pulled a U-turn and tailed him, from farther away this time, since he was rather conspicuous in a squad car. By the time he was a few blocks from Mama Dove's, he'd figured out where the man was headed. He pulled the squad car over a block from the brothel. From there he saw Underhill pull over, get out, and walk up to the front door, not even knocking as he entered.

He was there less than five minutes.

Rake then headed back to the station. The final two hours of his shift passed uneventfully. After clocking out, but still in uniform, he drove back to Mama Dove's.

The brothel was an old Victorian whose dark purple paint job did not look quite so garish at night as it did by day. At this hour, it almost blended in with its neighbors, except for the fact that in those other homes, the lights were out.

Rake parked beneath a crape myrtle whose sagging branches were years overdue for a trim. He could hear jazz from a record player calling through the open windows.

He hadn't even knocked on the door yet when it was opened by a black woman with long curly hair. She wore a scarlet silk dress with a purple design of dragons and Asian script, and several necklaces of varying lengths. Some were gold; others held red or blue or purple stones. The getup made her look like some Negro-geisha-gypsy blend, Rake thought. Her hair was gray in places and she might have been twice his age, but he was struck by the beauty in her powerful eyes.

"Well, hello, a man in uniform," she said theatrically. She was used to commanding a room, even one as small as this foyer. There was a closed door behind her, and through its beveled glass Rake could just make out human shapes. The bouncy swing jazz and the angled panes made those forms move in strange ways. "I assume this is pleasure, because you and I have never done business."

Her voice was dripping with innuendo yet he proceeded with the most officious voice he could muster. "Ma'am, I was hoping to ask you a few questions about a gentleman I've seen frequent this place."

She raised her right, fastidiously plucked eyebrow. "Really, you've *seen* a gentleman *frequent* this place? I'm afraid I don't know what you're talking about."

"I was hoping you could explain to me why Brian Underhill drops by here so often, but only for a couple of minutes at a time."

"Bad lay?"

"How about another reason?"

"I don't know. In fact, I don't know the name. Now, if you'll excuse me, I do—"

He grabbed one of her forearms before she could move. She gave him a scolding look, and he released her, but not without a rough squeeze to let her know she'd best not try again to slip away.

"Ma'am, as I'm sure you know, we have some Negro officers now. And I must say, they are rather anxious to shut you down. They don't like having a whorehouse in an otherwise respectable colored neighborhood. And you know what, ma'am? They shouldn't. I wouldn't want one in my neighborhood either. But it's cops like me who have been keeping them from raiding you. So I would appreciate it if you dropped with the playacting and just answered my questions straight for a moment. Or maybe I'll add a white voice to the black choir that's trying to convince the head of Vice to shut you down."

She sighed, then leaned against the door. "I hate dealing with rookies. You can be so tiresome with your ethics and procedure and whatnot."

"I'm sure I'll grow out of it soon enough."

"You will."

"Tell me about Brian Underhill."

"Aren't you supposed to identify yourselves when you come knocking on folks' doors?"

"My name is Officer Dennis Rakestraw, ma'am."

"All right, that's better. Now, why don't you start by telling me just how little you know about Mr. Underhill?"

"I know he's an ex-cop and he comes here so briefly that the only thing he could be doing is exchanging money."

"That's it?"

He felt belittled, so he said more than he should have. "He's also suspected in the murder of a young Negro woman." Which wasn't true—he wasn't officially a suspect, except perhaps in Rake's eyes. "So I'm asking again, why does he come here?"

"He's not a john, honey. He's a competitor."

"He does what you do?"

"He thinks of himself as a . . . talent scout."

"He takes your girls?"

"The right kind."

"What's the right kind?"

"Whatever his people are looking for."

"Who are his people?"

She laughed. "He certainly doesn't tell *me*."

"Come on. The girls he takes, you've never been able to ask them who it was he took them to?"

Her neck seemed to contract as her jaw lowered, and she didn't look like she'd be laughing again anytime soon. "Officer Rakestraw. We're talking about a former policeman who takes my best-looking girls to the nicest neighborhoods in town. People who wouldn't dream of coming down *here,* but want it all the same, and need it to come out to them. Now, who do *you* think his clients are?"

"What do you get out of it?"

"He gives me a little something, and I do mean a *little.*" So despite the fact that Underhill was only an *ex*-cop, he still managed to make her feel that he had enough friends in the Department that she couldn't cross him. He would come along and raid her roster whenever he needed to, and there was nothing she could do to stop him. "He thinks it's enough to make me not mind that I'm losing my girls. It's not."

"Losing your girls—you don't mean you never hear from them again?"

"I usually don't."

"Does anyone hear from them?"

"I wouldn't know."

Her face was blank, the kind of blank that shows a clear preference that some other subject be discussed. Rake felt chilled. He couldn't tell if she meant that the girls simply vanished into some other life or if she was implying that they were eventually killed.

"What can you tell me about Lily Ellsworth?" he asked.

"I've never had a girl with that name."

He wished he was better at spotting lies. And he had the feeling he was up against a true bullshit artist. He didn't have a chance against her, he just had to ask a lot of questions and try to piece her answers together later.

"Really? I would not be pleased to find out later that she was here and you lied to me about it."

"Officer Rakestraw, I'm being forthright. I've never heard the name Lily Ellsworth before. Now, that doesn't mean she wasn't here once, but under a different name. I'd bet half the girls in here are using names other than those their parents baptized them with, but how am I to know? If you really want to know if this girl was ever here, show me a picture of her."

She said that like it was a bit of obvious police work he was a fool not to know. He felt the blood rise to his cheeks.

"Light-skinned, long dark hair, birthmark on her right shoulder. Nineteen, thin, moved to Atlanta from Peacedale sometime in the last year. Last seen in a yellow dress and a silver locket. That help?"

She threw up her hands, red and blue stones catching the dim light. "Maybe. But light-skinned, long-haired girls from the country *do* grow on trees, so a photo would be better."

He was deeply tired of this woman. "If you don't mind my saying so, you seem remarkably unfazed by the fact that one of your girls was murdered."

"First of all, she wasn't one of my girls—at least, I don't know for sure without that photo. And second of all, alas, I'm remarkably used to it."

"So this sort of thing happens a lot to your girls."

"How new at this *are* you, son?" She put a hand on her hip and cocked her head a bit. "A black whore gets killed, that ain't exactly front-page news. The only thing I *am* fazed by right now is the fact that a cop is here bothering about her. Why? What was so special about *this* girl?"

"Maybe nothing. Maybe I'm just too hung up on my pesky ethics right now."

The hand fell from her hip and her expression changed to one of sympathy, or mock sympathy. Her fake emotions were difficult to keep up with.

"I know you're very tired, Officer. I know *just* the thing for a tired young man like you, something that will *truly* perk you up. I have an amazing array to choose from. Mr. Underhill doesn't take *all* my best girls, if you'd like to see for yourself?"

She stepped to the side, so he could see that one of her hands was at the inner door's knob, ready to turn if he said the word. It was unde-niably tempting as he stood there, realizing that behind that door were untold pleasures. Rake had been with only three women, two of them whores in Europe. He had sworn that nonsense off when he'd returned from the war alive, and he considered himself lucky to have Cassie, even if they were always exhausted lately, sex having become a distressingly rare occurrence. Still, plenty of other cops indulged, so why not him? Why did he have to be such a saint?

He could hear those voices whispering in his ear, but he did his best to ignore them. He held up his left hand, thumbing his wedding ring.

"This mean anything to you?"

She laughed. "Should it?"

He tipped his cap. "Good night, Mrs. Dove."

She laughed again, as if she'd never heard anyone address her that way.

He was halfway down the steps when she said, "It's rather sad, I must say. You coming to *me* for this information. I would think an officer in your position would be able to ask one of his colleagues what he needed to know about me. Yet you came *here*." He looked back at her and saw she was shaking her head, this time wearing not so much a sympathetic expression as a pitying one. With a trace of malice. "You must not have many friends on the force."

He would wish for a long while that he'd come up with a better retort than "Good night," before walking back to his lonely Ford.

19

BOGGS AND SMITH'S unofficial, off-the-books, and mostly amateur investigation into the murder of Lily Ellsworth was producing little in the way of information and much in the way of risk. They needed to limit the number of people they spoke to, to decrease the chances that McInnis or one of the other white cops might figure out what they were doing. Which hindered their efforts greatly. And they hadn't yet made the trek out to Peacedale to pick up Lily's letters back home. Though Boggs suspected the missives held a trove of information, he kept putting off the trip. Going out into the country, a land where the white men ruled even yet more ruthlessly than they did in Atlanta, was no minor errand. As he plotted it out in his head—he'd need to borrow a car, and go with Smith, and stash some guns in the car just in case—he realized how accustomed he was to moving about a city where he had a powerful family, important connections. But the country? It would be like that South Carolina army camp once again, and the horrible little hellhole of a town outside it, where the buses never stopped for Negroes and where failure to move off a sidewalk at the right time could be your last mistake.

So they'd done what they could in Atlanta, tracking down landladies and former roommates of the deceased and hoping they weren't causing enough of a stir to alert whichever white cops (all of them?) so desperately wanted this case unsolved.

The first place Lily had stayed in the city had been a rooming house, seven blocks south of Auburn, a place Boggs occasionally had reason to visit when trying to locate a suspect or witness. It was run by an older black couple, the Paulsons, who had moved to the city as teenagers themselves and now made a point of providing a clean, wholesome place for migrants to live as they got established. Or so they always claimed. From time to time, people rooming there had been arrested for this or that petty crime, but no one at the precinct had reason to think the Paulsons were involved in anything.

When Boggs and Smith visited, Mr. Paulson dimly remembered Lily. She had stayed with them for six weeks, he recalled. She had been polite and well mannered for a country girl, the old bald man had said, and had kept her room immaculate. That's all he knew. No visitors, and certainly no male guests (that was not allowed), and no reason to have suspected anything harmful might occur to her. He expressed surprise to hear of her death, but it didn't faze him. Many people came into and out of his three-story rooming house, and he seldom heard from them again. This was life in the city, he said, and he played his role as gatekeeper and hoped the people who moved on found better places, but that's not always what the Lord has designed. Sometimes those gates opened to dark things.

Paulson checked his books and said that Lily had moved there in the first week of March and left in late April. He knew no more.

Mrs. Paulson, who had been asleep that night but had called Boggs just two hours ago, knew a bit more. She had chatted a few times with Lily, especially when she'd first arrived. The girl had seemed friendly and more than a bit wide-eyed at this city she found herself in. Mrs. Paulson was used to seeing people who had fled one bad situation or another and had witnessed all manner of deception and evasiveness, but when she'd asked Lily why she'd left her family and come here, the girl's reply had simply been that she was tired of the country and wanted more. Mrs. Paulson had found her believable.

She also had the name and last known address of the girl who had shared bedrooms with Lily, which Boggs took down for later.

The next place Lily wound up in, for a mere two weeks, was another rooming house, in a better neighborhood, only a block off Auburn. The rooms there were larger, and each guest had her own space, so Lily had been moving up in the world. But the owner of the place barely remembered her, and couldn't think of anyone else who might. Boggs decided he'd drop by again; maybe he'd meet someone who knew something, but he didn't put much hope in it.

That left one more address: Mama Dove's. A brothel two blocks north of Decatur Street. A place Boggs and the other colored cops very much wanted to put out of business, but they had been told repeatedly not to invest their energy in that. The reason was clear: the white cops didn't mind the place, Mama Dove gave out good information, and it was in a Negro neighborhood, so no one on the force cared, apart from Boggs and his colleagues, but that was a battle they couldn't yet fight.

Which meant Lily had made her way from starter boardinghouse to better boardinghouse to working for a congressman to whorehouse, in barely four months.

How?

After a few repeat trips to the rooming houses where Lily had lived, Boggs and Smith finally found a couple of girls who'd boarded there at the same time as Lily, a few weeks ago. The first girl said Lily had been shy but warm, slow to open up to strangers. She'd thought they were on the verge of a friendship when Lily had taken on her job at the Prescotts and became so busy that they only met one other time, for a late ice cream. A second former roommate said something similar, and neither could think of anyone who would've wanted to hurt her, no rivals or beaus, not even any other friends.

The more Boggs heard what a sweet, nice girl she'd been, the more bothered he became.

So at six one morning he got out of bed, far earlier than he wanted to after another long evening of walking the beat. He got dressed and hurriedly drank a coffee and walked out. It was light already, his parents' small yard wet with dew. The birds sounded surprised to see him at that hour.

It hadn't taken him long to figure out the address of Miss Julie Cannon, Lily's replacement at the Prescotts. Between her last name and knowing what church her family worshipped at, he had more information on her than if he'd known her social security number. Finding her at home proved more challenging, as she worked long hours for the Prescotts. Catching her on the way to work seemed his only option.

She lived with her parents in a divided bungalow, two mailboxes out front and letters on the doors. It was a run-down block, just north of the tracks and in the area that Boggs's parents preferred to avoid.

He'd been there barely five minutes before the door opened and Julie stepped out, in a loose-fitting gray housedress and hair pulled into a bun.

"Morning, Miss Cannon."

"We know each other?"

"We met a couple of days ago but I wasn't straight with you. My name is Officer Lucius Boggs of the Atlanta Police Department."

She'd been giving him that *boy, I don't have time for your flirting ways* look of pretty girls the world over but now the edges softened, just a tad.

"You came to the Prescotts the other day."

He'd recalled her being attractive before, but she seemed to look twice as good this time. Perhaps he'd been too nervous the other day at the Prescotts, or he'd been put off by the coldness she'd so fully inhabited as part of her job saying *No* to unwanted visitors. Maybe it was just the low sunlight off her round eyes or the coffee he'd gulped too fast, but he found himself thrown off.

"I did. I was hoping to ask you a few questions."

"Are you trying to get me fired?"

"No, Miss Cannon. But I do need your help."

"I have a bus to catch."

"And I have an amazing ability to walk and talk at the same time."

That *boy, don't be flirting* look returned, but with it was the tiny hint of a grin. Then she was walking, and fast. She hadn't been kidding about being in a hurry.

She said, "So, you told Mrs. Prescott that you were the last maid's brother?"

"I lied to your boss about that. Her name was Lily Ellsworth. And she was murdered."

Julie stopped. She stared at him and he felt guilty for inflicting this look in her eyes, and for the way her right hand gripped her left forearm, as if he'd struck her. This certainly was the first she'd heard about her predecessor's death. Had the Prescotts deliberately kept it from her, or did they not even know?

"What?"

"Someone killed her. About a week ago."

"Wh . . . Why? How?"

"I'm working on the why. As for the how, someone shot her through the heart."

She lingered on that for a few seconds. "What are you playing here?"

"I'm not playing anything, Miss Cannon. I'm just trying to do my job, and do it discreetly so that, like you said, no one gets fired."

She shook her head and muttered, "I'm gonna miss my bus." She resumed her earlier pace. "If you have questions to ask you'd best get around to asking them."

The women he met through his church were so refined and mannerly, taught from a young age to be delicate and fair. Julie was more like the women he found himself dealing with on the job, curt and in no mood for dancing around subjects. He'd never found that an attractive trait before, but he was reassessing his feelings with every step she took.

"What can you tell me about Lily?" He told himself not to let her catch him glancing at her chest and calves but he ran the risk nonetheless.

"Nothing. I never met her."

"Have you ever heard the Prescotts talk about her?"

"Not really. I mean, I don't really talk to Mrs. Prescott much, you know? You met her. She's not the 'mingle with the help' sort. She don't ask me about my life and I don't ask about hers."

"But has she ever said anything at all about Lily, how they came to part company? She seemed to hint to me that she wasn't too happy with how Lily had worked out."

"I don't know. I mean, maybe things have been said. I assumed they weren't happy if she ain't there no more, but haven't asked her a lot of questions about the last girl."

They crossed the street. In another block they'd be at Auburn and the bus stop. He wished she'd lived farther away, both to get more out of her and because he was enjoying watching this girl walk.

"Has she ever said anything that made you think the last maid had stolen from them?"

"They sure don't leave their jewels out when I'm around if that's what you mean. But they're all like that."

"How about the congressman? Has he ever said anything about—"

"Never met the man. I've only been there a few weeks, and he's been away the whole time. Up in Washington. I don't think he's home much, or ever."

There were probably ways he could find out if Prescott had ever met Lily, Congressional calendars or something. The other day Lucius had asked his father for his opinion about Prescott; Boggs didn't mention the murder or the investigation, saying only that a former employee of the congressman was in some trouble. The reverend admitted he didn't know Prescott well, but he noted that the man's politics were as good as you could ask of a white elected official in Georgia. In addition to helping tamp down the state legislature's revolt against the mayor for hiring Lucius and the others, Prescott had recently dropped some hints that he might come around to supporting the latest version of antilynching legislation that kept failing in Washington.

"And their son?" Boggs asked Julie. "He lives in town, doesn't he?"

"Yeah, but I've never met him, either."

They were at the corner of Auburn now, and he could see the bus stop barely ten feet beyond her. Four other women stood there, three of them obviously maids and the fourth, too, probably.

"Miss Cannon, I need you to get back in touch with me if you ever hear them say anything at all about Lily. Even the most minor thing. You might not have noticed it before, but now that we've had this talk, hopefully—"

"This is my paycheck you're talking about. I ain't no one's spy. And why aren't you wearing a uniform?"

He saw a bus a block away. She'd hear it in a couple of seconds.

"Like I said, I'm trying to be discreet, for your sake as well as my own. And I'm not asking you to spy. I'd just like you to tell me if you ever hear anything, that's all."

She looked at him as if mentally flipping to the definition of *spy* and trying to determine how exactly his request differed from it. Before she could figure that out, he offered her a card with his name and number and the Department crest. He'd had to pay for the printing himself, as had the other colored officers. He'd also scribbled his home number on the back of this one.

She glanced at it, then recoiled.

"I can't have that on my person when I'm in their house!"

"Then may I leave it in your mailbox for you?"

She turned around and saw the bus coming. "Not *now*. My parents will see it and think I'm up to something."

"Do your parents often think that?"

She put a hand on her hip. "What would most parents think of their daughter talking to a cop?"

"Well, that's why I'm not in my uniform."

"And I don't need no card to remember. Your name is Officer Lucius Boggs and I surely can figure out how to phone the police if I need to." He liked hearing his name on her lips. Even if he could feel his mother flinch every time Julie dropped a syllable. "Look, I gotta go."

The bus stopped and the other ladies began boarding. She took a step toward it, then turned to face him again and asked what he'd expected her to ask far earlier in this conversation. The fact that she hadn't until now impressed him. "Should I be scared? Should I quit for someplace else? I mean, I *need* this job."

He wished he had a better answer for her than, "If I have any reason to think you're in any trouble there, I'll let you know. And you do the same."

He felt responsible for her then, as she boarded the bus and he caught a final glimpse of her smooth calves. Surely what happened to Lily would not be visited upon a second maid of the Prescotts'. Surely he would get to talk to Miss Julie Cannon again.

20

THE FARM OTIS Ellsworth had dedicated his life to was fifty miles south of Atlanta, though it felt even farther. The earth rolled gently out here, not so hilly as to be impossible to raise crops but not so flat as to be easy on those who tended the land. The farm grew sweet potatoes, green beans, and other vegetables for Ellsworth's family, but mostly it was dedicated to something his often-hungry family could not eat: cotton. Otis tended the land with his two sons and another family who lived in a small house a half-mile from his. Working from sunrise to sunset, from can to can't. As hard as it was, they were fortunate to have dodged the boll weevils that had decimated crops in so many other counties, sending desperate farmers into Atlanta or the grave or both.

Here the piney woods were thick and tall, and Otis remembered playing hide-and-seek as a child, remembered stealing first kisses and then running off as if the girls might pursue him and somehow take those kisses back. A few miles outside Peacedale there had once been a mountain, so Otis had been told, but the stone had been dynamited and quarried for so many years that Otis had never laid eyes on any such landmark. The area seemed to exist in shadow all the same.

He was driving toward town on a Saturday, a day that always held plenty of chores in store for him, as *weekend* was not a concept that applied to sharecroppers. Driving in his newly purchased Ford truck, which he himself had repainted just a few weeks ago, a bright red, beautiful, he thought, even if his neighbor had chimed in that it looked like a miniature fire truck now. His *envious* neighbor, Otis thought.

Fifty miles from Atlanta wasn't far enough.

How many miles away was Chicago? he wondered. Could this truck get them there? Of course it could. Only had nine thousand miles on it, good as new. There were seats in the front, so he and Emma Mae could sit there while his sons traded shifts between squeezing up front or riding in the back, without a roof. Surely he could jerry-rig some kind of tarp over it, in case it rained.

Unless he traded it for a sedan. The pickup had been a mighty big help on the farm this last month, and would continue to be as long as they stayed here. But if they were going to Chicago, a sedan would make more sense. Was he really thinking this? Just a few months ago, the idea of owning any kind of an automobile would have been so foreign as to be unbelievable, but here he was driving one. And yes, he truly did have enough money to trade it and pay more for a better car, one that could comfortably seat his entire family.

Blood money, his wife had called it. *That's why you painted it red.*

What had she meant by that? He still didn't understand it. True, it was an awful lot of money, and Lily's explanations didn't quite make sense, but *blood money* didn't sound right to him. Surely she'd acquired all that money in a fair way. Girl wasn't no crook.

The only other way she could have gotten it, he figured, was too wicked for him to believe. No daughter of his would have done that. Surely his wife didn't think it?

There was another explanation, there had to be. Just because he didn't know it didn't mean it wasn't so. With Lily gone, he'd never know what that explanation was. It would forever be untold. So that's how he would leave it. He was a man who could live without hearing the explanation of those things that appeared to make no sense. That strange colored police officer had felt differently, and Otis would show him those old letters if the officer really did come out here to see them, but it seemed wrong for the man to pester ghosts. Lily was gone. Otis saw no need to pick at his family's scars. He could only pick up his family and keep moving. That was the way he'd survived as long as he had, why his parents had survived long enough to raise him, why *their* parents—born slaves—had managed to do the same. You keep moving. You do not look back.

Yet look back is exactly what he did when he heard the sirens.

He had been driving down a road that cut through the piney woods, only a sliver of sunlight making it through the tall canopy, and as he crested a small hill he glanced in the mirror and saw two police cars a few hundred yards away, closing fast. With so little driving experience, he'd certainly never seen police in his rearview mirror before. It was like feeling the devil breathe on the back of his neck.

He pulled over. One of the cars moved in front of his and stopped there, and the other pulled behind. Dappled light creased in between some trees yet still the woods felt very dark here, and Otis very alone.

Sheriff Nayler emerged from the car in front. Otis had seen him around town, though the two had never had cause to address each other. Nayler was tall and thin, with a bushy black mustache and a strange scar like a half moon around the outside of his right eye socket, making the eye seem to lie more deeply in that crater than normal.

A young officer emerged from the passenger seat. He and Nayler stood at opposite sides of Otis's truck. They both wore dark blue uniforms and the sort of tall hats that would have been more fitting on cavalry men from an earlier time.

"Otis Ellsworth," Sheriff Nayler said. He stood with his hands on his hips, a disappointed schoolteacher. An armed one. In the rearview, Otis could see two other cops standing by their vehicle.

"Good morning, Sheriff, sir." His mouth dry already.

"Turn your truck off, Otis."

He obeyed.

"Mighty nice truck you got. Paint it yourself, did you?"

"Yes, sir, Sheriff."

"Ain't 'cause it's stolen, is it? That is what enterprising car thieves are known to do, disguising evidence of their crimes."

The young cop on the other side was tall, at least six five. He looked like he chopped down trees as a hobby. The Peacedale police did not seem to make uniforms big enough for him, as his short-sleeved shirt was straining from the muscles underneath.

"No, sir. Bought it myself. From Spooner Wells. He vouch for that."

"That's right, that's right. Ol' Spoon did tell us you paid for it. Paid cash. A *lot* of cash. Fact, he said he overcharged you, spectin' you to talk him down, only you didn't. You so flush you didn't seem to mind."

Had Spoon said that? It's true, they hadn't negotiated. Shame mixed itself into the other horrible emotions swirling in Otis's gut.

The sheriff put his hands on the door of Otis's car, leaning down to get a closer look. Otis knew not to look him in the eye.

"Come clean now, Otis. Come clean and make this easier on yourself."

He was staring at his dashboard, trying to figure out what the right answer was here. What did they want to hear? What would not get him beaten, or worse?

Movement in his rearview, then he felt the impact as the other two cops leaped into the back of the pickup. They seemed to be searching the contents of the truck, which were just some old crates and burlap left over from a recent delivery.

"I'm not sure what you want to know, Sheriff, sir."

The sheriff was as motionless as a copperhead that's already made its mind up.

"You and your people been in this country a long time, Otis. A long time."

"Yes, sir."

"Ain't never had no trouble out of any of you." Otis could smell stale chew on the man's breath.

"We good people, sir."

"Then why are we getting called by the Atlanta Police Department about you, Otis? Why they asking questions about you?"

He shook his head, but he couldn't think up a response. The other two cops were rustling around in the back of his truck. The big cop was still standing to his right, hands by his sidearm and club. The whole town of Peacedale couldn't have many more cops than these four, and all of them right here, watching him.

"Why they asking me about that girl of yours, what she been up to?"

He needed to say something. Yet all he had was, "I don't know, sir."

"Whole state seems to be interested in your family, Otis."

He tried to swallow. A honeybee flew in his open passenger window.

"They got a dead girl in Atlanta and I got a Negro here who's come into a suspicious amount of money. You win some jackpot I don't know about?"

He tried to answer, but his throat caught. He tried again. "Been putting just a little bit away for a good while now, and—"

"Don't you lie to me, son," the sheriff snapped. Otis had been a fool. He was betraying those ancestors who'd managed to stay alive, managed to skirt the narrow path between humiliation and death. "Where did you get that money?"

"I didn't steal it from nobody."

"That ain't what I asked."

He didn't say anything. The honeybee landed on his right wrist of all places. He shooed it away.

"We oughta take the truck," the young, big cop said to the sheriff.

"Really?" the sheriff replied.

"It's stole, obviously. Oughta impound it."

"That's an idea. That is an idea."

If they took the car, the family was in trouble. His wife was right, he should have just hidden the money away. That way, it would have been there when they needed to buy train tickets north. If the cops took the truck, did he have enough left to get north? Maybe enough to get there, but not enough to get there and then find a place to stay, and eat, while searching for a job and setting up their new lives. He'd wanted the truck, wanted it to help with fall harvest and, yes, wanted to show it off. Show the neighbors that he wasn't a nothing, that he aspired to things, that he *had* things.

The biggest mistake he'd made in his life.

It hadn't been far from here where the white people had killed Leo Milliner and the man's wife, too. Story was they hadn't been doing anything wrong, but a couple of white men had made some remarks about her that her husband hadn't appreciated. Milliner was a humble man, word was, and smart enough to avoid confrontation, but his wife had been three months pregnant and he'd felt the need to defend her. All he'd done was talk back, a witness claimed, but the white people felt otherwise. Two hours later a pack of whites came for the Milliners at their house, free of witnesses. Beat them both, burned them up. Five months ago, still casting long shadows.

Lily had left for Atlanta by then, but Otis had sat his two boys down, a good time to remind them of what not to do or say. Yet here he was.

The sheriff's hands were back on the door and his face was nearly in the truck again.

"I'll ask you one more time. How'd your girl get you that money?"

Tell the truth, he told himself. Tell the truth and let them sort it out.

But instead, his voice shaking, barely audible, he said, "I don't know."

"What's that?"

"I don't know." He felt himself near tears. He put his hands on the wheel to stop them from shaking, though he feared the sheriff would think he was trying to start the truck. "I don't know what she did. I don't know."

More movement from the back as one of the cops laughed about something. Otis hated the wetness in his eyes and tried to will it away.

Then Nayler swore, "Goddammit!" He stepped back. The young cop on the other side stepped back, too, and drew his pistol. All Otis could do was hold the wheel tighter.

"You all right, Sheriff?" asked one of the cops in back.

"Goddamn bee," the sheriff said, shaking his hand. He took his hand to his lips, sucking out the stinger perhaps, or kissing it better.

Otis was staring wide-eyed at the young cop's pistol, aimed at his head.

The sheriff took his hand out of his mouth, spat, and said to the junior cop, "Winston, I'd thank you to put that piece away before you shoot me by mistake." Winston obeyed. Nayler asked, "You transporting a goddamn hive or something, Otis?"

Otis tried to assure the white man he had nothing to do with the bee sting.

Then Nayler called to the cops in the back. "Anything?"

"Nope."

The sheriff shook his head. "Damned sorry mess this is. All right. Let's go."

Nayler started walking toward his car.

Otis didn't dare look at Winston, whose voice sounded insulted, almost hurt. "That's it?"

"C'mon," the sheriff barked, motioning for his subordinate to join him.

That's it? Otis couldn't believe it either, but one by one the cops got back into their cars, and their flashing lights were turned off. Still, he braced himself for gunshots.

The cars drove away. No gunfire. No curses. Not even a spit of tobacco juice.

Otis exhaled for what felt like the first time in minutes. *Thank you, Jesus.* But why? He'd thought they were going to take the truck, or shoot him in the woods. Had the sheriff decided there wasn't enough evidence? Had he decided it was a problem for the Atlanta cops?

Or were they waiting for later? While wearing different uniforms?

Otis turned around. Too shaken to run the errands he'd been planning. He needed to think, make a new plan. How was he going to tell Emma Mae? What would the boys say?

It didn't matter. Only one thing mattered: getting out.

He tried to test the best way of saying it to her. Today was Saturday. Tomorrow would be church. They would have to keep this to themselves, not arouse any more suspicions.

The road ran down a gradual decline and leveled out again, the woods retreating on either side, and there the country was before him, the grass pale green from the wet summer and not hay yellow as it usually was come July. Horses in the distance, gray mules dotting the landscape, the nearest ones inclining their heads as if to ask what newfangled beast Otis was riding on. This had been home all his life, and his parents' and theirs and Lord only knew how far back it went.

He wondered what Emma Mae would say, if she'd argue or resign herself to this as she did all the other calamities. He said it out loud, as practice.

"Baby, we need to put our things in order, right quick. We're going north Tuesday."

21

THOUGH REVEREND DANIEL Boggs did not live in the grandest house on Auburn Avenue, its deep wraparound porch was frequently filled with the business leaders and ministers who held sway over their community. It was less a home than a portal between other people's homes, where disputes among neighbors were settled, where theological crises were explicated, where marital advice was meted out and disagreements between siblings were calmed, where the heads of denominations put aside their differences to lay plans for the community's slow but determined march toward their God-given rights.

On Lucius's one night off that week, he was one of at least fifty people in his parents' house. Cousins and in-laws, children and adults and the elderly milled about the parlor and kitchen and hallways, the porch and the backyard. One of his cousins was moving to Chicago and this party was a bittersweet farewell. Count Basie had been playing on the family record player but by now the crowd had drowned him out. So much small talk had become big talk, everyone loosened by drink even though so many of the attendees were good Baptists who supposedly did not touch the stuff. Their glasses of Co-Colas held more than just cola.

Lucius felt a hand tap on his shoulder.

"These are some well-dressed colored folk," Smith said.

Lucius shook his partner's hand. He'd never invited him over before today. Smith wore a light blue linen jacket over a tieless white shirt. "Thanks for coming."

"My pleasure. That professor you mentioned here?"

"Kellen Timmons." They'd just learned through one of Lily's former roommates that Lily had been involved in a Negro rights organization.

The roommate hadn't remembered the name, just a few nouns that might have been in the wrong order, the Racial Cooperation League or Race Council of Something. Lucius had placed a few calls to old classmates and friends of friends before arriving at the actual name, the Racial Cooperative Council, one of whose founders was a Morehouse history professor and old friend of Lucius's brother Reginald. "He's here. Let's wait 'til he's had a drink or two."

Then they were intercepted by Lucius's uncle from Paris.

"Ah, this must be one of your fellow constables!"

"Yes, Uncle Percy, this is Tommy Smith, my partner most nights."

"A true pleasure to meet one of the gallant warriors of Auburn Avenue!"

"Pleased to meet you," Smith said, a half smile on his lips, not sure what to make of the man. Percy had been wearing an impeccably tailored black suit earlier, complete with a monocle dangling from the pocket, but he had since removed his jacket. His armpits were very damp indeed. He had not lived in the South in more than a decade and had lost his tolerance for the humidity, among other things.

"What's your weapon of choice, young man?"

"You mean, what do I carry?"

Percy laughed out loud. Though much thinner than his brother the reverend, Percy had a similarly imposing voice. His longish hair was combed in a wave that was perhaps the style among the Negroes who lived in Europe, not that Boggs would have known.

"What do you *drink,* my good man? We can talk firearms later."

"Oh, I'm fine, sir."

"Well, I simply *must* pry you two for some tales. Perhaps my next book will be about you."

"You write, sir?"

Percy was a novelist. Under an assumed name, he wrote historical adventures, and though he occasionally penned an ancient Greek or Roman epic, mainly he set his tales in early America. He was the best-selling Negro writer in America, and probably the world, partly because no one realized the writer of those stories *was* a Negro. Lucius had started reading Percy's novels when he was in grade school and had loved them, swashbuckling tales of pirates off the coast of the Carolinas and gold miners in the Georgia mountains, of lost Confederate battalions fighting off alligators in Louisiana swamps and Virginia cavaliers risking all to defeat the colonizing British. Seemingly every chapter ended with a lit keg of dynamite or a train careening dangerously toward a trapped stagecoach. It hadn't been until Lucius was in high school that he heard his father's low opinion of the books. That's when he started noticing that his own people were either absent from the stories or were represented in exactly the way the white readers of an antebellum Southern yarn would expect them to appear.

In the late thirties Percy had decamped to Paris to live the life of an intellectual unfettered by Jim Crow. How he had survived (and continued to publish a book every year) during the fall of France was a bit of a mystery, and Lucius had been told not to ask.

"He's a great writer," Lucius said, so his uncle wouldn't have to.

"I'm just a man with a typewriter. What *you* two are doing, however, now *that* is a true epic."

"We pretty much just arrest drunk folks and keep men from hitting their wives," Smith said.

"Don't forget the moonshiners," Percy said. "Your partner here was telling me how you've been turning off the illicit taps across town, isn't that right? Speaking of which, it appears there is a leak in my glass. I must return to the bar, then we shall continue this conversation."

"Interesting fellow," Smith said after Percy's exit.

"I have to go make sure he doesn't drink too much and kill himself."

"We all got drunk uncles, man. Mine don't write, they just sell whatever of yours they can steal."

"No, I mean literally. He tries to kill himself every time he comes home."

Lucius explained that Percy returned to Georgia annually for a week's stay. Each time, he seemed more and more disenchanted with the backwardness of the South. On every visit, there was at least one occasion when he drank too much and dramatically claimed that he would end his life. Two years ago he had tried to hurl himself out the third-floor window of a Spelman sociology professor's apartment, failing only when he couldn't open the window enough, at which point he was talked out of it, and then he fainted. Last year, at a formal dinner whose single floor offered no potential for deadly falls, he had announced he was going to throw himself before a streetcar. He was physically restrained, barely. Both times he had apologized the next morning and been very, very quiet for the remainder of his stay. This time, he had already been back five days with only two more to go until his return berth for the enlightened, demolished European continent.

"My father appointed me as his guardian for the evening. I'll be back."

"Sounds good. I'ma go meet some of your fine cousins."

➤

Smith had never been in the company of so many well-heeled Negroes before. He knew they existed, and had caught glimpses of them now and again, but such a collection all in one place was dizzying. He was glad he'd spent most of his savings on this jacket a week ago.

He felt newly conscious of his dropped *g*'s and propensity for cursing as he spoke with this doctor and that owner of a barbershop empire. He noticed watches and cuff links. More than once a mildly disdainful look faded when he mentioned that he was one of the city's new police officers, at which point his unpolished qualities suddenly became praiseworthy.

"You're making us all proud," said an insurance man.

"We need men like you to protect all we've built here," said the owner of the very haberdashery where Smith had bought his outfit.

It was nice to impress gentlemen who otherwise would have ignored him, but he was more interested in impressing their daughters. Every time he seemed to be making progress with one, however, another man asked to be introduced to one of Atlanta's new knights.

"Lucius tells me you were in an armored division during the war?" Reverend Boggs asked.

"Yes, sir, I served in the 761st Tank Battalion."

"I'm glad they teamed my son up with a proven warrior."

He hated conversations like this. "Well, they don't have us in a tank, sir. We're just on foot. Mighty different experience."

Then yet another reverend asked for an introduction. Though Tommy could see more than a few ladies admiring him from a distance, he felt his passage to them permanently blocked by important men.

➤

Later in the evening Boggs found himself in his father's den with his brother Reginald and Kellen Timmons, who was marveling at the bookshelves that lined all four walls. Lucius hadn't seen him in years, and the professor's waistline had grown, as had a goatee that seemed to be fashioned after photos of jazz musicians. They briefly caught up: married, two little girls, fourth year teaching at Morehouse. Timmons flipped through some of the books, asking if Lucius or Reginald had read the latest essay by Richard Wright, or that new poetry collection by Langston Hughes. Lucius realized how quickly he was falling behind on his reading now that he was busy not getting killed on the streets.

They talked current events, both the good (the ageless Satchel Paige, longtime star of the Negro Leagues, had recently made his major-league debut in Cleveland) and the bad (in South Africa, the newly elected Afrikaner National Party was making moves to further restrict the rights of colored people, calling its system "apartheid").

When Timmons asked how things were going with the job, Lucius did his usual routine of mentioning the best parts and omitting the other 95 percent.

"We're all just trying to do some good, right?" Timmons asked, his smile a bit too enthusiastic. The ginger ale in his glass was likely half bourbon. "That's what it's about."

"Speaking of which, tell me about this Racial Cooperative Council thing. My father mentioned it the other day"—a lie, but one that he knew would flatter Timmons—"and it sounded interesting."

Bored by politics, Reginald excused himself to make another drink.

"Well, me and some other professors got to thinking it might be good to have a different approach to encouraging our peers to be active politically. What your father and Reverend Holmes Borders and Reverend King have done, well, they're wonderful, of course. But we felt other voices should be heard." Another big smile, almost a laugh. Timmons seemed nervous. Nervous because he didn't want to offend the son of Reverend Boggs, or nervous for another reason? Boggs was about to tell Timmons that he wasn't offended, that he couldn't care less if the man was launching a splinter organization that competed with his father's for political space. But he liked that Timmons seemed to be struggling, so he didn't send him a lifeline yet.

In truth, Reverend Boggs and the other community leaders probably *were* upset that Timmons had started a new group. In recent years there had been several examples of former allies starting different organizations, or writing letters to editors that had not been approved in advance, or hosting lectures that had not been vetted. Minor disagreements could quickly blow up into blood feuds. Boggs tried to stay on the sidelines, but he knew that his father, for all his emphasis on brotherhood, wanted to know everything that happened in this community, as if seeking to duplicate the Good Lord's omniscience over these two or three square miles.

"We want to go beyond the Talented Tenth," Timmons continued, "you know, people like you and me, and everybody at this party. We want to do a better job educating those less fortunate, the kids who are stuck in the worst schools in the city, or dropping out because there isn't room for them. The ones out in the country, working in the fields all day instead of being educated."

Boggs had spent his entire life around people like Timmons. He could have chosen Timmons's path, and perhaps he would have, if he didn't equate such activities so strongly with his father. Part of him envied Timmons's lack of a family throne to occupy or ignore.

While at Morehouse, Lucius had envisioned himself becoming a professor just like the dignified, competent men he so painstakingly tried to model himself after. He had loved the place—and not just because Morehouse was on the West Side, which, like Sweet Auburn, was an oasis from Jim Crow. But what he'd loved even more than that was how it felt to be surrounded by other colored men with aspirations, to be encouraged so boldly by professors who pushed him harder not only to imagine a better world but to create it. That message, though inspiring, was compromised by those same professors' warnings to stay in the colored districts, to avoid the white neighborhoods, to avoid even the downtown movie theaters where Negroes were relegated to the balconies. "I wouldn't go to a segregated theater to see Jesus Christ Himself," one teacher had proclaimed. During Lucius's sophomore year, another Morehouse student who made extra money delivering papers confronted a white grocer about a delinquent bill, and the grocer shot him in the back. Boggs and his fellow students had protested outside City Hall for an afternoon, and Reverend Boggs and his fellow leaders had written letters to the mayor, but that grocer still happily ran his business and was never even arrested. Now his papers were delivered by some other paperboy.

"Are any politicians talking with your group?" Lucius asked, hoping to rhetorically lead Timmons to Representative Prescott. "Mayor Hartsfield, City Council? Senators?"

"Hartsfield only talks to Negroes when he fears we'll vote for someone else, and he knows that isn't going to happen right now, not after 'giving us' eight colored officers."

"How about Prescott? Have you talked to him?"

"We have written him a few letters, asking for better funding for Negro schools, in Atlanta and in the country. But I'm not holding my breath. Sometimes it's the ones who claim they're progressive who are the worst, because they act like they are the very boundary between the possible and the impossible, and they never let you cross them. Know what I mean?"

At which point Smith entered the den, smiled, extended his hand, and introduced himself to Timmons. Boggs briefly recapped what they'd been talking about.

"Oh yeah," Smith said. "I understand there's a girl who was involved in your group, Lily Ellsworth? Just moved to Atlanta from Peacedale. Very country."

It seemed to take Timmons a moment. "Oh yeah. Young girl, right?"

"Nineteen. Pretty, very light-skinned. New in town."

From the front parlor, a woman cried out and a glass shattered. Laughter.

"Yeah, that's right. Nathaniel's old student."

"Who's that?" Boggs asked.

"Nathaniel Hurst. He was her teacher out in Peacedale, said she was smart as a whip. She's exactly what I'm talking about, kind of kid who could really be something if only she was given the right tools. Lucky for her she winds up with a decent teacher, he opens her eyes, and she's off to better things. Nathaniel's an old classmate of mine, he's been helping our group out."

"He lives here now?" This was news. Lucius remembered Otis Ellsworth shaking his head angrily at some teacher who'd filled Lily's head with crazy ideas like equality and voting rights.

"Yeah, moved a few months ago maybe." Timmons stopped, as if he hadn't realized this was important information, or as if he hadn't meant to give it away. "How did you say you know Lily?"

"We don't, actually," Boggs answered. "She was murdered."

Timmons's face was fixed in place for a good second or two. Then his eyes widened, and his neck contracted a bit as he lowered his jaw, and he repeated the last word Lucius had said.

"Happened about two weeks ago. We were wondering if you might have heard anything."

"I don't— You mean . . . you're investigating a girl's murder?"

"Yes," Lucius said.

"You could have said that from the beginning!"

"We could have, you're right. There never seems to be a good way to say someone's been killed. Maybe we'll figure out how after a few more months. We'll probably get a lot of practice."

"Damn. But, why are you asking *me* about it?"

"We don't know much about her," Smith said. "One of the only things we know is she was reportedly very bright, she was new to Atlanta, and she was involved in this group of yours."

Timmons issued the kind of theatrical half laugh one does when someone else has the wrong idea and they're desperate to correct it. "I wouldn't say she was *involved*. I mean, she might have come to a meeting or two."

"Yet you remembered her name," Lucius said.

Timmons lowered his chin. "She was a very fine girl. Yes, I remember her. But I can hardly think of another thing about her, other than that Nathaniel had been her teacher."

"Tell us about him," Lucius asked.

"Morehouse man. Decided to use his degree to help poor kids out in the country, that's how he met her. But he never really took to the sticks, so he's back here. My impression is he left Peacedale because it was in his physical best interest to do so."

"He'd been threatened by somebody?" Smith asked.

"He never flat out said it, but . . . I had that impression."

"Or maybe he was following her here?"

"He's a married man."

Lucius rolled his eyes. "Oh, well in that case—"

"I can vouch for him. He is not that type."

What type? The type that might accidentally fall for a cute young thing who looks up to you and thanks you for opening her world? The type attracted to beautiful young women? Was Timmons too naïve, or was Boggs too cynical?

"And you've never had any contact with Congressman Prescott?" Lucius asked.

"No. Why, he dead, too?" An awkward laugh.

"She worked for him," Smith explained. "We figured, girl works as a maid to a congressman, she's part of some political group trying to get favors out of him, then she winds up dead. . . ."

Timmons's eyebrows shot way up. "We're not involved in anything that could get a girl *killed!*"

A middle-aged couple had been about to enter from the kitchen, behind Timmons, but on hearing these words they stopped, then turned around.

"Who has your group written these letters to?" Smith asked. "We'd love to get a list."

Timmons shook his head, appealing to Boggs. "Lucius, I'm sorry, but I'm not going to tell you everything we've done if it means that you're going to put the Police Department's nose in it."

"You had to know you'd make enemies," Lucius said. "There are plenty of folks who wouldn't agree with what you're doing, and a lot of them own guns."

"I just . . . I just don't believe that whatever happened to her could have anything to do with us."

By which he meant, he didn't *want* to believe that his group's politics might have put her at risk. He didn't want any guilt on his soul. Lucius knew the feeling.

"Okay," Lucius said. "Other than your group, did you ever have any reason to think she was mixed up in anything? Bad friends, loose morals, anything like that?"

Smith pressed, "She seem like the kind of girl who ran with white men?"

"Definitely not. She was corn bread pure, man. Wide-eyed and innocent."

An hour or so later the party was winding down, Smith was seducing the nineteen-year-old sister of Reginald's wife, and Lucius had escaped to the cooler air on the front porch. Distracted, he ran the known facts through his mind: *Prescott helps with the push for Negro cops, a little. He signals he may be more open to other Negro issues. His Negro maid is involved in a new, younger Negro rights group. She may or may not have talked to him about it. She may or may not have spied on him to report back to her allies. She may or may not have sent a suspicious amount of money home to her family. She later lists a brothel as her return address. She's spotted one night by me with a white ex-cop and a bruise on her face. She's shot and killed with a small-caliber gun, possibly that same night.*

"It's Officer Boggs!" boomed the unmistakable voice of Reverend King. "Put away the moonshine, everyone!"

He returned from his daydreaming and saw on the porch Reverend King from Ebenezer Baptist, Reverend Holmes Borders from Wheat Street, and John Wesley Dobbs, thirty-year veteran of the post office and Grand Master of the Prince Hall Masons, standing with his father by the small table that held their glasses. They seemed to have been looking over a sheet of paper they could barely read in the dark. These were some of the men who'd been instrumental in the push for registering Negro voters, Lucius knew, and though three of them were rivals for congregants, they were always working on some civic plan or another.

The others laughed and more good-natured ribbing ensued, comments about why wasn't he in uniform day and night if Satan never sleeps, and hey that's quite a scar there on your forehead, how's the other fellow look, and when are you going to get to drive a squad car?

The smiles had barely faded when the talk turned serious.

"We've been talking about the James Jameson situation," Reverend Holmes Borders said. "The community, as I'm sure you know, is very . . . concerned with how the Department has handled things."

Holmes Borders handed Lucius the sheet of paper. Lucius stepped back so enough light from the front parlor could seep through the window and make it legible. It was a letter addressed to Mayor Hartsfield, Congressman Prescott, and Herbert Jenkins, chief of the Atlanta Police Department, an allegedly reform-minded man who had acquiesced to the hiring of the colored officers and had even abolished the Klan-dominated police union a year ago (though Lucius had heard that an unofficial all-white union still existed). It remained to be seen how far such a man was willing to push such reforms, especially if another mayor should take office.

Lucius himself had proofread for his father many similarly officious letters over the years, their tone ranging from courteous to admonishing to outraged. This letter explained that the colored community was "extremely concerned" about the way the Department had handled the "homicidal apprehension" of Jameson, and noted that there were several "unanswered questions" that needed to be asked. The letter recommended a careful but widespread investigation. It requested some seats at that table. It was signed by these four community leaders, including Lucius's own father.

Lucius read the letter once and he read it again and still he stared at the page for a long while, too angry to reply.

"We were hoping you could deliver this to Chief Jenkins," Reverend King finally said.

"With my badge and gun?"

"I'm sorry?"

He looked up at them. "Why don't I just resign? Because that's what I may as well be doing if I handed him something like this."

The men all shifted on their feet, took their hands out of their pockets, crossed their arms.

"Son, let's not be so dramatic," his father said.

He tried to keep his voice calm. "You're asking me to throw a bomb at my employer."

"That's hardly a bomb," Holmes Borders said.

"We all respect what you're doing, Lucius," Reverend King said.

"Don't forget who helped you *get* that job," Dobbs snapped.

His father held out an appeasing hand. "Let's all talk this—"

"And now you want to take it away, Mr. Dobbs?" Lucius stared.

"We have been working *hard* for *years* to make things better—" Holmes Borders started.

"I realize that."

"Son, don't interrupt the man."

"But just because we finally have some colored men in uniform doesn't mean we're going to look the other way when the city pulls something like this."

Lucius tried to sound reasonable as he explained, "I didn't like Jameson's trial any more than you did, but it happened two years ago and there's nothing any of us can do about it. Him busting out and getting shot, though, there's nothing *abusive* about that. He was an escaped convict and he had a gun."

"He was shot in the back, I heard," Holmes Borders said.

"They tortured his sister."

Lucius shook the letter. "This is not the right battle to fight, gentlemen. I've seen plenty you wouldn't like and plenty that might deserve a letter, believe me, but Triple James getting himself killed is not one of them."

"*Triple James,* huh?" Reverend Holmes Borders shook his head. "So they got you thinking like they do already."

"I know how to think, Reverend. I respect all that you've done to get me where I am, but that doesn't mean I'm going to let you use me as some pawn between you and the chief and the mayor." He looked at his father. "I'm no one's sacrificial lamb."

"You watch your tone." His father was very still.

Lucius paused. The angrier he let himself become, the more likely they were to see him as some petulant, ungrateful child. Yet his anger was too great to contain.

"None of you have *any* idea what it's like. If you send this, all it will do is tighten the vise on me and the others. There are some of us, and you do *not* repeat this, there are some of us who might quit any day now. How do you think that will go over?"

"This is about more than eight officers," Reverend Holmes Borders said.

"You think we don't know that?" Did they think he'd be all too happy to act as their middleman, their spy into the white power structure? Or, worse, were they jealous to realize that the authority they'd built up over the years had not only crested but been transferred to the eight cops, these undeserving young men, and now the community leaders had to reassert themselves? "You think that hasn't occurred to us? You think we don't realize how important *everything* we do is?"

He dropped the letter, and the overhead fan accelerated its downward journey to the table, where it instantly stuck to the circle of condensation where someone's glass had been. The reverends and Mr. Dobbs were all watching that circle spread as Lucius walked off.

He needed to get away, and the house wasn't far enough, was too full of people, so he walked straight through every room and to the backyard. He was alone, or thought he was for the first minute or two, until his anger and self-possession faded enough for him to see the slender figure standing against the lone maple twenty feet away, smoking a cigarette with the aid of a narrow holder.

"Are you writing anymore, Lucius?" Percy asked.

Lucius walked closer to the silhouette. "I don't really have the time these days."

"So your new sword is mightier than your pen. That's a shame. You have a talent. Or perhaps I should use the past tense?"

"I didn't say I've given up on it. I just . . . need to spend all my time learning about policing these days. If I go a few weeks without writing anything, that's okay, I'll still live. But if I've got my head in the clouds while I'm walking the beat, maybe I won't."

Lord, what an evening. And the whole reason for the party was to bid farewell to one of his cousins, a young man who had decided to flee Atlanta and all the Boggs family had built, for the uncertainty of Chicago. The cousin had been rousted by white cops downtown a few months back, right before Lucius had joined the force, and had apparently made up his mind then to leave the South. Earlier tonight Lucius had asked him to stay, had promised him things were getting better. His cousin had replied, *I'm happy for you, but no matter what job you get for yourself down here, we're still just* niggers *to them.* The words were still ringing in Lucius's ears. *No matter how many college graduates and Negro-owned companies we get in Sweet Auburn, they'll still just call it* Darktown. *Half the people at this party haven't been downtown in years. They stay in this neighborhood, where they can fool themselves into thinking they have all they need, and don't dare wander out where they'll get knocked down another peg. So what's wrong with me looking for something better up north?*

Lucius had no answer. Just that afternoon, he had manned a complicated phone tree to see which car-owning relatives could offer rides to which great-aunts and -uncles to Terminal Station tomorrow to see the cousin off. None of his relatives wanted to take a downtown bus. Auburn Avenue was a private world they and their forbears had been cultivating for decades, since even before the horrible riot of '06. It was a protective bubble keeping them safe from the rest of the city, the South, America. They were the lucky few who could afford not to venture into those lands.

"How can you *stand* it here, Lucius?" Percy asked, reading his mind. "The looks on the street. The insanity. They're all mad here. We defeated the Fascists in Europe, yet here they rule."

"It's getting better," he said, repeating the empty promise he'd made to his cousin.

Percy coughed out a laugh, complete with a cloud of smoke. After he'd recovered, he asked, "Have you seen *The Big Sleep,* or *The Maltese Falcon?*"

"I read the books." The films had shown only briefly at Bailey's, the only theater on Auburn. They had played longer downtown, but Lucius would not subject himself to the colored balconies.

"Chandler and Hammett. Brilliant men. They write about detectives and police officers, so perhaps you'll find some truth there. Their heroes are good men who discover that their environments are far darker than they'd realized. Grand conspiracies afoot. But I look at you, Officer Lucius, and I can't imagine a darker place for you. You won't be the gumshoe who discovers to his horror that he's in a corrupt world, because you already know it. The evil is so garishly on display here, there's no mystery to it. It is sunning itself before us, and it will strike if you dare approach it."

Percy dropped his cigarette on the ground and stamped it.

"I suppose that living here all the time makes me tolerate it a bit better," Lucius said. "I've built up antibodies."

Percy grabbed him by both shoulders. Even in the darkness, their faces were close enough for Lucius to see the red in his uncle's eyes.

"You need to bleed those antibodies from your veins, Lucius. Understand me? *Bleed* them from your *veins.*"

22

WHAT'S YOUR STORY, *Underhill? What were you doing with Lily Ells-worth?*

Rake wondered this while he tailed the man late one night. He'd been staking out his apartment for barely half an hour when, at 11:30, Underhill emerged and walked to his car. Short-sleeved shirt, khakis, straw hat. Rake followed.

You're an ex-cop yet you're now a pimp? You steal girls from Mama Dove to meet the whims of clientele who don't want to be seen going into Dark-town. What else do you do? And once you take the girls from her, where do they go? Some other brothel? Or something worse? He wasn't sure whether he was on the verge of discovering some horrific conspiracy to steal, abuse, and kill colored girls, or whether such things happened all the time here, without need of any hidden machinations, and he'd been too naïve to realize it.

He needed to know more about Underhill. The man clearly had skeletons in his closet, though Rake always preferred the grislier German turn of phrase, *Eine Leiche im Keller haben.* Having a corpse in the basement.

They went south on Pryor, driving away from downtown and into the residential district of Mechanicsville, silent at that hour, all the factory workers exhausted. Rake had to hang back a ways, as there was so little traffic here he was afraid he'd be spotted.

He wondered whether he was doing this at least partially to get his mind off other things. Such as his brother-in-law, Dale. Cassie had warned him that morning that Dale had called for him, the third time in the last few days. Rake didn't want to hear about whatever nonsense complaint or damnfool errand Dale was thinking about performing. He was certain—*certain*—that his brother-in-law at least knew something about the bricks that had been thrown through their Negro neighbor's windows. In fact, the day after that incident was the first time Dale phoned to leave a message for Rake to call him back. A confession? More likely he wanted to know if Rake knew whether their new Negro neighbor, Calvin, had gone to the cops, though of course the odds of that were slim. Dale probably also wanted to know if Rake had changed his mind and wanted to lend his expertise to whatever escalation Dale was planning.

Up over a hill and then down again, into Pittsburgh, a colored district. They passed rows of bungalows where Rake spotted more than a few Negroes lying on their front porches in the vain hope that it would be less suffocatingly hot out there.

After Underhill took a third turn in less than five minutes, Rake began to wonder if he'd been spotted. The man was varying his speed, which Rake didn't recall him doing before. Maybe Rake was overthinking, maybe he was just desperate for something of note to occur. Or maybe he was a fool to be following a veteran ex-cop, and through such a quiet area no less. Maybe he was making yet another rookie mistake.

Earlier that day Rake had hiked Kennesaw Mountain with his father. For as long as he could remember, the trek had been an annual tradition for him, his brother Curtis, and their father. Always in the summer, when the air was so thick that they were bathed in sweat before they'd been climbing ten minutes. The battle back in 1864 had taken place in late June into early July, so Colson had felt it necessary that his sons experience what their great-great-grandfather had, at least climatologically. The malarial heat, the mosquitoes, the sense that things were only going to get worse. Once when they were kids, Curtis had complained about the hike, their father's pace, the blisters on his sore feet from his sweaty socks. So Colson had made the boy take off his shoes and complete the climb barefoot, as a lesson against further whining. *Your great-great-granddaddy went without shoes most of those weeks, you can try it for a couple of hours.*

Today the mountain had been the same as it had been in Rake's youth, the same as it had been for those troops and for the Cherokee before them. The spiked pods of sweetgum trees still littered the ground. The wet earth was still soft beneath their shoes. The mottled bark of pines, armored like alligator skin, still rose high all around them. The canopy still protected them from the worst of the sun, though they knew the sun was out there, patiently waiting for them to reach the top.

Rake had been amazed by how much he missed the South while at war. Even the crushing heat. Even the sharp pain of a yellow jacket sting. Even the sight of bread gone moldy in a pantry that hadn't been kept cool enough. Even the orange tint of kids' bare feet playing in a clay lot. Even the way the ground disappeared from view when so many shrubs and vines grew out of the earth. The thick overwhelming ripeness of the South, the sheer three-dimensionality, the way it grew everywhere and anywhere, vibrant and unstoppable. The beauty of the tulips in March and azaleas in April and the many-hued leaves of November. Even the suffocating humidity of a summer day like this.

Rake hadn't expected the ribbing he received in training camp, the Yankees laughing at his accent and marveling at some of his expressions. They asked if he knew how to tie shoes, did he use toilet paper. Called him "cracker" and "hick." And these were the ones who were being friendly. Then there was the drill sergeant who insisted they sing "Marching into Georgia" when they ran, and the New Yorkers who asked to see his KKK card and inquired whether he was a Grand Dragon or a Grand Wizard or a Grand Elf. He'd never felt such Southern pride as he did when fighting back at those Northerners and their indecipherably hard consonants, and despite the fact that he was miles from home, he felt a closer kinship with his father and departed grandfather, always so quick to denigrate Yankees for the way they belittled the proud old Confederacy.

Still, the annual hike up Kennesaw—the long slogs in memory of the Lost Cause—seemed irrevocably changed due to Rake's time in Europe. Fighting one's own war will do that. The bitter, cleansing tang of past sufferings no longer seemed in need of remembrance when one's own wounds were relatively fresh. He had tired of seeing Old Glory waving over wrecked battlefields in Europe, so he had little taste for seeing the Stars and Bars on this or any other formerly hallowed ground. The soldier in him couldn't even appreciate the ancient battle of Kennesaw Mountain anymore. Most textbooks described it as a victory for the South, as it slowed Sherman's march and forced him to retreat. But Sherman had kept on marching, simply taking a wider tack to Atlanta and the sea. Praising this as a glorious last stand seemed rather like an ex-pitcher regaling people with stories of an impressive strikeout but failing to mention the fact that the next batter had swatted a game-winning homer.

Rake had thought about asking his father's advice about how to handle Dale, and even what to do about Dunlow, but he'd held his tongue. He'd focused instead on climbing the mountain, pacing himself so the old man could keep up.

It was nearly midnight when Underhill headed northwest on Newnan Street, recrossing the invisible color line into a white area and then, half a mile later, turning onto a gravel drive. Rake continued past the drive, glancing at the cloud of dirt just visible in the dark. Underhill was driving into an old foundry, which had closed down two years ago. It had made railroad cars and engines, he recalled, but hadn't been used for anything in a while. What the hell was Underhill doing here?

Rake pulled over. He opened his glove box and removed his revolver, putting it in his pocket.

He hurried in the direction where Underhill's car had disappeared, avoiding the gravel and finding enough dirt and grass to keep his footfalls silent.

The foundry itself was three blocks long and as tall as a five-story building, most of its windows still intact. Its very size and dormancy put him in mind of the destroyed or abandoned factories and munitions plants—and in some cases entire towns—he'd seen in Germany. Some of the surrounding light poles were still lit, probably on the city's dime to make this place less appealing to those searching for late-night terrain to ply illicit wares. This wasn't Rake's beat but he was willing to bet a squad car made a point of driving around here at least a couple of times a night.

Rake walked alongside the building, hoping to stay invisible. He was more certain than ever that Underhill had deliberately been taking a circuitous route to get here. He was meeting someone, and for all Rake knew the someone was already here.

He stopped at a corner of the building. Twenty yards away, Underhill was walking up a two-flight fire escape, then across a long gangway from the main foundry building to a smaller one, his steps loud on the grating. Then he opened a steel door and closed it behind him.

Rake hurried after, gun in hand now, though when he made it to the gangway he slowed down again, mindful of the racket Underhill's feet had made and not wanting to repeat it. He looked behind him and below him, though there weren't enough lights for him to see very far.

Rake put his hand on the knob, which was so rusted he wasn't sure it would turn—or did he just need to push it open? It did turn. He could feel flakes of rust adhering to his palm as he turned the knob slowly, then applied pressure to the door, hoping it wouldn't make as much noise as it had when Underhill had walked through.

He realized it was a mistake before he'd even taken a step. Beyond the door, all was pitch black. He'd taken only one step inside when he felt a blow at the back of his head.

He wasn't sure if he remembered falling, but he was definitely on his ass now.

The part of his head that had been hit was leaning against the door, but he couldn't feel the door, at least not yet, because he felt numb. He tried to steady himself with a hand on the floor, but then the sole of a large black shoe appeared. He could make it out only because a trace amount of light was coming into the room from outside. He could see the shoe coming, inch by inch, but his body was curiously unable to do anything about it.

The sole pressed into his clavicle and pushed him flat on the floor.

The shoe stepped back into the darkness, and now what Rake saw was a gun.

He sat up, much more slowly than he was trying to, and Underhill's body began to materialize around the gun.

"Don't move."

Rake obeyed. He was sitting up now, but there was nothing behind him and he wondered if Underhill would kick him down again. He'd dropped his gun and wondered where it was.

The numbness was already being replaced by a throbbing pain in the back of his head and a pang of nausea in his gut.

He barely had time to think *Already the second time I've had a gun on me from close up* before Underhill leaned down, gun nearly in Rake's face, and patted Rake's pants pockets and his ankles in search of a weapon.

"You got another one? Roll over and keep your hands high."

Rake grudgingly did so, and then he felt Underhill searching for a weapon at the small of his back. Then Rake turned, sitting up again.

Underhill leaned back in the doorframe, enough light on him that Rake could study the man's expression. He hadn't shaved that day, and maybe not the day before either. He had a wart on the left side of his neck, which Rake remembered from the detailed physical description in his file. Like Dunlow, the man had a gut on him, but not as much of one, and he wasn't as tall. His straw hat was pushed back a bit, the brim not shielding his eyes from view. Rake's revolver was tucked into the ex-cop's belt.

Underhill was studying Rake, too, from a decidedly more comfortable vantage point. His face was alarmingly blank, like he was weighing pros and cons in his head.

"You're pointing your gun at a cop," Rake said, and he knew it sounded weak even as he spoke it.

"Big deal. *I'm* a cop."

"You *were* a cop."

"Really." The hint of a smile. "You so sure about that?"

Rake looked to his sides, wondering if there was anything he could grab and throw.

"Don't even think about it," Underhill said. Another pause as he assessed his prey. "They don't seem to teach surveillance so well anymore."

"I skipped that class. In favor of the one about how not to be a dirty cop."

"Oh yeah. One of them new classes. Didn't have those when I was a rookie."

"So I've heard."

"And what else have you heard?"

Rake wondered what the man was really asking. "I assume you recognize me."

"Remind me."

"That's right, you were fairly in the bag that night. When we pulled you over, the night you had Lily Ellsworth with you."

Underhill's expression was maddeningly difficult to read. Rake wondered, did the man have a particularly good poker face or was Rake just bad at this?

"And who might that be?"

"Come on. You got me sitting on the floor, you could at least have the dignity not to lie to my face. Let's do this like men at least."

Underhill chuckled. "You are an inscrutable little one, ain't ya?"

"She was in your car, with a bruise on her lip. Then you hit her again and she ran off. Dunlow pulls you over, lets you off with nothing but a slap on your wrist. That same night, she's shot."

"With a .22," Underhill said. "This look like a .22 to you?"

No, this was a .45 that was staring Rake in the face. Underhill seemed so insulted by the suggestion he might fire a ladylike weapon that he'd dropped his poker face, at least temporarily.

"How'd you know it was a .22?" Rake asked.

"Got friends in high places. Which oughta make you far more wary than you appear to be."

Rake sat up taller, partly because he wasn't comfortable and partly to see how much movement Underhill was prepared to let him get away with.

"So who was she?" He tucked his feet beneath his ass so that he was kneeling. It was awkward and would be painful if he stayed that way for long.

"You think you're conducting an interrogation here, son?"

"Who was she?"

Underhill laughed. This seemed to entertain him greatly. "She was a nigger."

"And."

"And you are exhausting my patience."

"You were sweet on her, but she didn't go for the older, portly types, and so—"

Underhill's foot moved quite a bit more quickly than it had before, but this time Rake was expecting it. He leaned to his right and the foot struck his side, rather than his stomach. Before that blow had even landed, though, Rake had straightened his legs, springing upward and driving a fist into Underhill's groin.

Rake heard the gun land but couldn't see it, as Underhill had nearly fallen over and was leaning on him now, his bulk pressing Rake's head into the wall. Rake swung twice with his left, hitting Underhill in what he thought was the stomach. It was almost like hitting a heavy bag, he was that big and solid. But deflating fast. Underhill stumbled, one knee hitting the ground. Rake pushed him with one hand and with the other he reached for the revolver in Underhill's belt. He had it in his hand now, but then Underhill batted at it and it hit the floor.

The two of them squared off, both of them standing on the landing outside the dark room—Rake still had no idea what was in there. They kept their eyes mostly on each other, but each glanced down at the ground occasionally, looking for the two guns.

Rake saw one first.

It was Underhill's, and it was no more than two feet to his right, just at the edge of the landing. Without fully thinking this through, he stepped forward and kicked it off the landing. He heard it clatter against the wall, then land in something wet.

"You son of a *bitch!*" Underhill yelled.

"You sure you want to do this, old man?" Rake asked, his fists at the ready. "You were smart enough not to shoot a cop. You smart enough to walk away?"

Apparently not. Underhill again showed that he was more spry and agile than his bulk would suggest, feigning with a right and then delivering a near-perfect jab to Rake's face. A fraction of an inch more centered and it would have broken his nose, but it still stung. Rake's right eye blinked a few times, watering despite himself, rendering him half blind.

Underhill stepped in to take advantage, but he was such an immense target that Rake landed two blows of his own, then the ex-cop staggered back. Underhill was leaning against the guardrail and seemed unsteady on his feet. His hat had fallen off somewhere along the way.

"*What* in the *hell* do you think you're *doing*, son? You ain't a detective. You're Dunlow's goddamn partner! You looking to dig an early grave?"

"You're not gonna put me there, old man."

"It doesn't have to be *me* that does it, son. You're making one hell of a mistake."

"Why? Tell me what I'm doing wrong. Explain to me how I'm putting myself in danger by asking an old ex-cop questions. Connect some goddamn dots for me."

"If you think I'm gonna spill everything to some college-boy rookie, you're damned mistaken." Underhill paused for a moment, as if hoping that's all he needed to say. "We can go ten rounds if you like, and we'll see how many teeth either of us have left, but you won't know a lick more than you do now. You'll only have a hell of a lot of injuries that you'll have to explain to your sergeant tomorrow."

Rake sorely wanted to hit the bastard again. The adrenaline was blasting through his veins with such ferocity he would have hit a *wall* if he had to. But what Underhill was saying had the unfortunate ring of truth.

Rake lowered his fists and stood taller, though he watched his adversary carefully. Underhill didn't look like he was in any condition to go even half a round, but he'd gotten the drop on Rake twice already, and Rake wasn't going to be thrice fooled.

Rake shifted to his side and felt something under his foot—his gun, most likely. He kept his foot there and tried not to give away his discovery.

"Glory be," Underhill exhaled, leaning over now, hands on his knees. It had been impressive how he'd managed to battle through that blow to the jewels, Rake thought. The big ox was able to endure a hell of a lot of pain. "I don't envy Dunlow one bit having to put up with the likes of you."

Rake wondered if he'd made a mistake, if he should have beaten Underhill until more secrets spilled. Or he could pick up his gun and threaten him. But even if Rake wasn't a detective, he was a cop, and even if Underhill was a former officer, he was a civilian, and the thought of beating up a man just to prove a point would have meant he was no better than his damned partner.

So if a beating wouldn't work, he would go for the tried and true method of insulting a Southerner and forcing him to verbally defend himself: "You got kicked off the force for running numbers, yet you like to kid yourself that you still have friends in high places. You're an old fat man with no pension, living in the past."

"You and damned Dunlow can issue all the traffic citations you want. Go lock up some drunk niggers, too." He tapped himself in the heart. "It's *us* that gets called in for the tough jobs."

"Yeah, you're a big man." Rake still had no idea what he was talking about. "I'll be seeing you around." He motioned for Underhill to head down the stairs first.

Underhill walked slowly. Rake bent down and put his gun in his pocket, then followed a few paces behind.

At the ground level, Underhill walked over the ledge, which apparently was where his gun had disappeared. "That was a damn fine gun you just got rid of," he said.

"Frightfully sorry about that."

The triumphant feeling seemed to fade with every step as Rake walked back through the lot, over the hill, and to his car. His head was throbbing worse than before, and he felt a bit dizzy, either from that first blow or the punch to his face. What felt worse was the realization of what Underhill had revealed. That he still thought of himself as a cop, or close to it. What had he meant by "tough jobs"? And he'd distinctly said "us"—"it's *us* that gets called in for the tough jobs"—so who was us? Underhill and Dunlow, or some larger group? It could have all been bluster, but the fact that Underhill knew the murder weapon was doubly troubling; either he had pulled the trigger, or had been involved, or was somehow privy to inside information.

He leaned against his car, waiting for the wooziness to pass. He wondered how bad he looked, and how much worse he might look in the morning.

Then he heard the shots.

Two of them, close together, but definitely not an echo, because he picked up a distinct, slight echo from each. Coming from the very place he'd just left.

He sprinted as fast as he could, his heart pounding and his stomach very much not in favor of this much activity after that blow to his head. He ran with the flashlight off, not wanting to expose himself to the shooter. He couldn't see very well but at least they couldn't see him.

He stopped at a corner, slowly peered around it, aimed his gun at darkness. He didn't see anyone else moving, didn't hear anything. Then he saw Underhill not far from where he'd been when Rake had left. Before he'd been on his hands and knees, looking for his fallen weapon. He was still on the ground, but this time he was on his back, one knee raised but the rest of him flat.

Rake spun around, calling out "Police!" and demanding that some-one come out. But someone did not reply. He was acutely aware of the fact that he was out in the open, and if someone had taken Underhill down with a rifle, he would be next. From the distance he'd been unable to determine if it had been a pistol or a rifle shot. His flashlight revealed nothing but old metal and dirt and decay and rust.

Then he heard something, small and far away, and he only realized it was a car door shutting when he heard the engine. Coming from the other side of the building, the sound fading already.

He walked over to Underhill and crouched down. A bruise was forming on his cheekbone from one of the punches Rake had landed. What was far more noticeable was the red chest and two gunshot wounds, the blood everywhere. Rake stood back up and looked at the blood on the ground, tried to make sense of it, and quickly. If someone had shot Underhill with a rifle, if an ambush had been set up along one of the catwalks or some other spot on this vast building, then there likely would have been a longer blood trail. And Underhill would have fallen differently, staggered. No, someone had shot the man from up close.

Shit, shit, shit. Could Rake call this in? Could he explain his presence here?

He looked at his knuckles. They weren't bad. They wouldn't look so bad tomorrow. He thought. He hoped.

His footprints? He beamed the ground again, checking the gravel where he'd walked. The ground was dry and he didn't think he'd left be-hind any tracks, nothing a plaster could be taken of, nothing to provide an investigator with even a guess as to what his size was. Of course, he also couldn't tell what size shoes the killer had worn, or even how many men there had been.

His heart was pounding but his hands were steady. He knew that he needed to make a decision, needed to do so now, and that whatever he decided would likely determine the next few weeks, or months, or years of his life.

"Us," Underhill had said. With such confidence. The calmness of knowing you're part of a group, that they had your back. Rake had felt that, too, during the war, but here on the force he felt the opposite, that his fellow officers were ready to drive the dagger into his spine.

Rake hurried back to his car, beaming behind himself again to make sure he hadn't dropped anything. He got in the car and closed the door. He drove home taking a circuitous route, checking behind himself, careful not to drive by any busy locations where any businesses might remember him.

Cassie was sound asleep in her bed, as were the kids. Rake washed his hands, the cuts on his knuckles stinging, before sitting down on his couch in a dark living room to think.

23

"ARE YOU STILL interested in that fellow you were asking about the other day? Underhill?"

Boggs had been filling out paperwork at his desk when the phone rang. It was the unseen woman in Records, the second one, who had called him back and actually helped him.

"Yes."

"Well, he's dead." Her voice, as before, was hushed. She was talking quietly while her colleagues were away from their desks.

"What happened?"

"Got the report right here. Officers Delroy and Reardon came upon the body at 12:31 a.m. Just filed their report a little bit ago. Shot twice, close range, small caliber. His body appeared to have been there for at least twenty-four hours, it says. Morgue's still working on it."

He asked her for the location, scribbling it down with the nearest pencil, then reaching for a street atlas. He didn't know the area well—it was a white part of town, blue collar.

"Body was found at a factory that's been closed a while," she said. "We make a few busts there most weeks, some reefer peddlers and prostitutes, and the occasional moonshine drop-off."

"Wonder what a guy like him would be doing out there."

"They're working on it, I can assure you. That last murder you were calling about, the colored girl? They could care less about that. An ex-cop is different."

He was amazed she was calling him with this, or with anything. And the fact that she referred to Lily as "colored" rather than the more derogatory "black" did not escape his notice.

"What else can you tell me about him?" he asked. "You mentioned he was forced out last time."

She told him how Underhill was one of the cops fired for being involved in running numbers.

"Do you know if he's still friendly with any officers today?"

"Hell, in this city you're a cop for life, even if you lose the job. I'm sure he has plenty of friends over here. Which is why you should be mighty careful if you're thinking what I think you're thinking." She let that sink in for a moment. "You should be able to ask your commanding officer for updates on his case if you want them. But if he stonewalls you, give me a ring."

"Thank you very much for calling me, ma'am. I appreciate it."

"We aren't all against you, you know."

"Thank you."

"Well, most of us are, I guess. But there's more of us for you than you'd probably think. We just can't advertise it."

"I understand." He didn't, not really.

"Anything else you want to know?"

"Yes, one thing." He took a breath. "Is there really a pool among the white cops, to have one of us killed?"

A pause. "Wish I could tell you otherwise, but yes."

"I appreciate your honesty."

"I mean, it isn't a literal pool as in an actual collection of dollars that they've passed around to give to the guy who finally decides to put a bullet in one of you. But it's real in the sense that people do talk about it a lot."

"And if people talk about something, then it must be real."

He could hear her smiling when she said, "Don't be smart, Officer Boggs."

He was smiling, too, when he hung up. So much so that he didn't remember until a few hours later that, the first time they had spoken, he had called simply to ask for the arrest history of Brian Underhill. He hadn't said anything whatsoever about Lily Ellsworth that time. Yet today she had noted that his earlier call had been about "that colored girl" who'd been killed.

So how did she know that when he'd called about Underhill, it was to look into Lily's murder?

The next day, Boggs stood waiting for his partner in the vast shadow of a magnolia tree in the Fourth Ward. Three little kids were climbing on the tree's thick branches, one of which was only a few feet off the ground and extended parallel for a good fifteen feet before suddenly plunging into the earth and emerging a meter away like some sea serpent turned arboreal.

It was that kind of late-afternoon hot that would only get hotter up until the moment the sun disappeared, the dampness in the air thickening nearly to the point of suffocation. Dark was still many hours off when Smith approached and they walked toward the home of Lily Ellsworth's former teacher. Boggs had visited the previous day and had been told by a pretty young woman that her husband wasn't in.

The narrow bungalow was in need of a paint job but Boggs had certainly seen worse. The garden was well maintained, thickets of seven-foot-tall brandy-wine canna flanking the house, their tropical leaves like wings and their red flowers like dragon's faces, jaws agape at the sun. Below them pink-veined caladium leaves, large as elephant ears, hung limp in the still air. The bungalow's windows were open, the sound of an electric fan whirring inside. This was a neighborhood they walked on their beat, but they seldom had reason to enter any of these homes except to take down robbery reports. The families here had decent jobs, and their accumulating possessions attracted thieves.

Boggs knocked on the door. Two hours before roll call, they were both in civilian dress.

The door was answered by the same woman as before: pretty and slight, eyes warm and round as chocolates. Bags under the eyes, though: the first time she'd had a little toddler with her, and this time she was holding a sleeping infant.

"Afternoon, Mrs. Hurst. Is your husband around?"

He'd not told her he was a cop yesterday, opting instead to lie and say he was an old friend from Morehouse. Not because he necessarily thought the man was a suspect, but still, he didn't see any reason to leave advance notice that a policeman was coming by. She had said her husband was at work, teaching summer school, and that late afternoons were best, so here they were. She didn't look suspicious to see him back again, and with another man this time. Maybe she was just too tired to be suspicious. She said she'd get her husband, the screen door snapping behind her.

Smith raised his eyebrows the way he always did after spying a good-looking woman.

The screen door opened again. Nathaniel Hurst was a tall man, two inches on Boggs and one on Smith. He looked the part of the teacher, thin and with glasses, his shoulders hunched forward a bit, as if he was used to lowering himself to reach his students. His forehead was shiny and his red plaid shirt was opened one more button than would be socially acceptable if it weren't so ungodly hot.

"Afternoon, gentlemen. Can I help you?"

Boggs extended a hand. "My name is Officer Lucius Boggs, Mr. Hurst." Hurst's hand greeted Boggs's after a two-second pause. "This is my partner, Tommy Smith."

Another handshake, and Hurst, taking them in now, unhunched his shoulders and grew an inch.

"We were hoping to ask you a few questions."

He said fine and motioned them to sit in the old wooden chairs on the cramped cement porch. "It's even hotter inside," he said, as if to excuse what could have been seen as a lack of hospitality.

Smith, rather than joining them on the chairs, chose to stand and lean against the porch railing, looking down at the teacher. Wasps as orange as tangerines zipped past.

"What can I help you with?"

The chairs were low to the ground, so Boggs's elbows were on his knees, his hands folded as he said, "We're looking into the murder of a former student of yours. Lily Ellsworth."

The teacher nodded, his expression appropriately somber. "Yes."

Smith asked, "You knew she was dead?"

"It was in the *Daily Times* a couple of days ago. I was . . . shocked. I still am. She . . . She was a very sweet young woman."

Boggs took out a small notebook and pencil and asked, "What else can you tell us about her?"

"Well, as you apparently know, I taught her in Peacedale. For a number of years. She was probably, I don't know, twelve when I met her? Could hardly read, like the other kids that age over there. I was the new teacher, just a year or two out of Morehouse, and I taught her for, I guess it was five years."

"So until about a year ago?" Boggs asked.

"That sounds about right."

Boggs wrote that down, and only mentally noted the fact that Hurst seemed to be saying "about" and "I guess" more than an educated man like him probably did in normal conversation.

Boggs asked more questions and heard what he'd already been told elsewhere, that Lily had moved to Atlanta because she tired of the limitations country life put on her. And no, I'm sorry, I don't really know who her friends were, don't know with whom she'd been consorting in her last days.

"When was the last time you saw her?"

"I don't know. It might have been . . . three months ago."

"At a Racial Cooperative Council meeting?"

He looked surprised. "Yes."

"What exactly was she helping you with?"

Hurst rearranged himself in his chair. They were pretty damn uncomfortable, Boggs had noticed. "We drafted a lot of letters. Petitions to elected officials, letters to other groups with whom we wanted to develop a relationship. Some outreach to Negro high schools and colleges. The kind of slow drudgery that some people have to undertake in hopes that it leads to something greater."

Boggs found it odd how everyone described the group in such boring terms. *Nothing to see here.*

"What brought you to Atlanta?" Smith asked.

"I was tired of the country myself. I went out there because I wanted to help kids, kids like Lily. And I feel that I did. Again, that girl could not read at an age when she was already starting to turn into a woman, and I opened the world for her, and for many others. At least, that's what I'd tell myself after really bad days when I wondered why I bothered. I did it for a few years. It was rewarding in some ways, but it was also grinding me down."

"Yet you're doing the same thing here, teaching?" Boggs asked.

"I got a job at Booker T., yes. That, too, has its challenges, but at least I get to live in Atlanta."

"So you and Lily moved here at about the same time."

"If we did, that's just a random coincidence. My wife and I left Peacedale a year ago, moved up to Macon, but after only a few months we decided to come back to Atlanta. I hadn't been in touch with Lily that last year, and only after she made it to Atlanta did I meet her again, at one of the Council meetings. I was very surprised to see her there, but also, honestly, flattered."

"What do you mean?" Boggs asked.

"My teaching had given her a political spirit—I'd seen that in Peacedale. And then to see her come to a political gathering here, it meant something to me. I was proud of her."

And proud of yourself, Boggs thought. His attention was diverted by a small lizard darting out of the tall grass past the opposite end of the porch. He looked back at Hurst. "What can you tell me about her family?"

"Not much. I only met them once or twice. Farm family. Sharecroppers. The conditions for our people there are not good. Again, I tried to help, but . . ." He shook his head.

"Her father gave the impression he didn't like you," Smith pressed. "Said you put all sorts of ideas in her head. Made her leave her family."

Hurst slowly took in some breath and leaned back, palms flat on his thighs. "I suppose it would look that way to an uneducated man. And yes, I suppose if I'd never taught in that school, Lily would still be illiterate, and milking someone's cows, and be pregnant and poor. And, I suppose, alive."

Boggs wanted to pause before asking another question, to see if those emotions would build, but his partner felt otherwise. Smith asked, "What did she think of the congressman?"

"Which one?"

"The one she worked for."

"That—oh, yes, that's right. Prescott. I don't know if she ever met him."

Alarms were blaring in Boggs's skull. He could tell by the way Smith slightly leaned back that his partner heard it, too, the completely false way in which the teacher had pretended to not remember and then remember something, the very thing he wished these officers had not mentioned.

"What did she tell you about working there?" Boggs asked.

"Nothing. I mean, I recall her mentioning that she worked as a maid for his wife. But I didn't exactly ask her for details about being a housekeeper. I assume it's rather dull." And to complete the fake act he grinned a bit, as if this were a joke now, three men rolling their eyes about the tediousness of women's work, as if they'd forget why they were here.

"You're absolutely sure she never mentioned anything else about working there?" Boggs asked. An obvious lifeline tossed to a man who was perhaps now realizing he was at risk of drowning.

Hurst wouldn't take the lifeline. "I'm sorry. And I'm afraid I'll be in trouble with the wife if I don't head back in and help feed the little one."

Hurst stood, as did Boggs, but Smith kept leaning against the porch railing.

"You were sweet on her, weren't you?" Smith said with a slight grin.

Hurst stiffened. "Excuse me?"

"You heard me."

"What are you trying to imply, Officer?"

"I don't think I implied anything, I think I stated it awful clear. Or should I go ask your wife?"

Hurst had appeared quite bookish before, but now a fire was lit in him, and Boggs saw him differently, catching a glimpse the way some women might see him, a tall and handsome man with a strong jaw and hands that were ready to do things.

Hurst said to Smith, "Are you threatening me?"

Boggs felt great envy at how Smith could appear so utterly cool in the face of someone who looked like he was ready to take a swing at him.

"Mr. Hurst"—Smith was still casually leaning against the railing— "are we wearing our uniforms right now? Did we park a squad car right there on the street for your landlady to see? Have we been unfriendly? Are you wearing handcuffs?" He let those images linger for a moment. "We could have done this different, but we were hoping you'd help us out. We were hoping you'd cooperate. Now, if you don't, and if we decide there *are* things you aren't telling us, then there *will* be uniforms, and there *will* be a squad car, and there *will* be handcuffs. But we wouldn't be the ones putting them on you. It would be white cops. Cops that *we ourselves* don't even like."

Hurst shifted his eyes between them for what felt like a very long time. Long enough for a car to drive past, long enough for the baby inside to start crying for one reason or another.

"You think I haven't been forthcoming with you. I can assure you, I had nothing to do with whatever happened to her."

Boggs asked, "What is it that happened to her?"

Boggs may have been mistaken—the moment felt so charged and his own emotions were swirling now—but it seemed as if Hurst was on the verge of tears.

"I respect that young lady too much," Hurst finally said, "to say another word to you about her."

Without bidding them good day or wishing them luck in catching her killer, he opened the screen door and left them there.

They waited a moment, then left. They walked along the west side of the street to stay in the shade.

"That was a stab in the dark," Smith said, "but damn if I didn't hit something."

"You hit something, all right. But do you think they had an affair, or he only *wanted* to have an affair with her? Or something else?" Asking half because he wasn't sure and half because he knew Smith had vastly more experience with affairs.

"I don't know. But we'd best keep our eye on that boy."

A few steps later, Boggs said, "He wasn't talking like she'd done something wrong. More like she'd done something shameful."

"Or something shameful been done to her."

Less than an hour later, after roll call, McInnis called them into his office. They avoided the temptation of glancing at each other guiltily. Yet each said a silent prayer.

McInnis sat down at his desk, sighed, and waved a file folder at them before dropping it on his desk. "Since you seemed so interested in it, I thought I'd let you know the Ellsworth case has been closed. It was the father after all. He confessed."

Boggs was stunned. "To whom?"

"Two of his friends. He told them, they told the Peacedale sheriff. When the sheriff showed up to arrest him, he ran. You can imagine the rest."

Boggs and Smith were silent for a moment. Then Smith said, "They shot him?"

"Yes. He's dead. It's over." McInnis paused. "I know you don't like it, and it don't look too good at all. But it's done and it's closed, and there's nothing we can do. I just . . . wanted you to hear it from me and not some other cop."

Boggs was shaking his head. He felt dizzy.

"You can read Peacedale's report on your break," McInnis said, tapping the folder. "But right now I need you to walk your beat, Officers."

"Yes, sir," Smith said, because Boggs had no words for what he was feeling.

Boggs felt Smith's hand on his bicep, pulling him away before he might open his mouth and get himself fired.

24

RAKE TRIED TO act nonchalant when he heard Dunlow, Peterson, and Helton discussing a body that had been found the night before.

"Who was it?"

Dunlow looked up at him before answering. "Brian Underhill. Ex-APD."

They were in the headquarters, fans circling above without seeming to move any air. All the paperwork on every desk weighed down by humidity. It was two days since Underhill had been killed.

"The one who was seen with Lily Ellsworth that night," Rake said, as if he was dimly remembering this.

Rake picked up the report. He tried not to look overly concerned as he read what the early morning officers had discovered. The body by the old plant, of course. Nothing about witnesses, thank goodness. A canvas of the neighborhood was ongoing, but Rake knew there were few houses in that area.

The fact that the body had laid there for more than a day before being discovered allayed Rake's fears—slightly—that the killer was APD. But the report noted that no shell casings had been found, which argued for a professional killer, or at least an unusually thorough one. Rake had run to the scene of the killing in less than a minute, yet the shooter had still cleaned his mess fast enough to vanish.

"It was your night off that night, wasn't it?" Dunlow asked his young partner.

"It was. Yours as well." He was glad the redness in his knuckles had faded.

Helton used a handkerchief to shine his brass buttons, sucking in his gut. "It is indeed a difficult time to be a former officer of the law." He glanced at Rake. "I'd hate to become one myself."

During his shift with Dunlow that night, news trickled in about the Underhill murder. Still no witnesses. The deceased's ex-wife up in Dahlonega had been notified. They had no children and few other relatives. Friends and former associates were being questioned. Detectives were searching the man's apartment, and Rake envied them, wondering what evidence might be hiding there, clues to the Ellsworth murder and Lord knew what other crimes.

As low as his opinion of Dunlow was, he still didn't think Dunlow was the type to plot in the shadows. If Dunlow truly had a problem with Rake, he would tell him to his face. Or just shoot him in the face. Men like Helton and Peterson, however, he was less sure about. Who were the other people Underhill had alluded to, the inside men he had on the force? How many of them were there, and how close were they to Rake?

The next day, as Rake drove down Auburn Avenue, he realized he had never been here before except in a squad car. It was a mercifully cloudy day, not nearly as hot as usual, a portentous breeze making American flags taut outside the pharmacies and restaurants and insurance agencies. He found the number he was looking for on a mailbox outside a well-kept bungalow with a large porch surrounded by tall hydrangeas, their blooms the color of a clear morning sky. He wondered if he had the wrong address.

Rake had been inside a Negro's house before—when he was a boy, his mother had been friendly with a Negro woman she'd met somewhere, though he didn't recall the particulars—but that was all. He had of course entered several colored residences in the line of duty, but what he was about to do was altogether different. He could not avoid the temptation to look over his shoulder as he crossed the street, to check the neighbors' front lawns for witnesses. He was walking faster than usual.

He rang the doorbell. The front door was open but the screen was shut.

An older, dignified Negro with gray hair and a confident stride smiled at him, pleasant but with unmistakable wariness. Rake was not in uniform and wore a light green short-sleeved shirt tucked into slacks.

"Can I help you?" the man asked, opening the screen door.

"Yes, I'm looking for Lucius Boggs."

"That's my son. Come right in." He extended a hand. "I'm Reverend Daniel Boggs."

Rake shook the Negro's hand, marveling at the palm's whiteness. It was a firm handshake. This was very strange.

"Officer Dennis Rakestraw."

"Good to meet you."

He wasn't sure what he had been expecting, but he was impressed by the spotless and shining wood floors, the paintings on the walls, the framed photographs of the reverend posing with people who seemed to think they were important. In the far corner of the living room sat a piano.

The reverend invited him into a dark study filled with more books than Rake had ever seen in someone's house. The walls were completely covered with bookshelves, apart from a small window. A rotating desk fan tried to make the room bearable. Rake felt too uncomfortable to sit, so he stood beside one of the chairs as the reverend excused himself to summon his son.

Rake read the spines of books on God, Frederick Douglass, the Apostles, the Crusades, Jesus, Thomas Aquinas, the Holy Spirit, Harriet Tubman, W.E.B. Du Bois, the Greek tragedies, the Civil War.

Footsteps, and the reverend returned with Lucius, whose face could not possibly have been any more scrubbed of emotion or betrayed thought.

"Rakestraw. Good morning."

Before Rake could say the same, the reverend made a show of claiming to have some errand to go on, and out he went through the front door, despite the coming storm.

"Please, sit. Can I get you some water or tea?"

Rake declined the drink but not the chair. Though it would have been less stuffy on the porch, he was grateful for not being on display. He figured the reverend had put them here for that reason.

"What brings you here?" Boggs asked.

And so began the gamble. "You and I, we have a similar problem. Dunlow."

Boggs was watching him carefully.

"I don't like him any more than you do," Rake continued. "I don't enjoy seeing the way he bullies Negroes and keeps all the gamblers and bootleggers and brothels running. Cops like him are part of the problem."

"There are a lot of cops like him."

"Well, only one of them is my partner." He took an extra breath to make sure he could dare say it. "And only one of them is a fellow who I think might have been involved in a murder."

"You like him for Lily Ellsworth," Boggs said, looking away now. Rake couldn't tell if that was a cue to end this line of inquiry or if the Negro was trying to appear deferential.

"I'm convinced he at least knows something. He and Underhill go back, yet the night that we all pulled Underhill over, they acted like strangers."

"McInnis altered my report, too. When we found her body, I put in my report that Underhill was the last man seen with her. I handed it to McInnis so he could take it to headquarters for me. He must have retyped it."

Rake figured before that Boggs had just made a sloppy mistake, leaving the name out of the report. Boggs's story seemed equally believable, but if true, it was bad news indeed. The more Rake looked into the murder, the more cops seemed involved in covering it up.

"I think," Rake said, "and I don't mean any offense to your people here, but I think an unusual amount of care is being taken to bury a crime against some poor colored girl."

"A poor colored girl who was working for a congressman a few weeks ago."

"What?"

Boggs told him that he had learned a few things himself, including the fact that Lily had worked as a maid for none other than Representative Billy Prescott.

"How did you find that out?"

"Let me just keep that to myself for now."

"Have you filed that in a report?"

"Of course not. I'm not a detective. I don't investigate murders. I walk a beat, that's all."

Rake thought this through. Maybe Boggs was doing the same thing he was, trying to solve it on the sly. Rake wondered if Boggs had a better-thought-out endgame than he himself did, or was Boggs, like him, simply hoping that if he solved the crime, the next steps would fall into place.

"And her father, Otis Ellsworth, was killed two days ago by the cops in Peacedale."

Jesus. Boggs knew a hell of a lot more about this than Rake did. Rake tried not to look unmoored as he asked for more.

"The official story is he tried to steal something from the county store, was arrested, then broke free, so the police shot him," Boggs said. "The Peacedale cops are also implying he stole a good deal of money recently, though they don't know where from. It was enough for a poor sharecropper to be able to suddenly buy himself a truck, and that won him some attention."

"So the Peacedale cops are involved in this, too?"

"I thought that at first. Then I thought, if I'm a white Atlanta cop and I committed a crime, the first thing I want to do is peg it on a Negro. So I try to beat Otis Ellsworth into confessing he killed his own daughter."

Rake leaned back in his chair. "But then an annoying rookie cop in the observation room mentions Underhill's name. And they realize that if they *do* just try to pin it on the wrong Negro, they still have problems, because someone has figured out the Underhill connection."

"I didn't know you were in the room," Boggs said. He watched Rake for a moment. "But the next step I see is, they call the Peacedale police and mention that they've questioned Ellsworth in relation to a crime, and they mention that he has extra money, knowing that will pique their interest. Knowing the way things work in towns like that, they just sit back and let nature take its course."

"And that's why they killed Underhill. He was the link. They knew someone—me, or you, or both of us—had connected him to the crime, so they got rid of him."

"So the only connection we have left is Dunlow."

They both sat in silence for a moment, replaying the conversation in their heads, trying to review the blank spots in their narrative. The rain came down, but silently, the sheets thin and without thunder.

"Clearly, I need your help on this," Rake said. "And you need mine. You can talk to some of the people I can't get at, or who won't be up front with me on account of my color. And I can access things in the headquarters you can't, not to mention get at some of the people you can't get to."

"I want to catch someone who thinks they can get away with killing a colored girl," Boggs said. "But it sounds like *you* want to take down a chunk of the police force. That's not going to happen."

"Why not? All Chief Jenkins talks about these days is reform, reform. We can find a big ol' twisted piece of APD for him to pull out by the roots. Besides, it's in your best interest for a fellow like Dunlow to get his hands out of your neighborhood. You'll never be able to do your job, I mean *truly* do your job the way you want it done, so long as cops like that have their fingers in the pie. That's what you want, isn't it, to get them out?"

"I'm trying to set realistic goals."

"If the point of Negro cops is to patrol the Negro neighborhood and keep your people safe, then you need the white cops out."

"I'm talking to a white cop."

"A white cop who would rather be policing a white neighborhood."

Boggs nodded after a pause, as if still determining whether he was talking to an ally or a foe.

"I didn't join up so I could keep colored criminals in operation and extort my share," Rake explained. "If we can make it clear that white cops can't do that anymore, and that you and your officers have control of the situation, then headquarters will get the message, this experiment will be judged a success, and they'll hire more of you. You can police your own the way you want to. And I can get myself reassigned, to a partner who isn't a thug and to a beat that isn't someone else's rightful territory."

"You want out of 'Darktown.'"

"Isn't that what y'all want? To be treated fair, to protect your own?"

Another pregnant pause. Christ, Rake still couldn't tell if he was making progress with Boggs or if it had been a horrible mistake to have said so much.

"Yes."

"You know damn well that most of the white cops want you all to fail so the mayor can call this off. *That's* why Dunlow is trying to tag you and Smith for killing Poe."

Boggs stiffened. "First, don't cuss in my father's house, please. Second, we did not kill Poe."

"I don't think you did either, but Dunlow believes it, in his bones. Last I heard, he's having trouble getting Homicide to pursue this the way he wants it done. The majors don't want this to blow up in the press as some cop-on-cop civil war. But that's not going to stop Dunlow from spending every waking second trying to nail you for it."

"So you're offering to keep him off our backs?"

The rain grew louder, the gutters talking to the downspouts.

"I don't think the devil himself could do that. But I am uniquely positioned to keep an eye on him. I can find out what kind of fake evidence and nonsense testimony he's going to wrangle up against you, like he tried on Bayle. I could pass that on to you, so you can find ways to protect yourself."

"You got a cigarette?" Boggs asked.

Rake did. He lit two and handed one to Boggs.

"So I try to find out who killed Lily Ellsworth," Boggs recapped, "and I pass what I find on to you, especially if it keeps pointing to Dunlow. And you keep tabs on Dunlow and give me advance warning before he does whatever it is he's fixing to do."

"Yes. But I'll do more than that. Any records you need at the headquarters, any white folks you want questioned, I'll do it."

Boggs raised an eyebrow. "Congressman Prescott?"

"Christ, within reason I mean."

Boggs shut his eyes for a moment, and Rake realized it was for the blasphemy in a preacher's house. Goodness, it must be strange to tread so lightly all the time.

"How about his son?" Boggs asked. "Or his wife. Someone who can tell us what went on in there, if anything."

"I'll think on it. But this only works if we keep this quiet. If Dunlow starts to think I'm spying on him, it all blows up. I'm taking a heck of a risk even telling you this."

"You think I'm not?"

"Just do me one other favor first. Chandler Poe. What happened?"

Boggs paused, and Rake wondered if he'd misplayed everything by asking this, if he was now making it look like this whole conversation had just been a ruse to goad Boggs into confessing.

"I have no idea," Boggs said.

"What about your partner?"

"What about him?"

"Well, you'll notice I came to talk to *you* and not him."

"He might not be as polite and diplomatic as I can be, but he's a good cop."

"A couple of bootleggers swear Smith beat Poe that night."

Boggs stubbed out his cigarette, even though it appeared to have plenty left. "I can assure you, Smith did not do anything that I haven't seen Dunlow do on occasion. Is that good enough for you?"

"So you're saying, no knife?"

"No knife. And neither of us has been within a mile of the place they found his body."

There was a lot of gray area in what Boggs was saying, but it made sense. "Okay. Still, I don't want Smith involved in this."

"He's my partner. I trust him."

"That doesn't mean that—"

"You hold up your end of the bargain and I'll hold up mine. But don't tell me how."

Rake decided to let it go. He reached into his pocket and handed Boggs a slip of paper. "My number. We'd best not communicate when we're in uniform. You need to reach me, call."

Rake stood and wished Boggs good luck. Then he shook hands with a Negro for the second time that day, and in his life.

25

MIDDAY. THE SUN was not taking prisoners. Movement and sound were things of the past, even the birds hiding silent in shaded branches.

Dunlow drove slowly past the house of James Calvin, the Negro who had dared to invade the white community of Hanford Park. Bricks through the man's windows had not yet convinced him that he'd made a horrible mistake in building that house, but it was early in the summer still, the nights sure to become darker and more miserable.

He had barely parked his car in his driveway when the eldest of his two sons, Knox, was asking to take the car off his hands. *What the hell was it boys felt they needed the car for so much, anyways?* When Dunlow had been their age he'd managed fine on foot, on the bus, on the street-car. He'd seen the city and got himself into a fair amount of trouble, even with his own father and police legend Arthur Dunlow keeping his eye on him. Yet his own sons seemed unable to function if they didn't have their hand on a gearshift.

"Why you need my car so badly?"

"Well, sir, I was hoping I could take Jenny-Beth to see the Crackers this afternoon." Knox was seventeen and with a year of schooling to go. Buddy, two years his junior, was greasing the chain of his bike about ten feet away, pretending not to be listening. Buddy wasn't yet legal to drive, but Dunlow knew the boy had taken the wheel for his brother a number of times, and was doubtless hoping to tag along to the game.

"She a baseball fan, is she?"

"Trying to make her one," Knox said.

"Her father allow her out like that without an adult around?"

"In the afternoon, sir."

Dunlow told Buddy to stop playing with the bike and come over here.

The kid's hands weren't even greasy. As much as Knox's bullheadedness grated on Dunlow, it was his younger son's sneakiness that had him more concerned.

When both young men—and damned if that's not what they seemed now, both of them as tall as Dunlow and Knox so muscled up that the football coach claimed he had a chance to make it on the Dawgs squad if he kept his focus—were right up beside him, Dunlow leveled with them.

"This here is my car. I work. I earn the money. It's mine when I'm using it, and it's mine when I ain't using it. Knox, you can find another way to impress that gal. And Buddy, you quit hiding in the shadows like a little girl and say what you want next time."

He walked past them toward the house. They knew better than to complain.

Then he stopped and turned. "And I thought I told you to do something about that nigger down the street. I don't expect to have to ask more than once."

⚡

Dunlow hadn't been any older than they were back when he'd helped his father clear the neighborhood the last time things had looked this dicey. Back in the twenties. Like now, a postwar housing crunch had caused some of the local coloreds to move into parts of town they'd previously avoided. He'd been but a boy when the houses of a number of coloreds had burned down. His father had taken him along, even let him toss some gasoline on a porch, then watch from the safety of the car as the men—cops and firemen and other trusted sorts—dropped the matches.

Sadly, he couldn't take his sons along for something like that. There were just enough spoilsports and pantywaists that, if word spread that a policeman had done anything extralegal, his job could be threatened. It was insane. First the crackdown on the numbers runners a few years back, then the crackdown on some Kluxers courtesy of the state BI, and now the worst insult of all, blacks donning the same uniform Dunlow proudly wore, the same uniform his father had worn. He knew that he and men like Helton and Peterson could easily run this Negro out of the neighborhood, but he figured it would be better to get his sons involved. Not only to keep his job safe but also because, if they were to be men, and if this was to be their neighborhood, they would damn well need to start defending it.

Inside, he saw that his wife was napping, thank goodness. He liked her at her quietest. He walked into the kitchen and picked up the phone, dialed Peterson to find out why the hell Smith and Boggs were still wearing badges.

"Word is, McInnis is shielding them," Peterson said. "Won't allow them to be questioned by detectives unless we can produce more evidence."

"It'll happen. He can't protect them forever."

"Well, the wheels of justice are turning a bit slowly right now."

"Like you said, Bo, I'm about ready to stuff those badges so far down their throats we can cut their balls off with 'em. I'll give the Department one more chance to do it straight, but if they can't get their pencils out of their asses, then I'll take care of it myself. I ain't waiting around for the niggers to kill someone else."

"Neither am I."

"Once they realize they got away with it, you know what they'll move on to, don't you? They'll take out a *cop*. Probably been their plan all along."

"They want a war, we'll give 'em a war."

"This ain't no time for burning crosses and hanging bodies in front yards," Dunlow said, looking out the window at his sons, who were literally kicking stones, hands in their pockets. "What we do has got to be done carefully, and quiet as quiet can be."

"You're not the man I think of first when I hear that word."

"Now there, Bo. You're forgetting a few things about me, boy."

26

RAKE PULLED HIS squad car over at a street corner in Druid Hills. Residential and forested, a tidy escape for people who made good money in the city. From downtown he'd taken Ponce, which turned windy and downright scenic in this stretch, poplars and red oaks overhead and the occasional trolley passing in its lane to his right. The houses on this block were larger than in Rake's part of town, the lots far more generous, the trees older and taller.

His heart was racing that he was even doing this, and he told himself to relax. He was lucky Dunlow was tied up with paperwork back at headquarters, but he needed to be fast.

He knocked on the door of a narrow bungalow that was sheltered by two white oaks.

The door was opened by a tall, slim, moon-faced man who was unable to disguise his shock at the sight of a police officer.

"Good evening, Mr. Prescott?"

"Yes?"

"I'm Officer Rakestraw. I was hoping I could ask you a couple of quick questions about someone who used to work for your family?"

Representative Prescott's son, Silas, looked Rake's age, not that that made them peers. His hair could have used a trim, the bangs falling across his forehead, probably the same haircut he'd had since prep school. He wore a dapper light blue sport coat even though he appeared home for the evening, a lone car in his driveway.

"Sure thing. Would you like to come in?"

Southern hospitality was a delightful weapon to wield against people who didn't want to talk to you, Rake had learned. He accepted the foolish invitation, his shined shoes tapping on the wood floor. Jump blues on a record player livened up the otherwise bare parlor. The room had less furniture in it than it should have, and nothing decorating the walls.

"Nice place," Rake said, as he knew it made people talk.

"Thank you. I just moved in a few weeks ago. Still need to decorate. Can I get you anything?"

"No, thank you, this shouldn't take but a minute." Rake sat in one easy chair and Prescott, after turning off the record, sat in the other one, as there were no other options.

He was William S. Prescott III but went by his middle name, Silas, Rake had learned. He'd worked for his father off and on and also owned a few restaurants downtown. From what Rake could gather, he was a professional rich kid and was trying to ride that into his thirties.

"I'm doing a quick follow-up about a girl who used to work for your mother." Rake made a show of taking his notebook from a pocket. The congressman's son was barefoot and had just the cutest uncallused feet a grown man could have. "Lily Ellsworth."

"Yes?" Legs crossed, Prescott's fingers were threaded upon his top knee. Rake was used to people being nervous in his presence, and this man certainly was.

"Unfortunately, Lily died a couple of weeks back."

"Oh, that's terrible."

"Did you know her?"

Prescott shook his head. "I mean, I probably saw her cleaning the house once or twice. And she probably served me dinner now and again. But I wouldn't say I *knew* her."

"Of course. I'm just trying to reconstruct where she was over the last few months. I understand she was working for your mother for two or three months but was let go in late May?"

Prescott inhaled deeply, like he was trying hard to remember. Emphasis on *like*. It seemed an act, overly theatrical. "I suppose that's about right."

"I know I could have asked your mother these questions, but it felt unseemly to bother her."

"Yes, I appreciate that. I'll have to let her know about poor Lily."

"Could you tell me why your mother let Lily go?"

"Goodness, if I had to tell you all the different maids and butlers

Mother has fired, you'd need a bigger notebook. The woman *is* demanding, as my father always says. I'm sure this girl laid a fork down at a slightly improper angle or something of that nature."

Rake smiled along as if he could relate. "You mentioned you moved here recently. Did you used to live at your parents'?"

"Ah, well, I suppose in a way. I've had my own place in the city now and then and have moved back in with Mother to help her through on occasion. It can be lonely for her with my father in Washington for long stretches. So, yes, prior to me moving here I was living there."

"So that would mean you were living there at the same time Lily worked there."

Prescott seemed to realize he'd painted himself into a corner. "Yes, that sounds about right."

"Is there anything you could tell me about her? Did she ever discuss having any problems, being in fear of anyone?"

Prescott uncrossed and recrossed his legs, the school ring on his finger catching the light.

"Again, we never really chatted. Mother is very strict about such things. I'm sure in some households there's more . . . blurring of the lines, you could say. But not in ours."

"Of course." A conveniently located clock on the dining room wall behind Prescott told Rake he'd been in there for five minutes. He was supposed to be somewhere else at this moment and would need to end this talk soon.

"Do you know the name Lionel Dunlow?"

Head shake, believably blank look.

"Brian Underhill?"

"No. Who are they?"

"You know, I'm honestly not sure. Just names we've heard kicked around when her name's come up. There's one last thing, Mr. Prescott, and then I'll be on my way. We have reason to understand Lily's family may have come into some money recently. They're a very poor family, but a few weeks after she started working at your mother's, they made a large purchase." He was exaggerating what he could prove, to see what he might get in return. That morning he'd read the deeply alarming "report" on Otis Ellsworth's death that the Peacedale police had shared with APD. "Some of their neighbors think Lily may have sent that money to her parents. So, naturally, our first thought was that she may have taken something from your family."

Prescott nodded once and turned his head, gazing at a blank wall and a window covered by a green curtain. Whatever he was about to say was something he was carefully arranging in his head first. He took his time with it.

"I suppose I haven't been completely forthcoming with you, Officer . . . what was it again?"

"Rakestraw." The brief anonymity of this visit seemed to be vanishing. There would be consequences. But he was finally learning something.

"Officer Rakestraw, Lily was indeed let go because she took something from my family. It was an unfortunate episode, and it's behind us now. We didn't see any reason to press charges so we simply let her go, chalking it up to an error in judgment on Mother's part for hiring her."

"What was it she stole?"

"I don't want this in any report. I'd like you to put that pen away."

Rake paused, surprised, but figured there was no harm giving this man a symbolic victory. He pocketed the pen.

"My family chose to handle this quietly. It wouldn't do to have us linked to some petty crime, especially one involving a Negro. Something like that can be construed however a political opponent would like to construe it, and we aren't in the business of handing ammunition to our enemies. We expect everything to be handled very discreetly, especially our dealings with the police. Frankly, I'm surprised they sent a young officer like yourself over about this."

Prescott had quickly pivoted from a skittish, nervous man into someone with reserves of power who was insulted to have to call upon them for something so minor.

"So," Rake asked, "you've already spoken with other members of the Department?"

"Of course. Not myself, but my father. He's close friends with several high-ranking members of the Department, as I'm sure you can imagine. Everything has been handled and all is in order. She was a girl who managed to conceal her criminal proclivities from my mother for a while, and then after we let her go she no doubt continued her errant ways and fell in with more of that crowd. Perhaps she finally stole from people who are less understanding than my family, and they chose to settle matters in a more brutish manner." He paused. "I suppose one could argue that their way was better than ours."

Rake didn't care for that. "I would argue against that, myself. It's my job to arrest people who commit murders, not philosophize about them."

"Of course." Prescott rose to bid Rake farewell. As they walked to the door, he added, "You know, they're a very deceptive race. They can at times win your sympathy, and you try to do right by them. And then you find they've been stealing from you all along."

Rake was surprised by the comment. He'd heard that Prescott was more of a moderate on the Negro question. It didn't sound like his son was.

"Did your father ever meet her, or was he in Washington the whole time she worked at the house?"

"Oh, he was in Washington. Mother did tell him about what happened. Told him what she stole, consulted him for advice, because of course *mine* is never good enough for her. But that was as involved as he was in any of this."

They walked to the door, Rake noticing how the man had gone from tight-lipped to full of information. Either Rake had stumbled upon the truth, or he had allowed Prescott time to draw a false picture and revel in its freedoms.

They shook hands and Rake apologized for bothering him.

"It's no bother. We've been in politics a long time, and it's a messy business. There's always some matter or another that needs tidying up, especially when people try to take advantage of you. But we respect the importance of maintaining appearances, Officer Rakestraw. Not just for ourselves but for our city. I'm sure you do as well."

Rake opened the door and walked through the wall of bugs that had been clinging to it, drawn to the overhead light's false promise.

After his shift, at home. Past two o'clock. Rake was dropping ice into a tall glass of water when the phone rang. *Who the hell at this hour?* He answered it on the second ring.

"Is this Officer Dennis Rakestraw?" The voice on the line spoke slowly and stilted, like he was foreign and reading from phonetically translated lines.

"It is. With whom am I speaking?"

"And would you be interested in learning why Brian Underhill was killed?"

Rake realized the speaker was trying to disguise his voice, clumsily so but effective all the same.

"I'd be interested in learning anything about any crime."

"Then I suggest we meet in person. Tomorrow, three in the morning, Mozley Park."

"Who's speaking?"

Silence. Rake asked twice more before hanging up.

27

THAT SAME NIGHT, Boggs walked up the steps to a whorehouse.

It was the day after Boggs's surprising conversation with Rake. He still wasn't sure what to make of it. He had done his best to steer clear of Rake just as he steered clear of the other white cops, especially because he was Dunlow's partner. He'd assumed Rake was every bit as rotten, only younger and less confident about flaunting his rottenness. Yet Rake's dislike of Dunlow seemed genuine. Boggs was not accustomed to hearing a white man express disapproval of another white man. It seemed to violate some code. That alone was worth paying attention to.

Unless it was all a ruse, another attempt by Dunlow to discredit the Negro officers, sending out his young accomplice to sweet-talk Boggs into a confession about killing Poe.

That morning Boggs had told Smith about it, and his partner had seemed equally wary. *Let's not trust him any more than another white man,* had been Smith's advice. *Neither of us tells him anything until the other has cleared it first. And whatever he tells one of us, we got to tell the other. God only knows what they're up to.*

Though Boggs and Smith had been conducting most of their unofficial investigation during off-work hours, an interview with Mama Dove would have to be different. They had gone as long as they could without asking her some questions, but if either of them dropped by her establishment while in civilian dress, someone might see them and report it.

At night it would be difficult to have their photo taken, and they would at least be able to claim they were there on official business. So they had waited until a good excuse came up, and finally, tonight, one had: a little boy from the neighborhood was missing. He'd been gone twelve hours by the time his panicked mother had called the main headquarters, which had then routed the call to the Butler Street Y on account of the kid's race.

Smith and Boggs had been knocking on doors, and they had known they were only a block from Mama Dove's. Why not knock on hers? While Smith waited a block away, Boggs rang the doorbell, which glowed red beneath his finger.

He heard an inner door open. "Come in," a voice beckoned.

He opened the outer door and entered a small foyer. Mama Dove stood there, one hand theatrically leaning against the wall. She wore a red velvet dress and a necklace whose single blue stone nearly disappeared into her cleavage.

"Well, well, it's the preacher's son!"

He tipped his cap. He'd never met her before and had no idea how she knew him, but he was used to the fact that others in the community knew his face.

"Good evening, ma'am."

"Ma'am! Well, how bad is that, I'm a *ma'am* to him. Course, that's short for *madam,* you know. And that's very much what I am. So I don't know why I'm so surprised to hear you say it."

He took a notebook and pen out of his back pocket, then asked about the little boy. She expressed faux-maternal sorrow to hear about a missing child but regrettably hadn't seen any.

"While I'm here, ma'am, I was hoping to ask you a few questions about a girl who used to live here, Lily Ellsworth."

"I don't know the name."

He described her appearance and background, but Mama Dove's very poised expression showed she wasn't ready to share any epiphanies with him.

"And what makes you think I know her?"

"A few weeks before she died, she sent two letters with this as the return address."

"Maybe she lived somewhere else on this street, got the numbers mixed up."

He was used to being lied to by now, but still, something about her blithe manner dug into him. He pressed, giving something away he hadn't been planning to: "She also sent quite a lot of money to her family before she died."

"I don't know nothing about that!" She half-laughed when she said this. In a way, that made her more believable. Which was strange. He had the feeling he'd told her something she hadn't known.

"You're sure you don't know her? See, when someone's leaving a brothel as a return address and sending a lot of cash through the mail, I can't help but put one and one together."

"Son, I don't have the foggiest where you're going with this."

"Might could be she didn't work here, but she stayed here? She's friends with one of your girls? Or you took her in or something, felt pity on her?"

"That's so nice, son. You think a lady like me knows how to feel pity. Been a good while since that was true."

He was tired of her calling him "son" and he wanted to correct her to "Officer," but it wasn't worth the effort. She'd only call him "son" again, pretend it was accidental. Or maybe it wouldn't be accidental—it was precisely that difficult for her to fathom a world in which a man with skin like hers could outfit himself this way.

"You have quite a way of not answering questions directly."

"Well, a woman in my station needs to be *direct* so very often, it's nice to do the opposite now and again. Come on, preacher's son, I don't know why you're troubling me about some dead girl. I don't know *why* I haven't seen you or your fellow Negro officers in my fine establishment." He was about to tell her not to hold her breath on that, but then she corrected herself. "Oh, wait, yes, there was that *one,* but he's the only one! And there are seven more of you, I don't know why you insist on hurting my feelings by not coming here, too."

She was baiting him. Surely none of his colleagues came here. Yet, even though he was 95 percent sure it was just a ploy, the other 5 percent of him was dying to hear her dirt.

He tried to ignore the comment and stay focused. "A girl was here for at least a couple of weeks, and then she got herself shot. Her body was dumped in an alley three blocks from here. That same night, she'd been riding in a car with a white man who'd assaulted her earlier, a man named Brian Underhill. Now, if you know anything at all about either of those people, you'd best tell me now instead of me finding out later it was a john who met her in this very goddamn house, which could make you an accessory to murder."

Her eyes were as wide as a silent movie actress's. "I wasn't expecting such words out of the mouth of the preacher's son!"

"I'm the minister's *son*, ma'am. I'm no minister myself."

"And thank *good*ness for it. I like my men with a bit of dirt to them. The grime of living is so much more interesting than the shine of eternity, I've always thought."

He put the notebook back in his pocket.

"Ma'am, allow me to give you a piece of advice. You should start looking into relocation. The white cops you pay off may be protecting you now, but they won't always be the ones working this neighborhood. And when they're gone, we *will* shut you down. I think it would be better for everyone if you just moved on now and saved us the trouble."

Her smile was gone yet her eyes had a way of retaining their twinkle. "You're very confident that you've found a permanent line of work, aren't you?"

"I will be in this neighborhood longer than you. I promise you that."

"You aren't as cute when you get all full of yourself. Now, do you know what the difference between you and me is?"

"I can't wait to hear your take on it."

"There *is* no difference. Not to them. We're both just *niggers* and you know it. How much longer you think they gonna let you parade around in that uniform, preacher's son?" She looked him up and down with a smirk, as if he were a twelve-year-old, too old to be playing dress up but too small to take seriously. "So let *me* give *you* some advice. You might want to drop this whole pompous nigger act, because when they do take away your badge and your gun and your paycheck, and you start feeling down and out and lonesome, we both know there's *one* place you're gonna turn. Same place all the ones turn. Mama Dove's."

He handed her his card. "Call me when you decide that a girl getting shot and thrown out like garbage is something you aren't in favor of."

She made a show of waiting an extra second before taking it from him.

He turned to leave, and just as he did so a white man stepped into the foyer. Early forties, overlong forelocks combed across a bald spot at the front of his head. He wore a brown suit jacket and a red tie and a look of horror to have stumbled upon a policeman, and a Negro one at that.

"What are you doing here?" Boggs barked at him.

The man backed up a step, and would have tripped if the door hadn't been behind him.

Boggs grabbed the man's left hand and held it up, squeezing the palm so that the fingers stuck out, including the adorned ring finger.

"Get back to your wife, now!"

The man's eyes were wider still, glancing back and forth between Mama Dove and this horrible vision of colored moral rectitude.

Then the white man was gone, running down the steps.

Mama Dove was laughing harder than ever as Boggs made his exit.

"Oooh, that man's look was *worth* the money you just cost me, preacher's son!"

⚡

"We need to go to Peacedale," Smith said.

They were five blocks from Mama Dove's now, her words still stinging. Boggs had found her indifference to Lily's fate more insulting than he'd expected.

"I know, but—"

"No 'buts.' You've been putting it off. Let's go. Tomorrow."

"It's not that simple."

"Didn't say it was simple. First, we need a car. How 'bout the reverend's?"

"Whoa, whoa." Boggs was stunned by his partner's confidence. He assumed it was mostly a front, but as he looked in Smith's eyes, he questioned that assumption. "The white cops out there killed him."

"I know. So we go armed."

"Tommy, we aren't in France. And you're not in a tank."

"And we ain't in no South Carolina training camp either. You aren't on the sidelines. We stood and waited, and someone else got killed. I'm done waiting. I'm going there tomorrow. You coming with me, or do I have to steal a car?"

⚡

Later that night, Mama Dove picked up her phone and made a call.

An unfamiliar voice answered. "Hello?" A boy not yet a man. That awkward phase, the one she had always loathed, though she saw it in her brothel so very often.

"Yes, may I speak with Lionel, please?"

"He's not here, ma'am," Dunlow's kid said. *One of* Dunlow's kids. And the "ma'am" again, the kid not noticing her voice was that of a Negress, or not caring. "He's working. Can I take a message?"

She said there was no need and hung up. She hated calling his house, hated the risk that she'd hear one of those boys' too-deep voices. The wife's voice she didn't mind, though they never spoke long enough, Mama Dove always feigning apologies for the wrong number.

But the son's? Abominable. That corn-fed, testosterone-dazed mulishness. They had his same stubborn whiteness, she could tell from the way they mumbled into the receiver.

Oh, but she would be in a foul mood the rest of the night.

28

AT TWENTY MINUTES 'til three, Rake drove to Mozley Park, as the mysterious caller had instructed him. He had hoped that being early might give him the drop on the caller, but he wasn't so fortunate. A blue Ford pickup waited in the small parking lot; its tailgate was open, and a portly, mostly bald man who looked to be past fifty sat on its ledge. He wore denim overalls and a white T-shirt and his large eyes seemed owlish in Rake's headlights.

The fact that the caller had asked Rake to come at three, which was one hour after his shift ended, gave Rake the strong feeling that the caller knew his schedule. If he'd said midnight, that meant Rake would have come in uniform, in a squad car with a radio. He'd clocked out and changed into his civvies, though he had known enough to bring along his revolver. He had thought about leaving a note of some kind, so that if anything happened, Cassie would know where he'd gone, but had decided against it.

He parked across from the pickup and got out of his car. "You the mystery caller?"

"That I am. I appreciate you dropping by."

"You picked quite a popular place for us to talk, Mister . . . ?" and he let that hang for the man to fill in the blank, but the man did not.

Instead what Rake heard was the unmistakable sound of a shotgun being pumped behind him.

"Put those hands up, rookie."

Rake slowly lifted his hands, feeling stupider than ever. His stomach seemed to drop a couple of inches as the bald man hopped out of the pickup and walked toward him. He was a few inches shorter than Rake but broad as a barn door.

"Whatever you gentlemen are trying to pull here ain't worth the trouble it'll cost you."

He could hear footsteps behind him as the man with the shotgun drew near. He braced himself for a blow to the back of his head. Instead, he felt hands from behind remove his revolver from his pocket. Then the bald man slugged him in the gut.

The wind rushed out of him, but he wasn't altogether surprised and he'd certainly had worse. As he drew himself back up, though, the blow to the back of his head finally came, and he stumbled forward. Someone very large pinned him down and his right cheek dug into gravel while his hands were yanked behind him. He thrashed as best he could but two blows to the back of his ribs diverted his mind plenty and then he heard another unmistakable metallic sound, this time that of handcuffs.

They pulled him to his feet and threw him forward. He was flung smack into the open doorway of the Ford's bed, like another blow to his gut. Someone put a hand on his head, pinning him against the dirty metal floor bed.

"What the hell do you think you're doing? I'm a cop."

"No shit you're a cop. What we want to know is why you killed Brian Underhill."

"What?"

The bald man took something from his pockets with a theatrical flourish. He held a rusty set of metal pliers before Rake's eyes. "Why'd you kill him?"

"I didn't kill him!"

Rake could hear the bald man step behind him, where the other one was holding Rake firm. With his arms behind his back and his center of gravity over the Ford, he couldn't wriggle or kick away. He felt something metal and cold clamp itself on either side of the base of his pinkie.

Rake's own hands had never felt so far from his body, while at the same time so horribly attached to himself.

"You want to maybe open up a little more, rookie?"

"I'm telling you the truth!"

The pliers clamped harder. Rake gritted his teeth.

"Last chance, Rakestraw."

"Fuck you!"

The muscles in Rake's shoulders and arms and fingers could not possibly have been more taut or bursting with all his strength yet the pinkie finger was yanked nearly from its base and he felt the snap and he hated himself for making as much noise as he did.

"Try again!" one of the men yelled. "Why'd you kill him?"

The pain from his broken finger was already shooting straight through to his shoulder and past it, to the base of his neck. His other fingers still possessed enough sensation to inform him that the pliers were now being applied to the ring finger.

"I beat the shit out of him but I didn't fucking shoot him! If I'd shot the son of a bitch, I would say so! I almost wish I had, but someone beat me to it!"

The weight leaning on him seemed to lessen ever so much, and though he couldn't quite hear their voices he could feel one of them, the vibration coming through that body that was pressed against his own.

Then one of them was just a bit louder. "Ah hell. I do, too."

The weight was lifted from him, and his feet were finally able to gain purchase on the ground and he pushed himself away, spinning awkwardly and landing on one knee. He could see them now, the bald man with his arms folded as if faced with a vexing problem, the pliers dangling from one of his hands, and the other man, unseen until now, tall and broad-shouldered and younger than his partner by many years, blond hair disheveled. The first thing Rake noticed was that the man wasn't holding a shotgun. Rake scanned the area before seeing the shotgun on the ground a few feet away.

The bald man slid his pliers into his overalls pocket and, having noticed Rake's glance at the shotgun, removed Rake's revolver from another pocket.

"Now just calm down there a minute."

Rake hadn't realized he was panting as loudly as he was. He gritted his teeth again, embarrassed and thankful they hadn't actually yanked the finger clean off but mostly goddamn enraged.

He slowly rose to his feet. He was still cuffed but he didn't feel like asking them for any favors just yet. Jesus his finger hurt.

"Who the hell are you, and what is this about?" he asked.

"We needed to be sure you didn't kill him," the older man said.

"I'm a *cop*."

"That don't mean shit. We would know, rookie."

They had seemed rather skilled at getting him into cuffs. "You're cops?"

The younger one said, "Not for a few years now."

"So, what, you worked with Underhill?"

"Yeah," the bald one said. "And he knew you were following him. Told me so, so's in case anything might happen to him, I'd know who to come after."

"Yeah, I was following him. As I believe I just mentioned, I'm a police officer, and we on occasion follow suspects. You might remember that."

"Except he ain't no suspect, and you know it."

If they weren't cops anymore, how were they so certain Underhill hadn't been an official suspect? Rake was so tired of playing against people who seemed to be peeking at his cards.

"So what happened to him?" the older one demanded.

"I followed him that night to an old factory in Pittsburgh. He was there to meet someone, I'd bet. But whoever showed up, showed up with a good bit more than he'd been expecting."

The two ex-cops were exchanging looks.

Rake continued, "But before that happened, it was just me and him. He got the drop on me and we tussled a bit. He wouldn't tell me anything, no matter how I tried. Though it did not occur to me to try breaking his fucking finger with a set of pliers. I suppose I should have considered that. We fought to a standstill and when I realized he wasn't going to spill, I finally left."

"Underhill would never spill," the younger one sneered. "Anyone who'd been paying attention in '44 would know that."

"I was a tad busy in '44. There was a war on. I suppose you got two clubfeet? Or you get the no-balls exemption?"

The younger one took a step and Rake was trying to decide between launching into a head butt or maybe kicking him in the no-balls, given his lack of arms, when the older one said, "Christ, Chet, you take bait quicker'n a starving bass. Just shut the blazes up and let him finish his story."

Chet stood stone faced. "Finish your goddamn story."

Rake paused a moment so as to demonstrate that he wasn't just following this lummox's orders but was in fact enjoying the telling of his tale. "I'd barely made it back to my car when I heard two shots. I ran back and there he was."

Chet said, "We gave up on the pliers too early I think."

"Take me out of these cuffs and see how far you get."

"Dammit, Chet, I said I believe him and I do. He don't know shit."

"He knows more'n I'm comfortable with him knowing."

"You two were kicked off the force the same time he was, weren't you?" Rake guessed. Their cold stares confirmed it.

The pistol in the older one's hands was still pointing at the ground. The shotgun was another three paces behind them.

"So you're his friends, and he told you he was afraid someone was out to get him. Who?" The two ex-cops looked at each other again. Rake pressed, "I know he killed that black girl, and I'm willing to bet whoever he was running from had something to do with it, too."

"He didn't kill her," the older one said. "We ain't fuckin' assassins."

"More like garbage men," Chet said, kicking at a stone.

"Damn right."

Rake waited. He was confident they wanted to tell him more, but asking about it too directly would just annoy them and make them hush up.

The older one started talking again, this time slipping the revolver back into his pocket. That motion alone was enough to get Rake to stand a bit straighter, free from his defensive crouch, and it was enough to cause Chet to step to the side as if he was about ready to get in his truck and drive off.

"We got reason to think that Underhill was killed on account of a job he did recently. It wasn't anything worse or bigger than the sort of jobs they give us these days, but for some reason someone—he didn't tell us who—seems to have panicked."

"Jobs, what jobs?"

"All he did was clean up the mess."

"You're saying someone else killed her, and then it was Underhill's job to remove the body?"

"Hey, give that boy a cigar."

"Who was it?"

"All we know is, he said he was paid to clean up a mess. That ain't all that uncommon, son. That's what they got the damned Rust Division for. We do the shit they don't want to deal with."

"Rust Division?"

"I figured you'd have at least heard of it. Could be you're still too green. Rust Division is what they call the ones let go in '44. We got the shaft for doing nothing worse than damn near every other cop in the city was doing. So sometimes fellows on the force take pity on us and offer us jobs that maybe ain't quite up to the legal standards of normal police work. We ain't an official division and we ain't even an official 'we,' just six ex-cops who get bones thrown our way now and then."

"Except now there are only five," Chet said, eyeing Rake in a way that suggested he did not yet find the rookie beyond suspicion.

Rake had never heard of the Rust Division apart from those few overheard words between Dunlow and Underhill a few nights back.

"So Underhill got called up by a cop and asked to dispose of a body to conceal a crime?"

"What I'm saying is that I can put one and one together, and it appears that with some helpful encouragement, you can, too."

"Why would Underhill do that?"

"Because they paid well."

"Who's 'they'?"

"We don't know. We don't even know who that girl was. He didn't want us to know."

Boggs had told Rake that the girl had worked for Congressman Prescott. That would certainly be the kind of person who could pay to hide an indiscretion. Had Prescott killed his maid? But she'd been alive and in Underhill's presence the night of her death, according to Boggs and Smith. You can't call up a fellow and ask him to dispose of a body if the person in that body is still alive: that's murder for hire.

He thought of mentioning the congressman, but held off. He'd rather keep that bit of intelligence to himself for now and go to them with it later, if he needed to. If he was alive later.

"He still hasn't explained why he was following Underhill," Chet said.

"I'll be glad to. I was following him because I had him for the murder of that girl, whose name was Lily Ellsworth. And since no one else seemed terribly interested in solving it, I figured I'd try." He almost didn't add this, but he wanted to hear their reaction, so he did: "And I wanted to figure out how he was connected to Dunlow."

"Dunlow?" The bald one again gave Rake an almost pitying look. "Dunlow ain't shit on a mule's ass. I never liked that bastard."

Rake said, "I know he was chummy with Underhill, and he's not the kind to have ethical qualms about how to make extra cash on the side."

"He's too stupid to realize that the whole point of the Rust Division is that it's *ex*-cops, so if we ever get caught for something, it's just us who gets nailed, and not the Department," the bald one said. "Even if one of us squealed, they'd never believe us, because we're goddamn felons. We're the perfect protection for them. Dunlow's still a cop—which is a goddamn miracle, by the way—so if he thought he could get in on a job for extra cash, he's a damn fool."

"The few who know about us," Chet said, "think we're something to envy. Or fear. Like we're the bogeyman swooping in for the dirty work. You know what I really am? I'm a blasted security guard on the night shift at a mill. That's what I am, thanks to that bullshit sting."

"We're just doing what we can to get by," his partner said. "Dunlow's a moron to think we're some underworld gang he can get rich with. Least he has a pension."

"Why are you telling me this?" Rake was still cuffed. "What do you expect me to do?"

"This Rust Division stuff has been going on for a while. And we felt there was a mutual respect, that the ones still in the Department realize they're lucky, and we're unlucky that we got kicked out. There but for the grace of God and all that, so they toss us some bones. But whatever Underhill's last job was, someone appears to have killed him to keep his mouth shut. That ain't mutual respect."

Rake tried to puzzle this out. "Why would they kill him? If they used him to insulate them from a murder, why commit another one?"

"We don't know. We're sure as hell trying to find out, from the outside. Maybe you can dig around on the inside."

With that, the bald man reached back into his pocket and took the pliers out. "Here, I'll get you out of those cuffs."

"How about using a key instead of those?"

"I don't have one. Stop being a pussy about it."

He heard metal on metal and felt the tug as the man pulled one of the cuffs apart, then another tug and the cuffs fell. Rake tried not to sigh with relief too obviously.

"Thanks," he said. Then he stepped forward and, with his uninjured left hand, punched Chet square on the nose.

Rake spun around, hoping to knock down the bald one, too, but the fellow had already backed up a step and had dropped the pliers in favor of Rake's revolver. He thumbed back the hammer.

"Why'd you go and do that?" the ex-cop asked.

Rake looked at Chet, who was out cold and already bleeding heavily from his nose. "He and I are square for the finger now."

"Once he wakes up, he ain't gonna feel you're square."

"Then he's free to come after me, but this time I'll see the son of a bitch coming."

"You're something, Rakestraw. You just might survive your job." He looked at Chet and shook his head. Blood was pumping out of Chet's nose but he still appeared to be breathing.

Rake asked, "You mind not pointing my gun at me anymore?"

"Why, so you can break one of my fingers to make *us* square?"

"Don't worry, I like you better than him."

The revolver's hammer was rethumbed and lowered, but the fellow held on to it. Then he walked over to the shotgun and picked it up. More heavily armed now, he walked over and placed Rake's revolver on the passenger seat of Rake's car.

"So," Rake asked, "how do I find you if I learn something that might interest you?"

"Drive up to Norcross and look me up at Second Baptist."

"So we can swap notes between hymns?"

"Careful there. I'm a man of God now. That's where I preach."

"You're serious?"

"Yes. I'm an ordained minister, and I don't take part in the nonsense of my past."

Rake held up his hand. "You just broke my fucking finger."

"I will pray on my knees for forgiveness tonight. But some things just need to be done." He nodded toward Chet. "Now buck up and help me get him in the truck."

"Hellfire. Do it yourself, *Reverend*. And don't waste any prayers on me."

Rake walked back to his car, thinking about which emergency room he should choose for resetting his finger.

The reverend replied, "I don't believe I will."

29

MAMA DOVE WAS halfway down the stairs after her customary afternoon nap when one of the girls told her there was a man here for her. Said in a very different tone than if this particular man was a john.

The fans were blasting in the windows yet still it felt too hot as she walked through the foyer. It was hard to predict the impact of weather on her business. Men were funny about the heat, and though they hardly lost their sex drive, there were times when they were just too lazy to leave their stuffy houses and get in their stuffy cars to drive out to Mama Dove's for some stuffy sex. Some of her girls had only had a couple of men a night lately, and she'd been thinking of letting them go, too many mouths to feed for too little income.

The door to the kitchen was open, the better for air to circulate. She immediately recognized his big old feet, kicked up on one of the chairs like they owned the place.

"I told you never to call my house, Marla."

"So nice to see you," she said, her voice flat. "Why don't you come in."

Dunlow was sitting at the table with a tumbler and an unmarked bottle of whiskey he'd helped himself to.

"You look fatter in your civvies."

He smirked at her and was unable to come up with a quick enough retort. He stood, not so much sucking in his gut as giving it more length to spread itself across.

"Janisse keeps me well fed I guess."

She motioned to the bottle. "Little early for that. You want any coffee instead?"

"What I want is for you to tell me why you called my house. At least twice that I know of."

"Well, my telegraph's busted and the smoke signals don't work so well anymore. How else am I supposed to tell you I need to talk?"

His eyes were colder now. He didn't need to say, *You're supposed to just wait your black ass until I choose to come here.*

She walked over to a carafe of lukewarm coffee. She drank it that way whenever it wasn't winter, adding some sugar that always sank to the bottom.

"I thought it was important enough to break your rules. You know all about breaking rules, remember, Lionel?"

And like that he was beside her. It always surprised her how fast he was, man that big. She hated herself for flinching.

"Suppose I do," he said. She could feel his belly against her own, and though he was still holding the whiskey he let his right hand help itself to her hip. She was wearing a white nightgown, cotton and thin, but even that was too much in this heat, and his palm felt even warmer against her. Her rubbed her, moving down and slowly around behind. "And I know you do, too."

She was pinned against the counter and could smell the alcohol on his breath (exactly how long had he been down here drinking?). Then he was kissing her. It was familiar even if it had been years. He was rough and needed a shave. His hand was acting like it owned her, because it had once and it believed things never changed.

When he stopped, she said, "You thought I called you for *that?*"

Slapping him wouldn't have been nearly as effective. He stepped back and the hunger in his eyes that makes even aging men look like puppy dogs was gone, replaced by the all-too-familiar pall of acceptance and defeat.

"Why don't you tell me why you were calling before I get even angrier and take it out on one of your girls."

"I figured you'd want to know that other officers have been by to ask about *your* girl."

"My girl?"

She slanted her head, practically eyeing him sideways. Did he really not know what she was talking about? What would be sadder, his stupidity or the fact that Lily Ellsworth meant so little to him as to be not worth remembering?

"The one who ain't alive no more. The one I took in for your friend Underhill."

"What cops came by?"

"Officer Boggs. Preacher's son."

"Don't you worry 'bout those YMCA cops. They can't hurt you, I'll see to that."

"Why you so sure *I'm* worried about being hurt? Maybe I was concerned that *you* had gotten yourself into trouble."

He smiled. At moments like this, fleeting though they were, the layer of fat faded, as did the years, and she caught a glimpse of the man he'd been, the confidence, the casual ease with which he used that smile and his body and the jokes that had seemed funny once, though never quite as funny as he'd thought them to be.

"Now, Marla, you don't need to be worrying about me."

"Who was she?"

"I haven't the foggiest idea."

"I don't believe that."

"Well, believe it. I don't mean to lower your opinion of me, but some things Underhill does, I don't get told any more than you."

"You mean to say you didn't even *ask* him what her story was?"

"Did you?" He stepped back to the table, pouring a couple more fingers into his glass.

"It's not my place. All he told me was she needed to be removed from a situation."

She wondered whether some of her girls were in the hallway or maybe around the corner in the parlor, straining to hear every word.

"Then that's the truth."

"Well, I don't appreciate having your fellow officers showing up and insinuating that I'm going to be arrested for helping your friends. It certainly seems to me there's things I deserve to know about."

"I'm sorry to hear that." Big sip.

"Why don't you just call him up and ask him what it was she'd done?"

"Because he's dead."

The ceiling above started creaking, quickly, so at least someone was making her some money right now. The sudden noise may have covered up her shock at his remark, but probably not.

"What happened?"

"Got himself shot."

"What the hell is going on?"

"Nothing you need worry about."

The girl was dead and so was the man who had demanded Mama Dove take her in, get her the hell away from the family for whom she'd been working and causing so much misery. *Just keep her in here, at all times. She ain't allowed out until we give you the word. Put her to work and let her see what that's like, Lord knows she can use it. But watch her close because she's a damned thief and she's got a particular taste for white people's money.*

Then why on earth are you giving her to me? she'd asked. *Put her ass in jail.*

Can't do that. Gentleman she stole from ain't the type to press charges. Ain't the type to like attention.

It had been explained to her that if this girl managed to extricate herself from Mama Dove's, many a foul consequence would ensue, and they would all fall on the madam's head. Lily was being put under house arrest, and Mama Dove was to provide the house. And the handcuffs, if the johns wanted that and paid extra.

"You know I don't worry easy, Lionel, but two dead bodies is enough to make my heart rate tick just the slightest bit up."

The ceiling stopped squeaking. The faster they were, the better.

"She's caused all the damage she's gonna cause."

"Then why are you drinking so much?"

He eyed her, then put the glass down. The bags under his eyes seemed about twice as big as usual, as if most of what he drank settled there rather than in his gut.

"You don't know who shot him, do you?" she said. "Or her?"

"Officer Dunlow's on the case."

That cocksure attitude had gone from grating to exasperating. "You . . . *men* really think women don't talk to each other? You don't think she might have opened her mouth and told me a few things, Lionel? You don't think she may have con*fided* in me?"

He stepped closer. "We know damn well how women talk. Hear your voices in our sleep."

"I'm glad you notice."

"And if I didn't know better, I'd say it sounded for a second there like you were threatening me."

Like before, his hands retook "his" property. One at the small of her back and the other at her neck. Not tightly but not gently either.

"I'm not threatening you," she said. "I'm just saying there are things I wish I didn't know."

He wasn't squeezing, yet. "The best thing to do in those circumstances, which you should know very well by now, is pretend you don't know, and pretend you don't know, and pretend you don't know. And then, eventually, you forget."

She could tell he was enjoying this, holding her this way, letting her wonder whether he was going to strangle her or grab her ass again, kiss her or slap her. All of which he'd done before, and never had she been able to predict it.

"And the next time a white cop comes by asking questions?" she asked.

"White cops?"

"Did I forget to mention that? One time it was Officer Boggs, the colored one. Another time there was a white one, Rakestraw."

He released her and backed up a step. "Rakestraw?" She had meant to hit some nerves before and hadn't. But now, with this name that had been meaningless to her, he looked like he'd gone sick to his stomach.

"Yes."

"Describe him to me."

"White. Dark hair. Your height, big. Not so hard on the eyes. In a way, he reminded me of you, minus a whole lot of long and tangled road."

Why had he needed her to prove who it had been? Who was Rakestraw to him? She decided not to ask. It was good to see him so unmoored.

He walked back to the table, shaking his head. He muttered, but she couldn't hear what.

Then he threw the tumbler against the cupboards not more than a foot from where she was standing. She screamed and raised her hands to her head too late, the feel of something glancing against it, glass everywhere in the room now, always so many more pieces than you'd think could come from something that had once been whole. She rubbed the side of her face and hoped she would not see blood on her palm when she pulled it away, but other than that she was standing there stock-still and barefoot in a sea of shards as Dunlow's boots crunched their way out of her house.

30

DRIVING HIS FATHER'S green Buick, Boggs pulled in front of the apartment building where Smith lived and tapped the horn. He'd never visited his partner's neighborhood before and he did not fail to notice the general disrepair of the street, the bits of trash strewn on the ground, the worn-out laundry hanging from clotheslines, the drunk old lady on the opposite side of the street, muttering to herself.

After less than a minute, Smith walked out, his white short-sleeved shirt ironed and tucked into gray pleated slacks. More noticeable was the jumbled blanket laying across his arms. Boggs reached over and opened the door for him.

The blanket was (barely) concealing a rifle. The gun was so long, part of it poked into Boggs's right leg as Smith sat down. He'd studied the maps that morning and guessed it would take them ninety minutes if they didn't get stuck at any train crossings.

"Don't shoot my leg, please."

"That's the handle pointed at you."

Boggs had borrowed the car under false pretenses, inventing some story about errands he'd needed to run. He was not accustomed to lying to his father, and it added to the sense of disquiet he felt as he drove beyond Atlanta.

After twenty minutes they were passing through a quiet interval between towns—it did not take long for one leaving that city to feel like they were already in the country. Now that they weren't at risk of being observed, Smith rearranged his belongings, the blanket falling to the floor. He held in his lap a Winchester rifle. The metal confidently gleamed from a recent cleaning.

"Cover that up again and put it in the backseat."

"That's too far away. It stays here."

"Then cover it again."

Smith shook his head, but a moment later he pulled the blanket back onto his lap.

In the glove box was a .45 revolver Boggs had bought after the war and had barely used in the first two years he'd owned it. Then, after he'd sent in his police application, he'd used it regularly for target practice in the vast backyard of family friends who lived down in Clayton County. He'd trained there for hours over the three-month application process, annihilating countless Coca-Cola bottles, hoping his lack of combat experience wouldn't doom his chances.

Smith opened the glove box, nodded at the weapon as if they were old friends, and added his own .38. The box, now crowded with firearms, could barely close.

They had packed sandwiches and canteens for water rather than risk not being able to find a lunch counter that would cater to Negroes. The guns would stay in the car, Boggs had insisted. Smith was right: he had delayed this trip because he was scared of the Georgia country. Scared of its people and their ways. The only other time he'd ventured this far from Sweet Auburn had been that awful training camp in South Carolina, the three worst years of his life.

He drove five miles under the speed limit lest he find himself in a rural cop's doghouse. The windows were down, but all that did was blow sweltering air in their faces. Smith seemed to mind it more, playing with his pomaded hair a few times. They both wore darkened glasses yet Boggs was squinting in the sun and gripping the wheel at ten o'clock and two o'clock. This would be the longest drive he'd ever attempted.

With every passing mile he felt less safe. He'd read *Heart of Darkness* at Morehouse and he felt he was on that boat in the river, venturing deeper and deeper into the wilderness of white men, the same effect if the opposite colors of Conrad's racist views.

They passed a Congregationalist church whose hand-lettered sign advised that they pray for their weak president.

"Don't like it out here, do you?" Smith asked.

"What gives you that idea?"

"I don't think you could be holding that wheel any tighter if you tried."

"Do *you* like it?"

"No. But I don't see how it's worse'n downtown."

He was right. Boggs, through his family connections and their car, had been able to live most of his life by avoiding downtown, the insulting buses, the company of whites. Smith hadn't been so fortunate. For all Boggs's education, it was his partner who was more schooled in dealing with white people.

They passed hog farms and silos, endless fields of cotton. Boggs had read in the papers that the summer's unusually persistent rains were wreaking havoc on Georgia crops, and more than a few times the sun glinted off stagnant water that lined the rows between crops. That year the peaches were all enormous and plump with water, but tasteless as cotton.

Two white men in a red pickup behind him were unimpressed by Boggs's adherence to the speed limit. Boggs stuck his left hand out the window and waved the truck to pass. It did so, engine roaring, and he saw an old man in the passenger seat eye him with what looked more like pity than hatred, *These damned Knee-grows and their cars not working right.*

"I have an aunt and uncle down in Clayton County," Boggs said. "He's a carpenter, has a good plot of land and grows vegetables, watermelon. He likes it down there. We visit now and again. And I can always see my daddy exhaling just a bit when we get back home."

They drove past a billboard proclaiming opposition to the United Nations. *Keep America safe from foreigners!* it warned, against an outline of other flags in flames. A hand-drawn sign on the other side of the street advertised an upcoming religious revival and pig picking.

"You've proven yourself good at keeping secrets, so I'll tell you another. I was born out here."

"Whereabouts?"

"Small town, Dunsonville."

"Why is it a secret?"

"The part that's a secret is my daddy was lynched."

Boggs was not remotely confident in his driving ability, but he turned his head to see the look on his partner's face. There was nothing to see but pursed lips and those featureless sunglasses.

Boggs turned his eyes back to the road and Smith told the story, his father the returning veteran, the parade, the end of one life and the derailing of his mother's, and then his own.

"Wasn't a secret so much as something nobody likes to talk about. Especially my uncle. But it's a secret now because I didn't mention it when I applied to the Department. I listed my uncle as my father, which is legally true, since he adopted me when I was a baby."

Smith was right, there was no way the city would have hired as one of its first Negro officers a man who'd lost a parent to white hands. During their battery of psychological tests, Boggs himself had been asked countless variations of "How do you feel about white people?" or "Tell me more about your family's experiences with officers of the law."

Boggs couldn't tell if he was sweating more now because of the story or if it was just the heat and the stress of the drive. "I'm sorry to hear that."

"S'awright. I didn't even know it 'til I was sixteen. I was raised thinking my aunt and uncle were my parents. Don't remember a thing about my real folks. Then my mom—I mean, my aunt—passed away when I was thirteen, and things didn't go so well with me and my uncle then. Fought a lot, and he picked a bad time to drop that little truth on me."

The road bent around a curve and down a hill and then it stretched out long and straight, the Piedmont shimmering before them and gradually giving way as they drove deeper into Georgia.

Smith added, "Though I suppose there ain't no delicate way of saying it, is there?"

They knew the address, but it didn't show up on the one map of Peacedale that they'd been able to find at the Auburn Avenue library, the only branch in Atlanta they were allowed to use. The Peacedale Police Department's files, which they'd been shown by McInnis, gave them only a rough idea of where the house was. Lucius had even visited his brother Reginald's insurance office to pore through their files—municipal records of Negroes were so haphazard and incomplete, Negro insurance companies were the true source of accurate information about the community. But the company hadn't done much business in Peacedale, so they weren't any help.

When they finally reached Peacedale—twenty minutes later than Boggs had expected—they drove down the small, one-stoplight Main Street, observing the surroundings while trying not to look too curious. A post office, a Methodist church, a soda fountain and pharmacy. A general store. A rebel flag hanging outside the greengrocer's. Several windows proudly advertising Coca-Cola and ice. A tiny town square with a stone obelisk memorializing the Confederate war dead (Boggs couldn't read the inscription, but he'd seen an identical one in his aunt and uncle's town). Hardly anyone was out, as it was nearing noon and the sun had a serious agenda that no sane person wanted to get involved with. Two older white men walking out of the post office appeared to gaze at these car-driving Negroes for longer than Boggs would have liked, but he couldn't be sure as he wasn't looking directly at them. Smith meanwhile had his right arm casually dangling out his window, like he was going out of his way to display as much colored skin as possible. Boggs considered asking him to pull his arm back in but could already anticipate Smith's reaction, so he didn't bother.

The post office might have been able to help find the address, but the clerks might tip off the local cops that two black Atlantans were in town, so Boggs drove past it without stopping.

Figuring that Negro farmers were less likely to be spies for the local police—a supposition they knew was risky indeed—they pulled into a long driveway when they saw two colored men rolling a wheelbarrow behind a small dilapidated house. More like a shack, the wood old and warped in places, a lone window in the front.

The farmers wore overalls without T-shirts and seemed on their way to the front porch, where a small overhang offered only a sliver of midday shade. They looked up as Boggs drove toward them. He left the engine running and Smith stayed in the car.

"Morning," Boggs said, though it wasn't anymore. "I'm having trouble finding the Ellsworths' place."

He saw now that this was a father and son, one of them a lanky teenager and the other thin and grizzled, both of them sweaty and rank. The father asked, "You kin to them?"

He didn't want to lie, so he dodged the question. "I wanted to pay my respects."

It was so quiet and bright out here. Boggs's running auto may have been the only one for miles.

"That ain't right what happened," the man said.

"You know anything about it?"

"You his brother? Cousin or something?"

"I knew Lily."

The man paused, then told his son, "Go on and fetch the water." After the teenager had walked out of earshot, the man said, "It ain't no secret. Ever'body knows. Sheriff don't like him, want to say he killed his girl even though he was miles from where she was, so sheriff gets two no-counts to say he *said* he done it one night when he was drunk. And ever'body know Otis ain't never take to liquor."

Boggs nodded along like he knew all this. "Why did the sheriff have it in for him? Could it have happened to anyone, or they take a special dislike to Otis?"

"I don't know what he was thinking buying that truck. It's a damn shame."

High above, three vultures were looping in vaguely concentric circles through a sky bleached white by the heat.

"Didn't know things had gotten so bad in this town."

The farmer looked offended by that, as if insulting the local white people was only acceptable if you lived here. "Most of us know how to get along."

Boggs's city accent and car were marking him an outsider. He asked again where the Ellsworths lived, realizing as he asked it that there couldn't be too many Ellsworths left alive.

The Ellsworth property was the sort of place that made Boggs deeply grateful for his many blessings. It looked like it had once been a one-floor house, its attic since expanded to become a bedroom, the nave a few feet taller than seemed proportionate. The white paint was chipping and the steps leading up to the porch were leaning to the right. Rusty wheelbarrows and pieces of boards that had once been an unrealized carpentry project leaned against the side of the building. The front lawn was recently mown and quite large—the house was set a good fifty yards from the road—and in the back Boggs saw rows of cotton and vegetables filling out what must have been a five-acre plot, or larger, shaped like a wide bowl, dipping a bit in the center and then opening out again to bake in the sun before hitting up against piney woods on three sides.

They hadn't passed an electric or telephone pole in miles. The furrows in the ground had no doubt been ploughed by mules, not tractors. And the truck that had aroused so much envy in his neighbor was not in the driveway.

They could see one figure far off in the cotton, but apart from that there was no sign of life except the loud barking of a dog.

Boggs drove to the end of the driveway and shut off the engine. Before they could get out, two enormous hounds, one of them dark brown and one a lighter, mottled white-and-tan mix, were circling the car and furiously trying to tell them something. The lighter dog leaped up onto the passenger side, spittle streaking Smith's window.

"Maybe I'll take my gun back out," Smith said.

Sweat was rolling down Boggs's cheek when he heard a voice calling out.

The dogs let out a few more barks, as if to warn the newcomers that their opinions still counted, but they otherwise calmed as a man walked toward them. He was slight and not tall, yet the beasts had been transformed to mere pets by his command. He wore a wide-brimmed straw hat, a white T-shirt, and dungarees gone deep orange in the legs from kneeling in Georgia clay. He walked closer to the car and Boggs could see now he was young, in his teens, with the same sad but watchful eyes Boggs had seen on Otis's face.

As Boggs sat in the Ellsworths' cramped parlor, he realized that he'd been so preoccupied with the physical risks he was taking that he had failed to brace himself for how emotionally difficult these conversations were going to be.

It hit him when he saw Jimmy Ellsworth's eyes up close. The kid was far too young to have eyes like that.

The water Jimmy had handed them was barely cold and there was no ice and it tasted of the earth and Boggs would have gladly drunk ten more glasses like it, but he made himself nurse it slowly so he wouldn't have to ask Jimmy to fetch more.

The parlor was spartan, the furniture obviously homemade, some with threadbare upholstery and others with none. Extinguished candles in the corner gave evidence to the lack of electricity. The light was provided by open windows, which let in air and flies. In an unframed photo on one wall, Jesus looked down beatifically from what may have been the torn-out illustration from a magazine, and nearby were old photos of kin. A few throw rugs curled up at the edges from the humidity. It was threadbare, yet no dirt or rocks crackled beneath Boggs's shoes as he walked across the wood floor. They didn't have much, but they'd taken care of what they had.

Jimmy told them his mother wasn't feeling well. She was in her bedroom upstairs and hadn't been about much lately. He and his brother had been taking turns tending to her, with help from neighbors, but those neighbors were at their homes right now.

"My brother, David, he out in the fields with a buddy of his. He's helping us out, there's a lot to do and just the two of us now."

He had looked tall and in his element outside, but now that he sat indoors his lanky physique vanished into a slouch and he fidgeted in the seat. It was like he reverse-aged ten years by entering the house.

"Y'all really policemen?"

"Yes, from Atlanta," Boggs said. "So to be up front about things, we don't really have any authority out here. In fact, I can about guarantee you that your local cops wouldn't want us here and wouldn't want you talking with us. So you can tell us to git if you want to. We'll respect that." The kid had broken eye contact after speaking and was staring at the floor. "But we've been looking into what happened to your sister, and now that we've heard what's happened here, we wanted to see you."

"Did the police come by after your father was killed?" Smith asked.

Such a long pause, Boggs wondered if the kid hadn't heard.

"They come by the next morning, tell Mama to come fetch his body." Jimmy's voice broke. The hounds wandered over and protectively sat on the floor beside him.

Smith asked, "What did they tell you happened to your father?"

Eye contact, blurred by tears. "They didn't need to tell me anything. I know what they done."

"Tell us," Smith said. Neither officer held a notebook, trying to keep this as informal as possible.

"We were going to leave for Chicago next day. But we couldn't tell, Pa said. We went to the general store to buy a few things he say we'd need for the trip. It was just me and him. We went there round lunchtime and the owner, Mr. Snelling, was asking him all these questions, why you buying all this, what you need that for, that kinda thing. Pa . . ." The kid wiped his eyes.

Waiting for him to regain his composure was about the hardest thing Boggs and Smith had done.

"Pa was nervous. He didn't seem so good at lying." Then the damnedest thing: the kid managed a half smile. "He always tell us not to lie, and he was there doing it, and he wasn't too good at it."

The half smile didn't last long.

"This Mr. Snelling give you any trouble before?"

"No, sir, not usually. He's not all friendly but he never be like that before."

"Then what happened?" Boggs asked.

"We'd almost made it back home when the police pulled us over. Said we'd stolen something from the store. Pa didn't want to get out, but they made him. They told me to walk home, and they put him in the back of their car. They wouldn't let me carry the groceries home, neither."

The ceiling creaked from footsteps above.

"We were up most that night, waiting. Me and my brother wanted to go to the neighbors and get a ride to the police station, but Ma forbid it. Lot of cars on the road that night, lot of them just stopping up there," and he pointed out the window, toward the end of the driveway, "like they watching us. Then in the morning, the sheriff come by."

They waited to hear if there was more. There wasn't.

Smith asked, "Where's your father's truck?"

Jimmy shrugged. "I ask Ma for us to ask the police about it, but she say not to. Say they only give us more trouble."

The futility was stifling. Boggs and Smith could never inspect the body. They couldn't investigate the crime scene, even if they could find it. They had no authority to question witnesses. Even if they tried anyway, they would only be able to question the Negro witnesses—if there were any, and only if those witnesses were brave enough to talk to them. And why should they be? Boggs and Smith could offer them nothing: not protection, not justice. The only thing they might possibly offer was the remote chance of a future in which such events would not recur, though this, too, seemed so unlikely as to be absurd.

Jimmy leaned forward then, elbows on knees, and sunk his head into his hands. The sound of his weeping was like a glimpse into a world Boggs never wanted to go anywhere near.

Smith stepped out onto the porch. He needed air. He needed to be farther away from this family and their pain. He needed to think.

He put on his sunglasses and gazed out at the front lawn, trying to imagine life out here. The town he'd been born in couldn't be so different from this. If his father hadn't been killed, perhaps Smith would call a place like this home. Maybe he'd be a blacksmith or a carpenter, hammering nails in the roof of a farmhouse as sweat poured from his body. Maybe a lawn like this would be his most prized possession, if he was lucky enough to own one.

Cobwebs clung in the corners of the porch beneath the awning, tiny insect caskets suspended there. Dirt dauber nests dotted the front of the house.

One of the hounds had followed Smith out and it approached him silently, the creature so tall its head was level with Smith's belt buckle. Its tongue was hanging out and it was panting loudly. Smith placed a hand on its head and stroked it slowly, unable to muster the kind of assurances a dog might want to hear.

Smith had been out there but two minutes when a tan Chevrolet slowly drove down the street. It stopped in front of the Ellsworths' driveway.

From the distance he could just barely see two figures in the front seat. White men. He stared at the car and willed it to drive away. After ten long seconds, it did.

Inside, Boggs waited for Jimmy's sobbing to at least slow down, or grow quieter. It took a while.

"You said your family was going to Chicago?"

"Yes, sir. Pa's big plan. Try things up there."

"He had mentioned that to me, too. But I hadn't realized it was coming so soon."

"About a week ago, he told us after dinner it would be in a couple of days. Caught us all by surprise. I mean, he'd already told my ma, I could tell that, but she didn't seem too happy about it."

Boggs heard the sound of weary footsteps on old stairs.

Then the front door opened and Smith walked back in. The darker hound leaped into action as if a new intruder had broken in, and the other hound darted in from the porch. Jimmy called out for them to hush. He stood; the dogs' misbehavior had given him a purpose and returned him from the isolated place he'd curled into.

"Let those dogs out, Jimmy," a woman's voice said.

Boggs turned and saw Mrs. Ellsworth standing at the foot of the stairs, thin arms crossed before her as if bracing for the next blow. Her hair was pulled back and her jaw was set tight and lines were etched across her forehead. Everything about her looked like it was on the verge of snapping.

She wore a blue housedress and the tips of her bare toes were startlingly white. But not the rest of her: Boggs had expected her to be light-skinned, yet she was as dark as her husband.

Boggs introduced himself and his partner. "We're very sorry for your loss."

"Why are you here? The police have already brought enough trouble."

She was eyeing them as if convinced they were complicit in the local cops' crimes. Boggs tried to explain what he'd said to Jimmy, about their not having any power but wanting to find the truth nonetheless. It sounded even more pathetic the second time. So much worse was seeing those words glance harmlessly off a face that had already stared into more pain than most can imagine.

"I don't want you here. I know you've driven a long way, but you can't help us. I'd like you to go now."

"I understand this is difficult, ma'am, but if we could ask you just a few things, it might help us in the investigation into what happened to your daughter."

"Investigation?"

"We've been talking to people who knew her in the city," Smith said. "People she lived with in the boardinghouses, other friends she made. Her old teacher, Mr. Hurst."

She scowled. "You tracked him down?"

"He's in Atlanta now, ma'am. Moved there just a few months before your daughter did. They got back in touch."

She waved as if at an invisible yellow jacket. "We don't need to be talking about those things now." She took a sudden step to the side and put a hand to the wall.

Jimmy led her to a chair. "You haven't eaten all day."

Boggs hated that he couldn't just leave her alone to grieve in peace. But he and Smith would probably never make it out here again, so now was the time.

"Ma'am, your husband told us Lily sent you some letters from when she'd been living in Atlanta. He'd told me he'd lend them to us, in case they might shed some light on someone who might have wanted to harm her. Would you mind if we took a look at them?"

"You don't need to read those."

"Anything at all might help, ma'am," Smith said.

"Mama," Jimmy spoke up, "we should let them see whatever they need if they can—"

"Boy, no one asked you your opinion. Now go get me some milk."

"Yes, ma'am." Jimmy hurried to the kitchen, the dogs happily following.

"Ma'am," Boggs said, "I give you my word I'll treat those letters like gold. We don't even need to take them with us—we can just read them here."

"There's nothing in there that will help you."

"I do understand, ma'am, but I'd prefer if my partner and I could be the judges of that."

"*Ma'am.* You're so polite. Raised right and proper, weren't you?"

"I suppose I was lucky. My father's a preacher and he takes those things seriously. My mother even more so."

"I'm sorry. But I'm not changing my mind."

"Mrs. Ellsworth," Smith said, "why didn't you want your daughter to move to Atlanta?"

"City ain't a good place for young ladies. And I'd say I was proven right."

"It's better out here?"

"Can be. You do things the right way."

Jimmy returned with a glass of milk and a plate of honeyed toast. She told him she wasn't hungry, but he insisted. She put the plate on her lap and took a bite.

"Did her letters tell you much about her job at the congressman's?" Boggs asked.

She glanced up from the toast like she'd bitten into something sharp. But she took her time chewing and swallowing and washing it down.

"She said she had a job there."

"Nothing else?"

"She said he seemed nice but she didn't get to meet him much. Mostly met his wife and son. Said they weren't all that friendly but weren't bad to work for neither."

"It must have been a little nerve-racking to be around important folks like that."

"Girl was good on her feet. Good manners. She was smart." Her eyes started to well up, and she reached for the toast as if it might salve the pain.

"Ma'am, I know the police here are saying your husband hurt her, but I don't think that's true. Do you?"

"Course not." The pain shaded to anger.

"They're also saying he came into a lot of money that they seem to think he got through her somehow, though they aren't very interested in figuring out how. Is it true that she sent you more money than you'd been expecting?"

"What did you say your name was?"

"Officer Lucius Boggs."

"Officer Boggs, I've worked hard to raise a good family." She was almost whispering now, the only way to sneak any of her voice through the tightening walls of her throat. "I had that little girl before I was a wedded woman, my husband probably told you. And that's not some-thing I'm proud of, but I found a good man and we worked hard and we tried to make a good life."

She stared out the window, tried to compose herself. Jimmy put a hand on her shoulder.

"Raised us a good family. I can tell you, I don't know what happened to her. And I don't know why anyone would have tried to hurt her. But that little girl did nothing wrong. Ever."

Minutes later, Boggs led Smith out of the house. He felt sick to his stomach. They were quiet as they approached the car, weighed down by a heaviness worse than the humidity that soaked their backs.

"When I talked to Otis," Boggs said as they reached the Buick, "he made it sound like the letters hadn't mentioned anything at all about the job at the congressman's. Yet she just said Lily talked about the Prescotts in them."

He opened his car door and got in. The seats were so hot through his clothes that he leaned forward as he turned the ignition. How people worked in fields on days like this was incomprehensible to him. Even the steering wheel hurt to touch, let alone a hoe or shovel.

They'd never even met the other son, and barely had twenty minutes with Mrs. Ellsworth. This entire day was a failure. All he'd done was make their day even less bearable. Every time he'd tried to help that family, he cursed it.

Boggs looked behind him so he could back out of the drive, and he was nearly back on the road when Smith stopped him.

"Over there."

Out in the fields they could see a figure running toward them. The older Ellsworth brother, David. He was about Jimmy's size, with a lon-ger face that took more after Otis than his mother. Both of the Ellsworth boys were a good deal darker than their sister had been, Boggs noticed.

David ran up to the car. He asked them nothing. In fact, he had come to give them some answers.

Ten minutes later they were back on the road. Boggs wasn't speeding, but he was anxious to get out of the sticks.

"Makes a lot more sense now, doesn't it?" Smith said.

"Yeah."

"We'd both been thinking it without realizing it. Explains why the mother was so short with us."

"Come on. She had plenty reasons to be short with us."

"She did." The nausea he'd felt earlier had faded, replaced by a quickened heartbeat, new connections forming in his mind. They had a long drive to plot out their next steps.

Five minutes later, he checked the rearview and caught his breath. A few hundred yards away, a squad car was pursuing them, lights flashing.

"Oh Jesus. We got the local cops."

Smith turned around. Boggs checked the rearview mirror and saw that a second car had accelerated to join the first. Boggs had driven through miles of farmland but now they were in the piney woods, the road narrow and straight, only a few gentle rises to the land.

"I have to pull over."

"Are you crazy?"

"I can't outrace them in this. If I even try, they'll shoot us down."

"And what do you think they'll do if we pull over?"

The squad cars were rapidly making up the distance. Smith popped open the glove box, removing his revolver and sliding it into his pocket.

"You just heard what they did to Ellsworth," he said.

Boggs smacked the steering wheel. Did Smith honestly want a shoot-out? Did he think they had any chance of surviving one? Did he just want revenge—for Ellsworth and his own father—and had Boggs stupidly let himself get drawn into something he'd never get out of?

"We're just going to talk to them," Boggs said.

"*If* that's all they do." As Smith said that, he reached to the backseat for the rifle.

Boggs said a silent prayer as he let his foot fall on the brake.

31

CUTTING VINES IN the midsummer heat was not Rake's idea of a pleasant way to spend the morning. Or anyone's idea. But he'd let things slide during the winter, when the work would have been the easiest, and in spring he'd been too busy with the new job. The previous owner clearly hadn't tended the yard in years, possibly decades. Virginia creeper and English ivy and something that looked suspiciously like poison ivy had completely wrapped the trunks of the five largest trees in their backyard, coating them in green from the ground to about twenty feet up. He crouched in the backyard with shears and a serrated knife and eventually had to trade up to a hacksaw for the thicker vines, which were as wide as his forearms.

To guard against the poison ivy, he was wearing a long-sleeved shirt, jeans, and work gloves. He used his sleeve on his forehead so he wouldn't touch his face. The only reason he was doing this was because Cassie was deathly allergic to the stuff—family legend had it she'd nearly died from it twice, the second time her face puffing up and darkening like a bruised peach after some idiot neighbor burned a patch of land, including poison ivy, and the smoke cloud paid no heed to property lines. Odds were, Denny Jr. and the baby had inherited the allergy. Now that Denny Jr. was moving around more, Rake was doing his fatherly duty, protecting the clan by combating Southern vegetation in ninety-degree heat.

The fact that he was doing this with one of his fingers in a splint made the work seem more like penance, which perhaps it was. The digit was swollen and he'd taken some aspirin—the doctor at the emergency room last night had offered him stronger stuff, but no thanks, Rake had seen what that did to plenty of men at the front—and in a way the brute exertion distracted the rest of his body from that one small damaged part.

He'd finished three of the trees and was contemplating the merits of some rest versus charging ahead when Cassie told him his partner was here. She was just inside the house at the back door, then Dunlow emerged through it.

"*That* looks like fun. Should have hired out one of my boys to do that, they could use the spending money."

A strange premonition took hold of Rake. While he crouched amid the scattered tools and piles of severed vines, partly obscured from the house thanks to the shrubbery, he folded the serrated knife into its handle and slipped it into his jeans pocket.

"No thanks," he said. "You've told me too much about your boys."

Cassie went back inside. Rake had invited Dunlow and his wife over for dinner once and had not repeated the gesture. Nor had it been reciprocated. Afterward Cassie had made some anodyne comments, too polite to criticize Dunlow's language or manners or more likely just not wanting to get in the middle. But he could tell she, too, didn't like him, and in the ensuing weeks he'd told her enough about Dunlow for her to want to give him the widest possible berth. And Rake had left out the bad stuff.

"Why don't you come take a break, talk at my place." There was no question mark at the end of that.

"I got two more to do. Maybe later."

Dunlow walked closer. Rake picked up a hint of liquor. "You and me need to have an overdue conversation and those vines can wait. If your pretty lady wasn't in that house, I would be dragging you by the scruff of your goddamn neck right now. So shut your mouth with the complaints and get on."

Rake was too proud to let someone, even his partner, threaten him on his own property, but he didn't want to get in a brawl in front of his wife and kids. He was down a finger and he was hot and exhausted and in need of some water, so the calculations he was performing in his head were unbalanced and swayed by physical factors. If all the sneaking and scheming he had managed the past few weeks were going to come to a head, he didn't want that to happen in his backyard.

Dunlow wore only a white undershirt, hanging past the top of his dungarees, and Rake couldn't quite tell if he had a piece on him. Small of his back, probably, but then again big fellows like this could hide pistols in their front pockets and hip holsters surprisingly well.

Rake kept his eyes on his partner and took off his work gloves, slowly, to show he wasn't going to be rushed or scared.

Then he walked toward the house, calling to Cassie that he needed to see something at Lionel's but would be back soon. She poked her head out the back door and looked surprised but not concerned, and he gave her a smile, nothing to be concerned about. Telling her he loved her would have set off alarms, so he kept his mouth shut.

Dunlow's house was only a few blocks away yet he was too lazy to make the walk. They drove back in Dunlow's Ford, Rake keeping his right hand near his pocket in case he needed to go for the knife, though he knew it would be an awkward weapon in such quarters.

"The nigger's house," Dunlow said as they passed Calvin's new place. "Bringing their trouble to our shores."

As far as Rake knew, there had been no other incidents. "I haven't heard of any trouble."

"Oh, you will soon enough. Don't you worry 'bout that."

Dunlow's low-slung bungalow was shaded by a monstrous white oak in the front yard, its massive boughs stretching the length of the yard. Dunlow parked in the driveway and said, "Out back."

Rake followed him as they walked through the door of a wooden fence that Dunlow himself had likely built. The yard sloped down and, true to Rake's comment, it didn't look like any teenagers had mown the lawn lately. Honeybees darted about as the men's walk disturbed their purchase on dandelions. At the edge of Dunlow's property was a wooded area that grew around a tiny creek, more like a very long and narrow puddle, but just before that an old work shed hid beneath a natural trellis of vines almost as completely as the main house hid beneath that oak.

"Step into my office."

The shed was surprisingly big on the inside. It seemed like a perfectly good place to work on home repair projects or slowly torture kidnap victims to death. Tools hung from pegs on one wall, a couple of wood horses leaning there amid piles of sawdust, a scent of paint or paint thinner or both. Faint light came in through a lone window, and Dunlow hit the switch on a small lamp atop a folding table that had perhaps hosted a few late-night poker games when the boys wanted to be free of women's eyes. Nails rolled across the floor as Rake stepped, dead moths hung from industrious spiderwebs in the corners, and a few old yard signs from elections Rake dimly remembered lay in a pile. It was roughly two hundred degrees in there.

"Have a seat."

Four old tree stumps had been arranged around the table as chairs. Dunlow lowered himself onto one and Rake sat opposite him.

A bottle appeared on the table, along with two glasses. Dunlow poured.

"No thanks," Rake said. Was this the last drink before the firing squad? He hadn't expected such hospitality.

"Can it and drink." Dunlow followed his own advice.

"No. Thanks."

"Drink it."

"I don't think you've had enough yet. You have mine and we can call it square."

He knew his rejection of the moonshine and the calmness he was trying very hard to project were enraging his partner. Dunlow stared at him and Rake maintained the stare. A platoon of very slow seconds marched by. Then Dunlow turned around to grab something from a shelf.

Rake let his right hand slide into his pocket and he grasped the knife's handle.

But the object Dunlow retrieved from the shelf was not a gun or any other weapon. It was a mason jar of something liquid, something that may once have been transparent or yellowish but was now greenish. Tiny flakes of something darker floated in the viscosity. At the bottom, bobbing a bit from the motion as Dunlow placed the jar on the table, was an object the size and approximate shape of a very large acorn.

"I'm sure as hell not drinking that," Rake said.

"It ain't for drinking, you dumb shit. It's for remembering. Know what that is?"

"I hope I don't."

Rake was beginning to form an idea just as Dunlow, ignoring Rake's full glass, poured another for himself and drank it. If Rake played his cards right and waited this out, Dunlow might be unconscious eventually.

"It's a nigger toe."

Rake tried to adopt a dispassionate expression and waited for Dunlow to explain.

"Uncle of mine got it, back in '06. Year I was born, matter of fact. He gave it to me when I was, I don't know, nine or ten."

"I got a baseball bat when I was ten."

"I believe he *used* a baseball bat to acquire this!" Dunlow guffawed. This was one of the funniest retorts he'd ever managed, apparently.

Rake couldn't resist the temptation to look at the toe again, even though he knew that was exactly what Dunlow wanted. It was hard to see if it was indeed a forty-two-year-gone toe, as whoever had mixed the formaldehyde had used too much of this or too little of that, and the chemicals were slowly degrading. Rake wondered how old the toe had been when it was cut off during those riots, when his ancestors had driven Negroes from downtown. He didn't see a toenail. He also wondered whether Dunlow was lying and perhaps he had "acquired" this more recently.

"What are we here to talk about, Dunlow?"

"You are a goddamn disgrace of a cop. You bring shame on me as a partner."

"That's funny. I've often been tempted to say the same thing about you."

"And what makes me sad, Rake, is that you remind me of me when I was younger."

"That certainly makes *me* sad. That's the cruelest thing you've ever said to me."

Dunlow placed a .45 beside the two glasses. His right hand remained upon it.

"The proverbial cards are on the table now," Rake said.

It was strange that he was so calm, but he was. He'd been waiting for this. He hadn't panicked in Europe and he hadn't panicked yet on his beat, and though this would have been a fine time to panic, his heart rate remained at its usual half-interested pace.

Still, he realized he had waited too long. He should have taken out his knife before Dunlow had revealed his gun. He never should have walked into this shed. He never should have joined the force. A series of turning points at which he'd pivoted the wrong way presented themselves to him now, like maps whose proper routes were oh so obvious in retrospect.

"Enough of your goddamn lip. I have something to say to you now and I should have said it a while ago, so you'll shut the hell up and let me do it."

Rake tried to adopt a shutting-the-hell-up expression. Dunlow didn't seem to notice or mind that Rake's hand remained under the table.

"You think I'm a bad cop, don't you? You think I'm an evil man, you think I'm bull-headed. And you think I'm too hard on the niggers, right? An unreconstructed Confederate who won't let those poor, good-hearted black folk be. That's what you think ain't it?"

"I wouldn't normally use a term like 'unreconstructed.' But yeah."

"Well, here's what I think of you, young man. You think you're a hero because you survived whatever the hell you survived over there and got your fancy medals to prove it. You think you're cultured and wise and that you know more about life than the bumpkins you left behind, and now you've returned to rule over us with that shiny badge of yours. You think you got something on everyone around you, and that by the time we figure that out you'll have moved on to some higher place above us and it'll be too late for us to catch up."

Sweat was rolling down Rake's cheeks. He should have drunk more water while doing the yard work, and now he was sitting in an oven facing a man with a gun and he didn't dare wipe his face lest he goad Dunlow into shooting him.

"Because I don't take bribes and rough up Negro kids? Because I won't put a hood over my head and firebomb that house down the block?"

Dunlow drank again. Distressingly, he wasn't yet acting terribly drunk. If Rake's plan was to wait until the man passed out, those odds were seeming slimmer.

"I was like you. You may not believe it. And I certainly wasn't as *irritating* as you are. But I did think I was better than the men around me. Especially my old man. He was a cop, too. He goddamn *ran* his part of the city, boy. People saw big-man Dunlow coming down the road, that road emptied out fast. He was one of the last cops to still ride a stallion down the streets, just to make himself seem even bigger. You think *I'm* hard on the niggers? You don't have a goddamn clue. One of my *uncles* gave me this toe, but don't you think for a second I don't know who really acquired it. The big man just wasn't the type to brag. Wasn't his style."

Rake was so hot he was getting dizzy. Unless it was nerves. Maybe he was only fooling himself about being calm.

"He had three little girls and then he had me and damn if he didn't put his heart and soul into making sure I knew how to be tough. I like to believe I learned most of those lessons eventually, but not all of them right away. Sometimes it takes us a while to learn the obvious stuff. See, the more he told me to steer clear of the niggers, the more curious I got. Even after that riot, there were still a few neighborhoods where the coloreds and us were on the same block, we'd cross paths, that sort of thing. And he always laid down the law good and thick on that."

Just keep him talking, Rake figured. The more Dunlow was talking, the more time Rake was not being shot.

"I do see a lotta me in you. And here's what I worry about, Officer Rakestraw. A good Christian man like you, with that pretty wife of yours." The mention of Cassie was enough to get Rake to tighten his grip on the blade's handle. "And those cute kids. You got so much to worry about, but at the same time, ah, I bet the wife won't stop complaining about the baby, and you can't stand the little one's crying at night, and life just doesn't seem that much fun anymore, does it? Being a strong respectable white man is *dad-gum* difficult work, and though that'd be more than enough to inspire most men to take to this"—he nudged with his left hand the glass that Rake still hadn't touched—"you're *better* than that, you take that police oath seriously. But the home life is getting tougher and your paycheck ain't going far enough and your job is taking its toll, and what's a fellow got to do to relax?"

Rake could push the table up and onto Dunlow, but it was so lightweight it would take Dunlow less than a second to knock it away and aim and fire. Or Rake could lunge over the table and hope Dunlow was too slowed by drink, then try to knock away the gun and at least it's a fair fight. Beyond that he saw no other options save waiting.

"So you decide to yourself, you'll go down to Darktown and have you some fun. Show off how enlightened you are, mix with the coloreds, because they always know how to relax and be lighthearted even when their lot in life ain't so good. So you hit those nightclubs even though you still ain't drinking, and you play cards even though that's illegal, too, but you ain't really betting much money so what's the harm?

"And the women! Now that's a whole 'nother story. You've heard the things they say about nigger women and damned if it don't appear to be true. Curves that white ladies couldn't even *draw,* and my Lord, they are free about it. Not *free* exactly, because at this one place you been frequenting, money is certainly exchanged with the ladies. But, you figure, money spent on *that* is a hell of a lot better spent than money at the tables, you get me? We coming to an understanding here?"

"Sure." He had no clue where this was going.

"So now you even got a regular thing with one of 'em. She gives you just the *best* damned time, she's wild and funny and the more you're with her, damned if you don't get to thinking. Thinking that she ain't all that dumb after all. She's got a brain on her shoulders. And you think maybe all this stuff they tell us about the coloreds and their women, maybe that's just a bit of hokum. Jealousy. Maybe it's just because us white folk are too stuck-up and hard up and we resent the way they can have so much damned *fun* despite having so little.

"Time goes by and your wife has probably noticed you ain't taking the family to church no more, but that's all right, you're busy with work and all and you got to sleep in the day. And you don't need to be right with no God right now anyway. It's the goddamn Depression and the things you see every day, Lord. You'd thought when you became a cop it'd be all hero stuff and saving lives and maybe busting heads and getting your rocks off like that, but no, it turns out you spend almost all your time trying to get good folks off the street, helping them find shelter, get a hot crumb somewhere. Hearing stories that just break your heart and seeing the looks in those little boys' eyes, kids same age as yours and they got *nothing* and they're skinny and their heads don't look quite right and you're just trying to get their parents a warm spot for the night. For one goddamn night. And then tomorrow it's the same thing for 'em again. That's your job, that's your life, every day. You don't unnerstand how no God could be doing things like this, and you ain't right in the head and your wife don't unnerstand you when you try to explain."

Dunlow had retreated within himself. His hand wasn't even on the gun anymore, just beside it. If there was a moment for Rake to knock away the gun, it was now.

Yet he wanted to hear the rest of the story.

"So you're going to that whorehouse more and more, and it's a shame the way those colored gals live, but hell, that's the hand life dealt 'em. You're there at the off-hours on account of your job, and they'll take you anytime and be happy about it, on account of your money. You eventually learn that more'n one of 'em has a kid there, these little boys who run around the halls when there ain't no john in the building. Sad as hell. Your own brats are driving you crazy at home, of course, but there are times at the whorehouse where you get to talking to those little kids and roughhousing with 'em. One of 'em's pretty damned smart, too, his name's Duke because his mother says she'd fallen in love with a Duke Ellington record back when he was born, listened to it all the time. It gets so you leave a nickel for him sometimes, or even bring him a bag of candy now and again. He's like your little mascot.

"Makes you feel sorrier for those girls, the way you and that kid get on. He's funny, and sometimes after you've had your roll in the hay with one of the girls, you bring him a book you brought from home, something your kids have outgrown. He ain't going to any school but he picks up the words quick enough. And he can play piano! They got one in their parlor, sometimes one of the ladies plays it, and he's picked it up just from watching her. One day he gets up on the bench and starts hammering away, and damned if he ain't carrying a tune. Not the greatest tune you ever heard, but for a four-year-old? Actually knows what he's doing. Sings, too, words he just done made up on the spot.

"That little boy. Calls you 'Mr. Down Low,' and first you think it's cause his pronunciation ain't so good, but you come to realize it's deliberate, it's a joke, he's a clever kid. So you're Mr. Down Low to him. And it sounds crazy, but you can just tell that little boy is meant for better things. Has a way about him. He looks at you and you feel like he's reading your mind, understanding you. Charisma in spades. No pun intended. And the more he plays that piano, you can just see him on a big stage, playing and maybe singing, charming folks in nice suits. Crazy, but maybe he *is* the next Duke Ellington. You read him these books at night, at an hour no kid that age should be up, let alone in a place like that, and you realize, this little kid has something, something truly special. You start wondering what you can do to really help him, not just reading him a book or buying him candy but getting him to a proper music instructor, something. Be like a secret sponsor to the boy, find a way to really make the most of that God-given talent he been given. Little ol' Duke."

Dunlow's hand was back on the gun. Not picking it up so much as ensuring it was near.

"Then one day you drop by the whorehouse place and it's all these other people there, some of them you know and others you never seen before, because you've been careful over the years to not be around when there's too many other folks, course, you can't have people realizing just how often you're frequenting the place. There's yelling and screaming and crying and you're still fighting your way through a crowd when the ambulance shows up. You don't see what happened yet, but folks are talking about it. Little boy ran out in the street. Hit by a car. Duke. And part of you wants to push that crowd out of the way and run up to the boy and see if maybe there's something you can do, and even if there ain't. . . . Comfort him that last time. But the other part of you knows who you are and where you are, and you can't do that. You just stand there and wait and listen to the crowd and you hear her screaming now, just screaming in a way you've never heard, not even the times you've had to give the worst news to parents on the job. . . . You just . . ."

Dunlow shook his head. His eyes were red and glassy and he tried to distract himself by pouring another drink. Half of it missed, spilling on the table. What made it into the glass he promptly swallowed.

Rake was wondering if he sat there long enough, would Dunlow's silence gradually turn into sleep? But good manners got the better of Rake, and he said, "I'm sorry, Dunlow."

"I didn't ask for your goddamn sympathy. This is a *lesson* for you, boy, like it was a lesson for me. Mothers drinking all day while their toddler walks off into traffic? Women selling themselves? All that lighthearted music and partying and laying about while good white people are working their tails to the bone trying to put this goddamn country back together during the Depression and then the war? I tricked myself into thinking they could be good as us, and then life showed me otherwise. Do *not* repeat that mistake. Do not be taking sides with these nigger cops. They ain't cops. We let them run around with guns much longer, this city will be in flames." The hand that wasn't cradling the gun slammed the table. "We are the last line of defense. Boggs and Smith have already killed one man that we know of, and they'll do worse soon enough. They'll be emboldened. Once they see they can kill a nigger and get away with it, they'll turn on white folks next. You want that, Officer Rakestraw? You want that on your conscience?"

Rake let a few seconds pass, hoping that might defuse his adversary some. Then he asked, "How does this end, Dunlow? You shooting me here because I don't see eye-to-eye with you? You building a case against Boggs and Smith, even though you've already passed on your so-called evidence to Homicide and we haven't heard anything since? Or will it be you deciding to hunt Boggs and Smith down yourself, maybe with a hood over your head, and you'll just assume no one in the Department will mind that two officers were killed?"

"They ain't officers."

"There was a time I may have actually wanted you to do something incredibly stupid, let yourself get fired or tossed in jail. But I don't want Boggs's or Smith's deaths on my conscience, or that Negro down the block. I've actually changed my mind on this, and I wish, I really do wish you *won't* do something incredibly stupid."

"Don't get your hopes up."

"Who killed Lily Ellsworth?"

"*What?*" The change of subject seemed dizzying to Dunlow.

"Who killed her, if not your buddy Underhill?"

"Hell if I know. He said he got paid to remove a body, not kill anybody."

"But she was alive and in his car when Boggs and Smith pulled him over that night. Removing a body when the body's alive isn't accessory after the fact, it's murder."

"He'd have no reason to lie to me 'bout that."

"You're a cop, and you're saying someone wouldn't have reason to lie about a murder?"

"You've changed the subject on me and I ain't too drunk to notice. What the hell happened to your finger anyway?"

"A wall mouthed off to me and I hit back."

"Then it wouldn't just be one finger in a splint like that." Spoken like a man who had punched his share of walls.

"My hair's about to catch fire it's so goddamn hot in here. I've heard you out and I thank you for showing me your family heirloom," and Rake nodded toward the toe, "but I'm going to stand up now and walk home to my wife and kids. I suppose I'm just going to have to hope you don't choose to shoot me in the back."

And with that, Rake stood. He had convinced himself he wasn't taking an awful chance. He had convinced himself that Dunlow did see him fondly in a way, that Dunlow truly did view him as a younger version of himself, that Dunlow felt more a fatherly need to beat sense into that self and not a homicidal need to turn this shed into a crime scene. Rake was reeling from Dunlow's story but he also saw that his partner was even smaller than he had thought before, and he was telling himself that smallness equaled weakness and therefore he had nothing to fear by standing up, and turning, and slowly walking toward the shed door. He chose not to think that this simple act constituted a fatal mistake.

One hand on the doorknob, he turned to look back at Dunlow one last time.

Dunlow was still sitting but he was holding the gun now, his arm straight and true, the muzzle aimed at Rake's head.

Bang.

32

THE SIRENS OF the Peacedale squad cars were louder now, the same sounds as the APD squad cars Boggs and Smith had become so accustomed to, but inspiring a very different reaction.

Boggs had nearly stopped, the first squad car no more than forty yards behind him when Smith said, *"Now."*

They had reached a bend in the road where the blacktop curved sharply to the left. Just before that bend, the road was narrower due to overgrowth of unkempt rhododendron and rose of Sharon shrubs. At Smith's command, Boggs swung the wheel counterclockwise. The Buick's wheels squealed and he felt it hydroplane a bit, dirt and gravel scraping beneath, the car swinging until they faced straight into the woods and they were blocking the road.

Next it was the squad car's wheels squealing. Boggs didn't turn to watch them, as Smith had already opened the passenger door and jumped out. Boggs crawled over the seat and did the same, closing the door behind him, so that the Buick stood between them and the cops.

The second squad car parked behind the first, which was a mere fifteen yards from the two colored officers.

The driver's door of the lead squad car was kicked open. The man who hurried outside it was so enraged he could barely stand up, nearly tripping as he exited. He had dark hair and something about one of his eyes looked funny even from this distance. Boggs saw from the stripes that this was the local sheriff.

"You get the hell back in that automobile, boy!"

At about this time, as doors from both squad cars were opening to disgorge the sheriff's fellow officers, the sheriff seemed to notice that one of the Negroes was holding a rifle.

Smith was not aiming it or even pointing it. He brandished it before him, though, muzzle pointing up at about ten o'clock from the white men's perspective. Standard infantry-at-guard position. Standard warning-not-to-consider-crossing-this-point stance. Boggs's hands were at his sides; the white men couldn't see his pistol because of the Buick's obstruction. He would let them imagine it.

"You're Sheriff Nayler?" Boggs called out, ignoring the question.

"You put that goddamn gun away, boy!"

By now the other cops had noticed the rifle, and quickly they availed themselves of their own weapons.

"Shit," Boggs whispered. He held up his left palm in what he hoped looked like mild appeasement, though the other hand he kept hidden. "Let's all stay calm here. We're just trying to head back home and don't want any trouble."

The white cops weren't pointing their revolvers at them, yet, since they were apparently awaiting an order from their superior. Beside the sheriff was another cop, big and much younger, staring at his master like a dog impatiently awaiting the command to attack. Behind them, from the second car, were two more white cops. They were too far away, so it was hard to tell how young or hard they were, though that barely mattered. All that was relevant was how good a shot either was, and how many more weapons they had stashed in those cars.

"Sheriff told you to put that gun away, boy!" the younger cop said. "And put both your damn hands up!"

All the cars' engines were still on, purring in the shade like barely stilled predators, waiting.

"We are police officers from the city of Atlanta," Boggs said, employing what Sergeant McInnis always referred to as *calm but barely restrained power.* Do not sound panicked or angry. Sound in control. And possessed of such inner wrath that they will fear the unleashing of it. "We are returning to our precinct and expect you to let us pass."

"The hell?" the younger one said to Nayler.

"You ain't police out here," the sheriff said. "You ain't got no call to be out in my town, son."

"We'll happily leave your town, Sheriff. That's what we were just trying to do when you pulled us over."

There were a hell of a lot of bees in the air, Boggs noticed. They were darting to and fro across the road, as the humans appeared to have stopped in the middle of some vital insect hub. The rose of Sharon were in bloom and nearly every lavender flower was being pillaged.

"What do you think y'all doing out here, boy?" the sheriff demanded. He hadn't asked them to show a badge, which they didn't have with them anyway. Even asking to see such a badge would have been to acknowledge the unmentionable, that these Negroes thought themselves worthy of the station.

"We were just expressing our condolences to the Ellsworths," Boggs said.

"That's a family of nigger thieves and you'd best stay away from them."

"I read your report, Sheriff," Boggs said, "but I didn't see anything about evidence of them committing theft, or any other crime."

"You're goddamn shifty niggers, ain't you? You may have tricked some pantywaist city folk over there, but you ain't tricking us."

Boggs said, "You'd know about tricking people, wouldn't you, Sheriff?"

The big cop whispered something to the sheriff, who nodded. Then the big one turned his head—slowly—and called something to the men behind him, though Boggs couldn't hear what. One of the rear cops nodded and opened his squad car door again.

"Y'all best stay out where I can see you," Smith commanded, trying to sound in control despite a growing sense of helplessness.

Hopefully these were the only two squad cars in Peacedale. If a third should happen to come from the other direction, they were doomed. The man in the other car may have been radioing for help, either in town or from another jurisdiction.

"Y'all are messing in affairs that don't concern you," Nayler said.

The cop who had reached into the back squad car now emerged with a rifle in his hands.

"*Shit,*" Smith whispered.

No one had aimed a weapon yet. Everyone but Smith was pointing their guns at the ground as if trying to hold the earth prisoner. Smith's rifle was still held before him, aimed at the canopy of pines.

The two cops from the back started walking toward their fellows. The one with the rifle was in the center of the road, the other brushing up against the shrubbery to the right, bees everywhere.

"We can't let them spread out no more," Smith whispered. "They try and flank out and we'll have to start shooting."

"Are you crazy?"

"I'm experienced. We let them draw a perimeter through the woods and we're dead."

Boggs called out, "My partner's a twice-decorated army sniper. You'd best not lift that rifle any higher."

"What do you think is stopping us, son, from just shooting you all right here and now?"

A bee landed on Boggs's shirt. He was tempted to brush it off, but he was afraid the movement would cause one of the whites to aim and fire.

"You outnumber us right here," Boggs said. "But our police outnumbers yours about a hundred to one."

"They ain't coming to your rescue, boy," the cop with the rifle spoke for the first time.

"You already got away with murder, Sheriff," Boggs recapped. "That and theft of his truck and his cash. You have a lot to lose if you call more attention to yourself. I think letting a couple of city cops drive home so they can just complain about you from fifty miles away is an awfully good deal for you."

Nayler was staring straight at Boggs. They were shaded from the worst of the summer sun yet still sweat was pouring down Boggs's back and he could smell his own stink, could hear his own heartbeat in his ears. His entire body was tense, arteries and veins compressed and loud.

"You tell your boys to start shooting, though," he said, "and you'll get a whole lot of attention."

"I don't know what you're talking about, boy," Nayler said. "And if you even consider trying to besmirch my good name, you will deeply regret ever having heard of me."

Smith's palms were sweaty and he was worried that if he had to aim the rifle hurriedly, he'd mishandle it. The Buick might not be thick enough to deflect many bullets. He was judging angles and who he'd shoot second, thinking of making his body thin, hiding behind the wheels, wondering which white man would panic first.

"We have no jurisdiction out here, like you said," Boggs said. "We just want to get back home."

The sheriff waited. "Then get your black asses in that car and get the hell back to Atlanta."

Boggs could breathe just the slightest bit easier, even though the big cop's head swiveled the sheriff's way, his eyes wide with shock and betrayal.

"Slowly," Smith whispered.

With his left hand, Boggs opened the passenger door, still gripping his revolver with his right. He climbed into the car, eyes on the white cops. Realizing that he now had less protection from them. Fearing that this was the sheriff's ruse and the command to fire was coming.

Smith put his left foot into the car and stood with his right on the running board, though this model seemed to be fading out the gangster-style boards and he could barely manage to stand upright, leaning with his chest against the roof of the car, the rifle pinned there but still in the white cops' view.

Because the car was perpendicular to the road, Boggs had to shift to reverse to give himself some space, backing ever closer to the white cops. They did not back up. Nor did they holster their weapons. There were even bees in the goddamn car. Boggs had to take his eyes from the whites for a moment as he shifted the car again—three-point turns were not something he had much experience with, let alone one-handed and with firearms involved.

Smith kept his eyes trained on the white cop with the rifle. Keeping all of them in his vision but focusing on that one. He wanted to give the sheriff one last glance, but it wasn't worth the risk.

The white cops were motionless as Boggs pressed the gas and the white men receded like two-dimensional props, Western-style shooting range targets looking more flat and lifeless with every second.

" 'Sniper twice decorated?' " Smith said when he got back in the car. "I spent the war in a goddamn tank."

"It scared 'em, though."

"Just drive, and faster."

Silence for a good ten minutes when Boggs finally said, "We need to warn them."

"When we're a hell of a lot safer than this. Back in Atlanta."

Boggs hated himself for agreeing with his partner. They needed to get out of the country. There was no telling where other white cops might have set up a roadblock, or just have a squad car ready to chase them down with more firepower and gunmen than Peacedale had mustered. Any minute they wasted by pulling over and making a phone call could make all the difference.

But what was happening to what was left of the Ellsworths? What would those Peacedale cops do next, after feeling like they'd been one-upped by a pair of Negro cops? What would happen to all that unquenched bloodlust, that sense that the order of their universe had been threatened?

He drove on.

After another twenty minutes, he couldn't take it. He pulled over into a filling station.

"Not yet!" Smith snapped. "We got longer to go."

"I'm not waiting any more." Boggs left the car.

Smith cursed under his breath and cradled a pistol in his lap. He scanned the area. Damn little to see: the filling station had two spigots, a long window, and a lone door. The pay phone was on the rear wall, and Boggs hurried toward it. Across the street was a ramshackle white house that *looked* abandoned but that possibly housed some unfortunates. Beyond that was nothing but peach trees baking in the late-afternoon sun.

Boggs dropped a coin down the slot, hoping a redneck wouldn't emerge from the building and tell him the phone was for whites only.

He hadn't seen any telephone poles out by the Ellsworths' place, and he didn't know which Peacedale Negroes, if any, owned phones. But he remembered one of the churches they'd passed on the south side of the tracks. "In Peacedale, Second Baptist Church of the Lord, please."

After a pause, the operator said, "Yes, sir," and connected him.

A woman answered on the second ring.

"Yes, ma'am, I'm calling from out of town and I have an urgent message I need to get to the Ellsworth residence."

Silence for so long he feared she'd hung up on him. "Who is this?" She was old, either a preacher's wife or a spinster so dedicated to the Lord that she spent her time helping around the office. He'd known such women all his life.

"Ma'am, I'd rather not say, but I'm very concerned the Ellsworths are in danger right now and need to get out of their house as soon as possible. Can you please see about getting that message to them somehow?"

She made a sound, like a sigh but more disgusted.

"You're too late. Fire trucks already done headed over there. Their place is on fire."

33

AFTERWARD, WHEN DUNLOW woke in his bedroom with a mouth so sandpaper dry that water wasn't so much something he craved but something that didn't even exist, couldn't exist, and his head was pounding and he felt nearly ill enough to roll over and empty his insides then and there, he closed his eyes again and waited and waited for the awfulness to pass and eventually just enough of it did for him to raise himself out of bed.

What the hell had he done?

Tonight was his off night so at least he had that to be thankful for, but here it was five o'clock in the evening and he was waking up with a hangover from all he'd done that morning. The house was quiet, which meant his sons weren't home, thank God, though his wife was probably in the kitchen or sitting on the front porch.

He sat there a while, trying to return to life. The phone rang.

"Yeah?"

"Hey, it's Bo."

"Hey."

"Listen, I thought you'd want to hear it from me first. There ain't gonna be no charges against the nigger cops, not murder anyhow. Homicide got someone else to confess to killing Poe."

"What?"

"Some moonshiner. Name Illinois Richard mean anything to you?"

Dunlow thought, which was hard. "Former boxer. Got here from Birmingham maybe three years ago."

"Well, he and Poe had a rivalry and were fighting over territory and he says he just happened to be walking down the street one night and there's Poe all beat up. So he used his knife to finish the job, then dumped him in that creek on the other side of town. Boggs and Smith may have roughed Poe up, like your witness said, but they didn't kill him."

Dunlow was standing now, pacing despite his headache and the short length of the cord. "Bullshit! Why the hell would the nigger confess to that?"

"Two beat cops caught him this morning at the scene of another homicide. His girlfriend. No question on that one, and I guess he figured he'd be all manly and let us know about the other big deeds he's done."

"Hellfire. Smith and Boggs put him up to it. Had to."

"Lionel." Peterson paused. "I don't like it no more'n you do. But Homicide is certain they got their man for Poe. There's no way the nigger cops are gonna take no blame for it. They get off scot-free."

"They still gotta answer to me, goddammit!"

Peterson's voice shrunk in direct proportion to Dunlow's. "I know."

"So get your ass over here and we'll make our plans."

"I'm on shift."

"That don't mean nothing."

"*Dunlow.* I'm calling you from the station."

Dunlow didn't care if some switchboard operator might be overhearing. Let them. Let them know that there were still some men willing to make sacrifices for everyone else.

"Get your ass over here later, then. I'm off tonight."

"Well, that's the other thing. It doesn't appear that many other men have the same appetite as you do on this."

"What?"

"I'm saying we don't like it any more than you do, but the idea of taking action against uniformed officers of the law don't seem like such a great idea, all right? I know they ain't real cops and you know it but the mayor doesn't seem to agree and neither does our chief."

"You're turning yellow, that it?"

"I ain't yellow."

"Yellowness is goddamn seeping out of this phone every time you open your mouth."

"*It ain't being yellow, Dunlow.* It's knowin' there's a time and a place, and this ain't it."

The next thing Dunlow knew he wasn't holding his phone anymore; it was smashed to pieces all over his bedroom. He would not lower himself to beg his fellow white men to aid him. He would not plead his case and he sure as hell would not repeat his mistake with Rake, trying to level with them and reveal things about himself he'd previously told no one. The time for talking was goddamn past.

He changed into fresh clothes, grabbed his keys and his gun.

34

"EVERY TIME WE tried to help that family, we only made it worse."

Boggs had hoped Smith might disagree, but his partner was silent.

"I never should have gotten the murder in the paper. I should have left the family alone out there to just wonder whatever happened to her. They would have thought she'd disappeared, married some fine school-teacher, and disowned them. They would have used that money to go north. The local cops wouldn't have been on the lookout for them."

Why were they doing this? Why continue with the sham of being "Negro officers"? They could do no real good. They were not permitted to correct the biggest problems, and when they dared try, they created worse disasters.

"It's not worth it," Boggs concluded as he pulled up to Smith's apartment building. So much had occurred since he'd picked him up that morning, it was amazing the sun hadn't yet set on the same day.

"We'll try to get in touch with them again tomorrow. See if there's anything we can do for them."

"If they're alive." He shook his head. "I wish I'd figured it out sooner. I would have known then, known to just stay away." Instead, he'd wanted the satisfaction of solving it, of being the hero. That pride had already destroyed one family—what would it destroy next?

"Just go home. Get some sleep. Things won't seem as bad in the morning."

Smith didn't sound like he believed his own words.

⋆

At home a note from the reverend explained that he and Lucius's mother were at a wake a few blocks away. At least one thing had gone right, then, since Lucius desperately needed to be alone.

He sat in the parlor for a good while. He hadn't turned on any of the lamps, and later twilight passed and he was sitting in darkness.

He walked into the kitchen, picked up the phone, and called Rake.

"I know why Lily Ellsworth was killed."

"Tell me." A baby was crying in the background and it sounded like Rake was walking into another room.

"She was Prescott's daughter."

"*What?* Says who?"

"One of her brothers said that their mother told Lily a few months ago. Lily and her brothers always knew she had a different father, and she's much lighter than her siblings. They'd wondered if her father was a white man. She was teased about it a fair amount. Then one day Emma Mae told Lily the story: when Emma Mae was fifteen, she and her family had moved to the city. A couple of years later she was working as a maid for the Prescott family. This was back in the twenties. The head of the household—the father of Congressman Prescott—was a state senator at the time. Billy Prescott himself was a young man, still in law school, and one day he took advantage of Emma Mae."

"Jesus Christ."

"According to Lily's brother, their mother didn't explain how it all came to pass. But she said she stopped working for them soon after that, and then when her own parents saw she was pregnant, they moved back out of the city. That's why she never wanted her own daughter to move here. Bad memories."

"So Lily just happened to wind up working for the same household? Why, so she could confront her father? Extort money out of him?"

"Maybe she did try to extort the family, and that's how she came into that money. Or maybe she just wanted to meet the man, look her daddy in the eye. Maybe she didn't have money on her mind at all, but once he laid eyes on her he saw who she was immediately, and he panicked and offered her the money to hush her up, and she was just too stunned to say no."

Silence for a few beats. "How could she have confronted the congressman?" Rake asked. "I thought he's been in Washington the whole time she was in Atlanta."

"I spent some time in the library the other day. A lot of time, actually, over a lot of days, and I finally found a short note in the *Constitution* that says Prescott came to town in late May, around Memorial Day. Went to some gala downtown, in honor of the Confederate war dead. He headed back up to the city two days later."

"And about two weeks later, Lily was shuttled off to Mama Dove's."

"That's right."

"Prescott's son lied to me," Rake said. "He claimed she'd stolen from them but they hadn't wanted to report it, and that's why they fired her."

Then Rake told him what he'd learned about the Rust Division.

Boggs tried to work it through in his head again. Maybe Lily had tried to blackmail Prescott, threatened to publicize her paternity. So he paid her off, hence the money, and hence the junior Prescott's lie to Rake about her stealing from them. Maybe Prescott *hadn't* killed her, and *hadn't* called in Underhill's help. Maybe one of Prescott's political friends had. Maybe Prescott had told someone else about his illegitimate daughter. Perhaps Prescott was softening his stance on Negroes precisely because of Lily, the memories she brought back of Emma Mae Ellsworth. Perhaps his affair with Emma Mae had been more than a dalliance—he'd buried all remnants of it, but they'd come back nonetheless, and now he was realizing that the races weren't so far apart as many liked to think.

"We're assuming the son knew, too," Rake said. "Maybe he didn't. Maybe they never told him, didn't want him to know he had a Negro half sister. Maybe it's such a family secret that only the congressman himself knows."

Silence on the line for a few seconds.

"But if they paid her off, then why kill her, too?"

No more than a minute after hanging up the phone, he was sitting at the table when he heard footsteps. His mother walked in from the hall.

"Sorry to startle you," she said when she saw his expression. She was tall, only two inches shorter than him, and her straightened hair touched her shoulders. She was getting thinner, almost in proportion with his father's weight gain over the years.

"I didn't realize you were home." He wanted to ask her how much she had overheard, but was afraid to. Something in her eyes told him that she'd heard quite a bit. Part of the job description of a reverend's wife is to be discreet enough not to eavesdrop exactly, but be helpful enough to tactfully act on any information she learned.

She sat down opposite him and watched him for a moment. Her face was very still. She asked, "Are you all right?"

"Not really." He realized the light wasn't on and that it must look strange to his mother for him to be sitting in the dark. But she hadn't turned the light on either. "Long day."

"Wasn't this your day off?"

"I didn't use it too wisely."

She was wearing a plain housedress and wore no makeup, the look she only allowed herself when it was late enough to be sure that no one would be dropping by. No sinners, no grievers, no one seeking counsel or the Lord or another supper.

"Maybe you should lie down."

"Did you think I was a fool when I signed up?"

"Of course not."

"You had this look on your face when I told you."

"I was just surprised. You . . . you hadn't seemed to like the army."

"I hated the army."

"And I thought the police would be more of the same."

"It's different. It's better in some ways, and awful in others."

"I do know that people are glad you're out there, Lucius. They tell us all the time."

It hurt him, in the back of his throat, to realize how badly he'd needed to hear this.

"Really? All I hear are the complaints. *Hey, why did you bust my brother's pool hall? Why did you arrest my cousin? How come you haven't kept the white cops off our backs?*"

"You've always been the type to fixate on the negatives. Or maybe people are more willing to tell me the positives about you. Mr. Thompkins said his pharmacy had been broken into four times last summer, but zero this summer. Mr. Royal mentioned he had a few knife fights at his club last year, but none this year, and he said the moonshiners aren't stealing his business as much. Principal Jones last week, he told me that seven different kids in his junior class wrote term papers about how they were going to be police officers."

Lucius nodded. The lump in his throat was getting worse. Sensing this, she stopped talking, and walked over to the counter to pour him a glass of water. She handed it to him, then said, "You don't have to keep doing it if you don't want to." Had she known he was thinking about quitting? Was it that obvious? "But I think you're doing more good than you realize."

He drank the water, washing away the thickness.

"The scar is growing on me, by the way."

He laughed. "Thanks."

"I'm sure the girls will love it."

"That hasn't been my experience yet."

Then the phone rang. She was about to answer it when he asked her to let him, as if he'd known.

A woman on the line said, "Is this Officer Lucius Boggs?"

He recognized her voice and the sassy way in which she said it.

"Yes it is, Miss Cannon." Like that, he perked up quite a bit. "What can I do for you?"

Julie said, "You told me to call you if I ever thought of anything or saw anything. Well, it's what I *haven't* seen that I think might be interesting."

An hour later, Lucius, on his one night off, was walking the streets he no longer felt qualified to protect. It felt different to do this now, in his civvies, no partner at his side. He'd hoped to escape from his thoughts but he was doing only the opposite. He realized then that the mere act of walking in his neighborhood at night would never be the same again, that if he truly did hand in his badge now, he still wouldn't be able to reclaim his old feeling about Atlanta. The experience had permanently marred all his earlier memories, and any possible future would bear at least some imprint of these last few months.

Unless he left Atlanta.

There seemed no more illicit thought than that. Leave the city. Leave his family. Leave his connections. Leave the South. Leave his history. Leave his grandmother and her parents who were born slaves. Leave slavery and the War Between the States. Leave everything but the future.

He had thought that by taking this job, he was helping his people, he was inching the rock of progress up the hill. But maybe he was wrong, and Uncle Percy was right. Maybe he was allowing himself to be fooled here, he was just another Negro casting down his bucket where he was, rather than moving someplace better.

Every day, thousands of Southern Negroes were doing it. Why not him? He had chosen a different struggle, a different way forward, and it sure as hell hadn't worked out. Here they were just niggers. Here he lived not in Sweet Auburn but Darktown. Here he was stubbornly holding on to the worst imaginable hand, as if hopeful that the next card would turn it into a royal flush. But the cards could not be read that way, and that perfect next card wasn't sitting atop the deck. Even if it was, some other hand would snatch it away, a white hand, and Lucius was making a fool of himself by playing along.

There were plenty of people he'd spoken to who knew more than they were saying, but he felt he had a decent chance with one of them. He got back in his father's car.

"Preacher's son." Mama Dove did not look surprised to see him. "But not in uniform. Finally decided to loosen that tight belt of yours?"

They were standing in the foyer, and though the quarters were small indeed he stepped even closer to her.

"Time to pick sides, ma'am. If you really feel like it, if you really think it's a smart thing to do, you could place a call to the Department and have a white cop show up and arrest me for frequenting a whorehouse. That'd be the end of me and the end of the colored cops. And I know you'd like that. You have that fate in your hands right now."

"Exciting. So why won't I do that? And why are you offering yourself to me?"

"I know that Lily Ellsworth was Congressman Prescott's daughter. I think they paid her off to keep quiet about it, but days later she's sent here. Why here? She wasn't a whore. I've talked to enough people who knew her and there's no way she up and decided to sell herself just days after working in a congressman's house. I'm thinking you were supposed to watch over her or something. But you didn't do a very good job."

"What a fascinating story."

"Whoever it is you think you're trying to protect, they don't deserve protection. And whoever it is you think might take you down for talking to me, I can protect you from them."

She laughed. "Boy, you had me with the first line, but you should have quit while you were ahead. That *second* line? I don't believe *that* for a second. And you don't either."

She was right, so he moved on: "They sent Underhill because they didn't want to send real cops, for the same reason they didn't want her in a real jail and put her here instead." He wished he had a better idea of who *they* was. Probably the Prescotts, but could it have been a rival, or a patron, of the congressman? Did anyone have *proof?* "They didn't want the publicity, didn't want anyone involved who might talk. And a colored madam who owes her continued existence to paying off the cops is a lady who knows how to keep a secret."

"I am pretty good at that."

"So Underhill eventually comes to take her away. That's what they told you, probably. But he kills her instead. And then someone else from the Rust Division—or, more likely, one of the high-ranking cops who bosses the Rust Division around—killed Underhill, too, to cover up the tracks, because he knew we were getting close to Underhill. And you don't feel the slightest bit bad about any of this?"

The mirth was gone from her eyes and her arms were folded.

"I want you to know two things, preacher's son. The first thing is that I'd already decided I was going to tell you when you got here, so don't be thinking you talked me into it or won me over with any of that fast-talking guff, got that?"

"Yes, ma'am."

Then she told him the second thing.

At a pay phone a block away, Lucius dropped in a coin and dialed Rake's number.

"Be there, be awake, be there," Lucius muttered.

Rake was. Lucius told him what Mama Dove had said, and they pondered what to do next. To Lucius's great surprise, Rake was ready to take a chance.

"I can meet you there," Lucius said.

"No, no. Not a good idea. I'm sorry, but . . ."

"White people only."

"I'm sorry. You did your job. Damn if you didn't. Now I need to do mine."

* * *

Dunlow couldn't believe his eyes.

For more than an hour now he had been circling the neighborhood he knew so well. He had stopped at a few informants' houses to ask if they'd seen the man, had finagled a bit more moonshine when he realized his bottle was running low, but apart from that he'd been on the prowl. The alcohol and endless circling making him tired. He'd just about gotten to the point where he was either going to put this off for another day *or* just break into Boggs's house so he could lie in wait for him, when who should step out into the street a mere fifty yards ahead of him?

Thank you, Jesus, for not leaving me.

He was a block from Mama Dove's. And there was the man he was looking for, jaywalking without an apparent care in the world.

Dunlow pressed his foot to the gas.

* * *

Boggs heard the car roaring toward him when he was nearly across the street.

He was used to this by now, but, to his surprise, this wasn't a squad car. And he wasn't in uniform himself, so perhaps this was different from those other times. This was a driver gunning for him, personally.

The car drove beneath a streetlight and he saw a white hand dangling outside the driver's window. Somehow he knew who was at the wheel.

Boggs was still standing in the street. If his rage had been a physical thing, it would have split the car in two. If his anger had been able to make itself solid, it would have been too vast and impenetrable for the Ford to drive through.

But that's not how these things work.

He stood his ground for as long as he possibly could have, then he bolted to his right and the relative safety of the sidewalk just before the car would have run him down.

Yet it ran him down anyway. Somehow. All Boggs knew was that the air was driven from his body and his body was driven to the air, and when he landed—after spinning around at least once—he landed hard and on his side.

He heard the car stop but didn't hear the door open, because it was already open.

※

Damned wily nigger had nearly leaped out of the way in time, but Dunlow had been expecting that, so he'd grabbed the handle and threw the door open, using his left foot for extra leverage, and the door had slammed Boggs with enough force to lift him into the air.

Dunlow stopped the car and got out. Boggs was lying on the ground. Nothing looked broken or bent the wrong way, yet. The colored officer was trying to get to his feet, but his body wasn't moving as fast he probably wanted it to.

There was a bottle in Dunlow's hand, and he swung it at Boggs's thick skull. The bottle shattered—Boggs's skull did, too, maybe—and then Boggs was flat on the ground and his eyes were shut.

He patted Boggs down, assuming the man at least had a knife on him, but he was clean. What a fool. He grabbed Boggs's feet and dragged him to the Ford. The keys were still in the ignition, so Dunlow had to leave the body there on the road while he walked back to retrieve them. Another car passed in the other direction, but Dunlow eyed it good and slow and the car didn't stop.

He popped open the trunk and lifted Boggs, pieces of glass falling all around. He dumped him into the trunk and shut it.

As he walked back to the front of the car, he saw an old black man standing outside the entrance to a shoe store. The light had been off, but the door was open, as this must be the proprietor on his way home after cleaning up for the night. The Negro was tall and gaunt, his hair mostly white, his eyes wide but shrinking fast, realizing he'd been caught watching.

"Get your black ass home, uncle, and be quick about it."

The cobbler muttered a quiet "yes, sir" and his head bowed as he walked off quickly. Dunlow smiling, easing back in the car and hitting the gas.

35

RAKE COULD NOT have planned it better: Silas Prescott was drunk.

"Officer. Hello." His cheeks were red and already Rake could smell the booze on his breath, seeping through the man's pores. He wore a white dress shirt and slacks, the tie only a memory.

"I'm sorry to bother you again, Mr. Prescott." Rake was not in uniform, yet he was not surprised Prescott had recognized him so quickly in his civvies. Manners would normally dictate that Rake ask if now was a bad time, but the last thing he was going to do was squander such an opportunity. "Won't take but a minute."

Again Prescott was either too polite or stupid to resist inviting Rake into his home. As before, a jazz LP was circling a record player. The house was no more furnished than last time. Rake wondered if Prescott drank alone like this every night, and the only difference between the two visits was that Rake had come by earlier that first time, whereas now it was nearing ten.

Prescott seemed too preoccupied to ask why Rake wasn't in uniform. Which was fine. Being in plainclothes made Rake look like a detective, he knew. He could get into all kinds of trouble for what he was doing right now. But a man is inclined to draw his own ethical borders on a day when his partner had actually aimed a weapon at his head. Dunlow hadn't pulled the trigger, but he'd silently mouthed *Bang*, and the expressionless way in which he'd done so left Rake with little doubt that Dunlow was warming to the idea of ridding himself of his troublesome young partner. Rake was tired of playing by rules that had been written in a way to empower bastards like Dunlow and made his own life difficult.

"I just wanted to ask why you lied to me, Mr. Prescott."

The jazz was still on, a slow kind of meandering thing not at all like the swing and big band tunes Rake was used to. This must be what the college boys played now.

"I'm sorry?" A lonely bottle of whiskey stood on the table of the kitchenette behind him.

"Lily Ellsworth did not steal from your parents. Not money, anyway. Not anything tangible."

An awkward smile. "I'm afraid I don't know what you mean. She stole jewelry from us."

"That's what your parents told you? And you believed them?"

"What are you trying to say?"

"Did you know she was your sister?"

Prescott's face could not have been more pale. "That's not true."

"It is true. Your father slept with her mother a long time ago, and she was born nine months later. That's how it works."

Prescott was shaking his head. Something in the man's eyes conveyed horror but not shock. It was more like he was confronting the awful realization that the world is indeed as twisted as he had been warned. A sense of rueful confirmation.

"You fucked your own sister."

Prescott backed up a step. Then he turned and ran, bumping into the table the record player was on. The needle jumped to the middle of another song, much faster, a saxophone firing off sixteenth notes while cymbals crashed.

Prescott pushed open a side door and Rake thought *Gun.* He's going for his piece, the paltry .22 he'd used on Lily. Rake's gun was in a holster in the small of his back, and he reached for it now, but then a sound informed him that Prescott was not going for a gun at all. He was throwing up.

Rake walked up to the open doorway and turned on the light that Prescott had been in too much of a rush to get to. The son of a U.S. congressman and grandson of a Georgia state senator was kneeling before his toilet, letting loose all that whiskey, the stench foul even from a few feet away.

"Oh God," Prescott said as he panted, spittle hanging from his lips. "Oh dear Lord."

"And when you found out she was your sister, you snapped. You killed her."

"No. No." It was hard to tell if that was a denial or if there was something else Prescott wanted to say, but couldn't, because he was throwing up again.

When Boggs woke, his head was screaming all kinds of cruel things and his body was being bumped up and down and left and right. His head ached through a dull fog, and he still felt the dreary awful vestiges of his dream, a car racing toward him, and then Dunlow swinging at him.

He realized he was in a car. The trunk of a car. He tried to move and his heart told him not to. No, not his heart, his ribs. Something was broken or fractured or at the very least pointing in the wrong direction. He was able to move both arms, but not very much, since he was crammed in there. He tried to roll onto his back and he felt something on his chest, lots of somethings. He used his hand to try to figure out what they were—then *bam*, the car hit a pothole and he sucked in his breath from the stabbing in his chest.

The things on his chest were shards of glass. The bottle Dunlow had broken on his skull. He picked at the pieces, some of which had torn through his shirt and were half lodged in his skin from his having been thrown on top of them. One of the pieces was big, smooth on one side—even rounded—and jagged on the other. The neck of the bottle, shorn in half. Sharp as a razor and just as long. Delicately, he clasped it in the palm of his hand.

Then he prayed.

He prayed to Jesus for forgiveness for all he'd done wrong. Which was a lot, lately. He prayed for forgiveness for the envy and scorn he felt toward his cousin who had fled Atlanta for Chicago. He prayed the Lord forgive the way he had not been honoring his father much lately, for the anger he'd shown the reverends, for talking back to the group of wise men who had handed him that letter to give to the police chief. *Lord, there is so much I don't know and don't understand and as I try to grow into this world I want to do the best I can, and sometimes I think I know what I'm doing, but I see now that I know nothing, and I should have done what my father asked and I should be selling insurance or even preaching your gospel at the reverend's side, though, as you know very well by now, Lord, I wouldn't make a very good preacher and you probably wouldn't have me anyway. Forgive the pride that allowed me to try to "solve" what had happened to Lily Ellsworth, for making everything so much worse for her family, for leading to the death of her father and now the loss of their home and—please, Lord, make sure that the others are safe, please ensure her two brothers are not hanging from branches or beaten half to death in some forsaken Peacedale cell. If it's your will to take me now, you may do so, but please spare them, please let those two Ellsworth boys grow old, and Dunlow can have me in their place.*

That last part of the offer vanished from his mind the moment the trunk popped open. Dunlow was aiming a .45 at Boggs's head. What Boggs felt toward this man was hatred so intense it didn't seem possible it could coexist with a loving God.

"Wake up, nigger."

Boggs didn't say anything.

"You killed Chandler Poe. And I'll hear you say it."

"I didn't kill anyone." Moving his jaw made the top of his head hurt.

"You're a damned liar. I'll give you one more chance."

They were in the woods somewhere. Full boughs hung behind Dunlow, though what kind Boggs couldn't tell. Dark. The night crawlers were loud and there was no other sound, no traffic or music or shouting or breaking bottles or anything at all human. He didn't know how long he'd been unconscious or how far they'd traveled.

"I don't know what it is you think of me, Dunlow. But I'm not a killer."

Dunlow waited for what felt like a very, very long time.

"Well, that makes one of us."

With the hand that wasn't holding his gun, Dunlow reached forward and then the trunk lid slammed the scant amount of light away.

A minute or so later, Boggs heard the digging.

⚡

"Enough," Rake told Prescott, backing up a step to get some air. "Get yourself together."

Prescott leaned back, wiped the spit from his mouth, and slowly went about getting to his feet. He washed his mouth out at the sink.

Rake walked into the parlor and turned off the jazz. When he turned back around, Prescott was leaning his elbows on the sink and staring into his own eyes.

"It's not like you said."

"It is. Your mother won't let you around the new maid because you took too many liberties with the last one. That's something of a family tradition, apparently." He didn't know this, but it was a guess—Boggs had told him the new maid, Lily's replacement, had realized she was always sent home before Silas was expected at his mother's place. "You forced yourself on Lily—at the time she was just the maid to you, because your father was still in Washington and she hadn't confronted him yet. After what you did to her, she probably wanted to run, but she felt she'd come too far, she had to meet your father. Or maybe you hadn't raped her yet at that point, I don't know." Prescott was still staring at himself, not denying anything or shaking his head or even seeming to breathe. Rake continued, "When he did come back for just a weekend, she and he had a conversation. I imagine he panicked, and he paid her off to keep quiet. But then something else happened. Maybe he'd told her never to come back, but she came back anyway. Maybe you were home that night, but he wasn't, because he'd already gone back north. Maybe she caused a scene in front of your mother, shouted or something, and that set you off. So your mama called your old man in Washington and then he called some people in Atlanta who knew how to clean up messes for important folks like you all."

"She was sweet," Prescott said, nearly a whisper. "She was a very sweet girl. We spoke a lot. I was around a fair amount then. One of my restaurants had gone under. . . . I didn't have much to occupy myself. Mother never liked it when I spoke to the help. I did it anyway, to spite her. Lily, she seemed like a smart girl." He spat into the sink again. "The kind of Negro that makes you think the things my father says about them maybe aren't true. People like my father say what they need to say to get what they want. It's a curious thing, to look up to someone like that."

"I'm sure you've suffered a great deal."

"I liked her. She even told me about this . . . group she'd joined. The sort of thing my father never would have tolerated, so of course

I encouraged her. And one night, maybe I'd had a bit too much to drink . . ."

He didn't fill in the blanks, which Rake appreciated.

"Only the one time. Just a few days later, my parents told me she'd stolen and they'd fired her."

"You really didn't know?"

"I was angry. Angry at my parents, at first, for what they were telling me and the way they'd driven away this girl I rather liked. I tried to find her, I drove all through Darktown, but she'd vanished. Then I realized she'd duped me. She'd made me *think* she was a sweet girl, she'd let me have a little fun, but it was just so she could get her hands on our money." The more he spoke, the less Rake liked him. Did Prescott really believe she'd enjoyed herself? Was he still telling himself it wasn't rape? When she knew all along they were siblings? "She'd waited for me to get my guard down, then she'd stolen from us. My father was right about them, you see. It's not very pleasant to be deceived by a Negro, Officer. And it's even less pleasant to realize a father like mine is right about anything."

So the congressman wasn't as friendly to Negroes as Boggs had wanted to think. Rake wasn't surprised. "Your father is wrong about quite a bit, actually."

"Then one night some men I didn't know were at Mother's, talking to her privately, but I put a few things together. They were police, and they'd taken her somewhere. I was so angry, *I* wanted to confront Lily, ask her who she thought she was to steal from us. At one point Mother stepped out and I heard the men talking amongst themselves, and they mentioned a brothel I've . . . heard of. A few days later I went there and the madam told me she wasn't there, but I knew she was lying. I waited in my car, and not more than an hour later one of those same men parks in front, walks in, and takes her away."

"Brian Underhill, an ex-cop."

"I never caught the gentleman's name. I followed them, but he pulled some crazy U-turn and hit a light and got flagged down by Negro policemen. I had to drive away but eventually I found him again, then lost him, and then I saw her running through the streets."

The lid of the trunk opened again and Dunlow backed up two paces to give Boggs room. "Out."

"You're making a mistake, Dunlow."

"I don't want your blood all over my trunk but I'll shoot you now if I have to. Out."

Boggs wondered how far away from Auburn Avenue he was. He had been hoping that perhaps by some miracle Smith might have been tailing Dunlow, that his partner was creeping through the woods to rescue him, but if so, that would have happened by now. It had taken Dunlow a good half hour to dig the grave that Boggs expected would be the last thing he'd ever see, and the white man was panting and sweaty and he smelled very drunk indeed even from a few paces away but the gun was steady in his hand.

Boggs slowly got out of the trunk. He held one of his hands to his ribs, as if they hurt—they did hurt, actually, quite a bit, but the reason he held his hand there was to conceal the sheared bottle neck that hand clasped. When he braced himself against the lid of the trunk to lift himself out, the neck cut into his palm but he took the pain because he couldn't drop the neck or let Dunlow see it. He stood and his head pounded, like the night he and Little had broken up a fight in the street. *Lord God, twice already I've had bottles broken against my skull.* The experience was not any easier to endure the second time.

"Step over there."

He turned and took one step to his right, then slumped over as if falling. He braced himself against the side of Dunlow's car and let his body go limp. His knees were buckling and he was about to hit the ground when he felt one of Dunlow's hands at his neck.

"Goddammit, nigger, don't be falling on my car."

But he wasn't falling, only pretending to. With Dunlow right behind him now, he swung around with his right hand, the sharp edge of the bottle neck facing out, and struck Dunlow. He'd spun around so fast he wasn't entirely sure where he hit him. Then an explosion and the sound of shattering glass. Boggs swung again, and again, and with his other arm he hit at Dunlow's right hand, the one with the gun in it, and there was another explosion and a cloud of gun smoke was hanging in the thick air between them. Boggs swung again with his right and this time the bottle's neck wasn't in his hand anymore, he'd dropped it, and Dunlow fell back a step and Boggs heard a metal-on-metal sound that hopefully meant the gun had fallen against the car and was on the ground somewhere.

Dunlow held a hand to the left side of his neck, then pulled it away and looked at it and his eyes were wide and white and now Boggs could see the darkness pumping out of his neck and flowing down his chest, like Boggs had simply reached over and opened the man up, turned a spigot. Dunlow was pressing his hand against his own neck as if trying to shut the spigot but there was no way. He tried to back up again and this time he fell.

Boggs's hands were shaking but he dropped to the ground and found the gun, which was hot because he touched the barrel first. He stood again and aimed it at Dunlow's chest. It was rising and falling so fast, as though he was full of life and breath, as though he could never die.

"Oh Jesus. You black son of a bitch."

The bottle neck had cut a four-inch gash in Dunlow's artery.

Boggs used his other hand to touch himself now, searching for a bullet wound, and though he felt the sting from some of the places where the shattered glass had cut him, nothing hurt enough to be a bullet wound.

Dunlow's chest was rising and falling less enthusiastically now. He was no longer looking at his foe, just staring into the sky.

The thought of offering some final words to Dunlow never even occurred to Boggs. The shock was enough, as was the thought that Dunlow might remember that he had another gun in his pocket or somehow heal himself.

Boggs was still aiming the gun at Dunlow's chest even past the point it was clear that the chest wasn't moving anymore.

Then Boggs sank to his knees and, seeing the shallow grave only a couple of feet away, scrambled toward it and threw up. After he was finished, he coughed, spat again, then sat back.

That's when he heard someone approaching on foot.

The son of Congressman Prescott continued his tale.

"I confronted her about the money. I told her all the things that had been percolating in my mind over those few days. I was . . . so angry at her."

"And you had a .22 on you."

"I would have been a fool to tramp through Darktown without it. I don't even remember taking it out of my pocket. I told her what she'd done to me, the shame she'd brought on me, and then she started screaming. Just completely mad. Saying that . . . she was my father's daughter. She just . . . seemed deranged. She wouldn't stop. She wouldn't stop."

"Until you stopped her."

Prescott didn't contradict him. Rake continued, "Underhill was circling the neighborhood for her, and he heard the shot, and that's how he found you. Does your father know?"

Prescott glared. "*I* certainly didn't tell him. I don't know. Underhill came to my place the next day and told me not to worry, that everything was being taken care of. I did not see fit to ask him how informed of all this my father was. I just . . . tried to forget about it."

Rake hadn't actually told Prescott that he was under arrest, and perhaps it was best not to. The words might jar him from the fugue that had settled over him. He was docile now, doing what he was told, and Rake guided him into the hallway where he could put on some shoes so he wouldn't have to walk out barefoot.

"I'd like to write a note for my father first."

"You can do that later."

"Please. Just . . . It will take only a minute. You can watch me. I've nothing left to hide, do I?"

Beyond the dining room was a small room with a desk and a mostly empty bookshelf. Prescott opened the desk's top drawer and it was as though Rake had seen this before when the man took from it a .22. Things did slow down this time. Rake reached to the small of his back and was pulling his gun from the holster while Prescott was lifting his own gun, held awkwardly in his fingers, held like someone who had used it often enough to know how it worked but not often enough to grip it properly or even lift it the right way, and now Rake's gun was at his side and his arm was swinging forward and he was just realizing how stupid he was, realizing that he wasn't going to get his gun in position in time, when Prescott's pistol pointed very much the wrong way and he shot himself in the temple.

Now Rake's gun was ready but there was nothing to aim at anymore, because Prescott had fallen to the floor. The entire body had folded into itself so fast, as though gravity is twice as strong on the dead.

Prescott's legs did not twitch and his eyes did not flutter—the lids were down, as he must have closed them at that awful moment. He was just *there,* a heap on the ground, blood flowing from his skull. There was more redness and a fleck of what might have been bone on the wall. The bullet hole was a few inches from the blood splatter. Rake paused to note how surprising it was that the bullet and the blood could land in such different places, and he wondered about that for a moment, because he was stunned and it was an easier thing to think about than the huge amount of trouble he was in.

Boggs was sure he wasn't imagining the footsteps. He pointed Dunlow's pistol before him, though he could see only the first few feet of trees before all became darkness.

"Who's there?"

"You put that gun down!" The voice was high-pitched but commanding. It wasn't coming from very far away.

"I said who's there!"

"I see your pistol but this here's a rifle and you don't drop that in three seconds I'ma lay you flat."

Boggs tried to focus on the region of darkness from where the voice seemed to be coming. He couldn't see anything but the intermittent lightning bugs that he half wondered were his own damaged neurons misfiring.

"I'm a police officer! From the city of Atlanta! If you have a rifle in your hand, you'd best lay it down, now!"

The unseen man's three-second warning passed, then twice as much time passed, then far more. Boggs felt dizzy from the blow to his head and weak from not having eaten in he couldn't remember how long, and he had no idea where he was or when the sun would rise.

"You ain't no cop." The voice was ratcheted down a few notches.

"How many colored men you think would lie about that, huh?"

Silence for a few seconds. Boggs still couldn't see anyone.

"Listen here," the voice said. "I'ma walk toward you a bit. I got this here rifle trained on you, so don't get to thinking nothing stupid. I'ma just get a bit closer so's we can talk. You so much as flinch and you're on the ground, got it?"

"I'm not lowering my weapon, if that's what you're asking. But come on over if you like."

"Just don't do nothing we gonna regret."

Twigs snapped and leaves crunched beneath the footsteps. A second later, a good many feet to the right of where Boggs had been pointing Dunlow's pistol, a figure emerged from the woods. The first thing Boggs noticed was the shine of the man's forehead, from the heat that would not abate even at night and from the terror of realizing he'd just come upon a crime scene. The second thing Boggs noticed was that the man was colored. He was wearing a gray T-shirt over brown canvas work pants.

The men were still aiming their weapons at each other.

"Sir, my name is Officer Lucius Boggs. I'm an officer with the Atlanta Police Department. This man tried to kill me."

"Looks like you beat him to it." When the man spoke, Boggs saw places where teeth should have been, as well as a few teeth.

"Just lucky."

"Looks like you just barely lucky."

"Where am I?"

"Tillsboro." It was twenty miles south of the city. There was a paper mill and the area produced amazing strawberries, according to the grocer Boggs frequented. Lucius had never set foot here before. "You really a cop?"

"Yes. You can call the Atlanta police and ask them if you want. Is this your property?"

"No. Mine about three hundred yards behind me. I heard shots an' came looking."

"Do you know this man? Any idea who he is?"

"No."

Boggs believed him. He'd wondered whether Dunlow had used this spot before, whether it was a favored destination for disposing of bodies.

Perhaps Lily Ellsworth had been bound for here once, until Boggs and Smith's traffic stop of Underhill had thrown that evening's plan into disarray.

Boggs asked, "This kind of thing happen around here a lot?"

"Not that I've noticed." The man was perhaps ten years older than Boggs, perhaps twenty.

"Now, you stop aiming that gun at me, I'll do the same."

"All right." The man pointed his gun at the sky. He'd been in a defensive crouch, but he stood taller and stepped closer. He stared down at Dunlow.

"Goddamn. Where's your knife?"

Boggs explained what he'd used as a weapon.

"You don't know this fella?" the man asked.

"Never seen him before."

"Where's your badge?"

"It isn't on me. I'm not on duty. I was just walking through the city and this man nearly ran me over, knocked me out, and stuffed me in his trunk."

"You arrest one of his buddies or somethin'?"

Boggs didn't answer, busily trying to construct a story in his head.

"I got a phone, you want to call your boys in."

"I can't do that."

"Why not?"

"What I just did was self-defense, but that won't matter. Even though I'm a cop, it won't matter."

They watched each other for a moment, then both stared at Dunlow, their mutual problem. Boggs felt ashamed of how he could smell his own vomit and was sure the man could, too.

"What's your name, sir?"

"Roland. Roland Dooley."

"I need you to do me a favor, Mr. Dooley. I'd like to use your phone to call my partner. Then he and I are going to bury this man right here, and get rid of his vehicle somewhere. We're never going to talk about this. And I'm going to have to ask you to never talk about it, either."

"That's two favors. The second one's mighty big."

"It is mighty big, sir." An owl echoed its own call in the dark. "Or you could tell it like you saw it, and I'll be arrested. I'll plead my case honestly, and even though this is just some bigot who decided it would be fun to kill a Negro, I'll at the very least lose my badge, and Atlanta will lose its Negro cops. That's the best-case scenario."

Dooley took another step until he was right next to Dunlow's feet. The earth near Dunlow's head and chest was shiny with blood. Then Dooley looked up at Boggs.

"We ain't got no Negro cops in Tillsboro."

It took more than an hour for Smith to find them. Boggs had called him from Dooley's phone, explaining as little as possible, then letting Dooley give Smith directions to wherever they were.

Boggs stood sentry at the body while Dooley waited in his home. When Boggs heard the faint sound of a motor, then silence, then two quick honks, he knew they were coming.

"Good God," Smith said as he got out of the reverend's car and surveyed the corpse. Some white people look so pale it doesn't seem possible they could be even yet paler until it happens.

"He was drunk. Drunk when he ran me down and a whole lot drunker when he tried to put me in that hole."

"It ain't near deep enough," Smith observed. So he got started. It was past one in the morning, so they had a few hours of darkness left. The owls and nighthawks seemed louder now to Boggs, as if this was the time of night they'd been saving themselves for.

Dooley told them he would honk his old pickup's horn again if he saw anyone venture down the road, then he returned home to wait for them.

"You trust him?" Smith asked Boggs while he deepened the hole.

"I don't have a choice."

Smith got out of the hole and handed the shovel to Boggs. "Your turn." He wasn't that tired yet, but he didn't like the vacant look in Boggs's eye. The man was no doubt exhausted, but Smith wanted him to move again, put himself to some purpose, even if he could only manage a few spades' worth.

"What did you tell my parents to get the car from them?"

"I didn't have a good story yet. Just told them you needed my help and you'd explain. Reverend looked like he was saying a prayer to Jesus in his head when he handed me the keys."

When the grave had been dug to Smith's satisfaction, they frisked Dunlow and found nothing but his wallet and keys. They chose to leave the wallet in his pocket, though not before looking in vain for some evidence into the Ellsworth crimes. They kept the keys. Then they each took one of Dunlow's feet and dragged him into the hole.

Dooley had offered to lend them an extra shovel, but they'd declined, lest he wind up with evidence in his toolshed. So the two officers shared the job of shoveling the fresh dirt on top of Dunlow.

"We're assuming he was acting alone," Smith said at one point. "Anybody else know what he was up to, and he goes missing . . ."

"I realize that. If you have a better idea, I'm listening."

Smith offered none. "Give me the shovel."

They hadn't covered up the grave very convincingly, Boggs could see, but here in summer all it would take was one good rain and the grave wouldn't look different from any other spot. In a month or two, nearby vines would be crawling their way across the surface, and in another year shrubs whose seeds were shat out by birds would be growing there.

The Lord would have expected some words to be said for Dunlow's immortal soul, Boggs realized. And Reverend Boggs certainly would have offered a benediction, even to a man who'd tried to kill his son. *Then perhaps my father truly is a better man than me,* Boggs silently said to the Lord, *because I have nothing to say.*

Smith tossed a few fallen branches across the spot. Then he spat on the ground. He was worried about his partner and worried what would happen with Dunlow's friends and worried that neither he nor Boggs would survive this, but at that moment his biggest regret was that Dunlow had not suffered more.

In Dooley's front yard, they paid him a few dollars for a can of gasoline.

He told them he worked at the paper mill. His wife and son were asleep, he claimed, though Boggs wouldn't have been surprised if his lady was sitting up in their bedroom at that moment, clutching her Bible and listening to everything. Dooley said that few people lived within a half mile of this spot; he had chosen it for the solitude it offered, though he sometimes heard rumors that the state wanted to turn some of the woods into parkland and kick him out.

They shook his hand. Boggs looked him in the eye and tried to impress upon him once again the gravity of this event, but probably all his blank eyes could convey at that moment was shock and the emptiness of death.

"If there's anything you ever need, Mr. Dooley, you call us."

With Boggs driving Dunlow's car and Smith the reverend's, they drove six miles north, closer to Atlanta but still safely far from where cops might search for Dunlow anytime soon. They were in woods again, and Smith knew these roads from days spent fishing. Eventually they drove down a dead-end road that went downhill sharply and ended in a wide clearing.

There had once been an antebellum mill building there, Smith explained, but it had caught fire a few years ago and all that was left was a bare skeleton of bricks whose outline looked spectral in the dark. Smith parked the car in the center of the clearing. Someone would find the car eventually, but it might be days, and they might not even be the type to bother telling the authorities of their discovery. Smith used a screwdriver he'd hidden in his pocket to remove Dunlow's tags, which he would toss into a drainage intake once they were closer to Atlanta.

They wiped the car down again, checking the trunk and floor for anything incriminating and removing some paperwork that would have traced it to Dunlow. Then Smith poured the gasoline, backed away, and threw a match. It caught slowly but then spread fast. They watched for a moment, checking to make sure nothing else caught fire, though if anything had, they wouldn't have been able to stop it.

It seemed they had spent most of the last twenty-four hours in this car. Smith said, "Well, you got your kill now."

"What?"

"You not getting to fight in the army. You taken care of that now."

He'd never said anything to Smith about any feelings of inferiority about his army experience. At least, he thought he hadn't. Had he been so obvious nonetheless?

"I didn't want this."

"Didn't say you did."

Boggs stared through the windshield and tried to remember what it had been like to wonder what it would be like to kill someone.

"If there's anything you want to say about the experience," Smith said, "now is the time. Because once we get out of this car, neither of us is ever talking about this again."

Boggs answered with silence that lasted thirty minutes, and then the lights of the looming office towers welcomed them back to Atlanta.

36

TWELVE HOURS AFTER Silas Prescott had exited this mortal world, Rake was sitting in the same interrogation room he had entered when he'd first arrived at police headquarters.

Shortly after Prescott shot himself, Rake had picked up the phone and dialed his home line. When he heard Cassie, half asleep, pick up the phone, he hung up. He'd then spent ten minutes cleaning the bathroom to kill the vomit smell, using only soap and water rather than stronger chemicals that might have tipped off other cops to the tampering of a crime scene. After waiting the ten longest minutes of his life, he'd called police headquarters.

His admittedly far-fetched story, when the squad cars and ambulance pulled up, was that Prescott had surprisingly called Rake at his house to say he urgently needed to speak to him. So Rake had dutifully come over, had then witnessed a shocking confession, and, before Rake could even mentally process it, Prescott had shot himself.

"Why in the hell did Prescott call *you?*" Rake's commanding officer, Sergeant Yale, had demanded. Rake had insisted he had no idea whatsoever.

Shortly after the first group of cops had shown up to take photos and gather evidence, two men whom Rake had been expecting showed up: Detectives Clayton and Sharpe, who had enthusiastically and brutally questioned Otis Ellsworth.

An hour later, Yale drove Rake back to the station.

"If there is anything else you want me to know, you had damn well better tell me now, because once we get back to that station you and me aren't talking a lick. There'll be a long line of folks ready to sink their teeth into you."

During the course of his half year working under Yale, Rake still had little idea of how far he could trust the man.

"Nothing that comes to mind, sir."

Rake's fingers had been shaking when he'd cleaned up the bathroom, but during the final wait before making the call his nerves had settled. He wasn't sure whether he was delusional to feel so confident. Perhaps he was suffering from some strange adrenalized spike of self-congratulation, but he wasn't going to whine and beg in front of the sergeant when he still had a few cards left to play.

In the interrogation room, he repeated his story to Yale's commanding officer, on the record. Twice. A third time. *Why did Prescott call you? Had you ever spoken to him before? How did he even have your number or know who you are?* He was asked to repeat exactly what Prescott had confessed, over and over, backward and forward, with adjectives and without.

Then a long wait in the otherwise empty room. It was likely past midnight when Sharpe and Clayton entered. Clayton was the former football player for the Bulldogs, the tough one who'd driven his fists into Ellsworth. Sharpe was older, gray hair, thin, with a fondness for suits that appeared more expensive than a police detective should be able to afford.

"Quite a night for you, Officer Rakestraw," Sharpe said. Rake was sitting in a chair opposite a small table. Clayton stood directly across from Rake, while Sharpe stood to the side, very close to Rake, easy striking distance.

Rake just stared at them, waiting for a question. It had not escaped his attention that this room had no observation window.

"Why don't we start from the beginning," Sharpe said. "Let's start with what Mr. Prescott said to you when you allegedly picked up the phone in your house, when he allegedly called you."

Rake rubbed at his chin. It was scratchy now and needed a shave.

He asked, "Which one of you shot Underhill?"

"Excuse me?"

"Underhill. That night by the foundry. Only thing I haven't figured out for a certain is why, though it was obviously one of two things. Maybe it was because he went back to you and asked for more money once he realized how important that girl had been. He hadn't known when he showed up to get her out of town that she was connected to a congressman. She mouthed off to him in the car, he slapped her, then she ran off. Then the junior Prescott finds her, snaps, shoots her, and when Underhill tracks them down he finds he's now dealing with a dead body. He gets rid of it, not doing a particularly good job, and now that he knows just how high-rent a crowd he's helping out, he decides that whatever fee he'd agreed to isn't enough, so he asks for more. And you decide he's too much trouble.

"Or," he continued, "maybe it was because you realized I was getting too close to him, and you needed to erase the trail. So, which of those two was it? And which one of you pulled the trigger?"

Sharpe smiled. Only now, though. During that long statement, the two detectives' faces had been cold and taut.

"I'm afraid the stress of this evening is getting to you, Officer Rakestraw."

"It's making you do very unwise things," Clayton said, making a show of folding his thick arms in front of his chest.

Rake was not cuffed. He scooted his chair back just a tad, so he'd have room to work with in a moment.

"Clayton, you can fold those arms as tight as you want, but if you even think of taking a swing at me like you did that Negro farmer, your partner will be picking up your teeth as keepsakes."

Sharpe laughed. "You think you're holding a winning hand, don't you? You're about to be booked for *murder*."

"People who are booked for murder have a habit of talking, a lot. They talk at their trial an amazing amount. They say all kinds of things that some people would prefer not get said."

Clayton swung. He got Rake in the cheekbone. The fact that Rake had been expecting it hardly meant that it didn't hurt. But it did mean that he rolled to his right quickly, flowing with the punch, his ass sliding off the chair and his right knee landing against the floor. Which gave him plenty of leverage as he stood back up, lifting the table with him, and using it as a battering ram as he flew into Clayton like a drilling lineman running into pads. Clayton tripped backward, the table slamming him into the wall. Rake heard the wind rush out of the detective. Then Rake let go of the table and hit the bastard square in the nose, twice, a third time, the back of the man's skull hitting the wall each time and Rake's hand getting increasingly wet with blood. Rake was gearing up for another swing when someone or something hit him and he was on the floor, and trying to get up, and seeing all kinds of feet coming at him, some running and some lifting themselves high above so they could plant themselves low.

An indeterminate amount of time later, Rake was sitting in the same room. This time there was no table and his hands were cuffed, one cuff each, to the chair legs behind him.

It had occurred to him, just before he lost consciousness, that the glaring weakness in his plan was that they could just kill him and no longer worry about his ability to talk. He was still alive, at the moment, but his lip was busted and one of his eyes was swollen shut. And regardless of how many of Clayton's teeth he'd punched out, he'd also lost one of his own.

He would have killed for a glass of water and a bottle of aspirin.

He still had no idea how many people on the force had been involved in the effort to remove Lily Ellsworth from life and any living person's memory. If there were as many as he was now beginning to fear—the entire police department except himself?—then Sharpe was right that Rake had no cards to play. Or maybe it was only a few dirty cops, but those few were still more than powerful enough to swat into nothingness the buzzing annoyance that was Denny Rakestraw.

The door opened and in walked a cop in a spotless uniform. He was tall and thick, an older man but, unlike Dunlow, one who had managed to keep himself in shape. He was holding about six inches of folders and paperwork. He looked down at Rake for a moment, then glanced out the open door and told someone named Kenny to fetch another chair. A chair was handed to him by the unseen Kenny, and the door was closed, and Chief Jenkins sat down opposite one of the most vexing officers in his city.

"Discretion is not one of your strengths, Officer Rakestraw." Jenkins had blue eyes and a ruddy face that had spent years in the sun. Those eyes still looked youthful but the skin around them was lined with wrinkles that stretched nearly to the gray hair above his ears.

"No, sir." Talking hurt. He clenched his stomach and forced the words out. "I felt it wasn't in my best interest to be quiet tonight."

"Why is that?"

"It's the people doing things wrong who want to stay quiet about it. Sir." He breathed. He didn't think his ribs were broken, but they weren't particularly happy either. "No questions, no whispers, no one bothering them. Being loud is the last thing they want."

Jenkins regarded him.

"A United States congressman has boarded a plane for Atlanta," the chief finally said. "By the time he lands, he is going to want to know exactly why his son is dead." He opened one of the folders and flipped through it. Rake wasn't a good enough upside-down reader to know what Jenkins was looking at, plus his one "good" eye was getting fuzzy.

"It's not a very palatable story, sir. And I've been saving the worst parts for you."

Jenkins looked up from his paperwork. "How's that?"

Rake had been gambling on the fact that the reform-minded Jenkins, who had moved to arrest the cops who ran the numbers operations a few years back and who had thrown the Kluxers out of the police union, would not side against Rake if he heard the whole story. The fact that the chief himself was in this room made Rake feel all the more strongly that he was right.

So Rake mentioned that he'd had suspicions about his own partner and thus had gone this alone. He told the truth about how he'd questioned Silas Prescott a few nights ago, and how he'd confronted the man tonight. When Jenkins asked how Rake had learned certain things, he did not mention his collaboration with Boggs, afraid to touch that third rail, instead making it sound as if he had picked up tips from Negro informants.

"You did a lot of things wrong, Officer Rakestraw."

"I realize that, sir."

"And you're laying quite a mess at my feet."

"I'm sorry for that, sir. But the way I see it is, there are cops here you wish you didn't have, and there are cops you wish you had more of. I'm the second kind."

"You don't lack for confidence."

"Probably just got hit in the head a few too many times."

"Don't let that become a habit."

"Sir, there are a lot of things I'm not good at. But I think I'm a good cop. And I was a good soldier. If you think it's best for you and your department for me to go away and keep my mouth shut, I can do that. But if you think it would be best to have me stick around and keep my mouth shut, I figure I can do that, too."

Jenkins drummed his fingers on the desk. "If there's anything you've been fixing to ask me, you'd best do so now."

"Sir, if you do decide I'm to remain an officer here, I'd surely appreciate a new partner."

Jenkins folded his arms across his chest. "Funny you should mention that. We've been trying to reach Officer Dunlow ever since we brought you in here, but he's nowhere to be found. Any clue where he might be?"

37

THE DAY AFTER burying Dunlow, Boggs and Smith had reported for duty like any other. Despite suffering the headache of his life, Boggs had no bruises on his face, as the bottle had hit the back of his skull. His ribs ached, and only through prayer and great force of will had he been able to walk without leaning over like the invalid he felt he was.

They tried and failed to reach the Ellsworth family. Various calls placed to different churches in Peacedale had brought them only bits of information. Their messages were routed to different phoneless households by messenger or letter or gossip or God's will. The Ellsworths had fled Peacedale, perhaps to some relations of Emma Mae in a county farther east. Or perhaps, Boggs wondered, they were trying to go to Chicago after all, even though the white cops had stolen all the money Lily had sent them, the hush money her father had paid out in hopes that it would undo his history. Undo her. Perhaps the few surviving Ellsworths would make it up north, would wind up living in an apartment only a few blocks away from some of Boggs's relations who had also made the migration. Or perhaps they would spend the remainder of their days as they had lived them, barely scraping by beneath the boot of another white landowner, a different town and a different county but the same unbreakable rules.

Two days later, no one had come to arrest or fire Boggs.

He had only spoken to Rake once more since that awful night, and briefly: Rake called simply to say that they'd been right about Prescott, but that the truth would never be acknowledged. When Boggs asked why not, Rake had rushed off the phone, promising to explain soon.

The official story, which ran in the back pages of the local paper only a few hours after that phone call, was that the only son of Congressman Prescott had committed suicide for reasons unknown. It would not do to invade the family's privacy, although a few writers pointed out that the young man had recently presided over a failed restaurant and had yet to make a success of himself the way his father and grandfather had. The governor and mayor offered their condolences, but otherwise this was a private matter.

Boggs heard conflicting rumors that Rakestraw was going to be fired, then that he was going to be promoted. And he heard that the other white cops hated Rake almost as much as they hated the colored officers. Whatever bargain the man had struck, he'd won one thing but lost something else.

❧

Lucius wasn't sure how long it would take for him to relax. If he would ever relax. One day, surely, someone would find Dunlow's body. Even if that didn't happen, at the very least someone would find his incinerated car and track it to the missing cop. Even if *that* didn't happen, surely Dunlow had friends wondering where he was. He was not the type to run off. Boggs wasn't sure how many people knew that Dunlow was coming after him that night or if it had been a random attack, didn't know which accomplices might make the next strike.

Perhaps, if he was very lucky, months and then years would pass, and he would eventually conclude that he had gotten away with it. Then he might be able to exhale.

Until then, the uncertainty was a clamp around his rib cage, squeezing him every day.

❧

One afternoon he walked into the basement precinct an hour early, intending to get a head start on some paperwork. He was surprised to find McInnis down there. After a brief hello, the sergeant—in an untucked blue shirt and khakis—told him, "I received a rather agitated call from the Peacedale sheriff a few days ago. Forgot to mention that."

"What was he agitated about, sir?"

"He seemed to believe that two Negroes who claimed to be Atlanta police officers had come down to his little town to stir up trouble."

"That's quite a story, sir."

McInnis sat down on a desk. "It is. I reminded him that Atlanta police would have had no jurisdiction in Peacedale, and that besides, a Negro officer would know better than to stick his nose in a town like that. I told him any Negro who caused trouble down there could surely be handled by a big man like him."

Boggs was having trouble figuring out McInnis's angle. After a moment of indecision, he realized his own silence looked rude. So he said, "Thank you, sir."

McInnis nodded to one of the chairs. "Have a seat. Now, have you ever thought to wonder why I was given the honor of leading you Negro officers?"

"I've wondered it, sir."

"Then I have a story for you. Have you ever heard tell of the Rust Division?"

"A little bit."

"Couple of years ago, I was one of the cops given the task of investigating the Atlanta police officers who were deeply involved in numbers running. Not just the ones who were *involved*—cause that was damn near everyone—but the ones who were in charge. It wasn't the kind of job any cop would have asked for, and I don't know why they gave it to me. Thirteen cops lost their jobs because of what I had to do. Four went to jail, and they're still there now. Another nine *could* have gone— should have, in my opinion—but the evidence wasn't strong enough to convict. It *was* strong enough for them to lose their badges and pensions, though."

"They deserved it."

McInnis grinned. "Things do seem awfully black and white to you, don't they?"

"I just mean—"

"I don't care what you mean. My point is, I made a lot of enemies. Didn't have a choice, though, did I? If I'd done a bad job, I would've been demoted, or just sent to rot at some desk. If I'd done a *really* bad job, it might have looked like I was colluding with the very men I was investigating, in which case I might have gone to jail myself. So I did a damned excellent job. And lo and behold, when a sergeant was needed to watch over our Negro recruits, I got that job, too."

Then he explained what Boggs had already learned through Rake: the Rust Division of cops who'd been laid off but were still available for dirty work, for a price.

"This is unofficial. But I've heard enough to believe it. 'Rust Division,' I kind of like that, a play on cop, copper, but it's old dirty copper so it's got some rust to it. Rather creative for cops." He shook his head. "Except copper doesn't actually rust."

"So . . . what sort of things do these ex-cops do?"

"Maybe they don't exist. Maybe it's just a bogeyman story told to keep other cops on their toes. To know that there's a parallel police force out there, off the books, small but operating with impunity because they're being watched out for and paid by some very high-ranking officials."

"Who are these officials?"

"That's far beyond your pay grade."

"But you're saying these Rust people are still out there. And the cops who control them, they're out there, too." He and Rake had concluded it was Sharpe and Clayton, the two cops who had roughly interrogated Ellsworth and then tried to beat Rake into nothingness afterward, who likely hired and then eliminated Underhill. Rake had pointed Chief Jenkins in their direction, but there had been no arrests that Boggs knew of. "They're still on the force, drawing pay."

"Which should keep all of us on our toes, shouldn't it?"

"Yes, sir." After a pause, Lucius asked, "Why did you remove Underhill's name from my report? Why not call more attention to this phantom division if it's killing people?"

"Number one, we can't prove they killed anyone. Number two, we are talking about men I tried to put away, men who should have gone to jail after the lottery sting but instead only got fired, and for my trouble, I got sent to the basement of a colored YMCA. So perhaps I am lazy, perhaps I am immoral, or perhaps I am merely loath to reengage battles I'm not permitted to win. And, though this may shock you, Officer Boggs, I've been impressed by you. I think you're becoming nearly adept at this job. I think you may well become good at it one day. And I think that, if certain people in APD had realized that you were looking into a man like Brian Underhill, your already low odds of surviving would have plummeted yet further, and perhaps I don't think that's fair."

Boggs needed a moment to make sense of this. "You changed my report to protect me?"

"As I said, shocking." McInnis rolled his eyes. "I don't know what the hell is happening to me down here. The good news for you is, I don't think you have much to worry about with those Rust boys. What happened to Underhill has no doubt scared them. But what you *do* need to be worried about—far more worried than you seem to be—is pretty much every other white cop in this city. If you and your partner decide to take on any investigations of your own again, you will at least be fired, and, at the most, whichever white cop you piss off will decide to permanently remove you from his list of problems. Is that clear?"

"Yes, sir."

"Good. I intend to be a cop in this city for a long while, Officer Boggs. And if you do, too, then we're going to have to find a way to put up with each other."

The next afternoon, Boggs was walking home from the grocer's, past a row of vibrant orange lilies, when he heard a car door close. He looked up and saw Rakestraw crossing the street. He hadn't heard or seen the car drive up—Rake had been sitting there waiting.

They met in front of the reverend's house. They stood in the shade, the low branches of the oak nearly touching their heads.

"I was wondering if you were going to stop by," Boggs said.

"I've been meaning to. Been a bit hairy lately. But I didn't want you to think I'd forgotten. I appreciate all you did to help me out."

Lucius didn't appreciate the way Rake had phrased that, *you* help *me* out. He said, "There's a lot I'm still not straight on."

Rake explained again what had happened at Silas Prescott's house that night, the confession and the shooting. All he said beyond that, however, was that the deceased Silas Prescott would never be charged with Lily's murder. Lucius wanted to object, wanted to say the least they could do was officially clear Otis's name, but he knew that wasn't true: there was always less they could do. And that's exactly what white people would do.

His heart had broken for Lily so many times, but it did again. And it broke for his father, and for himself. They had both wanted to believe that Congressman Prescott was an ally. An important white politician who had seen the merit of their arguments against Jim Crow. A convert to their cause who would work the halls of power for them, strive with them to achieve their goals. When in fact the extent of his regard for Negroes seemed to be that he liked sleeping with the cute young ones. He knew what speeches to make to win enough of their votes, now that they were permitted to vote. But he was no better than the rural legislators who openly invited white mobs to keep them in line with nooses and guns. He took advantage of a Negro girl, and a generation later his son did the same thing, and both times, when those girls became problems, they did what they had to do to remove them.

Boggs hadn't told his father the truth about Prescott, and he probably never would. It was a moot point anyway: word was that the congressman would not run for reelection, succumbing to grief.

"Well, I'm glad to hear things have worked out for you," Lucius said, barely even trying to conceal his bitterness. He dared stray into dangerous territory with, "I heard you got a new partner."

"Yeah. He's a good fellow. Teaching me a lot."

"Good. Thanks for dropping by. You take care."

He had taken a few steps down the walkway when Rake called out, "Wait." Boggs turned.

Rake took a few steps toward him, glancing around, clearly afraid someone would see a white man talking to a Negro like an equal, or some rough approximation.

"You've heard that Dunlow's missing, I'm sure."

Boggs tried to keep his face blank.

"The last time I saw him," Rake continued, "he was drinking in the morning and ranting about you and Smith. There any chance he came looking for one of you?"

Boggs had practiced in front of his mirror what he would say, many times. "If he had, do you think I'd be standing here right now? He probably drove into a wall somewhere."

"Then there'd be a wreck, and a body."

"Then he up and left town."

"Doesn't sound like him. Seemed like he was about ready to restart the War Between the States that day, not run off."

"Who knows, then. Don't ask *me* to explain the behavior of a man like that."

Rake looked down for a moment, then back at Boggs. "You should know, in case you haven't heard this yourself. But plenty of white cops figure something happened between you and Smith and Dunlow. Fellows I'm not so fond of myself. They say there's no way Dunlow would have turned tail, that he would have come after you. And that something happened."

Lucius paused only a moment. "First they had us for Poe, and now they have us for Dunlow? I can't wait to see what unsolved murder they pin on the colored cops next."

"I know it," Rake said, and sighed. He seemed convinced.

Lucius felt perhaps too much relief then, because he pushed too far with, "Maybe it was whoever on the force was behind Ellsworth. Sharpe and Clayton, or whoever it was that we can't touch? Maybe they got tired of Dunlow for the same reason they got tired of Underhill. Or maybe it was whoever it was you worked out some deal with to stay on the force."

Rake scowled. "What the hell is that supposed to mean? What 'deal,' what have you heard?"

"Nothing. Forget it. We all had to strike crazy bargains to get where we are, right? You and Dunlow. Me and Smith. Me and you. Who knows what bargain Dunlow struck with whom?"

Boggs hoped Rake wouldn't wonder why he wasn't making eye contact anymore. Hoped he wouldn't wonder why he was staring at the ground and then turning, walking away as if fleeing before any more questions.

38

RAKE COULDN'T SLEEP again, even though he'd just finished a grueling shift with his new partner. A man had stabbed his brother to death in front of the dead man's wife and two young children, Rake arriving minutes later, everyone screaming but the dead man. Blood everywhere, expressions on faces that he feared he would never forget.

After lying in bed for thirty minutes, he got up, dressed, and went for a walk.

The killer tonight had surrendered immediately. He hadn't even fled the scene, had simply been waiting outside for the police. Hands slick with blood, he explained that he'd done what needed to be done, that his brother had lent him money once and never shut up about it, the man had shamed him over and over, he was all proud of himself for having a pretty wife and cute kids and a good-paying job, he needed to be taken down a notch. Derangement could be so matter-of-fact sometimes.

It was past three in the morning as Rake walked in the middle of the street, the silence as thick as the humidity.

He was still reacting to the evening's horrors, he knew, and the two little boys screaming, but somehow the experience merged in his mind with Dunlow. He knew Dunlow was dead. There was no way the man had simply run off, and Boggs's theory that someone in APD had decided Dunlow was a nuisance seemed wrong. Dunlow hadn't been involved in the Ellsworth saga at all; he had *wanted* to be involved, as he would have liked the extra money, but Underhill had held him at arm's length. The Rust Division men who'd broken Rake's finger had confirmed it. Dunlow was dirty and racist and a horrible cop, but he hadn't been involved in the Ellsworth murder other than letting Underhill off without a ticket that night. There was no reason he would have been killed in connection with that crime.

Rake did not like the thought that Boggs or Smith had killed him, but it had been there in his head for days now. He had wanted to see how Boggs would react to Dunlow's name, and the Negro's reaction had felt staged.

Now that Dunlow seemed to be dead, Rake felt a guilt he'd never expected. Had he killed Dunlow somehow? Had he driven his partner to do something stupid? He'd reviewed the events of the last few weeks in his mind so many times now, and the attenuating fear and stress was mixing everything up, confusing him, timelines getting fuzzy, cause blurring with effect.

He stopped when he heard glass shatter. It had come from his left, far enough away to have been barely audible, and he wondered if he'd imagined it. Then he heard it again.

Few things are as disorienting as being lost in a thought and then realizing that something of great import is trying to interrupt. It's hard to notice what's happening, hard to step away from the insular inertia of one's self. The job had been helping Rake get better at this, though, as the outside world's unexpected action tended to invade monotony at least once each night. When he saw a figure darting to his left, he turned and was about to follow it when he saw something else, to his right. A brightness. He turned toward it, losing the figure so he could better take in the fire. It was Mr. Calvin's house. From the distance he could just make out its silhouette, but he could certainly see the yellow blaze running up one of its walls. So bright he couldn't look at it directly, the glowing yellow and the angry oranges and it was spreading so fast. When he blinked he saw the round blue burns inside his eyelids.

There was no car in their driveway. No screams, at least not yet. For a moment Rake stood there.

Then he turned and looked for the figure. He didn't see it but he heard the scuff of a shoe on pavement, so he ran. There it was, darting a few houses ahead of him, cutting now into a backyard.

He could have yelled, "Stop, police!" and if he'd been in a different neighborhood, perhaps he would have.

He ran because it was easy and sudden and the longer he ran, the more he wondered if he was running in the wrong direction. The driveway was empty, but the house?

Chasing the figure, Rake nearly tripped over a shovel that someone's back light warned him about just in time. Then he saw the man, trapped by the fact that a neighbor had decided to put up a fence. The man was moving to his side now, hoping to find some new escape. He sped past some shrubs and Rake was just behind him, the two of them emerging in another yard and then Rake sprang forward like the free safety he'd once been, a perfect tackle as he grasped the man's ankles and held on.

Before the man could get up, Rake was on top of him. He knelt on the small of his back and grabbed his right wrist, pulling it behind him.

"Let me up!" Sounded young. Rake wasn't surprised. Not a man but a teenager.

"What the hell do you think you're doing, kid? You want the electric chair?"

"Nobody's even home, we checked!"

"Who's 'we'?"

No reply. The kid was panting and so was Rake.

With his free hand, Rake patted the kid down. He couldn't reach everything since the kid was pinned down, but he felt reassured enough.

"I'm going to roll you over real slow. Don't even think about getting up."

Rake stood and took a step to the side so he'd have space if the kid pulled anything. Then he prodded the kid's shoulder with one of his feet and told him to roll over onto his back.

It was dark out, but the nearly full moon provided just enough illumination for Rake to see himself gazing back in time. The bone structure and eyes were unmistakable.

"You're a Dunlow, aren't you?"

"Yessir. Lionel Junior. Folks call me Buddy." He'd seemed nearly as tall as Rake when he'd been running. He was thin but not scrawny, the cords of his neck taut and his white T-shirt bulging softly beneath his chest. "How'd you know?"

"I work with your father."

"Do you know where he is?"

Rake sighed and shook his head.

"He's working on some secret mission, ain't he? Something they needed to send only the most special cops on?"

Rake heard footsteps coming from the next yard, quiet whispers against tall grass.

"That may be," Rake said. "I'm not told such things."

"Me and my brother are doing what we need to do. He asked us to before, but we didn't get to it. Maybe he's upset at us for not doing it sooner, and this way he'll finally come back and—"

"Shut *up*, Buddy!"

Rake saw another new figure a few feet away. It was too far to see a face, but the voice sounded like another Dunlow, older than this one, thicker looking. And holding a knife.

"Son, you can either put that blade back in your pocket right now, or underhand it to me real slow."

"You ain't taking my brother," the kid said, not moving. "Our old man's gone but you ain't taking him, too."

"I never said I was taking anybody. Are you two morons? Trying to kill someone?"

"No, sir," the older one said. He folded and pocketed the knife. "We checked the windows that no one was home. We waited for the right time. We know what we're doing."

"Yeah, you're goddamned criminal masterminds." Rake was not surprised that no sirens were calling, no neighbors yelling. He looked at the younger one. "Get up. Go the hell home, and mind your business from now on."

The younger one stood and walked, with a limp, over to his brother. Rake stared at them and they looked back, dark shapes without faces. Rake was tempted to ask them if they'd *come to an understanding* but he bit his tongue. It was only going to get harder for these two.

Then the two Dunlows backed away, swallowed by the overgrowth of summer gardens.

Rake was closer to his own house than to the Calvins', so he ran home first. Cassie and the kids were still asleep, blissfully unaware. He picked up the kitchen phone and called the fire department. He didn't identify himself as a cop, didn't identify himself at all. He asked for a fire truck—and an ambulance, which he hoped wasn't necessary—and they assured him one was on the way.

It would be a very slow truck, he knew. He hurried back outside and ran to the burning building. The flames had made quite some progress over the last few minutes. Fire was very good at its job. The entire building was consumed now, black funneling upward in the thick air until it disappeared into the matching night. None of the Calvins had emerged. No one was screaming and there was no sign of life. He hoped the Dunlow boys had been right.

From the road, a good ten feet from the edge of the yard, the heat felt like an angry hand against his breastbone, warning him back. His eyes went dry, his throat tightened.

It was a corner lot. The house to its right was closer, and the bushes between them were at risk of catching. He ran to that house and tried the front door, but it was locked. He pounded on it and yelled, "Police! There's a fire next door, you need to evacuate!"

Something from inside the fire popped, or the fire popped as it expanded, or maybe it was his nerves as he ran to the neighbors' back door. It was unlocked. He turned on the lights and ran to the stairs, repeating his warning as loud as he could. He saw kids' pictures on the walls. He ran up the steps, yelling still, and found a bedroom, the bed empty. So was the bed in the other room. He found the parents' room and that, too, was abandoned.

He ran to the next house and found it empty as well.

Outside again, the burning house was a black skeleton already, no longer enclosing its angry soul. Rake walked backward so he could see the fire churn as he headed home. When he was far enough away to no longer feel the heat on his skin, he turned and made his way home through the quiet night.

39

IT HAD BEEN weeks since they'd found her, so the weeds in the dumping grounds may have been an inch or so higher, but other than that it looked the same. Crabgrass rose shoulder-high in places, waist-high in others. Trash was strewn everywhere, some in bags and some loose, some of it freshly laid on top, and some nearly subsumed into the earth itself. The only real differences between that first night and now was that the sun was out and there wasn't a body here anymore.

Tommy Smith parked the pickup truck that he'd borrowed from a friend. In shotgun was Champ Jennings, who had been one of the first officers at the scene the night they'd found her, and, conveniently, was the strongest man in the precinct.

The redbrick wall of an apartment building in front of them offered a bit of shade at that midmorning hour, though it would be taking that shade back shortly. They would have been smart to get an earlier start, but cops who pulled night shifts weren't much for morning yard work. They grabbed machetes and hedge clippers from the bed of the truck. Then they got to work on their city beautification project. First was the swinging, as they chopped away at the highest weeds and got them down to a manageable, possibly mowable height. Smith realized immediately that this would be a much harder job than he'd been hoping it would be.

"I don't think my machete's sharp enough," he said.

Champ laughed. "I don't think your shoulder's sharp enough, boy."

Smith swung harder, then Champ laughed again. "Hold up, hold up." Champ was a farm boy, and after Smith steadied his blade, Champ stepped forward and demonstrated. "Hit it this way, down like." Smith watched as the big man split the sheaths in a smooth stroke. "That, and add thirty pounds of muscle, and you should be fine."

They alternated between hacking at the growth and pulling out pieces of trash, stuffing the loose garbage into paper bags they'd brought and tossing them into the truck.

They wore gloves, long-sleeved shirts, and boots to protect themselves from snakes and thorns and poison ivy, not to mention the general nastiness of days- and week-old trash. Every now and then Smith caught a whiff of nearby honeysuckle but mostly he smelled the almost sweet ripeness of refuse. Within an hour the sun was leaning on them hard and Smith's shoulders were on fire. Eventually Boggs arrived, fresh from some church event and wearing nicer clothes than the task demanded.

Stray dogs came and went, some to watch, others to use the dumping grounds for their own waste-disposal purposes. Smith, digging out an old tire that had become encased in vines and roots, shook his shovel and hollered at the mutts, who trotted off.

Two neighbors joined them for a spell, Samaritans intrigued by the chance to show some solidarity. Could this dumping ground really become a park? Could this spot actually be used for picnics or a playground, or were such thoughts laughable? Was it even worth it to try?

Smith was wiping his brow when he heard a scraping noise. He looked to the right and saw a young man, maybe eighteen, dragging a metal garbage pail toward them.

"No!" Smith yelled, the same tone he'd used to shoo the mutts.

The man stopped and took in the surprising scene before him.

"What am I supposed to do with this, then?" he asked.

"Leave it on the curb. Collection for this neighborhood is Tuesday morning."

"Yeah, same day as Jesus comes back to save us all, right? When's that ever happened?"

Smith walked over to the man, who was slight and thin and sweating himself from dragging his trash around the building. He reached into his pocket and handed the man one of his cards.

"We spoke to the Sanitation Department. They'll be here every Tuesday. If they're not, you call me. Officer Tommy Smith. All right?"

The man read the card. Or appeared to read it. Smith couldn't tell. "All right."

Smith heard the pail scraping its way back home as he attacked a patch of bamboo.

Hours later, the group had whittled back down to Smith and Champ. One by one the others had tired or remembered other things they had to get to. The bed of the truck was piled high with weeds and branches on one side, man-made garbage on the other.

"If we're gonna drive this to the dump before roll call, we need to stop now," Champ said.

Smith surveyed the lot. They had cleared perhaps a third of it, down to the last few inches thanks to a mower they'd brought with them. The other half, however, was still sneering at them.

"It's a start," Champ said. "It's a start."

Smith wanted to agree. But he kept his mouth shut, as he loathed unfinished jobs.

40

THE DEPARTMENT OF Public Works had taken its sweet time, but the lamppost that Brian Underhill had nearly knocked down was finally being repaired. Three white men in hard hats, sweaty T-shirts, and aggrieved expressions arrived one day around noon, the sun high and punishing as they took ladders from the roof of their truck.

A block away, the seven remaining Negro officers were having lunch together at Mae's Spot. In the back, they'd dragged together two tables to accommodate them and were feasting on ribs and collards, mac and cheese, and pitchers of sweet tea.

"Good luck at Morehouse," Smith proclaimed.

Glasses in the air, they toasted to Xavier Little, who had worked his final shift the night before.

Little had decided to go back to school and finish his degree. Maybe he would rejoin them once he had the diploma in hand, he told them. Lucius didn't believe him, though. The job was not for him. So now there were seven, and each wondered which of them might make it six.

They swapped stories about their families, trying to talk about the job as little as possible. Those conversations could occur in more discreet surroundings, far from civilians' ears. In public like this, though, they were all honored to have the job, they deeply respected their community, they worked well with the white officers, and none would ever think of relinquishing such an exalted position.

"Buddy of mine," Smith said. "He just told me his uncle's house burned down, in Hanford Park."

"There aren't any colored folk in Hanford Park," Champ Jennings said.

"There ain't *now*. He was the first. Built it about a month ago. He and his family were away for the weekend, and someone burned it down."

"I heard the fire department didn't get there until there was nothing left," Boggs said.

After they'd finished eating and were sitting there too full to move, Little got emotional. He said he was sorry for letting them down. He told them he'd wanted to be better at this, wanted to be stronger. His eyes were watering and some of them nodded and others looked away.

Then Smith made a joke about Spelman girls, and they all laughed even though it wasn't that funny, everyone relieved that the spell was broken and they could get up now and leave.

Outside they all shook Little's hand again and told him not be a stranger, then they went their separate ways for a few hours, until roll call.

Lucius walked toward an apartment he wanted to check out, as he had decided to start looking for a place of his own. Not least because he had a date next week with Julie Cannon, and though he certainly didn't expect to be taking her home that night, he also didn't want to let slip that he lived with his parents. A rented room would be a waste of money, he could hear his father saying, and he would be better off saving for a mortgage that one of the Negro-owned banks could extend to him, but Lucius didn't care. He needed his own space, needed to escape some shadows.

As he walked down Auburn, he passed the lamppost repair. Two of the white men were rifling through tools in their truck, and the third was high above on a ladder.

The man on the ladder hocked and spat. A circle of saliva landed not far from where Lucius had been about to step.

Maybe the man had just spat from up high and hadn't been looking. Or maybe he had aimed it that way. Lucius thought he heard a mutter from above but he wasn't certain. Nor would he look up, as that would have meant staring into the sun, not to mention giving the man the satisfaction.

The white man was very precariously placed indeed. All it would take is a gentle shove to knock the ladder down. Just the lightest push.

Officer Boggs kept his shoulders straight as he walked past the ladder, looking forward to seeing the lamp aglow when he'd next walk the Auburn Avenue beat.

ACKNOWLEDGMENTS

THANK YOU!

The Mullen and Strickland families; Susan Golomb and Writers House; Dawn Davis and everyone at 37Ink and Atria; Rich Green and ICM; Amy Pascal; Charles McNair; Professors Stephen Mihm and Joe Crespino; Thomas Lake, Tony Rehagen and the writers at the Auburn Chautauqua; Terra Elan McVoy; David Huntington, John Carter, and Sparks Grove; the Decatur Book Festival; Joe Davich, Bill Starr, and Georgia Center for the Book; Rebecca Burns, Steve Fennessey and *Atlanta* Magazine; Chuck Reece and *The Bitter Southerner*; booksellers everywhere.